It was irksome, thou... the kind of authority ....at had people jumping to attention but still fail to get served in a wine bar until every other person waiting had been dealt with. If it had been a pub it could be put down to male chauvinism of the kind exercised by barmaids as well as men, but in a place like this where the waiters of both sexes were young and reasonable it had to be a facial defect, some fatal lack of presence, that allowed them to ignore you.

'Yes?' said the earringed barman. Judy put from her mind the notion of a course in counter-assertiveness and ordered.

A. R. Beven has worked in advertising, is now a journalist, and is working on a new novel. A. R. Beven's second novel, *The Sanctuary Man*, is available from Hodder and Stoughton.

The Seldom Girls

A. R. Beven

CORONET BOOKS
Hodder and Stoughton

First published in Great Britain in 1994
by Hodder and Stoughton
A division of Hodder Headline PLC

First published in paperback in 1995
by Hodder and Stoughton

A Coronet paperback

10 9 8 7 6 5 4 3 2 1

British Library Cataloguing in Publication Data

Beven, A. R.
Seldom Girls
I. Title
823.914 [F]

ISBN 0 340 63797 8

Typeset by Keyboard Services, Luton, Beds

Printed and bound in Great Britain by
Cox and Wyman Ltd, Reading, Berks

Hodder and Stoughton
A division of Hodder Headline PLC
338 Euston Road
London NW1 3BH

For Lesley, Patrick and Lisa

Thanks to all the commissioners of music, words and manual labour, who kept the wolf from the door.

1

Work That Body

Sophie Attwood stood under the shower, her mop of auburn curls imprisoned beneath a pink nylon bath cap from Boots, and recalculated. Her last period had started the day after Daddy's birthday which was 30 March and now it was the . . . 25th, almost certainly, which meant . . . twenty-six days. Safe.

She had worked that out last night with Mikey licking her thigh and no sign of a condom, but then she had been under the influence of a bottle of white Rioja and a certain desire. Mind you, it could do her no good to discover now that she had been mistaken . . .

'Who's in this bloody bathroom?' The doorknob rattled.

'Me. I won't be a minute.'

'Oh, hi Sophie. Well, get a move on. We've all got to get to work. I'm surprised you're up at all,' the disembodied voice continued slyly.

'Why?' asked Sophie, wrapping herself in her towel and glancing at her watch to confirm that it was the 25th.

'Twice in one night. You lucky cow.' There was a peal of laughter.

The bedroom, with Mikey still in it, must be within earshot.

1

'Shush, Carol, I'm coming now,' she said somewhat frantically.

There was another hoot, 'Again?' and the sound of feet padding away down the corridor. Long experience had taught Carol that in the parlance of shared bathrooms 'now' meant in five minutes' time.

Rubbing in talcum powder reminded Sophie that she was slightly sore. She hadn't particularly wanted to do it again this morning but Mikey was off on location for a fortnight so she'd consented. Knowing she would be late if it wasn't a quickie she'd had to work fast though, which meant rough, so . . . She tramped across the landing, remembering to whip off the shower cap and shake out her hair before entering her room.

She needn't have worried about Mikey's sensibilities. He was still buried under the duvet, either in a post-coital haze or dreaming about directing feature films instead of chocolate commercials. She kicked the lump.

'Come on. I'm leaving in five minutes and so are you.'

The room was glowing with sunlight fighting its way around the edges of heavy velvet curtains. Shafts of it held specks of dust in their thrall. Before the full-length mirror, its corners draped with scarves and headbands, Sophie dressed, half-conscious of her potential audience. Pants. Bra? Yes if lacy shirt, no if Breton striped top. She stretched, arms above head, adopting a balletic pose and waiting for her deodorant to dry.

A rumpled head emerged from the bedclothes. 'No time for a bath then. I could let myself out.'

'You couldn't,' she said, watching him in the mirror watching her. 'I've only got one key and I'm not going without it.'

The Breton then. Sometimes, if Mikey was there, she felt

embarrassed putting her small breasts into a bra in case he asked why she bothered.

'Why not?' he asked. 'I'll give it back to you – and I promise not to have a copy made.' He smiled.

Having wriggled her long legs into the tight, white jeans she coaxed them over her bottom. 'But I'm not seeing you again before you go.' When she buttoned them up she realised that today their skin-fit might be an uncomfortable mistake.

Mikey was up now and hauling on his jeans and a sweater. She had expected him to argue about the key, suggesting biking it to her or meeting for lunch, but all he said was, 'What are you doing tonight then?'

'Something interesting,' said Sophie, embarking on her make-up, and blew him a kiss.

Judy Hucknell put her mug with the cereal bowl on the rack to drain and removed her rubber gloves.

'For God's sake, Barty, I don't cook that stuff for fun.'

Receiving no response she took the car and front-door keys from her handbag and put on the jacket of her blue suit. She switched on the answerphone on the breakfast bar and gathered her umbrella and raincoat from the hall. Having checked her face in the mirror – a touch too much blusher but that could be rectified before her meeting with the Research Group at ten – she returned.

'Look, I know you've had a terrible experience but sex is no fun anyway. As far as I remember.' She planted a kiss on his head. 'Bye-bye, my darling, and be a good boy while I'm out.'

She opened the front door and paused, juggling brief-case, handbag and umbrella while she fiddled with the mortice lock.

'And I'll be late tonight.'

Bartholomew stared back unblinkingly.

'And quite probably drunk.' She shut the door.

He waited in case she had forgotten anything and was about to come storming back into the house. When the silence seemed complete he jumped carefully down from the dresser and crossed with the delicate gait of one who has recently been neutered to enjoy the shredded chicken in his bowl.

'No,' said Vanessa Tierney to the junior government minister being interviewed on the radio. The traffic at Vauxhall Cross was as awful as ever but the interviewer's inept questioning was letting this politician off the hook.

'If company car drivers could be persuaded to drive in together, or better still to use public transport, then there would be no need for better roads in the capital,' he said smugly.

Vanessa rapped the steering wheel of her company BMW in irritation. She knew she was vulnerable to this line of attack, but how else was she to deliver Josh to the childminder's? Today, as most days, just getting him dressed, breakfasted and into the car had been a chaotic and wearing business. And he was never at his most angelic once she had told him that he would have to stay with Aunty Eileen until bedtime.

Crossing the Thames she noticed that the water was high, lapping only feet from the tops of the restraining walls. One of her recurring nightmares was that the river would flood and her house, being in lowland Battersea, would be engulfed. The dream, she assumed, was yet another manifestation of her Josh-related guilt complexes.

Whatever its cause it was tangible enough to have had her not only in the pool with Josh and his waterwings but

4

also taking the ferry down to inspect the Thames flood barrier at Woolwich. According to the badly-written guidebook the barrier was the eighth wonder of the world, yet it seemed rather flimsy and certainly appeared not to take into account the predicted raising of sea levels caused by global warming. She had returned less than reassured and persevered with the swimming lessons.

'It's eight o'clock on the 25th of April 1989,' said the radio, 'and here is the news.'

She switched it off, hitched her spectacles up the bridge of her nose, and allowed her mind to range over the forthcoming day. A tricky meeting with the snack food client whose latest sales figures were declining despite a new campaign, and then lunch, hopefully with the crisis averted. Afterwards a meeting with the creative director whose department's work on the Dolphin swimwear account could not be presented without major changes. As she parked the car in the basement of the agency's building in St James's she was humming to herself.

'Don't sit on that radiator, Timothy.'

'Why not, miss?'

'You'll get piles.' Oh God, what reflex had made her say that – the time-honoured response of teachers from her own schooldays.

'Piles of what, miss?'

Twelve-year-old smartarse. Still, she'd asked for it.

'Piles are a medical condition, as I'm sure you know perfectly well. They cause extremely uncomfortable swelling around the—'

The bell rang. Milton hovered.

'Off you go to assembly, Timothy.'

'Swelling where, miss?'

'Around your ear if you're not careful. And before you

say it I know we're not allowed to hit you any more. Assembly.'

'But the piles, miss?'

'Around your rear.' He looked puzzled. 'Think about it, Timothy. It's a schoolboy joke. You should have made it, not me.'

He did think, and suddenly smiled. 'Good one, miss.'

And then he was caught in the flow of pupils surging to the hall, disappearing like the Cheshire cat, so that the image left on her retina was of a jumble of white teeth in need of a corrective brace.

Becky Fishman leant back on the radiator herself, feeling its warmth against the base of her spine.

'Don't run. And keep to the left.'

The last of the blazered ants vanished round the corner, leaving her alone in the green and white corridor. She patrolled its length, checking the classrooms for malingerers. Perhaps that little exchange with Milton would improve her standing with 2C.

The dense quiet of an empty school was broken by the faint strains of six hundred voices plodding through 'To be a Pilgrim'. One of the benefits of early duty was missing the awful hymns and headmaster's homilies, retiring instead to the staffroom for the day's first fag before GCSE Shakespeare.

Lighting the Silk Cut she thought about tonight. Drinks with the girls – a fortnightly institution that had survived Vanessa's baby and the vicissitudes of their various careers. Others had come and gone but this hard core had kept up their friendship since decamping to London from university nearly ten years before.

They were her best friends but sometimes, anticipating a group meeting, she experienced a *frisson* of inferiority which angered her. The trouble – one of the troubles – with being a teacher was that while other people's jobs were only vaguely understood everybody, having been to school, thought they understood hers completely. Consequently it had no mystique, hardly rated a mention in any discussion of careers among these career girls.

Becky knew logically that interesting children in English was as important as marketing shampoo, like Judy, if far less well paid, and that Sophie's job in TV production was not as glamorous as the images it conjured up.

However, she had lived through the eighties and absorbed the social superiority of marketing to mere selling, and the growing importance of the media until they rated a weekly supplement in the *Guardian*, just like her own profession, presently so reviled.

She could no longer make the mistake that she had when Vanessa had announced her first appointment as a lowly account executive. Then both she and Sophie had failed to appreciate the distinction between Account and Accounts, assuming that Vanessa was to spend the rest of her life doing something to Bought Ledgers rather than ... well, rather than whatever she did do. Vanessa was now an Account Director at the advertising agency Breughel Thomas but Becky had always been hazy on what Vanessa's working day might entail apart from meetings, which, considering her salary, were presumably rather more productive than school staff meetings.

A clatter on the stairs warned of the return from assembly of those members of staff with a free period. As she didn't have one she stubbed out her cigarette and checked her briefcase for *Love's Labour's Lost*.

It was always a bit of a scramble to get to the wine bar by six, driving back into London from the suburb where she worked, leaving the car at her flat in Clapham, and catching the tube to Leicester Square. But they had to meet early so that Vanessa could get back to her son at a reasonable time.

Becky stood at the railings and looked down. The bar was not yet crowded and Judy and Vanessa were at their usual table beneath the basement window. Vanessa was engaged in a characteristically animated monologue, the padded shoulders of her striking red jacket rising and falling as her hands swooped across the table. Judy, pale, passive and blonde, was her antithesis. Judy looked up, saw Becky through the glass and smiled. Becky coloured, feeling absurdly as if she had been caught spying, waved and hurried down the stairs.

As she sat down and Judy asked what she would like Becky was discomfited to see that the other two were drinking Perrier.

'Is Sophie coming?'

'Yes, but—'

'In that case a bottle of Muscadet. I know that sounds greedy but if you buy it by the glass you just get Vin de Table. But I'll get it.'

'No, I'll get it,' Judy said mildly. 'I'll be helping you drink it once I've quenched my thirst.'

'She doesn't need any help,' said Vanessa. 'Implying that it would take Sophie to make it worth getting a bottle. You old soak.'

'You're only drinking water because you're driving,' Becky said indignantly.

'She's not even drinking water because she's driving,' said Judy. 'Do you want another vodka and tonic, Nessie?'

'Don't call me that. One day you'll do it in front of Josh and he'll go on saying it for bloody years. Yes, I would like one. And that must be my last,' she added, as they were left alone. 'But I need a pick-me-up after the day I've had.'

'Bad, obviously.'

'Looked very black at one stage. Mr Tortilla Chip was spoiling for a fight – in fact I thought he was going to put the account up for review.' Becky looked questioning. 'It's the next worst thing to being sacked. It means you have to compete to hang on to the business against a load of other agencies, all of whom have novelty on their side.'

'And did he?'

'No – but I had to be particularly obsequious to him over lunch, and I took out my frustration on the creative director this afternoon, thereby no doubt confirming his view that all account persons are complete philistines.'

'And are they?'

'Well, you've seen the flying ducks on my sitting-room wall – judge for yourself.'

Becky laughed.

'Anyway,' Vanessa went on, 'how about you? Nurtured any talents? Given any detentions?'

'Managed to avoid being lumbered with the summer play. Although I don't think I'm quite safe on that one yet.'

'But I thought you liked producing plays,' said Vanessa, and Becky explained the power politics of her own workplace.

Having already done three school plays she was being taken for granted and support for her efforts was diminishing. Forcing someone else to cope with intransigent timetables, recalcitrant child actors, and an ageing lighting system should result in her being welcomed back with open arms and more resources for the Christmas production.

'Unless of course Mr Wilkinson proves to be an undercover agent from the National Theatre. In which case I shall never be invited to direct again.'

'Well, let's hope your tactics succeed. It would be awful if you lost the plays. I thought they were one of the great compensations of the job.' Becky was silent. 'Aren't they?'

'I suppose so. Perhaps I just need the break.'

It was irksome, thought Judy, that you could wield the kind of authority at the office that had people jumping to attention but still fail to get served in a wine bar until every other person waiting had been dealt with. If it had been a pub it could be put down to male chauvinism of the kind exercised by barmaids as well as men, but in a place like this where the waiters of both sexes were young and reasonable it had to be a facial defect, some fatal lack of presence, that allowed them to ignore you.

'Yes?' said the earringed barman.

Judy put from her mind the notion of a course in counter-assertiveness and ordered. As she was asking for a tray she saw Sophie drift across the room like some Pre-Raphaelite Ophelia and bend to kiss the girls. The big green eyes turned and focused on her.

'Jesus,' she said. 'I'm gasping. Pour us a glass, Jude.' And the bony arms enfolded her in a hug.

When she had removed her coat and scarf Sophie lowered herself gently into a chair, grimacing a little as she contacted the seat.

'What's the matter?'

Sophie giggled. 'Jeans too tight. Probably have thrush by the morning. Ah well, at least I'm not pregnant.' And they had all known each other too long to take the bait.

By the time the bottle was finished they had rounded up the gossip and offered moral support over life's various tribulations. It was comforting, thought Becky, but slightly unreal. The criticisms either remained unspoken or, like

10

serious questions, were voiced only in conversations for two.

Vanessa was collecting the second bottle and Judy had gone to the lavatory when Sophie offered her a menthol-tipped cigarette and asked, 'How's your PE teacher?'

Becky, who disliked St Moritz and had never accepted one in all the time they had known each other, shook her head and lit herself a Silk Cut.

'I don't think I'll be seeing him again.'

'Why?'

'You know. He was the kind of guy you can go for an Indian with and talk about what's happening at school, but that was about it.'

'Sexy?'

Becky smiled, and then shook her head. 'No, I thought, maybe, but—'

'Not plug-ugly then.'

'No, not . . . not at all ugly really. But . . . no spark.'

'So what? Not too bright?'

'Oh, bright enough but simply not interested in films, plays, books . . . he would try to discuss them but what's the point of talking to someone about something when it's so obviously an effort for them?'

Vanessa was now back in her seat and Judy was threading her way across the bar.

'That makes me sound such an old bluestocking. But there'll be no more cosy chicken tikkas there.'

Vanessa refilled Becky's glass and she took a gulp. 'Unfortunately I think one of the most off-putting things about him—'

'Yes?'

'We're agog,' said Judy.

'Spit it out,' said Vanessa.

'—is that he's a teacher.'

11

Vanessa frowned.

'What a let-down,' said Sophie. 'I thought we were in for some juicy piece of gossip – at least poor personal hygiene.'

'So,' said Judy. 'You're no longer attached.'

'I never was.'

'Whatever. And neither are you, Vanessa.'

'Except to my sprog.'

'And neither am I.'

'So what is this statement of the obvious?' asked Sophie.

'And are you at the moment?'

'I'll decide when you tell us where this is leading.'

'And has anyone booked a holiday yet?'

The moment of silence said it all.

Look at us, Becky thought. Four attractive women, well, three attractive women and me, and none of us with a holiday fixed up. Pathetic.

I could have done, Sophie thought defiantly, it's simply stupid to tie yourself down too early. When I'm ready . . .

Vanessa was riled by the reminder that as a good mother she should have found something wonderful for Josh to do. Rather bad-temperedly she said, 'Judith, get to the point.'

'I don't believe it. She's going to suggest a week in Great Yarmouth,' said Sophie. 'Even Josh might balk at that.'

'Sadly,' said Vanessa, 'I think he'd love it.'

'I've never been to Yarmouth.'

'For God's sake, Rebecca, this is like Chinese whispers. I'm not suggesting Norfolk. But I have got an option on a villa in Tuscany for three weeks in August.'

And slowly, with the assistance of another bottle of wine, Judy talked the group through the facts: that the availability fell within Becky's school holidays, that not being a hotel it would be suitable for Josh, that they didn't have to stay for the full three weeks. She reminded them of the virtues of Italian cooking and orchestrated enthusiasm with photographs of the views and the pool; agreement seemed certain.

At which point Vanessa realised the time and left in a rush, promising to check dates, and the others realised that if they did not eat they were in danger of being drunk and adjourned for a pizza.

Over the *cappuccinos* Judy returned to the subject of Sophie's capricious love life and Sophie confided that she had 'in fact, got involved with' – which meant been to bed with – 'someone new'.

'Anyone we know?' asked Becky and, although Sophie replied yes, expected to hear a name which would mean nothing to her, just one that Sophie had mentioned in quite another context some weeks earlier.

Instead the new man turned out to be Michael Rodgers, with whom Becky and Vanessa had appeared in a somewhat shaky production of *The Duchess of Malfi* at university. Judy did not remember him and Sophie maintained that she had not recognised him when they met and that it was he who reminded her that their first meeting had been when she was doing props for that play.

He had been in his final year then while they had only been in their first. Although Becky was already friendly with Vanessa the two of them were only aware of Sophie as the dippy redhead working backstage. Becky had played a minor role but Vanessa had auditioned for, and won, the female lead. At the last-night party she had disappeared with her co-star and returned to college the next morning dishevelled but happy, a condition that lasted until it became apparent that Michael was notorious for one-night stands and regarded his relationship with Vanessa as terminated at about the time that the posters were removed from the front of the theatre.

As far as Becky knew it was the first time that two of them had bedded the same man. Odd that it should have happened not within the hothouse atmosphere of under-graduate society but by bizarre coincidence twelve years later.

It was clear that Sophie knew nothing of Michael's fling with Vanessa and Becky decided not to enlighten her. Judging by Sophie's previous form he might well not last long enough for them to meet in any case. She wondered whether it was sinister that Michael had not mentioned it to Sophie himself, and then realised how silly that was; in the first flush of romance you were hardly likely to pick the bones of the casual lays of ancient history.

'So how long's this been going on?' Judy asked.

'A few weeks.'

'And this is the first time you've seen fit to mention it?'

'I don't tell you everything.'

'Since when? You rarely spare us a sordid detail.'

'You make me sound like an alley cat.'

There was a pause.

'I think that is what is known as a discreet silence.' Becky giggled.

'You two are just a pair of puritanical cows.'

'Certainly not,' Judy said.

'Jealous puritanical cows.'

'There's no need to rub it in.'

'It's nothing special.'

'That,' Becky said, 'is what we were afraid of.'

'And anyway,' Judy added, 'your self-satisfied smirk suggests otherwise.'

'All right, all right. Call off the Spanish inquisition.'

'So it is special.'

'I don't know.'

They waited.

Sophie laughed. 'OK, maybe. Maybe this time the alley cat thinks she's got the cream.'

Saturday felt like the first day of summer, and Becky was sitting at the window of her second-floor flat toying with a bacon sandwich and the idea of going to Sainsburys when the phone rang.

'Do you want to come over?' Vanessa asked. 'It's so warm we could have lunch in the garden, and Josh says he hasn't seen you for ages. Unless you're busy, of course?'

Becky, who immediately felt guilty about the bacon sandwich and happy at the prospect of a sunny lawn, accepted.

'And bring your leotard or leggings and a top or something.'

'Why?'

'I thought we might go to the gym. Don't pout. I can tell that you are. You've never been so you can't possibly say that you'll hate it. You only have to do a little exercise and then we can have a sauna and jacuzzi.'

Becky groaned.

'Pain before pleasure. When will you be here?'

'I'll just do my shopping. An hour.'

After the plasticky heat of the battered Renault 5 Vanessa's house seemed more than ever like a shadowy art gallery – all bare wood, white paint and an esoteric collection of framed prints and photographs. They drank coffee and watched Josh rattling around the tiny garden – a lawn the size of the handwoven rug in the sitting-room and a brick patio on which stood an elaborate wrought-iron table and chairs.

Then Vanessa suggested taking her son to Battersea Park to wear him out before lunch, and they walked by the lake and fed the ducks.

Watching Becky push Josh on the swings, his silky, golden hair blowing in the wind, Vanessa felt one of those surges of love like adrenalin that overcame her occasionally and that she had never experienced for his father. Getting pregnant was an accident, or at least something she had not consciously intended. It was mere coincidence that Charlie was both conventionally handsome and intelligent, unlike some of her previous boyfriends, and that for the first time she had the house and the salary to be truly independent.

But when it happened she had not hesitated. Charlie was honourable enough to offer to stand by her but patently relieved to be assured that it was not necessary, that he was free to continue his career at the Bar and in the fullness of time to marry the daughter of the aristocracy that he so obviously deserved.

Advertising agencies are not known for their puritanism so there was no stigma attached to her partnerless state. Her difficulty was in explaining why she wanted a baby at all if she were truly wedded to her career. Too many of her female colleagues had decided, when the crunch came at the end of maternity leave, not to return to work. Vanessa knew she would have to and willingly did, but even now, nearly two years after the birth, she was still on probation and more likely to suffer sideways glances and sly comment if ever she needed to leave early than men who had wives at home to run the kid to the dentist.

Her biggest problem had been with her parents. Even though illegitimacy ranked second only to adultery as a subject of gossip in their home town of Haslemere, her wilful acceptance of her condition was inexplicable to them. Throughout her pregnancy her mother had offered no advice or comfort and when she went into labour a minicab had taken her to St Thomas's Hospital. Married friends had expressed concern that she had to face the birth alone but, as she pointed out, this made her no different from generations of women who had had babies before togetherness and the National Childbirth Trust imposed their norm on parenthood.

It was after the delivery, when the first elation and the drugs had worn off, that she wanted someone to share her experience with. Becky, monitoring progress by phone, had arrived as soon as school was over, and Judy soon after.

Becky irresistibly reminded Vanessa of a young Parisienne. She was attractive rather than beautiful, slender but not remotely boyish, her soft, spotted skirt and loosely-knotted neckerchief suggesting the inexpensive style glimpsed so often on the Métro. Her fine, mousey-brown hair was cut to hang perfectly around the nape of her neck and flick away from her forehead, but a characteristic gesture was to push it back behind the ears as if it was in constant danger of obscuring her vision. She was doing that now, explaining something to Josh, the sun catching the gold sleepers that were the only earrings she ever seemed to wear.

'Ice-cream,' said Josh.

'Not now,' Vanessa replied. 'Lunch now.'

The small face puckered.

'Ice-cream for afters. In fridge,' she continued, in the pidgin English of a missionary placating an angry native.

The face relaxed.

Vanessa winked. 'Strawberry AND chocolate,' she flourished and was rewarded with a gap-toothed grin.

They lunched frugally on tuna salads, with Josh alone enjoying crisps and a dishful of Wall's Neapolitan. Becky's tentative suggestion of a glass of the chilled rosé she had brought was sternly dismissed.

17

'You might manage the gym but it's very bad to drink alcohol before the sweatbox.'

The health club was in a converted warehouse, its car park full of the German cars of the successful corporate executive, their serried ranks broken only by the occasional Citroën of those with artistic pretensions and the Range Rovers of the rurally ambitious.

'Although heaven knows what they're doing here at the weekend,' said Vanessa. 'What's the point of having a Range Rover without at least a weekend cottage in Wiltshire?'

'Sophie's got a jeep,' said Becky. 'And she lives in a bedsit in Camden.'

'Quite,' said Vanessa, and they went in. 'Can you hold Josh while I sign you in?' she asked, and once Becky was occupied with the boy she handed over the £10 for a day's guest membership along with her own card. Knowing how much less Becky earned she occasionally subsidised her when she wanted her company, but it had to be covert.

They left Josh in the crèche and went up to the changing room. In Becky's experience such places either smelt of chlorine, like the municipal swimming baths, or old socks, as at school. But this room held the confusion of a hundred perfumes and deodorants, overlaid with scorching wood. A blast of heat pushed this scent towards them as a woman emerged from the sauna and vanished into the showers, affording a brief glimpse of firm, tanned and glistening flesh.

It was unnerving. Becky had always disliked communal changing rooms in shops and as it was years since she'd swum anywhere except in the sea on holiday she hadn't had to consider the prospect of public undressing. At the doctor's you were behind a screen and in the bedroom the lights were low or even off. Luckily for her self-consciousness the locker area was empty and she concentrated on getting into her leggings and a baggy sweatshirt as quickly as possible.

'Can affect your morale tremendously, this place,' said Vanessa with the alarming telepathy that she often displayed. 'If you're lucky it's other young mums with stretchmarks and tummies or matrons who make you feel like a stick insect who's never even heard of cellulite, but once I came in on a Thursday morning and it was full of out-of-work dancers. Made me want to strangle myself with my own leotard.'

'Can't see what you've got to worry about.' Vanessa's black, footless tights revealed strong and shapely legs, and the pale-grey leotard and loose vest over it accentuated her olive skin.

'Wait till you see me in the sauna,' she replied, and they went down to the gym.

After twenty minutes on the exercise bike, even set on the lowest level, Becky thought her lungs would burst, and her heart was pumping so fast it must be juddering in its cavity like a washing machine on a spin cycle. The rivulets of sweat pouring down her back and chest threatened dehydration. Her scalp itched and she knew her face must be beetroot with exertion.

The only way to distract her brain from this torment had been to examine her fellow-sufferers although, with the exception of a balding, fat man on the rowing machine in matching pastel-green shorts and vest, highly unsuited to his age and figure, none of them appeared to be suffering.

On the mats a slender Scandinavian with too much eye make-up executed a series of stretch exercises requiring disturbing flexibility, and a heavy girl endlessly raised

19

plump thighs against a machine designed to reduce them. Two muscle-bound men with the leathery faces of the bed-tanned encouraged each other to lift impossibly heavy weights. It was hard to decide whether their bulging pectorals and the tendons of arms and legs exposed and quivering with effort were sexy or repellent.

Etiquette seemed to dictate that none of the gym's occupants looked at one another, and despite the walls being entirely mirrored even narcissistic self-regard was hard to spot. A dreamy, unfocused gaze into the middle distance seemed par for the course.

'OK, long enough,' said Vanessa.

Back from a stint on the jogger her vest was stained with dark patches and a couple of locks of black hair were plastered to her forehead. She looked positively Amazonian.

'We'll just do a few machines – and then your reward.'

So they strengthened their calves and firmed their busts, biceps and triceps.

'Where are my triceps?' asked Becky as they stood before yet another Heath Robinson contraption, and Vanessa pointed to the back of her upper arm. She felt her own soft flesh. 'Don't think I've got any muscle to build.'

'It's hardly surprising. It must be years since you did any exercise. It's just depressing for the rest of us that you look so well on it. Shall we have a sunbed?'

One of the things that all the members had in common was golden-brown skin. 'I'd better. Looking at this lot I feel like something that's been kept in a dark cupboard.'

The cubicles were small and empty apart from the giant toasted sandwichmaker. For some reason Becky hadn't liked to say that she had never used one of these things before, and during their walk from the changing room she had been preoccupied with whether her small white towel would continue to cover her body unsupported by hand. Having read the instructions she climbed on to the machine and lay flat, pulling the canopy down over her. It was very close to her face. A good job she wasn't claustrophobic. Clutching her goggles she stretched out her other arm to pop the token in the meter to start the machine. Her outstretched fingers were a good six inches from the slot.

The only way to insert the token was to roll on her side, which meant lifting up the canopy, but that in turn meant several movements to make after the process had begun and the instructions specifically stated that goggles had to be worn at all times. She balanced them on her nose. Not only would they fall off unless held in place but once on rendered sight absolutely impossible.

She practised the manoeuvre a couple of times while trying to decide if her arms were particularly short. She didn't think they were so presumably lots of people had this problem. Was being brown worth this aggravation?

She pushed the token into the slot with her left hand and just as she was transferring the grip on her goggles and reaching for the canopy with her right the motor started with a clattering roar and she was bathed in the ghostly blue light of a thousand black-and-white televisions. She squealed and the goggles dropped to the floor.

With her eyes squeezed shut she felt blindly around until she found them. The colour behind her lids was far brighter than it should have been. A vision of herself crossing the road with a white stick, no, a guide dog, was obliterated by the pain as she struck her elbow against the canopy and her fingertips fizzed. But she had got the goggles back on. Keening with distress she subsided on to the bed and pulled the lid down tight. Above the noise of the engine she became aware of a faint voice.

'Rebecca. Rebecca. Are you all right?'

She took a deep breath. 'Of course,' she shouted back and gave herself up to the penetrating warmth. It was so easy to believe that you were lying under the Mediterranean sky with your eyes closed against the midday sun that when the bed switched off, the silence and darkness were as shocking as a sudden explosion.

It was disappointing that she seemed only faintly pink whereas Vanessa looked browner than ever. 'And I always thought your colour was natural,' she said.

Vanessa had the grace to look slightly shamefaced. 'I just top it up now and again. Jacuzzi.'

'Is there no end to this box of delights?'

'You have to have some compensation for pumping iron.'

Set in marble like a Cleopatran bath filled by Dr Frankenstein, the bubbling surface of the jacuzzi had the heads of two women bobbing on it. They looked up as Vanessa discarded her towel and climbed the steps to join them. Resisting the impulse to avoid their curiosity by doubling up and scuttling like a crab Becky followed suit.

'Has Judy been on to you again about the villa in Tuscany?' Vanessa asked.

'Yes. Are you definitely going?'

'I've got the time off work so yes, if everyone else is.'

'Right.'

'What's the matter, Becky? You sound uncertain. Don't you think it will be fun?'

Unused to having conversations in a bath occupied by four people Becky glanced at the women but one seemed to be in a trance and the other was clambering out, puddles of water forming on the floor around her as she groped for her towel.

'It's just the cost,' she said. 'The villa split four ways, plus the air fare and spending money. I just wonder if I ought to stay at home and put the money towards a new car. The Renault's on its last legs.'

Vanessa closed her eyes. She had anticipated this problem, but she wanted to go and having Becky there would be more fun for her and a help with Josh.

'Well, you can't go without a holiday,' she advanced, playing for time.

'Of course you can. Or at least take a cheap one.'

'On your own? That won't be much fun. Unless you're planning to reinstate your PE man.'

She wondered whether she had misread that situation but Becky smiled.

'No chance of that. My disillusion with sports masters is complete. You're right. It won't be so good but rather that than the car dying in the autumn and me cursing because I can only replace it with a moped. It's a long way to Beckenham every day.'

'Is Sophie coming?'

'Yes.'

'Well, that's OK then.' Vanessa had the makings of a solution. 'It won't be split four ways but five.'

'Who's the fifth?'

'Sophie, Judy, you, me, and Josh of course.'

'You can't pay for him. He's only two.'

'The airlines don't agree with you.'

'But he'll be sharing your room.'

'So if I brought a lover to share my bed would you expect him to get free board?'

'No,' said Becky uneasily. She could sense she was being outmanoeuvred. 'But—'

'And Josh won't even be sharing my bed. Unless he's frightened or I need a cuddle, of course.' She splashed her face with water. 'There's something else. Car hire in Italy is phenomenally expensive and it's probably impossible to get a child seat – plus I'm going to have so much stuff I wondered if you'd help me out.'

'Yes,' said Becky, confused. 'But how?'

'I thought I'd drive the BMW down but I can't do it on my own. Will you share the driving?'

'Of course.'

'Great. So you are coming?'

'Vanessa. I—'

'Well, if you help me out you've saved yourself the air fare so now it's a really cheap holiday.'

'But even going by car there's petrol and it's going to take a couple of days so there's hotels.'

'I'd have to buy the petrol anyway and if you come with me you'll be saving me from a nervous breakdown so the least I can do is cover the hotel expenses.'

'No.'

'Yes.'

The remaining woman got out.

'Excuse us,' said Vanessa. 'Look, don't do me the favour. But you've got to come. You've been out-argued and you know it.' She slid forward and kicked Becky under the water. Becky smiled momentarily but the little frown returned.

Vanessa lay back. 'Oh,' she gasped, hamming it up.

'What's the matter?'

'I'm just getting a jet in a very peculiar place.'

And Becky laughed and Vanessa knew she had won.

If the sunbed had warmed Becky's bones and the jacuzzi relaxed her muscles the intense heat of the sauna seemed to be ironing the contents of her brain. Or at least her inhibitions, although she hadn't felt able to strike up a conversation with Scandinavia who was occupying the highest shelf and whose thighs and stomach were at eye-level. Instead she watched the sand in the egg timer on the wall run out, and the growing pool of water beneath the bench, which must be partly her own sweat. The silence lasted a beat after Scandinavia had departed, pausing only to invert the timer.

'I've never been able to talk to strangers in here,' said Vanessa. She stretched. 'But it should help to get the spare tyre off before Italy.'

'What spare tyre?' Sitting on a pine-slatted bench which spread the thighs was not the most flattering of poses but Vanessa still looked fine. She was tall and muscular and Becky had spotted no sag to her bottom.

Vanessa pinched a small roll of fat on her stomach between her thumb and forefinger. 'I haven't been able to get rid of this since Josh was born. Still, I'll need a one-piece swimsuit to hide the stretchmarks. That will cover a multitude of sins.' She looked down at herself. 'But not this, unfortunately. The cream and the razor, I think.'

Vanessa's pubic hair was prolific. A narrow strip of fur ran down from her navel and her inner thighs were covered with a dark down. Becky wasn't really surprised because a drift of soft dark hairs lay on Vanessa's forearms and if she thought back she could vaguely picture the merest hint of hair on her upper lip, but that no longer existed and her lower legs were perfectly waxed so . . .

'I don't go swimming, and I've not fucked since Josh so I've had no reason to get rid of it,' Vanessa said, reading her thoughts. 'Do you know Judy's hairs are so pale she's never shaved her legs?'

'I wish I'd never started,' said Becky, thinking ruefully of painful ministrations to her stubble in the bath. 'But when you're fourteen it's another of those things that makes you feel grown up.'

'I wish I'd had a choice,' said Vanessa. 'But I didn't want to go on my first date looking like a chimpanzee who'd stolen a pair of American Tan tights.'

When they got back to the house Vanessa prepared supper while Becky gave Josh his bath. This was an activity they both enjoyed but it made her worry that perhaps Josh didn't see enough of his mother – presumably hardly at all during the week and then today he had been banished to the crèche for two hours. And now she was splashing the water over him while Vanessa was making a casserole and sipping her first glass of Sauvignon.

Perhaps Vanessa didn't want to see any more of Josh . . . This disturbing notion stayed with her until she had tucked the boy into bed, kissed him goodnight and gone to fetch Vanessa to do the same. And then as she sat in the cool of the sitting-room, a languor in her limbs from the afternoon's pummelling and the glass wet with condensation from the cold wine within, she heard the giggling that accompanied the expertly told bedtime story (Vanessa was still a very good actress) and felt guilty for ever having doubted.

It was when they were sprawled on the sofas after their *boeuf en daube*, and a glass of Cointreau was adding to the abandonment induced by the wine, that Becky mentioned Sophie's new boyfriend.

'He calls himself Mikey now,' she said, 'or at least that's what Sophie calls him but it's Michael Rodgers, who was in *The Duchess of Malfi* with us our first year at Durham.'

The silence that followed was long enough for her to wonder whether Vanessa had no recollection of this incident or was so shocked that she was speechless, but when she looked up Vanessa was simply in the middle of swallowing a slug of liqueur.

'Well, well. He must be, what, thirty-four now. What does he do, I wonder?'

'Film director. Or at least of a sort. He's done some pop videos and one or two TV ads, apparently.'

'Does everybody end up in advertising?'

'I haven't.'

'That's because you're too sweet-natured. How did they meet?'

'Sophie had applied for a job at his production company and although the job's nothing to do with him he'd seen her CV and said hello when she came for the interview.'

'Has she got the job?'

'No, don't you remember? She's staying at the BBC.'

'That interview was back in March. So she's been going out with him since then?'

'I think so.'

'Has she slept with him?'

Becky nodded.

'Does she know that I have?'

'No,' Becky said. 'I didn't mention it and Judy doesn't remember him.'

There was a pause. 'How many times have they slept together?'

'I don't know. Blimey, Vee, that's not the kind of question you ask.'

'More than once, anyway.' Another pause and then Vanessa giggled. 'So she's lasted longer than I did.'

'He's probably changed. We all have.'

'Is it serious, do you think?'

'Well, he's not a louse that she's trying to get out of her life.'

This was an expression of Sophie's that had remained unchanged for ten years.

'He'll have to have changed a great deal not to be a

louse,' Vanessa said lightly. 'But perhaps he's met his match.'

'That's not a very nice thing to say.'

'No. It must be the booze talking. Have some more.'

2

Spiritland

The car's engine had barely started when a violent screech rent the air, making Becky jump.

'Jesus, what's that?'

Concentrating at the wheel of a borrowed Peugeot estate both larger and heavier than the Toyota that was her own company car, Judy sighed.

'It's Barty,' she said. 'He's been complaining ever since we left home. He'll settle down to a sort of low moan in a minute.' On cue the cat did. 'Unfortunately his volume seems to be related to our speed, so pray for heavy traffic until we reach Canterbury.'

'But that's nearly the Channel,' protested Becky. 'Fifty miles down the motorway.'

'I know. But they don't seem to have catteries in London. We'll just have to turn up the radio, I think.'

They might not have catteries in Islington, Becky thought furiously, but surely there must be some sort of feline boarding establishment closer than that. She would not have imagined that Judy could become so devoted to a creature that was a reluctantly accepted gift from parents who didn't like to think of her all on her own in the big city.

It was Judy's appetite for organisation that left Becky undertaking this journey with her rather than with Vanessa and Josh in the BMW. Once the original plan had been discussed its flaws – to wit the BMW being too small for all five of them in Tuscany and it being a very long drive for a two-year-old – had been examined and the solution – the Peugeot of Judy's colleague Alan – was produced like a rabbit from a hat.

It was ideal for their purpose, being very big and having an optional third row of seats, but Becky wasn't looking forward to driving the beast. She wondered how Alan's wife and children were managing in the back seat of Judy's Celica which they had received in the swap. It barely took a briefcase and an umbrella.

They had left early and it was only nine when they drove on to the ferry at Dover. Judy had spoken hardly a word since collecting her in Clapham, even after returning forlornly from depositing Bartholomew at his temporary quarters.

'I'm sure he'll be all right,' Becky said again as they leant over the rail and watched the not very white cliffs diminish against a cloudy sky.

'Oh, I know he will. I feel stupid for minding but somehow I've got very fond of him. I've only had him five months and already I'm worrying about his life expectancy.'

Astonishingly there seemed to be a lump in her throat. Becky hadn't spent time alone with Judy for ages and on the strength of this rather shaky start she wasn't altogether sure that the journey would be fun.

Their progress along the autoroutes, infrequently punctuated by stops for coffee and sandwiches, was light on conversation. Judy, presumably not still brooding about the moggy, was preoccupied by something, and while

Becky was happy to watch the landscape drifting past this was so unlike Judy – who would normally have talked if only to be polite – that Becky felt increasingly ill at ease. The thought of their having dinner together was alarming.

When they sat down to it, in a small hotel dining-room run by a plump grandmother who kept her cheeses and her red wine in the same linen press in the corner, Becky broached the subject. 'We've got three weeks in Tuscany ahead of us; you should be happy and you're not so something is wrong. What is it?'

'Nothing. Do you think the veal kidneys in Dijon mustard will be good?'

'It can only be one of four things. The cat, your job, your family, an affair you've kept secret, or you've remembered you've left the immersion heater on at home.'

'That's five things,' said Judy, but she smiled. 'We both know that I'm far too organised to have done the last and an affair, secret or otherwise, is something I could do with. It's months since I went out with anybody.'

This was true but Becky could not imagine why, unless it was that Judy was too choosy to accept any offers. She was pretty, with long, fair hair that she wore mostly in a French plait. Her eyes were a pale blue, her nose snubbed and delicately freckled, and her lips full; as was her figure, with the kind of bust and hips best suited to formal clothes and perfectly to ballgowns. In the guernsey she had been wearing today her breasts looked over-sized, but as far as Becky understood men did not find exaggeration in this department a problem.

She expressed her opinion.

'I haven't had any offers,' Judy said. 'Apart from you lot my social life revolves around work and it would be career death to get involved with anyone there. Anyway I'm number two in the marketing department now so anyone asking me out apart from the director would be propositioning their boss. Would you do that?'

'No,' said Becky, thinking of the head of English, appositely called Chrome-Dome by his pupils. 'What about your boss propositioning you, then?'

'Ah well, he is a problem. But not in that way. He's fifty-eight and overweight. Shall we have another bottle?'

Hugo, her boss, would, according to the custom of the multinational for which they worked, be compulsorily retired in a year's time. At this point Judy would have been his deputy for four years and might hope to step into his shoes.

'Brilliant,' said Becky. 'So what's the problem?'

'Personnel. They've offered me a job in another division.'

'I don't understand.'

'It's a sideways move for me. The salary's a little better but nothing spectacular. In the ordinary course of events it would be flattering but I haven't asked for a change and there must be plenty of other people who'd like that job.'

'So maybe you're the best qualified.'

'Maybe I am but I also think I'll be the best qualified for Hugo's job. Personnel offering me this sop now implies that I won't get Hugo's and they're moving me to avoid embarrassment later.'

'Perhaps it's age. Thirty-two is young to be a marketing director, isn't it?'

'Not unprecedented. There's a guy in detergents who made it at thirty-two. But there's no woman at director level of any age.'

There was a long pause.

'So what are you going to do?'

'I've got to decide whether to take the job in deodorants by the time I go back to work.'

'And will you?'

'I don't know.'

The next evening Becky drew the short straw and had to drive to Pisa airport to collect Sophie, Vanessa and Josh. They had masses of luggage despite the fact that most of it was supposed to have come in the Peugeot. Josh was on the dangerous cusp between wide-eyed excitement and tearful fractiousness, and Sophie, although her face was half-hidden by Raybans, looked sulky. Vanessa seemed tense and Becky found herself burbling with over-enthusiasm as she bundled them into the car. The evening sunlight which had been stinging her arms, over-exposed during an afternoon sunbathe, on the journey to Pisa, had now vanished leaving a flat, grey light and a cool breeze on the road. She stopped speaking and concentrated on finding the way back. The silence left by the ending of her monologue became as solid as an extra passenger.

'It must have been a terrible flight,' she said eventually.

Sophie merely shrugged but Vanessa roused herself. 'I'm sorry. It's been a bit of a trying day, what with working and rushing to Gatwick and—'

At which point Sophie, sitting in the front, suddenly leapt in. 'Anyway we're here now. What's the villa like?'

'Better than expected.'

'Better?'

'Well, you know what a difference there usually is between brochures and reality. And I must admit the pool is about half the size it appears to be in the photos but the views are unsullied and it's got the right number of rooms and beds.'

'Unsullied?' said Sophie. 'What have you been reading, Barbara Cartland?'

'Judy must be relieved then,' said Vanessa. 'It's always a worry if you've booked a place for other people.'

'She is,' said Becky. 'We danced the usual *pas de deux* over who would have which room but I stopped that by pointing out that you and Josh should have the largest and that as organiser she should pick next. I guess that's all right with you,' she said to Sophie who nodded.

'As long as it's big enough for two,' said Vanessa.

Becky was puzzled. 'I just said, it's the biggest one, it's got two beds—'

'She means my room,' said Sophie. 'She's cross because I said Mikey, who just happens to be in Milan on a job, could drop in if he had some time to kill.'

Becky looked in the rearview mirror but Vanessa's expression was studiedly neutral.

Inside Vanessa was furious. She knew that her attitude was dismissed by Sophie as ridiculously jolly hockey sticks but the whole atmosphere would be changed by having a man there. It wouldn't be so bad if there was more than one but there wasn't. And if there had to be just one, why this one?

She didn't see how she could have told Sophie about her and Michael without sounding bitchy but if it came out now it would look as if she had been hiding something. As they drove towards the villa Vanessa played scenarios of accusation and recrimination, featuring herself and Sophie and a long-haired boy – she had no other way of picturing Michael. Mimicking Josh, who had genuinely fallen asleep, she closed her eyes to remove herself from the conversation.

Becky, having said how nice it would be to see Mikey again after all this time, had adroitly manoeuvred the discussion through one of his commercials that she had seen on the box, to the programme that had been on after, to the programme that Sophie was working on at the moment.

Michael either hadn't told Sophie himself because he was a shit, Vanessa thought, or because, like her, he hadn't found an opportunity and now it seemed too late. She hoped he had the sense to continue to keep his mouth shut. Or better still not to turn up.

She was gloomily contemplating the prospect of several days on tenterhooks when an entirely different reason for his silence occurred to her. As a Lothario of the worst order maybe he simply didn't remember sleeping with her at all.

Hurt pride aside, following his example was the solution; if by any chance the subject came up she would claim to have entirely forgotten. What a relief – she must remember to prime Becky. She began to go through the motions of waking up.

The first day they did nothing but lie by the pool or explore the village shops. Judy and Vanessa had piles of paperbacks with them; Becky pored over guidebooks and in this found an unexpected ally in Sophie who alternated between long periods of lying comatose in the sun and bouts of restlessness which usually culminated in her splashing about in the water with Josh. When none of the four could be persuaded to play with him he would creep up behind one of the aunts and place a cold, wet hand on a warm, bare back, soliciting a satisfying squeak of surprise from the unfortunate victim.

When Becky suggested a trip to Florence the next day only Sophie, whose pale skin needed a break from the sun even though it had been smothered in Factor Fifteen, was enthusiastic. Vanessa, believing that Josh could do with another day to get bored with the pool before seeing any sights, and Judy, happily halfway through a blockbuster, demurred.

They took a stopping train through a countryside littered with toy trees and, closer to the city, the dilapidated blocks of flats that would have looked terrible in an English climate but here seemed almost as charming as the farmhouses themselves.

The Stazione Centrale was an odd mixture of the clean lines of modernism and the marble and gold of an earlier municipal pomposity.

'It's really rather attractive,' said Becky as they hovered, unwilling to make that first break into the uncharted territory of a new town.

'Oh dear – first you complain about the train being late and now you're excited by this corporatist stuff. How you'd have loved Mussolini.'

'I would not. He was a fat man who wore a sort of nightcap to military parades.'

'But lovely soft leather boots. And very well-cut breeches. Come on, let's go and get some atmosphere.'

They went first to the cathedral, that being the Grade A site nearest to their starting point, and came upon it almost too soon. Tantalising glimpses of its enormous dome were succeeded by the reality of the Piazza del Duomo, its perimeter pulsating with traffic and the centre subject to the troop movements of tourists, each column headed by a guide brandishing the inevitable furled umbrella above her head.

Being used to the overstuffed Westminster Abbey and the opulent choir of St Paul's, Becky was startled by the Duomo's spartan, cavernous interior.

They made the arduous climb between the inner and outer skins of the dome to the lantern and circled it in the hot sun. Beneath them the entire city was laid out for inspection, its network of narrow streets punctuated by squares, or more accurately rhomboids, each dominated by a church. From this height any modern redevelopment of shopfronts was concealed beneath the jumble of terracotta roofs, so that they might have been in a sixteenth-century time warp.

Becky felt her pulse speeding and the commonplace niggles of the recent end of term fading away. She had never been anywhere that looked so beautifully complete, and turned to say so to Sophie. But Sophie was gazing dreamily at the glittering River Arno, Raybans wedged on her head, a cigarette burning unregarded in her hand. Eventually she looked at Becky and smiled slowly.

'I could stay here all day. And I wouldn't even have bothered to puff up all those steps if you hadn't made me. You're in charge from now on. Where next?'

'The Ponte Vecchio via the Uffizi, I think. Although now I've seen what it's like I could just wander aimlessly.'

'No you couldn't. You're a teacher. You'll have this overwhelming urge to tell me about the rise and fall of the Medicis as we gallop from work of art to work of art.'

'At least I'll have an attentive audience.' Becky gestured minutely over Sophie's shoulder to a gaggle of Italian adolescents regarding her rear with an admiration more sullen than smouldering. Sophie, giggling, wiggled her hips at them as she straightened from the rail.

'They wouldn't understand a word you said,' she said uncharitably.

'It hardly matters. I don't think they have eyes for anything except your bum.'

'Quite flattering really. At my age.'

'Yes,' said Becky. 'It must be worrying when your years are greater than your hip measurement.'

The rest of the day was the standard sightseeing roller-coaster. When they saw the queue for the Uffizi they decided to leave it for another time. The picturesque buildings on the Ponte Vecchio turned out to be tatty jewellers' and the bridge's pavements were littered with latterday hippies.

Making up for that were the churches, their darkened interiors revealing endless frescos, not neglected, 'but not tarted up,' said Sophie. 'I suppose they've got so many they can afford to be cool about them.' And the streets themselves, the stone softening the harsh sunlight, the smells of lunchtime cooking, the absolute quiet of early afternoon when everything was shut and they walked through the formality of the Boboli Gardens to drink coffee and be repulsed by a grotesque statue of a dwarf riding a giant tortoise. And afterwards Santa Croce, where Donatello's disturbingly realistic *Crucifix* hung above the altar, its ponderously faded colours riveting against the backdrop of bright stained glass. They sat transfixed as the rosary was intoned hypnotically by a stubby priest with a stained cassock and a breathy microphone.

'I wish being a Catholic was just a matter of aesthetics,' Becky said as they returned to the station. 'I'd take instruction tomorrow.'

'Oh no, think of all those terrible plaster statuettes of the Blessed Virgin that you get in England or France. It's not the theology that makes Florentine churches gorgeous, it's just . . .'

Sophie tailed off, her arms flapping in a fruitless effort to find some explanation for the concentration of beauty they had just seen.

'I need one more fix before we go,' said Becky. 'Let's go to the Medici chapels. They're on our way.'

But this was a mistake. She stared in horror at the vast

walls of marble in lurid shades – oxblood, lemon curd, gorgonzola vein. How could they have wanted to be remembered like this, in dizzying expanses of material that she had previously only seen employed with some sense of scale to create intricate mosaics on altar rails?

'You can see where Mussolini got his ideas from,' Sophie whispered.

'At least he did it in off-white. This is a bad dream.'

'I'm trying not to take it in.' Sophie was pressing her body against the wall, her eyes closed. 'Perhaps they suffered from sunburn. It's very soothing on the skin.' Her bare arms looked white as lard where they touched the red marble.

'Calamine would have been less distressing to future generations,' said Becky and they went for their train.

The next fortnight acquired a pattern; one day's touring followed by one by the pool. At first Vanessa and Judy went on only half the outings but they were gradually drawn in by the others' enthusiasm. Some of their trips were to other parts of Tuscany and once they ventured as far as the sea but mostly they returned to Florence and its inexhaustible supply of things to look at. In-between-times they baked and basted and only desultory conversation punctuated reading and daydreams.

The hostility to Mikey coming, made obvious by Vanessa but palpable in the others, had evaporated on their first morning. He hadn't been mentioned again and, apart from one rather sexy dream in which they had become Dante and Beatrice while making a film about the Inferno, Sophie had also stopped thinking about him. When Judy asked her one evening what had happened to her guest it took a momentary effort to recall who she meant. Sophie couldn't imagine why she had invited anybody.

Judy ate up her Jilly Cooper and Julie Burchill and allowed her mind to roam about the recesses of her life without directly approaching the job offer. She thought of her mother's increasingly laboured hints that time was running out for her in the maternity stakes – after all, her sister Cheryl was three years younger and already had two kids – and she didn't even have a steady boyfriend. This last thrust was always delivered with the desperate hope of a rebuttal but none came and the conversation would then move on to stage two in which it was made clear that if Judy followed the example of her friend Vanessa it would be the finish of her father. Watching Josh splashing about now Judy knew, sweet as he was, that her mother need have no worries on that score. If she was going to have a child she would need the support of a husband, but she certainly wouldn't give her mum the satisfaction of saying so. Thank goodness for Darren and Kelly anyway; if there were no grandchildren to soak up the available affection Mum would probably already be sending her articles from *Woman and Home* about artificial insemination.

Becky felt dazed by the intensity of her own enjoyment. Her mind flickered with triptychs and diptychs and the life's work of Fra Angelico on the walls of the monastery of San Marco. They were a constant internal accompaniment to the long lunches and boozy suppers, to monitoring the progress of the lizard across the villa's kitchen wall, to Sophie flinging off her clothes and hurling herself into the pool after dinner, dragging Judy, protesting and still dressed, behind her.

They went to the Accademia to ogle Michelangelo's nude David.

'Beautiful,' said Vanessa.

'I don't know,' said Becky. 'I think there must be

different rules for sculpture but it doesn't get to me like the pictures.'

'Vanessa's just reaching the age for toy-boys,' said Sophie, 'and this is the granddaddy of them all.'

They sat at an open-air café in the Piazza della Repubblica drinking grappa, sambucca or amaretto and watched the Florentines promenade before the hoardings of another Italian general election. If their photographs on the posters were to be believed all of the candidates, whether Communist, Fascist or Christian Democrat, were handsome, middle-aged businessmen in Armani suits and Dior spectacles.

'If their sartorial style is indicative of their policies,' said Vanessa, 'it's no wonder they spend so much time in coalition.'

The angry buzz of dawdling Lambrettas reminded Becky that if they were watching the Florentines then the flower of Florentine youth was watching them. Or at least some of them. The fan club that Sophie had attracted on top of the cathedral was aped by a gathering of the sallow and sharply dressed wherever the girls settled. It was not only Sophie who drew them but Judy with her blonde hair piled above a delicately tanned neck and the tight bodice and flared skirt of her sleeveless Laura Ashley emphasising the right curves while concealing the wrong. Vanessa seemed of no interest; perhaps her colouring after a week in the sun was too familiar or perhaps the aura of power scared them even from window-shopping.

Becky didn't count herself; when she had attracted a 'bellissima' from a passer-by it was an ageing roué in suede blouson and matching moccasins.

'Sugar daddy,' Sophie had said. 'Get one of those and you'll be able to give up the comprehensive and devote yourself to La Dolce Vita.'

* * *

Apart from an attempted reconciliation with her parents, a week in a cottage in Devon with inclement weather and a frosty emotional climate, Vanessa hadn't had a holiday since Josh was born. As the four girls had never spent this amount of unbroken time together before she had been concerned that disagreements would erupt, but the reverse was true; the tensions apparent in the first couple of days had vanished. She couldn't imagine why they hadn't gone away together before.

Even Josh, who she thought might get on their nerves after the novelty of having a child around had worn off, still seemed to be in favour. She had thought that he might distance her from the others and had occasionally held back from some expedition to give them breathing space from him but invariably Judy or Becky, and once even Sophie; had pronounced themselves happier also to stay behind. Judy had taken him off to feed the pigeons in the Campo in Siena, and Becky had suggested a bus ride up to Fiesole when she would probably much rather have returned to the Uffizi for another spin around the Caravaggios.

Becky's fascination with religious art – her pupils dilated at the mere mention of Bartolommeo – was the revelation of this trip and Vanessa wished she was more able to share it, but her toddler was not entirely responsible for her truncated exploration of churches and galleries. She and Judy were simply more ardent sunseekers than art *aficionados*, and Judy had set the cat among the pigeons by saying that she preferred the nineteenth-century medievalism of Burne-Jones and Dante Gabriel Rossetti to the genuine article.

'Why not just have photographs and be done with it,' Becky had said, infuriated. 'The Pre-Raphaelites were a bunch of sentimental pedants.'

'Pictures for lovesick adolescents,' Sophie had added.

'Don't beat about the bush,' Vanessa had felt obliged to take Judy's part. 'If you think we're artistically retarded then just come right out and say so.'

This difference of opinion led to a surprising balance of company so that, as this morning, the two of them were on adjacent loungers while Becky and Sophie were stickily driving to Lucca for some cultural experience or other.

The sound of a car engine grumbling up the hill only intruded upon her unfocused thoughts when its changing-down gears coincided with a break in the tune Josh was humming as he trundled his toy bus up some hill of the imagination. Thinking for a moment that it was the others returning she rolled over on to her back and squinted into the sun. She realised that the engine note was too thin and laboured to belong to the Peugeot as whatever it was turned into their drive and stopped at the villa. She hauled at the straps of her swimsuit, pulling it over her oily torso and letting them slap painfully back on her shoulders. She looked across at Judy. 'We've got a visitor.'

'Who is it?'

'I don't know. Aren't you going to cover up?'

'No,' she said, her eyes still closed. 'You're not going to bring them over here, are you? Anyway, I'll lie still. I'll look just like a statue.'

Even breathing made Judy's breasts vibrate as if they were being blown by a gentle breeze but this was hardly the time to debate the point. Eager to head off some lecherous Italian postman (postman, why postman? . . . who could be writing to them here? . . . well, dustman then . . . in a Fiat?) she jumped up and grabbed her glasses. They transformed the blurred, black silhouette into a tousle-haired man wearing Levis, deck shoes and a T-shirt proclaiming 'Cinecitta – Pellicola Ben Cotto'.

Gathering her resources Vanessa began, '*Buon giorno.*'

He looked at his watch. '*Buona sera.*' There was a pause. 'Ah . . . *parla inglese?*'

'*Si.* I mean yes.'

'You are English. From your accent. It's just that you look . . .' His hands jiggled fleetingly at his sides. 'I'm looking for Sophie Attwood.'

This conversation had taken an unexpected turn. She swallowed. 'And you are?' As if she couldn't have guessed.

'Michael Rodgers.' He held out his hand diffidently.

She extended her own and he had taken it before she realised it was slick with suntan lotion. 'Sophie's not here at the moment.' There was a loud splash from behind which made him look up.

'And you are?' He was wiping his hand on the seat of his jeans.

'Vanessa. Tierney.' She turned away. 'Come and sit down.'

In her confusion she had forgotten about Judy but the sun lounger was empty; Judy was threshing round in the pool with the ungainly movements of one trying to fasten a bikini top while treading water.

Sitting out on the terrace after dinner with a grappa in one hand and a Marlboro in the other Mikey felt faintly uneasy. He hadn't really contemplated what it would be like being the sole man in a sort of free-thinking nunnery. The conversation had flowed well enough but he suspected it would have been entirely different if he wasn't there. Not only different but they would have been having a better time. Even Soph had seemed surprised to see him, dislocated.

The first few minutes had been a bit sticky; getting out of the car, which was too small for him and had left him with backache, to see what he took to be a tall Italian girl trying to shake a wasp from her swimming costume while a page-three model slept beside her and a cherub prostrated himself at their feet. When he discovered that the first was Vanessa and the last was her son he was shocked. She bore no similarity to the girl he remembered playing the Duchess.

When he'd first read Sophie's CV and recalled that year, Mikey thought he'd slept with Vanessa and had considered telling Soph once he realised they were still friends but the moment had never arrived, or at least he'd never been able to think of an unembarrassing way of bringing it into the conversation. And just as well, because now he wasn't sure that he had.

His vague memory of the angular, angry, furry body beneath the sheets was so unlike this sleekly powerful woman discussing advertising beside a Tuscan swimming pool that he thought it must have been someone else. Sophie's legs wrapping themselves around him had more in common with his mental picture of Vanessa than her actuality.

And his sharper recollection of their stage partnership, for which evidence existed, was distorted so that her lines were now delivered by a face deeply tanned rather than crudely highlighted with five and nine, and the long tresses gathered loosely in a cloak were replaced by shorter, curlier locks wet from the water.

Vanessa and Judy had gone to bed and now Becky was saying her goodnights. He and Sophie were on their own.

'Have you missed me then?' she said and sat herself on his lap.

'Of course,' he said and meant it. He breathed in the smell of white musk and kissed her neck. 'But I don't think you've missed me.'

'What do you mean?'

'You looked quite startled to find me here this afternoon. I felt like an invader.'

'That's not very fair,' she said, nuzzling at his ear. 'Everyone's been very friendly. They all like you,' she added, hoping it was true.

'Maybe I just feel surplus to requirements. What can I add to the idyllic set-up you've got here?'

'There is one thing.' She passed her tongue over her teeth, moistening her lips. 'But before I show you what that is I must just down this—' she swallowed the grappa remaining in his glass, 'otherwise you'll taste like an old Rotarian.'

'Why?'

'Because they always taste of brandy, and you've had some and I haven't. It's like garlic: if you've eaten it yourself you don't notice the pong.'

They progressed slowly towards her bedroom, shutting doors, switching off lights, tidying glasses as they went. Most untypical of Sophie, he thought.

'When did you last kiss an old Rotarian?'

'Even you couldn't get through Christmas at my parents' without one sticking his tongue down your throat. Or perhaps more, as you're a handsome boy.' She pinched his bottom and propelled him through the door of the bathroom. 'You go first.'

Sophie in turn drifted out to clean her teeth, her silk kimono trailing behind her, and Mikey was lying in bed when he realised just how quiet the house was. He could hear Sophie gargling from here, and if he could hear that . . .

A *frisson* of panic. Sophie's lovemaking was extremely noisy, which was exciting but not with an audience consisting of her three best friends. He closed his eyes.

Suddenly he felt very unenamoured. A headache was out of the question. Perhaps they were all heavy sleepers. Perhaps it was only from the bathroom that sound travelled, owing to the acoustics of early Medici plumbing. He was being stupid – other people lived in her house in London and it had never bothered him there. But apart from the leaden beat of the stereo he'd never heard sounds from any other room there, masked as they were by the traffic on the Camden Road.

He heard her return and the slither of the kimono on to the floor. The lamp was switched off. The bed moved under her weight and an ice-cold hand and the filaments of her hair simultaneously touched his chest. Soft breath crossed his cheek and a wet tongue licked the tip of his nose. His qualms were forgotten.

Probably no one except Vanessa would hear the steady sound of Josh's breathing even if they were in the same room but its regularity was a source of comfort to her, just as any deviation in its rhythm when he was a baby had frightened her far beyond reason. She pictured, dozily, his first school blazer and cap and somehow saw herself waiting for him outside the quaint Victorian gates of an infants' school carrying another child, a girl. She wondered whether Charlie had married his deb – perhaps he could send her a sample even if he could not be present at the conception – but when she pulled the shawl back from her daughter's face it smiled up at her with Becky's smile. She wouldn't have time to do the school run because by then she would have set up her own agency to handle all the haircare business that would be in Judy's pocket once she had become marketing director.

Sophie and Michael were on the landing. Sophie sounded a bit squiffy.

It was hard to believe that Michael had not recognised her nor she him at first. Then as they had sat talking about advertising, a nice safe topic, the occasional expression, the voice – although deeper and rougher around the edges (it presumably didn't do to sound too actorish when directing pop musicians and film crews) – had come back to her and she had been able to marry up the lined face of today with the youthful countenance of 1977. Turning to her as the curtain fell and hugging her through the ringing applause, heaving over her as the iron college bed squeaked . . .

Had all of her lovers forgotten her? Peter and Gary the biker and Michael and Lennox and John and Jon who now worked in Hong Kong and Russell the obnoxious copywriter and Danny's friend the accountant – what was his name? – there, it was easily done – and Martin who had blue eyes like Paul Newman and a house in Blackheath and who once tried to knock her about a bit, and then Charlie who wouldn't have dreamed of such a thing.

From beyond the wall came a squeal which Vanessa wouldn't have recognised as Sophie except that it was followed by an unmistakable half-giggle cut short.

As the succeeding procession of gasps and groans rose in frequency and intensity she was at first curious, then appalled at herself, then angry at being forced into voyeurism, and finally worried that they might wake Josh. She got out of bed to check but his sleep seemed deep; she wished hers was. Standing by the window she realised she was sweating profusely and pressed her nightshirt against her body to soak it up. For God's sake, she didn't begrudge anybody an orgasm but this was ridiculous.

She buried her head beneath the pillow but somehow the sounds were still there and with her eyes closed they began to intermingle with re-runs of her own couplings. She sat up to hear Sophie's final sigh and then silence.

Thoroughly awake, she felt resentful, but how could you resent someone else's pleasure? Presumably it was that and not faked – she couldn't imagine Sophie bothering to salve any man's feelings in that way although she'd heard nothing like it outside the cinema. Her nerve-ends were tingling. Resolutely she put her mind to the problems of the Dolphin swimwear account.

The last few days of their holiday passed very quickly; after Mikey had left there seemed only time for one last trip to Florence and a final delicious day by the pool, sunning and swimming, eating and drinking everything that was left in the house. They'd staggered to bed very late, leaving Becky to wake up on a sun lounger, covered by a blanket, as the dawn broke. It was a beautiful sight but she was hardly in a state to appreciate it and so it was Judy, herself under the weather if not still the influence, who drove the others to the airport.

They had all had such a good time that only the hangovers saved them from an outbreak of tearful sentimentality at the departure gate – that and Josh's burning desire to see the planes – but on the way back to the villa, alone in the car, Judy indulged in a couple of stern blows into a tissue.

The house she found empty and forlorn, all signs of their revelry tidied away. Becky was on the terrace with her suitcase, the plastic rubbish bags and an open packet of Paracetamol. There was nothing to do but load up and set off. The prospect of an overnight stop in France was now strangely unappealing; once the villa had disappeared behind the row of olive trees in the rearview mirror all Judy wanted was to get home as quickly as possible. She calculated the odds of making directly for the ferry but couldn't drive the full distance unassisted, and looking at

Becky – eyes closed and window wound down to ward off nausea – she knew it would not be possible.

It was lunchtime, or rather 'just coffee time', before they had a conversation.

'It was good.'

'It was brilliant. The best holiday I've ever had,' said Becky.

'That's a sweeping statement. What about your honeymoon?'

'Different, obviously.' A pause. 'Don't think I have a proper perspective on that. Anyway, I'm not prepared to rake over the ashes just to make a comparison. Not with this head.' A montage from her post-nuptial tryst in Israel whizzed past . . . She blinked, 'And what about you?'

'I think me too.'

'You don't harbour a secret longing for the sandy beaches and giant ice-cream cornets of childhood?'

'I don't think so. If I'm honest the sand was usually blowing against the windbreak and stinging my goose-bumps.'

Becky laughed, and winced. 'And it was always miles to the sea.'

'It'll be nice to get home, anyway.' It was the sort of thing people say in motorway service areas.

'Really? Oh well, I suppose you've got the cat to look forward to.'

'Poor Bartholomew. Do you know, I've hardly thought about him since we arrived. I ought to feel very guilty. I wonder if he's missed me?'

'Shouldn't think so. They've only got ten-minute memories, cats, so he won't have the faintest idea who you are.'

Judy looked shocked. 'Are you sure? No, you're laughing at me. If you want to take the piss out of me and my one true love you can do the next stint of driving.'

Later, when the autostrada had become the autoroute, Judy asked, 'So aren't you looking forward to getting back?'

'Why? Two weeks more of the supposed holidays, bit of preparation, and then back into the grind of another bloody term.'

'But you love it. Don't you?'

'Why does everybody assume I like being a teacher?'

'Because you've been doing it for eight years. You've got a vocation.'

'If I ever had one I think I've lost it. And that leaves me with a mortgage, a rusty car and . . .'

'And what?'

'Nothing. Nothing at all.'

'You've just got a premature dose of post-holiday blues. Last night's Chianti talking. Cheer up.'

And anyway what could I do instead? Becky thought. 'What about you? Are you going to take that promotion?'

'No. No, I'm feeling very positive. I'm going to make them make me marketing director.'

Somewhere above the Massif Central Vanessa read Josh a story while Sophie, whose trace tan seemed to have faded as their altitude increased, nursed a cognac she described as medicinal and stared at the clouds through dark glasses.

Eventually, with the story over and the child sulking in silence Sophie said, 'When I invited Mikey to join us I thought three weeks with just us girls might be a bit . . . claustrophobic.'

'You say the nicest things, Sophie.'

'Well, we'd never done it before, not for more than a long weekend.'

'And did we fulfil your expectations?'

'No. Or yes. I'm not quite sure what you mean by that

51

question. I had a fun time. So when he turned up I sort of wished he hadn't. I mean the sex was nice but he unbalanced everything. Good job he could only stay two days really. I hope I wasn't too offhand.'

'No,' Vanessa said carefully. 'I wouldn't say you were that.'

'Anyway – you were right. About him upsetting the equilibrium. I just thought I'd gracefully concede that.'

'I wouldn't bother. He was fine.'

'Oh, good. Do you think they'll let me have another brandy? I'm starting to feel quite perky.'

3

The Trick Cyclist

The autumn term was only a week old when a souped-up Cortina went into the back of Becky's car at a zebra crossing in Dulwich. Its owner turned out to be an uninsured, unemployed divorcee. 'You could take him to court,' said her solicitor, 'but you'll only get a pound a week for however long it takes, assuming you win. You'll be the first year or more simply recovering the legal costs. Frankly I'd advise against an action. Can you bear the repair costs yourself? What's the damage?'

The damage, according to Ernie at the Renault garage in Stockwell, was £800-worth of new body panels and respraying, and although the car was drivable without, it was not legal. Even before the accident it had only been worth £500 and now his advice was to sell it for spares. 'Or, if you're very lucky you might find someone who can do the work themselves and'll pay a bit more.'

'How much?'

'I'd advertise it for a ton ... or near offer.'

Despairingly, she had, but in contradiction of her gloomy expectations the car had been bought almost immediately for the full £100, in cash, by a softly-spoken man with a leather jacket, Mediterranean features and a surprising Irish brogue.

Becky was condemned to travel to school by tube and train until she had plucked up enough courage to take out a bank loan and it was as she stepped off the up escalator at Victoria that she saw the poster. HAVE YOU RENTED A ROOM RECENTLY? SOLD A CAR FOR CASH? it demanded in urgent, official black and red print. And because she had done just that she stopped to read the rest, causing a great deal of annoyance to the commuters piling up behind.

The statistical improbability of the purchaser of her car being a terrorist enabled her to ignore the request to contact the police, but that night she found it hard to get to sleep and when she did it was to dream of the Renault, parked among the chauffeur-driven Daimlers in front of Vanessa's office building, erupting in a sheet of flame. Logically, the casualties included the Kensington matron who presided over the reception desk and her young acolyte whose imitative upturned collar and pearls implied rigorous grooming for the succession. Fantastically, the blast also claimed Chrome-Dome, Becky's head of department, and a boy she went out with when she was fifteen.

Unsettled, she worried about what to do. The idea of her Irishman planting bombs was ludicrous, but presumably that's what everyone thought until the person they knew was proved to have done exactly that. And was it normal to buy a car without a proper test drive or any haggling?

But what could she tell the police if she went to them? She had no address and goodness knew how many people could have seen the ad in *Loot*, added to which her only grounds for suspicion were his accent, which made her as prejudiced as the boys in blue who would make his life a misery if she reported him. A disturbing vision of his handsome face under the interrogator's lamp together with *Guardian* headlines on police brutality made up her mind. Almost.

The next evening three people rang about the car for sale – the only ones to have done so since he had driven it away. Then it clicked that as *Loot* had only been published that day he must have seen her other ad in the window of the newsagents. She had given it to Mrs Patel on Friday night and he had rung Saturday lunchtime.

Feeling very stupid but hoping to salve her conscience she went back the following Saturday and described him to Mr Patel in case he was a regular.

'It's the man with the bike,' said a doe-eyed junior Patel, after his father had regretfully shaken his head.

'Does he come in every day?' she asked.

The boy nodded.

'Same time every day?'

'Morning.'

'He can't know that,' said Mr Patel. 'He is at school.'

But not on Saturdays, she thought, and crossed the road to the workman's café where she bagged a table by the window and, armed with a mug of tea and her paper, settled down to wait. Just for a bit. Because she had nothing else in particular to do and because if she saw that he was a local using the same shops as she did she would know he was an innocent with a perfectly legitimate use for an unroadworthy Renault.

What sort of bike? The leather jacket hardly allowed for his riding a Tebbitesque sit-up-and-beg – the kind of cycle that went with allotments and coming home to a lunch called dinner. But somehow he was too stylish and well-pressed for a Honda 250. And, buying the Renault, too poor for a big BMW. Eventually she settled for a mountain bike; pedal power to go with his slight but muscular frame, and trendy enough to match his ponytail.

When he did appear she almost missed him, expecting as she was a man on two wheels. He was on foot, his Levis freshly laundered, the black jacket adorned by a red silk scarf hooked through the right epaulette. He was more attractive than she remembered and looked about as much like an IRA zealot as Ian Paisley. Without any idea of what she might do next she paid fat Stan, the café proprietor, and stumbled on to the street as the cyclist emerged from Patel's.

Had his attention not been engaged by the *Sporting Life* he might have seen her but as it was he crossed the road and set off across the Common. Still caught up in a muddled detection fantasy, mildly triumphant at her success so far, Becky followed, tracking him at what seemed a discreet distance. Even after he had swung off at a tangent from the main path she was confident that should he turn round she would merge into the sprinkling of perpetual dog-walkers that made up the Common's staple population.

As they passed through the ride of oak and beech decimated by the big storm of 1987, one mutilated stump now for every living tree, she saw the barbed-wire enclosure containing a gaggle of caravans, lorries and Portakabins around a marquee. Along the fence was draped an enormous banner reading 'Cirque d'Apocalypse'. The Irishman jumped lightly over the crash barrier blocking the gap in the fence and vanished into a garishly-painted double-decker bus serving as a gatehouse.

Slowly she approached the encampment. The lorries had foreign number plates, as did the black Cadillac attached to the largest caravan. All the vehicles looked worn, with none of the loving care that fairground machinery paintwork normally exhibits. Apart from the marquee, boldly striped in blue and white, and the kaleidoscopically-coloured bus, it could have been an abandoned construction site.

Traces of life became apparent. The ashes of a fire smouldered between the cabins; a peroxide-blonde head, sex indeterminate, could be glimpsed through a caravan window; inexplicably the sound of a chain-saw starting up came from inside the marquee. She leant over the barrier to read the ticket prices and performance times displayed on the side of a bus.

'It's a good show,' said a voice behind her. She jumped. Blood rushed to her head. It was an effort to turn round without falling over. She swallowed. He was close and smiling. 'Have you come to see what's happened to your poor old car?'

In some ways it was bad luck that Mikey rang Sophie only two hours before the Wednesday recording of *Churchill's People*. One of the guests was running late and the minor American film star who had arrived was an absolute bitch and was refusing to answer questions that had been agreed at her preliminary interview. The chat show's genial host, the eponymous Jerry Churchill, had switched off his famous charm and was cursing anyone unwise enough to show their face. Sophie, who had no choice, had been mauled twice, so when Mikey suggested dinner that evening she snapped an unembroidered refusal and told him to call her at the weekend 'which is the only time some of us have off'. As Mikey was unhappily between assignments she could hardly have been more unpleasant.

After the show she had a couple of large ones in the hospitality suite and felt better disposed towards him and the rest of the world, but the traffic on the Euston Road was a pig and by the time she got home her benign mood had evaporated.

Carol was cooking a chilli in the communal kitchen and, a rare occurrence, offered to share rather than freezing the surplus. They ate it with far too many pieces of garlic bread and tumblerfuls of sour Vin de Pays. Having damned all employers – Carol was exploited by the customer service department of a tour operator who used her considerable cheek as a first line of defence against the complaints of dissatisfied returnees from the Costa del Sol – they both went to bed in high spirits and Sophie slept soundly.

It was only when she woke early with a dry mouth, an inevitable consequence of drinking too much, that she thought again about Mikey. She knew she had been rude, and she would apologise, but she hadn't wanted to see him last night and didn't know whether she even wanted to see him at the weekend.

She couldn't work out why. Normally it would be because some new man had come into view . . . but at the moment there was no one.

They had had six months . . . but that was not unprecedented.

He was getting a little settled into their coupledom . . . but not to a degree that she couldn't live with.

So what was the problem?

Perhaps that friendship with Mikey, as with any man, was indelibly bound up with sex and at the moment she didn't seem to want that, a feeling she recognised as extremely unusual. Because they only saw each other two or three times a week they seemed to do it every time and although she knew that didn't happen when you saw someone more frequently she didn't actually want to see him more often. Apart from anything else the trade-off was absurd – seeing more of someone to avoid screwing them.

Feeling guilty, she rang Mikey and agreed to go to a dinner party with him on Saturday.

To assuage her guilt at not wanting to go to the party she let him take her home after it and make love to her.

Feeling guilty about not enjoying that, she faked an orgasm for the first time in her life.

Then she lay awake against his sleeping back feeling guilty about that and angry with herself. What was the matter?

Becky was going to the circus. She hadn't done that since she was seven, but at her unorthodox second meeting with Dermot she had had to imply that she was already considering coming to see the show. What other possible explanation for her presence by the bus could there be? Luckily he claimed only to have spotted her from the window of his caravan so she hadn't had to explain why she had trailed him.

So flustered was she that when he asked her if she was coming alone she had answered no. Then he had simply said that he hoped she would enjoy it, and they had parted.

'Well, why don't you go alone anyway?' said Vanessa, when she had heard the story so far. 'At least then you might get to see him after the performance. Unless, of course, you still think he's a gunman or a bomber or whatever.'

'Of course not. I never did really.'

'Either way you're mad. Following a strange man like some demented Sherlock Holmes. You would like to see him?'

'Well . . . yes. I mean, why not?' Becky added, glimpsing Vanessa's predatory expression. 'He's probably quite interesting. I mean, living in a circus.'

Vanessa was openly smirking. Becky jabbed at her.

'But there's nothing to say that he wants to see me.'

'Oh, nothing much,' Vanessa scoffed. 'The entire conversation was a pick-up. Sometimes I think you're regressing to pre-puberty. But yes, I will come and hold your hand as long as you promise me elephants.'

'I don't think there are any animals at all.'

'What sort of a circus is it, for God's sake?'

'The sort that has cuttings of reviews from *Time Out* and the *Guardian* on its posters.'

'Oh. Post-modern plate twirlers and feminist clowns, I suppose. I can not bring Josh with a clear conscience then.'

Inside the marquee there was tiered seating on either side and at one end a raised stage housing the amplifiers, drum-kit, keyboards, guitars and microphone stands of what was obviously going to be an extensive band. At the other end was an arrangement of ramps and slides fashioned out of metal so blackened and twisted it might have been debris from an oil refinery fire.

The lights dimmed to black, leaving only the winking orange and green bulbs of the equipment on-stage. Whispers and giggles replaced conversations about arthouse movies and mortgage rates. The first heavy chords of Latin post-punk burst out of the darkness as fireworks exploded in the arena, provoking inevitable screams. Two pairs of car headlights stabbed out from either end of the auditorium and caught in their beams was a midget riding an electric wheelchair surmounted by an elaborately shaded standard lamp. His amplified cackling reverberated around the audience as more lights returned to reveal a world of swirling smoke and the red glow of distant fires.

The music gathered in pace and density as from the mouths of the tunnels came a ragbag army of holocaust refugees, clothed in torn tights and tattered cloaks – here a German helmet, there a top hat with a long silk scarf fluttering above its brim – faces daubed with warpaint and hair dyed and spiked.

One of them was juggling flaming brands and another bowling a huge iron hoop. In the mêlée two barbarian warriors were bundling the shrieking midget into a dustbin when cars roared in, painted in nightmarish streaks, their missing body panels exposing sheafs of wiring and rusting engine parts. The performers scattered, screaming and shouting, some climbing into the audience. A pair of matadors produced chain-saws from their cloaks and skipped around the ring, avoiding the charges of the ungainly motors and hacking at them with the saws whose rotating teeth created showers of sparks.

Vanessa, the sharp stench of cordite in her nostrils, looked at Becky. She was bent forward, thumb pressed against her chin, hair unattended and fallen forward across her ears. At a particularly painful screech of metal on metal she started.

'That's my car.'

The next act was a pair of gymnasts – a man and a woman – each wearing a black leather thong and shining with body oil and sweat beneath the lights. To a slow and sensual number from the band they created a number of impossibly balanced tableaux, their tense muscles vibrating with the strain of apparently supporting a whole body on toe or finger. Their dreamy movements had the eroticism of slow-motion film, focusing attention on the perfection of their glistening forms.

'It's not him, is it?' whispered Vanessa and Becky shook her head. 'Perhaps you could arrange a double date then. What a bum. Have we seen yours?'

Becky shook her head. The driver of her metamorphosed Renault had been in shadow; she assumed it had been Dermot but if so he had not reappeared.

A trapeze team were followed by jugglers and as they disappeared a large bicycle wheel rolled in from the tunnel, traversed the arena and vanished on the other side. As, without explanation, it came back at a stately pace there was a blur of movement and it was snatched from the ring by the rider of a pushbike that had flown down the ramp at extraordinary speed. He wore a skin-tight black suit and goggles and a gold band held back his ponytail.

Vanessa realised from the shift in Becky's position that this was her Irishman. He performed an astonishing series of manoeuvres at speed including jumps that elicited gasps from the audience and then rode backwards out of the arena while the troupe's groundlings assembled an obstacle course of scaffolding and narrow planks along its centre. He returned on a motorbike and roared up and over this tortuous route in a pall of exhaust fumes. After a skidding turn and a roll on the drums he brought the bike up on to its rear wheel only and covered the course again at a snail's pace, never letting the front wheel touch the planking.

'I don't know much about bikes,' whispered Vanessa, 'but that looked bloody difficult.'

When the lights came up they realised it would be impossible to defy the crowd and remain in their seats so let themselves be carried out into the cold of late evening. It was obvious to Becky that unless they waited until the place was deserted he would never find her, assuming that he even tried. They hovered in the lee of the marquee for some time, Vanessa subconsciously fiddling with her car keys. Eventually Becky, on tiptoe, cast one final fruitless glance at the caravans, now curtained and lit up, and said, 'Come on, let's go back to my place for a coffee or something.'

The next morning Becky didn't know whether she was

disappointed or not. Skilful and daring as his act was, there was something boyish about cycle tricks that was as shameful and ultimately pointless as train-spotting. It lacked the nobility of, say, trapeze work. As she crossed her tiny hall to the kitchen she saw the envelope caught in the letterbox.

The note said, 'I don't know if I missed you last night by accident or design. If you would like to see me I would like to see you. I will be in the Crown at one. Dermot.'

Accident or design. Not the wording of a train-spotter. She thought about the cosmopolitan looks that belied the bikes and the voice that belied the looks and went to run a bath.

The Crown was a small pub that had carpets on the floors and a couple of lank strings of horse brasses but no jukebox. Of the many bars within walking distance it was the most anonymously respectable and not one that she would have put on his shortlist. He was sitting in a corner with a crumpled Penguin paperback and a half-empty glass of stout. Although the book was raised he was looking straight at her as she came through the door. He smiled and stood up gracefully.

'I hope you don't mind this place. But there are some inherited desires you can't escape if you're Irish and decently served Guinness is one. After all, I thought I might be drinking alone.'

That day they talked until closing time and then walked across the Common.

'Because of my unsociable working hours,' he said, taking his leave, 'I won't really be able to see you again until next weekend. We sit up into the small hours but you can't do that if you're teaching at nine on the other side of town.'

Well, she thought, you could try me, but he seemed disinclined to do that and she wondered who precisely he sat up into the small hours with. A brief, disturbing vision of the oiled torso of the female gymnast flashed like a red-light district.

'How do you fancy a late movie in Brixton on Friday, if there's something good on?'

She accepted and he kissed her hand in farewell.

When she had first seen Dermot she would have said, if asked, that he was good-looking but not sexy, not her type. Too trendy, too ... well, too short. But what had begun with curiosity and embarrassment seemed to have evolved.

She found herself commuting with an inexplicable spring in her step. On Wednesday she decided that perhaps her hair needed cutting, nothing special, just a trim. On Thursday, passing the Body Shop, it suddenly occurred to her that for ages she had been meaning to get a face pack. On Friday she ironed her clothes for the evening before she left for work and missed her customary train. Normally this would have made her furious but it faded into insignificance against the vexed question of what they would do after the film. Everywhere would be closed. Would he invite her back? Should she accept? Was circus etiquette different?

Waiting for him outside the cinema she acknowledged that she was excited, and fretted. Should he find her sitting on the bench or lurking seductively in the shadows by the doors? Did her coat collar look better up or down? She tried it both ways, twice. She suffered the almost-forgotten fear of being stood up, and her consequent relief at Dermot's arrival was mingled with shame that his first view of her had undoubtedly been of her minutely scrutinising her face in her compact mirror. When he tapped her on the shoulder, having come from a totally unexpected direction, she was just putting it away for the third time.

Safely in the darkness of the cinema she dismissed such dating anxieties as stupid, or at least as harmless fun. What did it matter? Then they were in the street, walking, at the end of her street, outside her house, and no further arrangements had been made. She invited him in for coffee. He only stayed fifteen minutes, sat politely on her sofa, and when he left he kissed her equally politely on both cheeks. But he had asked her out again. She went to bed feeling warm, wanted, successful.

On Saturday, after his evening performance, they were the last customers to arrive at a Chinese in Clapham High Street where they discovered a mutual liking for crispy duck. He ordered coffee in the restaurant, which rendered redundant the beans sitting in her coffee grinder and the tray with *cafetière*, mugs and milk jug ready prepared in her kitchen. They parted on the pavement outside her flat, but there, for the first time, under the sodium glare of the street lamp, they kissed properly, lips to lips, tasting the salty legacy of plum sauce.

Lying in bed later she realised that she did not know how long before the circus left town. And that, perhaps, it really mattered.

The creative team had finally come up with a script for the Dolphin swimwear cinema commercial that Vanessa thought the client would accept. It involved vigorous cross-cutting between a group of beautiful girls dressing and laughing, and an underwater scene. Tropical fish, sandy seabed, and so on. The girls would emerge on to a catwalk at a fashion show and parade, discarding their clothes to reveal the Dolphin swimsuits beneath. One by one they would drop through a hole in the catwalk and be seen swimming along the seabed before emerging from another hole by means of a typical pool ladder to rapturous applause and the flashes of many cameras.

This scenario neatly incorporated the client's requirements that his costumes be positioned as fashion items but immensely practical, and be seen wet and dry.

Together with the storyboard, Max, the creative director, had three showreels of film directors' work for the client to see. The first director was an underwater specialist but with no fashion experience; the second a safe pair of hands with plenty of glamorous vacuity to his credit; the third was Mikey.

'Why this one?' asked Vanessa.

'Good lighting and pace on the pop videos, and some unusual close-ups on the deodorant ad. It's more exciting.'

'And cheaper?'

'Of course. He needs the work more. But he's also the best.'

'What about the underwater stuff?'

'He's got a clip from a vid that was done in a swimming pool, but the truth is we'll insist on Doug Arthur as cameraman – at least for that sequence.'

Vanessa did not say that she knew Mikey; a 'suit' endorsing an artist could only lessen his chances as their creative judgement was widely assumed to be non-existent.

As there were only three weeks before the circus packed up and embarked on an extensive tour of France, Becky believed her next meeting with Dermot would be pivotal. Their 'thing' was going to stop immediately or acquire the other-worldly amorality of a holiday romance without, as she said to Vanessa, the inconvenience of a flight home at the end of it. Surprisingly Vanessa had not issued dire warnings of the consequences of unprotected sex, but wished her luck with the wistful manner of one who was finally having doubts about her own self-imposed celibacy.

Becky had invited Dermot to her flat for a meal and he arrived at eleven so hastily showered after the evening's performance that his ponytail was still wet and traces of eyeliner remained below his lashes.

With an innocent charm he produced, in addition to the obligatory guest's bottle of plonk, a small bunch of freesias. A nice touch this – a smooth seducer would have brought roses and her realistic accountant of an ex-husband a box of chocolates, which might be what a girl wants deep down but are extremely unflattering to her self-image.

They ate *coq au vin* and a piece of ripe Camembert.

'I didn't used to like this stuff,' he said. 'Before I left Dublin it was all meat and potatoes and suet pudding.'

'And when did you leave Ireland?'

'I came over to see my brother. With my motorbike and a rucksack. I worked on the building sites for a couple of months, had a couple of good wins, and it was summer so I decided to cross the Channel and bum around Europe for as long as the weather was good.'

'And is that where you found the circus?'

'Yes.'

'And could you already do the tricks?'

'Some of them. But I started just as a labourer, I suppose you might say. Helping rig the tent and so on. Three years ago now.'

'And when did you become a star performer?'

'We don't have star performers.'

His tone was lazy but she felt she had in some way overstepped the mark, offended his sensibilities. 'Become an act then,' she said defiantly.

He grinned. 'That's more in keeping with our egalitarian spirit. Just the twelve months.'

They sat on the floor in front of the sofa and Becky added the sibilant glow of the gas fire to the distant table lamp and the candles now guttering on the dining-table. She asked him to choose a tape and with tact he picked a soft rock album very like those she had been playing. It was that, the inability to get him to reveal any more of his charming self, that decided her. She had felt, thought she had felt, the responsive tingle when they had kissed and a tension in his arms which added up to desire but he seemed set on proceeding at a stately pace and there was no time for that. The wine had given her the temporary insouciance to test her theory to destruction. If she was wrong and he backed off she would regret it in the morning but not now. When, at three, no further forward, he suggested he should be heading back to camp she said that he didn't have to.

'Is that an invitation to your bed or your settee?'

'To me,' she said and then blushed, astonished by her own boldness. To hide it she scrambled to her feet and reached out her hands. 'This is always the embarrassing bit. Hanging about wondering whether to go straight to the bedroom or start in the sitting-room.' Jesus, her mouth was racing ahead of her brain. They were halfway down the hall when she realised just what the 'always' implied.

In the dark she kissed him once and then broke away to remove her clothes. She had intended to be beneath the duvet before he had ceased to be preoccupied by the encumbrance of his boots but somehow the familiar fastening of her bra eluded her and she pulled off her tights and knickers aware that he was watching this undignified movement from her pillow.

Sleep did not come deeply enough to prevent her waking at the first sign of light through the too-thin curtains. Beside her Dermot's breathing was as measured as his earlier lovemaking. He even slept neatly, neither foetally curled nor extravagantly sprawled but straight as if lying in state. By the radiator his clothes were carefully folded.

The radiator was on and with an extra occupant the bed was far too hot. She began to replay events in her head but a part of her brain was attempting to compare Dermot with past lovers, with Danny ... and she couldn't handle that with him here. Luckily she wasn't on the wall side so she slipped out and, pulling on the long T-shirt that she normally slept in, she crept to the kitchen to make some tea. She was watching the kettle, ready to pull its cord in the millisecond after it had boiled and before it buzzed, when the back of her neck prickled and he was standing in the doorway, circumspectly dressed in his jeans and vest.

'Hello,' she said.

He smiled but did not move.

'Tea?' she said and he nodded so she got another mug from the cupboard and then the kettle was boiling and buzzing and the pot needed warming and filling and the milk getting from the fridge and somehow they were sitting at the dining-table with the formality of supper and he was asking her whether she wanted to come with him to see his brother, which seemed like some parody of family approval and far too premature ... and they still hadn't touched.

While he was explaining that it was a fair distance but he had a spare helmet Becky was considering their lack of contact. What she would have expected was him to come up behind her in the kitchen and curl his hand round her tummy; even, possibly, to feel the prod of an early morning erection against her back, but that was Danny again and with Dermot being shorter it would be somewhere nearer her bottom. But he hadn't even announced his presence, let alone kissed her on the head.

She offered him a bath and he accepted, saying it was a

luxury he didn't often experience, so she went to start it running and by that stage all that it seemed reasonable to do was to ruffle his hair as she passed. Her fingers itched to do this but, already gathered in its ponytail, it didn't look as if it would ruffle without extreme discomfort so she contented herself with touching his shoulder.

It was years since Becky had ridden pillion on a motorbike and then it was a sort of souped-up moped, nothing like this large and noisy machine. They crossed the river, weaved through an empty East End and by the time they reached the M11 she had got the hang of leaning into the corners with confidence. For a while longer the speed deterred her from taking her hands off the tail rack but her arms were getting numb. Eventually, when they seemed to be on a particularly long, straight stretch she let go and, leaning forward, wrapped them around his waist instead. Although he must have been surprised he didn't flinch.

They left the motorway and boomed along winding Essex lanes, eventually stopping by a large, wrought-iron gate, the intricate pattern of which somewhat laboriously spelt out 'Rathkennen Kennels'. She pushed up the visor of her helmet as he fiddled with its bolts.

'Is this where your brother lives then?'

'And works.'

'I thought he was in the building trade.'

'Did I say that?'

'Yes ... well, no, maybe not. It was implied.'

'Not intentionally.' He smiled. 'What were you expecting? A big bloke with tattoos and his bum exposed by his low-slung jeans?'

'No, I don't know.'

'Come to think of it,' he said, remounting the bike, 'his arse does hang out of his trousers but not in that way.'

They went down a long drive on either side of which were paddocks enclosed by high wire fences. A pair of emaciated black and white dogs in the paddock to their left kept pace with them. He parked outside an enormous, ugly 1950s house and as soon as the engine was switched off she could hear the barking of what sounded like hundreds more dogs.

'I didn't realise boarding kennels had so much exercise space,' she said.

Dermot stood at the paddock fence. 'Do you not recognise these creatures?' he asked, as a couple came up, wagging their tails. She realised that they were all of the same breed.

'Whippets?' she hazarded, hazily recalling a frowned-upon uncle who had reputedly hunted rabbits on the Thames marshes as an antidote to his shift work in the paper mill.

Dermot snorted with derision, the strongest expression of his she had encountered. 'They're greyhounds – racing greyhounds.'

She really had no mental picture of this at all.

'It's a good living,' she said, gesturing at the house.

She wondered whether Dermot liked houses like this – there were so many things you didn't know about a person until circumstance thrust their opinions in your face.

'That's not his – he's just the head lad. He's got a caravan round the back.'

Sean was a little older than Dermot and thicker set. He wore a stained white coat in the manner of a butcher or fishmonger and seemed immune to the smell of urine and disinfectant which filled the enclosed range of cubicles, each containing a wooden bed covered with shredded paper, a galvanised bucket of water and a pair of hounds. As they passed by the dogs stood on their hind legs against the wire doors, pressing their wet noses through the mesh

71

to be petted, their flailing tails contradicting the perpetually doleful eyes.

'Do they like running?' Becky asked, when she had been shown the kitchen where the dogs' daily meal of beef and vegetables was prepared. It was far better kept than Sean's caravan; in fact it was obvious to a casual observer that the animals lived in luxury with their muscle-toning machines and indoor swimming pool, but their whole lives were geared to running round a track and she wondered whether they did it naturally or had to be bribed.

'They wouldn't be here if they didn't. There are pups who don't like it or aren't very good at it but they get weeded out.'

She decided not to ask what happened to the weeds.

'You'll see one run in a minute. I have to give Smokey a solo,' he added to his brother. 'Before the rush.'

'Sunday's a big day,' explained Dermot. 'The owners all come to visit their dogs, and the select few get to have a brandy and some cockles afterwards with the boss.'

He indicated a dumpy man who had emerged from the house, a white coat pulled on over a travesty of English country casuals and a cigarette wedged between his lips. Smoothing back his curly, greying, Brilliantined hair, he ambled across the yard.

'Morning, Mr P,' said Dermot.

'Eh, you come on your bloody bike wakin' up my wife.' The cigarette oscillated violently during this speech. 'Where's that lazy mick your brother?' He grinned hugely, revealing several gold teeth, letting the butt fall and grinding it beneath his heel.

'Getting Smokey for a trial,' said Dermot, also smiling.

'So that's why you're here. You come for a red-hot tip. I refuse to let you watch but your bloody brother only tell you anyway. Who is your friend?'

He beamed at Becky, and turned to Sean who had returned leading a handsome blue-grey hound. 'So you're selling tickets now?'

'This is Becky,' said Dermot, 'and this is Mr Patzaki.'

Becky half expected the exuberant trainer to give her a hug or kiss her hand but he merely shook it delicately.

'So, are you a big punter?' he asked.

'No,' she said. 'In fact I've never been greyhound racing.'

'Good,' he said. 'We're safe then. She won't know whether the time is good or bad, eh?'

And with that he set off towards the field beyond the kennel range, the others trailing behind.

'Smokey,' said Dermot quietly, 'or Zakis Minotaur, to give him his full name, has been on the sick-list for some time but if this morning's run is satisfactory they'll enter him for a big race at Walthamstow.'

'What's all the hush-hush business?'

'If they know he's running well but no one else does they'll get longer odds on him before the competition. That's the only way you sometimes make money at this game.'

Now they had arrived at its perimeter Becky could see that the field was bordered by a low-fenced, oval-shaped track. Sean and the dog peeled off in one direction and they followed Patzaki up the rickety staircase of a wooden watchtower.

'This is about the size of a real dog track,' said Dermot. 'What they're doing is giving him a mock race.'

'But he's on his own,' said Becky, watching Sean pushing Smokey's hindquarters to get him into a small box on the track. 'Who's he racing?'

'The bunny,' said Patzaki, hanging out of the tower's window.

'Not a real one,' Dermot interjected, seeing Becky's face.

'No,' Patzaki said proudly. 'He's never needed a live one. Not like his sister.'

'He'd be no good at public relations,' Dermot said, sotto voce.

But Patzaki was hauling down the sort of lever that would have done justice to a Victorian signal box and the loud hum of an electrical motor filled the air. From inside the trap came a yelp of excitement. Sean waved to indicate that he was ready and through the trap's wire front Becky could see Smokey's eager snout. Patzaki checked his stopwatch and handed round cigarettes. They were Rothmans but, swept up in the prevailing sudden tension, Becky took one. The harsh, tarry smoke made her head swim.

'OK,' said the trainer, pressing a red button on the control panel. Along the far side of the track there was a flash of movement and, refocusing, Becky saw that an incongruous furry pink rabbit, attached to a buggy, was speeding along a rail around the track's outside edge. As this hare passed the trap Sean released its wire door which sprang upwards and Smokey came out in furious pursuit of the mechanical lure. His pace, from a standing start, was extraordinary.

It was only afterwards that Becky realised that Patzaki was controlling the speed of the hare to keep it the requisite distance from Smokey's questing jaws, always in sight but enough out of reach to encourage maximum effort. At the time all she registered was the huge galloping stride of the dog, how graceful it was in flight, and the speed with which dog and hare completed their circuit and came to a halt. Smokey was distracted from his adversary by Sean throwing a rabbit skin on to the track.

'Exciting, isn't it?' said Dermot.

Sean joined them. 'What's on the clock?' he asked Patzaki.

'Is a good time. We will enter.' He rubbed the dog's ears.

Smokey's mouth hung as far open as the muzzle would allow and his pink tongue was flecked with saliva. His ribcage was heaving; he looked exhausted.

'Is he all right?' Becky asked.

'Sure. Let's get that muzzle off. Give him a cuddle, he'll like that.'

She hesitated.

'He won't bite. The muzzle's just to make it like the real thing.'

She bent down to the dog who gazed at her blankly. She ran her hand along his flank and felt the bones beneath the soft fur. She stroked the solidly muscled neck and as her fingers felt his fragile front legs Smokey nuzzled her cheek experimentally with the wet tip of his nose.

By the time they got home Becky was feeling somewhat lightheaded from a combination of the bike, the fresh air, a lack of sleep and the generous slugs of Cypriot brandy that had washed down the seafood and cold pheasant at the Patzaki house. Dermot had a matinee so she kissed him goodbye and ran herself a hot bath with plenty of jasmine foam. She slid beneath the hot water and let it soak into her skin. Dermot's lifestyle was so similar to her own in some ways – the cinemas, cheap restaurants, walks on the Common – and so vastly different in others – the glitter of the circus and the adrenalin-inducing speed of the dogs that so obviously fascinated him. When they left Rathkennen Dermot had handed his brother a wad of rather crumpled notes with which to back Smokey in his upcoming competition. She hadn't felt able to ask him directly how much but as Sean had riffled through the pile she had guessed at £200.

75

'Will Sean have a big bet, too?' she had asked as he started the bike.

'Not "too". Mine was the sort of small wager that makes men like Patzaki laugh. Sean'll put on everything he can spare which, who knows, might be £500 or so.' She thought of the squalid caravan. 'And Mr P, if he really thinks he's got a winner, will do a couple of grand, I should guess.'

'On one race?'

'Three races. Heat, semi and final.'

'As short as that trial?'

'Yes.'

'But that only lasted thirty seconds.'

'If you've got your shirt on the result it seems an awful lot longer, let me tell you.'

Topping up her bath with more hot water, Becky wondered how Patzaki, a Greek Cypriot, had got into a game that was so dominated by the Irish that he felt obliged to name his kennels after some hamlet in Co. Wicklow. She wondered how Sean could live in comparative squalor when he had several hundred pounds available for a bet. She wondered whether Dermot's caravan was as decrepit as his brother's.

She wondered what their mother thought of her two itinerant sons – educated, charming, and both seemingly living on a knife-edge of speed and poverty. She wondered how often she and Dermot would sleep together again. It was certainly surreal enough to be a holiday romance. Her mind was just drifting back to the early hours of that morning when the phone rang. She padded to it wrapped in a towel and leaving a trail of footprints across the hall carpet, assuming illogically that it must be Dermot because she was thinking about him.

'When are you going to get an answerphone?' said Vanessa. 'I've been trying you all day.'

'What's the matter?'

'Nothing.' Vanessa sounded slightly taken aback. 'Josh and I just hoped you might want to come round for tea . . . supper . . . call it what you will.'

'I'd really like to but—'

'You're going out with Pagliacci.'

Becky didn't laugh. 'No, it's just that I'm really tired and I'm in the bath and—'

'Don't say another thing. Call me soon and fill me in. Don't catch a chill. Bye.' And she was gone.

Becky stomped back to the bath, now too tepid for enjoyment, feeling guilty that she had upset Vanessa.

Vanessa wished she hadn't made that stupid crack about Dermot being a clown and that Becky was coming round for a chat. She and her son had had a disagreeable day and needed an injection of fresh company, if not a mediator. She went into the kitchen to look for the chocolate biscuits.

'Why don't you come with me?'

She was lying against his chest on the sofa. It was seven thirty on a Wednesday morning and she should have been leaving for school but was still in her old dressing-gown with the piping on the collar and cuffs. Dermot was wearing one of her baggiest sweaters but he was still shivering. His ribs felt as prominent as a hound's.

'And do what?'

'Anything. Help with the ticket sales, make-up, costumes, until—'

'Until what?'

'Until you get your act together. So to speak.'

'I think I'm a bit old to learn to juggle,' she laughed.

'What languages can you speak?'

'French, a bit. I did German at school but I can't really remember much.'

'You don't need much to sell popcorn or programmes.'

She sat up. If she could feel his ribs he must be able to feel her heart thumping through her squashed left breast. 'It's getting late. Can you make some tea while I get dressed?'

'I'll run you over if you like.'

'It's miles. And miles.'

'I've got all day.'

'It's very sweet of you but – perhaps you could just run me to Victoria.'

'OK. Whatever.'

She needed some time alone to compose herself before the school day, besides which, unless she made him drop her off round the corner, someone at school was bound to see her dismounting his Yamaha and then she would be the butt of jokey curiosity for the rest of the week.

She resolutely read the *Guardian* on the train and as she walked on the last part of her journey. She did not want to give herself time to think. But when she had her first free period the images that had been jostling at the edge of her mind lurched through . . . a convoy of caravans on some dusty French highway in a late sun filtered by the poplars bordering the road, camp fires on a frosty morning, the heat and lights of the ring on her face, cooking garlic on a primus stove, Dermot cleaning his bicycle parts on the floor . . . The whole thing was so sudden and surprising it was hard to take seriously and yet, and yet . . . she had scarcely noticed the term passing these last few weeks.

If he went and she stayed behind what was there but an increasingly lacklustre routine? Becoming head of department eventually – maybe. Moving to a flat with an extra bedroom – for what? Remarrying another schoolteacher out of boredom and insecurity, buying a neo-Tudor semi . . . stop it. She had only known him for forty days.

That afternoon she asked her union rep the implications

of a sudden resignation, which proved to her that at least part of her brain was behaving rationally. When she got home she spent a fruitless hour trying to contact Vanessa at her office. Finally the reply 'in a meeting' became 'no one's answering, must have gone for the day' and she got soaked waiting for a bus to Battersea. Vanessa, arriving home with Josh, found her sheltering beneath the inadequate protection of the lintel.

They had gin and tomato soup and discussed the pros and cons, with Becky acutely aware that Vanessa was trying to conceal an opposition verging on the pathological.

'I ought to go and see him,' she said at eleven.

'Are you sure? I'm definitely squiffy, so I'm sure you are. Don't you want a clear head to discuss this with him?'

'No – I might change my mind. Let's call a cab.'

It dropped her at an encampment already deserted, the taxi-driver concerned at leaving a respectable but inebriated woman in such a place. He watched her climb awkwardly over the crash barrier and approach a caravan.

Dermot was chatting to a stocky, peroxided girl who showed no sign of leaving until he suggested they finish in the morning. She said neither hello nor goodbye to Becky although the cramped confines of the caravan meant that they brushed in the doorway.

'Glass of wine?'

'No, I feel like a distillery already. Dermot—'

'Sit down . . . please.'

'Dermot, I've thought about what you said all day and I can't come with you.'

It was far blunter than she intended but he accepted it with his usual equanimity. He didn't try to persuade her, simply said how he would have liked it had her decision been different. For the first time she slept on his narrow mattress.

Four days later the circus left town. It was a Sunday but she didn't see them off. She stayed in the flat until teatime, occupying her body with dusting, vacuuming and eventually, somewhat desperately, rearranging her books alphabetically. She had hoped that the deadly reassurance of long-standing radio programmes – the everyday story of countryfolk, discs for a desert island and topical gardening tips – would occupy her mind but it persisted in wandering off into dangerous territory.

One minute she despised herself for not having the courage to jump out of her rut, out of the rat race. It wasn't as if she was a particularly successful competitor or happy in her work. Rather the reverse.

Ever since her divorce she had plodded on in a dis-illusioned way – no great excitement or happiness – and when something thrilling finally did pop up she was turning her back on it. It was ludicrous, throwing up the chance of a handsome, sexy, thinking, seemingly considerate man – perhaps her last chance judging by the infrequency with which they seemed to come along.

On the other hand Vanessa was right, the timing had put her in an impossible position. She might like going to the cinema, the park, to bed with Dermot but she had never spent more than a day with him and weeks on end in a tiny caravan was a different proposition. Besides, if she went away with him he might be all she had. Apart from the occasional hello she knew no one else from the circus and they might all turn out to be insufferable or cold-shoulder her. And for that she would be giving up friends of long standing, the frequent moves making it almost impossible for them to phone or even write.

Vanessa had put these arguments so clearly that Becky was tempted to blame her for the decision. But that wasn't fair. The true culprit was Becky's failed marriage. She had once before invested everything in one person – Danny – and been disillusioned. Faced with a proposition that required her to do the same again it was not just cowardice that made her back down but a cynicism cultivated over the years into a protective coating.

In the late afternoon she decided to buy some crumpets. In theory she could have gone in and out of Patel's without looking at the Common but, having caught a glimpse between the houses at the end of the street on her way in, she somehow found herself turning towards it as she came out, comfort food clasped in her mittened hand.

She knew, of course, that they would be on the motorway by now, but in the blurring dusk she saw, for a second, the silhouette of the big top between the trees, and her heart raced. Then it became a distant gable and, when she was standing where it had been, all that remained were a selection of wheel ruts and a discoloration of the grass.

4

I'm Not in Love

Judy sat in a darkened gallery on a black leather chair, iced Perrier by her side, concealed by the mirrored glass of the window through which she looked out at an interior designer's notion of a normal, suburban lounge. Bland prints hung above rattanwork sofas with muted floral cushions and on the glass-topped coffee table a plate of shortbread and chocolate digestives lay beside the teapot.

With her back to the unseen audience the qualitative researcher – Joy, forty, plump, comfortable, could have been a social worker or a psychotherapist – was discussing the attributes of a new shampoo formulation with a panel of 'normal housewives'. Half of these women had children; their age range was approximately twenty-five to forty-five; their social class was in dispute as the old A, B, C1, C2 system was discredited and no other universally accepted classification had replaced it.

At four o'clock these women would be released to collect their kids or cook their husbands' tea or whatever and the observers would write up their impressions of the discussion and replay on video the high points that might make up the entertaining crux of a presentation to convince the board of the need for a new product launch.

At seven, with the teapot replaced by bottles of white wine and fruit juice, and nuts and crisps substituted for the biscuits, a new group – the 'working women' – would be ushered in and Joy would put them at their ease and draw out their reaction to the idea of a combined shampoo and conditioner.

Judy had looked at potential areas for new product development and identified two. One was suggested by simple demographics; the population was ageing and older women, or at least some older women, had more money than ever before, so why not develop a stylish haircare brand positively targeted at the over-forties? Over-forties really meant over-fifties, of course, but marketing double-speak uses a vocabulary kind to the consumer's self-image. Hugo, her boss, had put his weight behind this project, thereby rendering it useless to Judy as a means of career advancement, so she had turned her attention to the second.

The scientists on the Pasco payroll had devised a means of combining all the practical benefits of shampoo and conditioner in one liquid, which was a technical advance but not of immediately obvious sales use. After all, one liquid meant one bottle and it was generally doubted whether purchasers could be persuaded to pay as much for that one bottle as they had previously paid for two. However, if one could find a niche where the use of one bottle became a positive advantage, then the immense cost of launching a new brand might be justified, and this was what Judy was looking for.

Building a new brand was exciting because it was risky and, no matter how much research you conducted, in the end you proceeded partly by hunch. If you were identified with a launch failure you had wasted a lot of the company's money and at least stalled, if not reversed, your prospects of promotion. But the opposite was also true and at the back of Judy's mind was the thought that if she was right about this then the directorship would be hers.

It was after nine by the time their second set of guinea-pigs had been shown off the premises and Judy and Joy sat down for a glass of wine of their own. Judy knew Joy too well to ask for opinions; anything she said would be riddled with caveats and it would be only a week before the report was on her desk, inconclusive but at least a considered reflection. So they made small talk about the business and past successes. But as Judy got into her car in a deserted Kennington street she hugged to herself the nuggets of hope engendered by the panels' comments and knew that privately Joy would be appreciating them too.

The best was that basic belief in the product was there; women did find it credible that a conditioner's attributes could exist in a shampoo. Probing to find out why this might be useful suggested that time-saving was not important in the privacy of the bathroom, where in some cases the reverse was true – it was seen as a refuge. But the convenience of only taking one bottle in a holdall to the swimming pool or gym, and in luggage when travelling, was appreciated.

Contemplating baked beans on toast and an angrily ravenous Bartholomew Judy thought she just might have found her niche.

The next day was a busy one with an agency meeting to finalise the media schedule for an existing brand, but Judy had time to call up some statistics on the increasing number of women either participating in sport or attending exercise classes and was consequently in a buoyant mood when she reached the wine bar. Sophie, unusually punctual, was not.

'What's the matter?' Judy asked.

'My contract's up for renewal at the end of the month.'

'Don't you think they will renew it?'

'Oh, I expect so – I mean, I have the occasional spat with Jerry, and Kate, the executive producer, is an absolute bitch of course—' She paused, as if contemplating the exact nature of Kate's bitchiness.

'Of course,' said Judy, herself wondering what it would be like to have the mercurial Sophie in your employ.

'But I'm pretty good at my job so I guess they'll offer me another twelve months.'

'So – what's the matter?' repeated Judy.

'I've done two years already. There's nowhere up for me to go on *Churchill's People* – Kate's been with him for years and even if she wanted to leave I don't suppose anyone else would take the old harpy on. Anyway I never really wanted to work on a chat show, I just took it to get my feet on the ladder. I really want to shift to arts or drama and the longer I carry on getting credited for this dross the less likely that becomes.'

'Have you applied for anything else?'

'A couple of things earlier in the year, which I didn't get, and now there's a rumour of a job going on *Backdrop*, that arts documentary series, but it's not official and if I don't do something soon I'm going to be saddled with his nibs and her ladyship for another season.'

At this point the others arrived and it was apparent to Judy that Becky was even more miserable than Sophie.

'It's her leprechaun, I suppose,' Sophie said to Vanessa while Becky was at the bar.

'Yes, or rather the lack of him.'

'Did anybody ever meet him?'

Judy shook her head.

'Once, for Sunday lunch,' said Vanessa.

'And what did you think?'

'Handsome, in a sort of snake-hipped, gigolo-ish way. Quietly spoken. Not boring but—'

'But what?'

'Well, she was a bit obsessed by him. Probably more than he deserved.'

'Perhaps that was just because she knew it couldn't last. I expect she would have got it into proportion if he'd been working nine to five down the road.'

'I hope so. She actually thought about going with him.'

God, I shouldn't have said that, Vanessa thought.

'Seriously?'

'No, only for a couple of hours.'

'You mean you talked her out of it,' Sophie said.

'No ... well, yes, she discussed it with me but it wasn't as if I changed her mind, I mean she hadn't made it up.'

'You'd have missed her if she had gone.'

'We all would have done,' said Judy quickly.

'Of course,' said Sophie, 'I didn't mean—'

'She's coming back,' said Vanessa, 'so let's talk about something else, shall we?'

'Are you going to this awards do at the Grosvenor House tomorrow night?' Judy asked Vanessa.

'Yes, to accompany Mr Tortilla Chip, who wishes to bask in the reflected glory of his last commercial having been voted best in the snack food category.'

'Is that for making the most fraudulent claim or for being the most expensive to film?' asked Sophie.

'Or for best use of an old hit song?' Becky chimed in.

'None of those. It is actually quite funny, as you very well know.' Vanessa had, of course, been subjected to all these gibes about her profession before and usually managed to avoid climbing on to her high horse, but tonight she was nettled. 'I don't think you should take such a lofty attitude;

your boss Jerry Churchill certainly hasn't disdained hosting the ceremony.'

'He'd do anything for a fiver and a round of applause,' said Sophie.

'Help me out here,' said Vanessa to Judy, who grinned. 'I don't understand why you regard your client's presence as an intrusion. After all he's paid for the whole thing. Why shouldn't we be invited?'

'I'd momentarily forgotten she was one, too,' said Sophie wearily.

'Are you going then?' Vanessa asked Judy and received a nod in reply. 'Have you won an award?'

'Don't be silly. Shampoos never win awards. But I think my agency are hoping that if I see all these other clients collecting them I'll give them stacks of money to make weird ads with next year.'

'New frocks for both of you then,' said Becky.

'No, just my little black number,' said Vanessa. 'Hope it's still in fashion.'

'The day you're turned out in anything unfashionable I'll eat my hat.'

'You haven't got a hat, Soph. An idle threat as usual. Are you still all right to look after Josh, Becky?'

'What would you do without her?' Sophie asked. 'I hope she pays well, Beck. In Battersea they'll do anything to hang on to a babysitter.'

'I do it for love.'

'Oh, so it's the traditional set-up. She leaves you out a box of chocolates and warns you not to touch the drinks cabinet or have sex on the sofa with your boyfriend. Oh God, sorry Becky. Have another glass. Don't let it get to you. They're not worth it.'

'Does that apply to Mikey?'

'I haven't seen him for a week.'

'Is he away filming?'

'No, it's just that I'm not ready to become a couple yet.'

'Yet?'

'If ever.'

Vanessa had booked her client a room at the Grosvenor House Hotel and arranged to call him there from the lobby when she arrived. She didn't want him roaming round the bars falling into conversation with sirens from other agencies. She had a minor crisis when she laddered her tights while changing in her office but sent out for a replacement pair and gathered her taxi load together only ten minutes late. Once in the hotel she dispatched Graham and Billy, the writer and art director of the award-winning commercial, to start tanking up on champagne or lager or whatever the lads were tippling this month. It would be better to make sure Mr Doherty had a few himself before being exposed to their natural exuberance.

Then she went to the marble and mahogany cloakroom to check her make-up and relieve her bladder before the rigours of the evening ahead. A few early arrivals were fiddling with mascara and chatting before the mirrors. Vanessa resisted the temptation to have a cigarette and listen to their high-octane babble and went to the reception desk.

George Doherty was, as self-made industrialists go, normally quite presentable. He had avoided the pitfalls of grey shoes, very pale summer suits and combing hair over his bald patch. His ego and his belly were publicly restrained. But a dinner suit is worn so rarely that a man tends only to change it when it ceases to fit and George's had obviously fitted him since the late 1970s. The lapels were long and wide, the single-breasted jacket too waisted and the trousers slightly flared. Ah well, thought Vanessa as she beamed in greeting, at least it's not velvet and the cummerbund is black.

Unlike middle managers, who were presumably under instructions to recoup as much as they could from the agency's entertainment budget, George always bought his fair share of drinks and he now ordered gin and tonics for them in the quiet of the residents' bar, anticipating the crush that would exist in the bars around the ballroom. They sat on stools and she was aware, just for a second, of him appraising the yardage of ten-denier leg displayed by her short skirt.

She had been quite surprised, when sorting out the tickets, that he had not requested one for his PA. Sandy was young, blonde and bouncy enough for agency gossip to assume some extra-curricular activity between her and her boss, but if that was so he was either too scared to advertise it so publicly or fancied his chances with some of the talent always on show at functions like these. Vanessa did not think he would be crass enough to compromise their business relationship by attempting anything more than a sedate dance with her but you could never tell what brandy and port might do to a man's judgement.

She suggested they made their way to the ballroom to rendezvous with the rest of the agency's party. They were ensconced at a table on the balcony with a view over the body of the hall, where the dining-tables were as yet sparsely populated, the stage empty, the waiters adding finishing touches.

George already knew Max, the creative director, so Vanessa effected introductions to Billy and Graham, and Malcolm and Emma from TV Production. Then Guy, another account manager, introduced his clients Ralph and Adrienne from the confectionery giant, Orion.

Vanessa made sure that George had a glass of fizz, offered him an olive from the choice of nibbles on the table to pre-empt his pontificating about the relative merits of his own products and those in the glass dishes, and made sure that Max was exerting his considerable charm on him before setting about a few tasks of her own. Guy, who guessed what these were likely to include, followed her with his eyes but could do no more as he was the recipient of one of Ralph's golfing monologues.

She stopped at the head of the stairs to check the overall table plan, both for the position of their own – not as close to the stage as she would have liked but at least they wouldn't be looking at Churchill's back like the poor sods on Tables 2 and 3 – and to see who else was in attendance. Judy's agency, Miller Markwick, was on the other side.

Then Vanessa descended the sweeping grand staircase, enjoying the fact that she was more or less alone on it rather than part of the crush that would occur as soon as dinner was announced; knowing that her earrings would be flashing and her dress shimmering in the light from the enormous, twinkling chandelier above; unable to stop herself imagining, just for a moment, that she was a film star. When she reached the bottom she opened her clutch bag and got out the place-name cards that one of the illustrators had knocked up for her that afternoon.

If people straggled to the table and chose their own places one could end up with some very unfortunate combinations, but Vanessa knew from bitter experience that marshalling her guests into some sort of order meant drunken jokes about bossiness later in the evening; the card system she now used had never been questioned.

She decided to put herself and Max on either side of George. The round tables were too large for it to matter conversationally who was opposite him but for decorative reasons she settled on Emma of the wiggly bottom, giggly laugh and pert urchin cut. Having ensured her own client's safety she was as fair as possible to Guy by giving Adrienne Max's other ear and sticking Ralph between Guy himself and the nymphette. The creative and production teams would be much happier bunched together on one side of the table.

Mission accomplished, Vanessa sat back, lit up and watched the hordes pour down the stairs. It always surprised her how many good-looking women there were and how few cases of mutton dressed as lamb, or perhaps like herself people felt and therefore looked more glamorous in this setting. The jobs of most guests of either sex could be ascertained from their style of dress.

The clients, account persons and production people tended to be smart – the men in conventional dinner suits and the women in ball gowns or cocktail dresses, always a fair smattering of black and other colours dependent upon *Vogue* and the like. This year the grosser excesses of silver lamé and gold taffeta seemed to have made way for rich reds and blues.

White tuxes, brocade waistcoats, tieless shirts, drapes and drainpipes tended to be the province of writers and directors. Women with responsibility could show as much cleavage and thigh as they dared but a bare midriff or opaque tights inevitably signified a female creative.

One or two poor souls in imitation leopard skin and garishly coloured spectacles were either jingle writers or directors whose careers were on the skids.

Vanessa's eyes were drawn by the beauty of a blonde woman on the staircase before she recognised her as Judy.

Judy's hair was piled up, and long diamond drops hung from the soft, white lobes of her ears. She wore a strapless dress in jade-green, tightly bodiced and with a wide-flowing skirt. Her heavy bosom was invisibly supported, presumably by fiendish underwiring, and looked as if it might pop out at any moment but she exhibited no anxiety. She negotiated the stairs on high green heels with delicate steps and head erect. Even from this distance you could see that her escort was as pleased as punch to be in the same photo opportunity.

The meal suffered from the usual problems of mass catering – bland, traditional and lukewarm – but the wine flowed and by the time Jerry Churchill came to the podium cheeks were glowing and spirits were high. The sound system was poor but as the audience would know most of the work were it shown back to front, that hardly mattered, and a film played at the wrong moment was drowned out by personnel from the appropriate agency shouting the words of what should have been on the screen. They laughed at Jerry's poor jokes and booed those of competitors. A continuous procession of hacks went to and from the stage to press the flesh of various luminaries and collect their imitation gold cameras, allowed a brief moment of glory before the real cameras but mercifully debarred from making gracious speeches of acceptance.

While Graham and Billy were weaving their way back through the congratulations of their peers and mutual back-patting had overwhelmed the Breughel Thomas contingent, George, who had abstemiously contented himself with a single cognac and an acrid, fat Havana, summoned a waiter and ordered some more bubbly. The boys, looking more than ever like Regency bucks, set about improvising champagne cocktails with gusto.

After the last trophy had been borne away there was a collective pause for breath before the Capital Radio Big Band played for dancing. Vanessa was just excusing herself to George, intent on the loo and a search for Judy, when in mid-remark his gaze left hers and fixed itself on a point above her left shoulder. Afterwards she would have sworn she saw his pupils dilate but in truth it was far too dark for that kind of observation.

'Hello,' said Judy. 'I just came to offer my congratulations.'

'Well, this is the man who deserves them,' said Vanessa. 'George Doherty, Judith Hucknell.'

George stood and took the proffered jade-green evening glove. 'I just approved it,' he said, shaking too firmly as was his wont. 'These blokes thought it up.'

'You won't find Judy underrating the importance of the man with the purse strings,' Vanessa said. 'She's one herself.'

Oh God, she thought, I hope he doesn't let himself down by picking that up and saying she's the prettiest man he's ever seen, ho, ho, ho.

'Really? What company are you with?'

'So that's Mr Tortilla Chip?' said Judy when they had escaped to the cloakroom. 'He seems pleasant enough.'

'I think the feeling is more than mutual. You look fantastic. I don't think you'll have any shortage of dancing partners. Do you think your dress will stand up to it?'

'It's my feet I'm worried about. I know my tits are secure.'

'How?'

'I've tested them. Look.' She stretched her arms above her head and pouted at the mirror. Then she jumped up and down vigorously, much to the surprise of the ageing head of television applying another layer of fuchsia lipstick. 'See?'

'Well, it bounces and wobbles – but I suppose it's not indecent. Back to the fray?'

Billy had just lost to Ralph the race to invite Emma on to the floor.

'Family hold back,' Vanessa said softly into his ear.

'Let's keep it in the family then. Come on.' He took her hand.

She checked George's availability but he was engrossed in conversation with Max.

'OK then,' she said.

The intricacies of the vigorous rock 'n' roll number which began the band's set eventually defeated Billy, whose co-ordination was somewhat impaired. After they had become inextricably tangled for the third time they gave up and simply jigged and swayed in time.

'If I didn't know you were drunk, I'd suspect you of groping me deliberately.'

'I value my life more than that. Oh look, there's our Dolphin director.' And there was Mikey, sitting alone with a bottle of port, looking as carefully unbothered as those left alone at a social event try to look. 'Come on, I'll introduce you.' He grabbed Vanessa's arm and dragged her in his wake. 'Mikey, hi. Having fun?'

'Plenty,' he said. 'Pull up a chair.'

And then he saw Vanessa and it seemed to her that the quality of his smile changed. Billy introduced them and she left a beat but his mouth hadn't started to move so she said, 'Yes, we've met. How are you?'

'Really?' said Billy. 'Oh, well, good.' He slumped into the chair next to Mikey.

'I'm fine,' Mikey said. 'And you?'

'Listen,' said Billy, 'my feet are a bit fucked – not to

mention my brain – so why don't you two have a bop and I'll catch you later.'

Mikey looked enquiring. 'Well, that would be fine—'

Vanessa nodded and they returned to the floor, now full enough to force you close to your partner. Over his shoulder she could see that Billy's head was resting on the tablecloth.

'I think he just wanted to politely get rid of me before he passed out. You were the nearest port in a storm, so to speak.'

'I'm happy to be used. I'm sorry I didn't admit to knowing you but I wasn't quite sure of the politics, you know.'

'Not a problem now we've had this dance. Anyway I think you could have told Billy we were brother and sister and he wouldn't remember it in the morning.'

Or that we slept together once, she thought, but you have a history of not admitting that. She concentrated on the music.

After the fourth number she was hot, and buzzing gently.

'Look, I've enjoyed this but I must go and attend to my client. Thanks, I'm sure I'll see you on the shoot.'

'Sorry to have monopolised you for so long. Thank you.' And he disappeared into the crowd.

'Who's your friend?' said Max, when she reached their table.

'He's the director of—'

'Not him. The lady in green.'

'Oh, you wouldn't like her – she's only interested in brand share, Max, not art. Where's gorgeous George?'

'Taking his turn with young Emma. I think her patience is wearing thin. Can you keep a discreet eye? Suggest if she's had enough she hides in the ladies until their attention has been attracted by something else. We don't want an incident.'

'I don't think Doherty is a groper.'

'Maybe not but there must be some slow ones coming soon and I don't want them fighting over her. Her bare back will be hard to resist.'

'Well, Billy's out of the running anyway.'

The band stopped and seconds later George and Emma returned, George's hair and shirt collar awry and his face a dangerous shade of red.

'I think that's my lot. I've got a breakfast meeting tomorrow so I'll be away to my room. Thanks for a great evening, Vanessa.'

'I'll walk up to the lobby with you. I could do with a breath of fresh air.'

'That'd be nice. I'll collect my jacket and tie.'

'All right?' she asked Emma once he was out of earshot.

'Oh, yes. The old ones you can wear out very quickly.' She giggled. 'I'm not getting caught by that Ralph when they turn the lights low though. He's got wandering hands.'

Vanessa waited with Doherty for his key.

'We must have a dance next time,' she said speculatively.

'A waltz would suit me.' He winked. 'Save the last one, eh? Goodnight.'

Turning away she saw Mikey watching from across the lobby.

'Are you spying on me?'

'I've got no one left to play with. I thought I might be able to interest you in one for the road.'

'Drink?'

'Well, yes, but perhaps another dance, too.'

'OK.'

And so they were together when the band slowed down and a hundred couples, willingly or unwillingly, drew close together. He danced carefully and well, one hand in the middle of her back and the other at the base of her spine, not taking too many liberties, the little finger resting on her buttocks. They were just close enough for her breasts to brush his shirtfront occasionally and her right hand was on the nape of his neck. Gradually her mind became disconnected, drifting, aware not only of his touch but also of the charged air between them. It was a long time since she had felt the crackle of sexual electricity and she tingled deliciously. She wondered whether when the phrase to melt into someone's arms had been coined it was this sensation that was being described.

Emma shuffled past with Graham massaging her bottom and their tongues apparently embedded in each other's mouths. It didn't look like sexual harassment.

Vanessa's cheek touched his and she could feel his breath against her ear.

'Thank you very much and goodnight,' said the singer and the brass swelled into their final chords.

They pressed together, the music stopped, they jerked apart.

'Well,' he said, looking round at the wreckage on the tables – ash, butts, empty bottles, streamers, the odd shoe – 'I guess it's time to go.'

'My babysitter will be pacing the floor.'

'How is Josh?'

'Fine. Thanks.'

'See you on the shoot, then.'

'Oh . . . yes . . . of course . . . see you then. Goodnight.'

'Thanks for the dance. Goodnight.'

* * *

A hand on her shoulder as she was queuing for her jacket made her jump.

'What were you dreaming about?' Judy said.

'A mug of Ovaltine.'

'As long as it wasn't the mug of Sophie's boyfriend.'

'It was just a dance,' she said, far too defensively.

'But a steamy one.' Judy's hair had partly fallen from its clips and her earrings were missing.

'No. Anyway you look as if you had one or two yourself.'

'Ah, but those were with people I don't know.' Judy laughed. 'And don't want to. Much safer.'

As they passed through the lobby and out into the cold night air Vanessa glimpsed Graham and Emma attempting to book a room at the Reservations desk.

In the taxi she considered her actions or, more accurately, her reactions. She had felt aroused but perhaps she would have done with any halfway to decent man this evening.

Maybe she had felt less inhibited because she had already slept with Mikey, although that must be purely a psychological barrier as not a single cell of the Mikey she fucked remained. Or was the seven-year replacement cycle a myth? If nothing else it explained why she hadn't recognised him in Italy.

Judy had certainly put the damper on her evening by reminding her about Sophie, but why should she feel guilty? Only last night she had distinctly heard Sophie say that she and Mikey were no longer a couple.

And anyway, what had she done? Nothing, a peck on the cheek, that was all.

Only the kitchen light was burning when Vanessa got home. It was after one. She carefully opened the door to the sitting-room and there was Becky asleep on the sofabed. Upstairs Josh was also sparked out, lying on his tummy. She desperately wanted to pick him up and hug him hard but it would wake him, which wasn't fair, so she cleaned her teeth and slid between her own cold sheets.

Sophie was in what was grandly referred to by Jerry, who had once worked in newspapers, as an editorial conference but which was known to everyone else as a production meeting when her contact in personnel rang.

'Who was that answering your phone?'

'Yes?' said Sophie, hoping that no one but her could hear the other end of the conversation.

'Is it a bad time to talk?'

'Yes.'

'OK, call me later. Just wanted to tell you the job on *Backdrop* is definitely up for grabs. Good timing, eh?'

'Yes, thank you very much but I'm tied up just at the moment. I'll call you when I get back to my own office.'

'OK, mum's the word. *Ciao*.'

Not for the first time Sophie wished she hadn't diverted her calls to Kate's phone.

'Problem with Personnel, love? Perhaps my clout would sort it,' Jerry was saying.

'Oh no, nothing like that, thanks, Jerry. It's just—' think, think, 'that I'm taking out a pension and they offer advice on that kind of thing.'

'Do they?' Kate said curiously.

Sophie didn't really know but was saved by Jerry starting to prattle on about how good his broker was, he'd done him a great tax-saving deal so a little pension for a girlie would be no more than a flicker on his calculator.

Kate, who could foresee the anecdote about his offshore funds recurring, moved to head him off at the pass. 'I wonder whether we could get the highest paid kid in the city

– you know, champagne, coke and currency dealing – to contrast with the Governor of the Bank of England?'

'Makes the programme a bit heavy, doesn't it?' asked the host, and they were just settling down for a 'discussion' as to whether a teenage star of Australian soap provided sufficient raising agent when the phone rang again.

'She is here,' said Kate, and Sophie knew she would be fuming at being upstaged on her own territory. 'Who's calling?'

The reply caused an arching of eyebrows, and then a grimace. 'He says he's from the Broadcasting Standards Council.' Jerry twitched, immediately nervous, and plumes of cigarette smoke poured from Kate's nostrils in annoyance at having momentarily been taken in. 'And that his name's Lord Reith.'

'Sorry,' Sophie said and took the receiver.

'Soph—' said Mikey.

'I'm very busy. What do you want?'

'Dinner this evening?'

'Where?'

'Oh God, I don't know, er—'

'I'm going to have to go—'

'Rani's? At eight?'

'Fine. See you then.'

Rani's was an Indian restaurant in Camden with no particular merit other than its position opposite the cinema. As a result its trade was largely a post-film one, supplemented by a second wave when the pubs closed. At eight it was more or less deserted.

Mikey knew it was a mistake to have suggested it even before he arrived; a curry on top of a hangover is a desperate measure. But he was feeling desperate, and his despair was not induced by the surfeit of port, and one or two other things, still lurking somewhere in his system.

Once he was seated beneath gloomy flock wallpaper, with the wailing voice of a singer apparently lamenting some major catastrophe and dismally failing to make the place seem less empty, he wished he had picked an atmosphere more conducive to what he had to say.

When Sophie breezed in Mikey ordered his second pint of cold lager to go with the poppadams and pickles, and between them the alcohol and the mango chutney contrived to bolster his determination.

'You look a bit rough. Been on the razz?'

'I had this awards junket last night. Saw Vanessa and Judy. Had a dance with her.'

'Yes, they said they were going to some bunfight. I hope you didn't tread on Judy's toes.'

'It was Vanessa I danced with.'

'Vanessa? Blimey, you are privileged. I thought she only danced for money these days.'

'What?'

'Business. I thought she only jived when the customers demanded it. In private life she's a nun. Well, since she had the baby. Nobody's tried to claim that was a virgin birth.'

'They're called clients, not customers. And in a way I suppose it was business. I'm directing an ad for them.'

'Really? She never said.'

'Perhaps she didn't know. She's not in the Creative or TV department.'

But she must have done. Just when he was clearing his conscience there was the conspiracy of silence again.

Their meal arrived, far too many dishes as usual – why had he ordered spinach? He asked for another beer and added a little chicken to the plain rice on his plate. Sophie was eating in characteristic fashion, fork in and out of all the dishes, torn pieces of naan bread and desecrated onion bhajis littering her plate, but the only thing she seemed to have swallowed were a couple of tandoori prawns.

'The thing is, Sophie, I wanted to have a talk, about us, but it's been kind of hard to find the right time.'

She put down her fork and fixed him with her wide, untroubled green eyes.

It was hard to go on but she said nothing.

'We've been seeing each other for, what, six months and it's been really great—'

Shit, she thought, he's dumping me. I can't believe it.

All Mikey saw were her eyes cease to focus on him.

'But I sort of believe that all relationships are going up or down, like, they don't stand still,' he looked at her for some sign of agreement or disagreement but there was none. 'The thing is, ours seems to be less together than it was and I want to change that direction if I can, so—'

Relief coursed through her – she didn't quite know what she felt about Mikey but she didn't want it to end. Was that just pride – if someone was going to call a halt it should be her? What was he saying?

'—if we've got a ... well, a future ... then maybe we should try living in the same flat ... my flat really 'cos it would be a bit impractical me moving my day-to-day things into your room?'

This seemed to be a question rather than a statement. She put her hand over his on the table, stopping his fingers tapping.

'Are you asking me to live with you?'

'Yes.'

This was moving too fast the other way now. Far too fast. She could feel herself blushing.

'Mikey, can I think about it? I mean, I can't decide about it just at the moment. It's not you but it's a big thing, apart from anything else I've lived here for nearly ten years, and then I've just applied for this new job and . . . don't get me wrong but I just need some time to sort myself out.'

She was turning him down and her face was red. Was she lying? He said, yes think about it, Soph, and asked her about the job.

Later they went back to Camden Road and before she got into bed Sophie, red again, said that she was sorry but she had her period and all she could do was give him a hug. He couldn't tell if it was the truth.

'So who else was there?' asked Becky. It was Saturday and she had no desire to go out but Judy had rung and in an effort to avoid agreeing to go to the pictures she was feigning interest in a dinner party Judy had been to the night before.

'Paul and Sue, Tim and Ellie, Danny . . .'

'I haven't seen him for ages. How was he?'

'OK.'

'On his own?'

'No. He had his fiancée with him.'

A very peculiar shiver ran through her and the hairs on the back of her arms stood up.

'Becky?'

'Sorry, bit of a weird thing to hear about your husband . . . ex-husband even. What was she like?'

'Do you mean what did she look like?'

'Let me guess. She was a regular Jewish princess, long black hair, heavy make-up, perfect pointy tits – how am I doing so far?'

'Very good,' Judy laughed nervously.

'What a shame. So she's pretty?'

'Yes.'

'No blackheads, greasy skin, goitres of any description?'

'Afraid not.'

'Not even an enormously fat bum?'

'Well, like me she probably looks better in skirts than trousers.'

'Judith, you know perfectly well you haven't got a fat bum. So what you're saying is that she has a wonderful hour-glass figure?'

'She can't do her own make-up though.'

'Tell me, tell me.'

'Bright-blue eyeshadow—'

'Dress sense?'

'Cutesy, white shoes.'

'Thank Yahweh for small mercies.'

'Listen, why don't you come over, or – I've got a car – I'll come to you—'

'Honestly, I'm fine, Judy. I've been divorced a year and separated for four. I've got a lasagne in the oven and programmes ringed in the *Radio Times*.'

She hadn't but she wasn't hungry so she poured herself a gin, lay on the sofa and thought about Danny.

They had met in their first term at university; she was reading English and he Oriental Studies. He took her virginity, and she had understood then that she had taken his, although now she sometimes wondered.

They both continued to live in their separate colleges but it seemed perfectly natural when, in the final week of their last summer term, he proposed.

For the first time that seriously raised the question of religion. Becky knew that because of her name his parents had assumed that she too was Jewish, and Danny had allowed them to go on thinking that. Even after they realised she wasn't they were friendly on her occasional visits, but when the news of the engagement was broken to them she discovered that their relaxed attitude had stemmed from a belief that their son would never consider marrying outside the faith. As Danny had never displayed any religious feeling to her – merely a historical interest in the land of his ancestors – she was in turn surprised at their surprise.

She embarked on her teacher-training course and Danny, accepting the quid pro quo for his time at Durham, joined the accountancy firm in which his father and uncle were senior partners. During the week he lived at home in Finchley and at weekends he drove his new Ford Escort to Loughborough.

He railed at his parents' intolerance but assured her he would win them round and she believed him because he was as stubborn as a mule. He moaned about the soulless nature of accounting but explained that, once qualified, he would be able to use his skill in some more congenial area. Becky wasn't so sure that she believed this. To her it seemed that by even entering the firm he had more or less conceded the battle for his career, but if he could cope with his job and remain the companion he was then who was she to complain? They would have to indulge his interest in history on holiday rather than skiing and playing golf as other accountants seemed to do.

However it had been achieved she detected a softening in the Fishmans' manner and at Passover they announced a date for their wedding to general and sincere acclaim. The ceremony was at Chelsea Register Office, fixed by Mr Fishman to fulfil Mrs Fishman's wish that if you couldn't be joined in the local synagogue then at least you could be chic, and after lunch and a champagne reception at the Dorchester the happy couple left for Heathrow and a gruelling flight to Tel Aviv.

Her first clear recollection of their honeymoon was lying on the beach at Netanya with her eyes closed and hearing above the very gentle wash of the sea the approaching rumble of a helicopter. It took her back to childhood holidays in Tenby and the air–sea rescue men waving as they flew overhead but when she opened her eyes, expecting to see the yellow whirlybird with RAF roundels somehow transposed to the eastern Mediterranean, instead there was a gunship in military camouflage, rockets slung beneath and a soldier pointing a machine-gun from the open hatch.

When they moved up the coast to Akko two days later the 'safe' sections of beach were marked out with barbed wire but already the sight of young conscripts sitting at café tables with carbines hanging from the back of their chairs was familiar enough not to warrant comment.

Despite the evidence of a country on war footing Becky could detect no animosity between Jew and Arab – the conflict was one of culture. Around the old, walled Crusader port had sprung up modern Jewish suburbs of flats in the style of Majorcan hotels, and factories had brutalised beautiful, rugged landscapes throughout northern Israel. But the architects of this progress had also literally made the desert bloom; enormous orange groves and banana plantations flourished and there was an infectious vitality everywhere. Sitting by the swimming pool of a kibbutz in the mountains behind Haifa you could truly feel this was God's own country. Why did there have to be a dispute over whose God?

In Jerusalem they were elbowed aside by the worshippers in their black coats and hats sweating beneath the Wailing Wall, and virtually trampled underfoot by a scrummage of Filipino nuns intent on laying hands on the site of Christ's tomb in the dank Church of the Holy Sepulchre. The calm of the Dome of the Rock – soft carpets under bare feet, cool air, everyone behaving with polite dignity – inspired her to say, 'Comparing these religions by their holy places, who wouldn't be a Muslim?' It was meant lightheartedly but Danny scowled and buried his head in the guidebook.

Back on the beach she watched an old man in black trunks, nut-brown and wasted, gazing out to sea with a distant stare, still and intense and sad. Then he turned his arm to wipe the sweat from his brow and Becky saw the number tattooed on his wrist and felt that she would fight to secure the right of these victims to live here, there, anywhere they chose.

Every way you turned you got a different and contradictory perspective. On their last night they had walked through the Akko street market, now deserted and profoundly dark apart from the open doorway of a little printer's. Inside on old presses young Palestinians were running off Arabic leaflets which despite the conspiratorial lateness of the hour might have been commercial not seditious. They emerged from the covered way steeped in the sharp smell off the cobbles of crushed fruit and butcher's blood, and stood in a courtyard beneath the bright stars. The last, scratchy call of the muezzin competed with the canned laughter of a TV game show from an open window.

Their flat in West Hampstead was modern and predominantly beige. After they had hung their respective pictures it looked like a college study with a thyroid problem.

They lived there for three years during which Danny passed his exams and Becky learnt the difference between teaching theory and teaching practice. They had friends round for dinner and stockpiled possessions. Danny's Escort became a Sierra and he took her to look at a house in Golders Green. It was inter-war neo-Tudor with four bedrooms and a conservatory. This seemed like a serious child-rearing property and she expressed her misgivings. His assurance that they need only stay until he became a partner when the serious money would start rather begged the question of his leaving accountancy for that something more congenial. He rationalised that with just a few more years under his belt he would be able to pick and choose.

Becky suggested looking for a property in another part of London, wanting to detach herself from the Fishman clan, but was hoist by the petard of not wanting to change jobs herself. They compromised on an Edwardian house which patently never met with Mrs Fishman's approval, but it still had four bedrooms and the hints about pattering, tiny feet began. Becky asked Danny to explain to his mother in no uncertain terms that she was not contemplating a child in the foreseeable future – and he asked why not.

It had taken some time for Becky to realise that there was something of the chameleon about Danny. His stubborn streak had belied it, and not until their honeymoon had she seen him in circumstances other than student ones, because whenever he had visited her in Loughborough he had naturally fallen back into her way of life. But over the working years the protective colouring he had adopted to get on in his job had become so ingrained that he no longer knew or cared that it was there. He had been assimilated.

The dispute over children had marked the beginning of the end, she could see that now. Sex became an activity with a purpose, or rather no purpose, and as a manifestation of their disagreement was not welcomed by either of them. Other differences of opinion which any couple might let pass in a spirit of altruism began to surface. She did not know how long they might have carried on like this – as it was they lasted two years – had it not been for her visit to the Fishman office. It was half-term and she had gone to

John Lewis to buy some new curtains before meeting
Danny for lunch. Normally they would have agreed on a
venue beforehand but today they had not done so, because
they had been arguing in a weary way about what to give his
squash partner and girlfriend for dinner. Consequently she
presented herself in the reception area of Fishman Spink at
a quarter to one.

There were two girls behind the desk – both about
twenty, one dark and one blonde. The blonde girl was the
prettier of the two and at the perfect age for her looks. She
had a ripeness that could not last long – soon her cheeks
would become pudgy and her chin soften and her breasts
and bottom sag, but not yet. She had a sing-song voice and
a bland smile and she announced Becky's presence with
neutrality. She would have got away with it but her friend
looked at her in such a way – half-amused, half-fascinated –
that Becky suddenly knew the blonde was having an affair
with Danny. Then she leaned forward, the unbuttoned
collar of her blouse shifted and beneath her gold chain
Becky could see the inadequately disguised bruising of a
lovebite.

'Having an affair' sounded so ridiculously middle-aged
that she had never suspected it befalling any of their
contemporaries, let alone Danny. But it was true and it was
terminal. Two days later she moved out of the house she
had never liked and, after a spell on Vanessa's sofa, into a
spare room at Sophie's rented place in Camden Road.

Many people could not understand how she had abandoned a nine-year relationship so quickly but in her head
the abandonment was much more gradual and Danny's
infidelity merely the shocking catalyst.

Since then he had reportedly had a succession of what
she liked to think of as 'bimbo' girlfriends – all blonde, and
all as different from her as chalk from cheese. But now he

was marrying again he was playing by the book. She assumed – hoped – this was tantamount to a dynastic marriage. A pity it wasn't to an old boot. Mrs Fishman would be pleased.

But here too there were different and contradictory perspectives. She wanted him to miss her, but she didn't want him unhappy. She didn't want him back but part of her still loved, if not him, then the man he once was.

After Danny she too had had a sporadic succession of boyfriends but none had evoked anything like the strength of feeling that he had, right from their first date.

Until, maybe, now. Perhaps Danny's engagement was a sign that it was time for a fresh start for herself. It would certainly take the wind out of his sails for her to demonstrate a similar new commitment. Nellie the elephant . . .

Fresh start. Wind out of sails. She would be rearranging the deckchairs on the *Titanic* if she didn't have something to soak up the gin. But she still wasn't hungry so she had another and resigned herself to maudlin reminiscence.

5

Going to the Dogs

Vanessa went to the Dolphin shoot on day two. The dressing-room footage was done and today they would be filming the models on the catwalk, diving into and climbing out of the imaginary pool. The underwater sequences were still to come.

Like most clients with their first commercial, hers was fascinated for half an hour and then bored by the apparent lack of progress. The same small piece of action was filmed repeatedly from different angles, and on many of the takes a voice would cry 'Cut' for no obvious reason before the manoeuvre was complete.

When they broke for lunch she introduced the client to Mikey, who exchanged politenesses for five minutes before leaving the table to approve another set-up. She rather hoped that Derek would have had enough by then but he settled down in his chair, saying he would just stay and see his products wet as well as dry.

The black one-piece and the tropically-patterned bikini were in the can when Shona, modelling a fluorescent-yellow costume, emerged dripping from head to toe and stood beneath the lights. The fabric had become see-through to the point where her nipples and shadow of pubic hair were clearly visible.

'Very nice,' said an electrician. There were a couple of laughs and wolf whistles.

'Act your age,' snapped Mikey, and the principals gathered around her for a conference.

'I take it that effect is not intended,' he began, 'and even if we like it the advertising standards people probably won't pass it.'

'I know we use sex to sell,' Graham said, 'but that's probably a bit blatant.'

'I have some other suits,' Derek reassured them.

Malcolm, the agency producer, arriving from the corner in which he had been totting up some expenses, looked alarmed. Vanessa stepped in delicately before some other pair of size-nines ruined the still amicable atmosphere.

'I think the problem with swapping at this stage is that it would involve us in some reshoots, and the cost of those reshoots.' Which is why I told you that for continuity we had to be absolutely sure from day one that we had the right costumes, she didn't add.

Mikey took his cue. 'We'd certainly have to do Shona's parade again, which would mean overtime tonight, and without reviewing the dressing-room stuff I'm not sure we can cut together those scenes without that suit in the background. If not, that would mean another day redoing all yesterday's material.'

'How expensive would that be?' asked Derek, who now seemed a bit shell-shocked.

Malcolm looked at Tim, Mikey's producer. 'I think we'd need the computer to work it out exactly—'

'Ballpark,' said Vanessa.

'Thirty thousand and several days' delay at the very least.'

'Give us five minutes and we'll try and work out a way of shooting her without showing the naughty bits,' said Mikey.

'Great,' said Vanessa. 'We'll go and get a cup of tea then,' and she escorted the hapless client away.

'Take five everyone,' said Tim.

'Do you want to whip that robe off and hop back into position,' Mikey said to Shona, who had covered up.

'I've never done topless or, you know, men's mags,' she said, 'so if I'm going to be seen I think you ought to talk to my agent.'

'Don't worry, you won't be. Now, what if we run the camera from behind to get the bum and the back, and then from the side like this, and then we'll have to get Jenny out again so that we have a full frontal on the black one?'

Vanessa reappeared, having left Derek talking to Emma. 'Solution?'

'Means changes to the agreed storyboard,' said Billy.

'He'll buy that, I'm sure,' she said, 'as long as it doesn't cost anything. Can you get an accurate price on reshoots in case we have to pressure him, Malcolm?'

Derek did buy it, and Vanessa walked him to his car very soon after. He was probably keen to escape the site of a potential disaster so lightly, and showed no inclination to witness the underwater filming the next day, preferring to wait and see an edited version of the commercial on Friday afternoon.

Vanessa was called to the editor's in Soho on the Thursday evening just after six, and arrived to find Graham, Billy, Malcolm and Mikey sitting in the anteroom surrounded by the overflowing ashtrays, curling sandwiches and abandoned coffee cups that normally accumulate around an edit.

They watched the roughcut on the Steenbeck, crowded round the tiny screen as the spools of film were rolled back and forth.

'So you reckon it's worth transferring this one to video for Derek the Dolphin to have a look at tomorrow?'

'Well, he's got to see something,' she answered, 'and this looks fine to me. Are you all happy with it? Best to know now if there's anything you have reservations about.'

There was general assent.

'First cut, absurdly known as the director's cut,' said Mikey, 'although I can't imagine why, given the number of people hanging around here,' and the others laughed with the camaraderie of those who have endured much boredom together, 'you always go for what looks the best. So this is the best we've got.'

They sorted out how many copies she needed and in which formats, and ritual horror was expressed that the client was going to see something lovingly crafted on 35mm film stock reduced to the crudity of a VHS video cassette. Malcolm offered Vanessa a lift back to the agency in the cab he had ordered but her car was outside so she declined and finished her coffee, and suddenly there was only Mikey left in the room.

'You must be tired,' she said.

'In need of a drink,' he said, 'and a conversation that doesn't start "You know that shot where dot dot dot". Have you got the time – or the inclination even – to join me?'

'It will have to be a quick one,' she said, glancing at her watch. 'Why are you laughing?'

'Because I know that you probably mean it whereas for

just about everyone else who says that it's a precursor to a long night in the pub.'

They went round the corner and had spritzers.

'How's Josh?' he asked, and her heart warmed to him.

She talked about Josh's increasing vocabulary and how excited he was about Christmas – 'Frightening as it's only November 16th. So much anticipation can only lead to disappointment. How's Sophie?'

There was a pause. She watched Mikey's face but he didn't look guilty, merely depressed.

'I think she's OK. You probably know more than me. After all you've been friends for a lot longer than I've known her.'

She wanted to mention *The Duchess of Malfi* but she didn't. She wanted to say, 'About the other night' but she didn't. Instead she said, 'As far as I know she's fine. Look, I'm sorry but I must go.'

'That old babysitter again?'

'Child-minder. And more importantly, child.'

'What time will you be back from Dolphin tomorrow?'

'Not until the evening,' she said, misunderstanding. 'But I'll ring the agency from Leicester and I'm sure they'll call you if there's any major problem with the cut.'

'I'm sure they will too,' he said. 'But I wasn't thinking about that. I was wondering if you would have dinner with me?'

'I can't,' she said. 'I couldn't leave Josh at such short notice, and I've hardly seen him this week.'

'Saturday then?'

She sat down again and swallowed carefully. 'This might sound childish but I don't think I should have dinner with you while you are ... going out with ... one of my best friends. I mean I'm not saying it has to be cleared with her or anything but I'd rather know that she knows, if you see what I mean.'

'I can see your point,' he said. 'But the fact is Sophie and I are not . . . are not an "item" any more. So asking her permission or whatever would feel sort of odd to me.'

He didn't look upset so she didn't say she was sorry.

'OK then.'

When the post came on Saturday Becky was out of bed at the sound of the letterbox, but it turned out to be another glossy circular about investment opportunities. She hadn't realistically expected a reply from Dermot so soon – she had only written six days ago to a poste restante address in Paris – but a part of her hoped that a letter from him might have crossed with hers. After all it had not been agreed that she should write first or, she had to remind herself, at all.

Once again an empty weekend yawned before her – she seemed incapable of organising entertainment for herself. So she did as usual in the circumstances; rang Vanessa and left a message on the answerphone. It still hadn't been answered when Sophie called at twelve.

'Not seeing Mikey then?'

'Left a message for him' – Sophie had actually left two but it sounded rather pathetic to admit that – 'but he hasn't called back. He might be away the whole weekend for all I know. He's been filming all week and I don't usually see him while that's going on.'

They decided to go to the National Gallery and have another look at the early Renaissance collection that they had visited in a burst of enthusiasm on their return from Florence. Becky said that she had left a message for Vanessa who therefore might join them and Sophie wondered whether they were the only two people left in London without bloody answerphones.

In the event Vanessa didn't call back before Becky left the flat and so it was just she and Sophie having tea in the gallery's cafeteria and considering how to spend their evening. After rummaging in her bag for a *Time Out* Becky half-emptied it on to the table and produced that day's *Sporting Life*.

'You're a dark horse. What are you doing with this?'

Becky explained how she had seen Zakis Minotaur and noted the dates of his races. Having qualified from the heats he was in the final tonight and she wanted to see how the paper rated his chances.

If Sophie thought this behaviour obsessive in one who had never displayed a previous interest in racing of any kind she did not say so. She probably recognised the truth, which was that Becky would maintain any link with Dermot, however vestigial.

'Why don't we go then?' she said. 'I've never been dog racing before but the horses are fun; it'll make a change from the pictures anyway. Do you know where Walthamstow is?'

As the *A–Z* showed the stadium some distance from the nearest tube they went via Camden and took Sophie's jeep. Any fears they had about not finding it were dispelled by the slow-moving traffic off the roundabout in an otherwise deserted semi-suburban area and seconds later an enormous neon sign of galloping dogs with 'Welcome to the Stow' beneath. Following the example of numerous other punters they abandoned the Suzuki on a grass verge and walked across the already full car park. The expected Nissans and Montegos of the North London family man were augmented by lots of souped-up Fords, the preferred transport of 'lads' with leather jackets and white socks, and a surprising number of Jags and Rollers.

Ahead of them, picking their way through the ruts and

puddles, were two girls in short fur coats and extremely high stilettos.

'Do you think we're underdressed?' Becky giggled.

'No,' said Sophie. 'It says they've got a nightclub – they're probably hostesses, poor cows.'

But they weren't. When, having bought their pro-grammes – 'Racecards, darlin',' the man on the turnstile corrected Sophie – and climbed endless flights of stairs, they emerged into the hubbub of the grandstand bar and realised that they were the inappropriately dressed.

'You can't say underdressed,' said Sophie. 'We're wear-ing more each than these girls have got between a pair.'

Very short, tight skirts, some in black leather, and heels that imperilled stability seemed *de rigueur* for the under-forties, and were most commonly teamed with sparkling boob tubes. Necklaces bearing the wearer's initial and ankle bracelets glittered against improbably golden tans. Although many of these heavily-coiffured creatures were pretty, possessing a suitable build for the costume had not deterred them, and acres of bare shoulders and deep cleavages were not complemented by the sprinkling of visible panty lines on show. The archetypal escort was smooth-suited and coarse-featured; the fingers gripping glasses were adorned with chunky rings.

'Talk about gangsters and their molls,' said Sophie.

'I can't decide if we're on the inside of a tropical fish tank looking out or the outside looking in.'

Becky gestured at the wall of plate glass beyond which the grass of the track was unnaturally green beneath the floodlights. In the centre of the stadium a dispirited municipal garden was illuminated by purple and orange spots. She couldn't see anyone who looked like Sean nor could she imagine him or Dermot buying brandy and ginger ales here, so when they were getting their drinks she asked the tired barmaid if there was somewhere the kennel staff hung out and was directed to another bar in the bowels of the stand.

Just then the TV screens slung all over the place suddenly switched from incomprehensible numerical displays headed 'Forecast' and 'Treble' to live film of hounds being paraded in brightly-coloured jackets. Becky and Sophie manoeuvred to get a real view of the track and as they squeezed into a scarcely vacant space all the lights in the stand went out, making the view through the window like a giant movie screen itself. In the stirring crowd and the subsequent explosion of colour and movement Becky could see more similarities with the circus.

'Gosh,' said Sophie. 'It's much more interesting than the gee-gees. You can see what happens all the way round. Shall we have a bet on the next one?'

So they looked at their racing cards but these were full of lines and lines of unfathomable form.

'Perhaps we'll be able to tell when they come out. Or shall we just pick the best name? I like Hick and Benzol.'

Becky suggested they sought out Sean, who would know, but when they reached the other bar it looked about as easy to find him as the proverbial needle in the haystack, despite Becky's feeling that she would recognise him anywhere. Down here the hot air was even thicker with smoke and the almost exclusively male crowd far scruffier and more loudly opinionated. But when the tannoy announced that the next race was three minutes away the enormous room suddenly emptied through double doors which led to the bookmakers by the finishing line, and among the flotsam remaining at previously hidden tables she spotted Patzaki.

In this context his raffish appearance made sense – he was one of the few people she had seen who could pass muster in either bar. Becky approached him somewhat

warily, but after a short hiatus Patzaki recognised her and
sped to replenish their drinks. And not a moment too soon
because as he returned the crowd surged back in, carrying
Sean with them.

He had no news of his brother.

'And how's Smokey? Will he win?'

'We hope. Don't talk too loudly. Bars have ears.'

'We wanted to have a bet,' said Sophie. 'Can we put it on
now?'

She indicated the temporarily queueless windows of the
tote kiosks.

'Don't put your money on there,' said Sean with the
horror of the true gambler. 'You don't know what odds
you've got until the race has started. We'll do it with the
bookies outside, and they won't take bets on the final until
three minutes before the off.'

'Can you do it with us?'

'No, because I shall be leading out the dog, but if you
give your money to Mr P he'll put it on with the rest at the
best price he can get.' He paused. 'In fact—'

He leant across the table and mumbled in his employer's
ear. The Greek looked at them and laughed.

'We've got an idea,' Sean said quietly. 'But I can't tell
you here. Come with me.'

He said this so confidently that Becky followed him and
Sophie her. It occurred to Becky that neither man had
expressed the least surprise at them being there – perhaps
they thought everyone went dog racing. In their small
world she supposed everyone did. When it was obvious
they were heading for the car park Sophie touched her arm
and raised an interrogative eyebrow.

'He's OK,' Becky whispered. 'Don't worry.'

Sean unlocked the back doors of the van and gestured
them in to perch among the empty wire dog boxes.

'Sorry about all the cloak and dagger but it won't work if we're seen together.'

He explained that in the frantic three minutes before a race when the bookies were taking bets the odds were changing constantly depending on how much money was being placed on each dog, and that each bookie had at least one assistant in the crowd around their stands watching the others to let his boss know if the odds he was offering were out of line.

'So they all try to give the same odds?'

'More or less. The punter's art, apart of course from picking the winner, is to judge the right moment to place his bet to get the highest odds. If it's a big bet no one afterwards will get odds as high because the risk has to be laid off, balanced out. You understand the maths, yeah?'

'Well, the principle,' said Sophie. 'I can't imagine how they work out the new odds in their heads.'

'It's not all arithmetic,' Sean said. 'If it's a big bet from someone the bookies recognise as being in the know like a trainer—'

'Like Mr Patzaki?'

'Yes, then the odds will come down more than the figures justify. Our problem tonight is that between us we've got three grand to put on. No one bookie will accept a single bet of more than a grand and, like I said, once the governor's placed one bet he'll get lousy odds from the next bookie. We thought you might like to have some fun and help us beat the bookies, which, after all, is every gambler's dream.'

'OK.'

He outlined what they would have to do.

Patzaki arrived with a fat man in a blazer who was Smokey's owner. He gave them a pile of £50 notes each.

'How do you know we won't run off with it?' Becky asked Sean as they returned to the track.

'I trust you,' he said. 'You're a friend of Dermot's. Good enough for me.'

'Is that good enough for Patzaki?'

'It doesn't have to be.'

'Why?'

'Because he'd be able to find you and get his money back, I should think.'

Once the race prior to the Goodwood Cup Final was over both girls went and stood on the cold, concrete terraces. Their breath came in ghostly blasts of white smoke. Neither of them had risked another alcoholic drink. 'God, I hope we don't make a mess of it,' said Sophie.

'We won't. Isn't it exciting?'

The terraces slowly filled up and they moved down to stand close to the respective pitches they had been allocated. These consisted of nothing more than an upturned crate for the bookie himself to stand on and a blackboard on a pole behind his head detailing the runners. A battered briefcase containing his money hung from the pole. At his side stood his chief assistant with the book in which the bets were entered.

When Becky saw the dogs led out on to the track she looked up and, exactly where he had said, stood Patzaki. Betting opened, slowly, as he had warned. Smokey, who had won his heat but had only come third in his semi-final and whose time was the fourth fastest of those in the final, opened at four to one.

She concentrated on looking as if she was following the progress of chalk on blackboards while keeping an eye on Patzaki. Grasped moistly in her pocket was £1,000. The price lengthened to five to one and she thought, quick,

quick. Dimly in the distance she could see Sean in a white coat among the dogs and handlers processing to the traps. Closer were Sophie and the fat man, both hovering by pitches of their own.

Becky had been frightened that she might miss it but the six-inch sheet of flame that erupted from Patzaki's lighter as he raised it to the cigarette dangling from his lips was as clear as a lifeboat-summoning maroon.

Somehow there were now two people between her and the man in the mac and it seemed an eternity before she thrust her bundle of notes into his hand and said, just as she had been instructed, 'A grand on Zakis Minotaur.'

Another age passed before he replied, as he counted, 'One thousand on Trap 5', and then she had her orange card and was pushing away. In the crowd the tic-tac men were frantically shouting and their bosses wiping Minotaur from their boards.

'I got five to one, did you?' Sophie asked, hopping from one foot to the other. Becky had. 'He was right, Patzaki, they're showing one to one now.'

'That's called evens. They're starting.'

The sound of the hare motor, remembered from her morning at Rathkennen with Dermot, was clearly audible out here. A bell rang. 'Hare's running,' announced the tannoy.

They had to stand on tiptoe for a clear view of the traps, which sprang open as the bunny passed. The dogs came powering out.

'Which colour is ours?' squealed Sophie.

'Yellow jacket.'

Becky's heart leapt into her mouth as the two leading dogs bumped at the first bend but Smokey was on their outside and once they were on to the back straight he began to gain inexorably on the leader. The roar of the crowd was deafening. In between the third and fourth bends there was nothing more than a head's length in it and then they were running for home. Because of the angle it was impossible to tell who was leading but suddenly the red dog was up there with the other two. Sophie was screaming mindlessly and pulling at her hair. It was only as the winning dog crossed the line, a surprisingly comfortable two lengths clear, that Becky realised her throat was sore from bellowing 'Come on! Come on!'

Sophie whirled her round as if the triumph was personal. 'We've done it! We've done it!'

The celebrations of the Minotaur camp were raucous. After the presentation the girls and the fat man collected £6,000 each from furious and tight-lipped bookmakers and all repaired to the restaurant where Patzaki had a table and a running order on champagne, although he stuck to brandy.

Sean joined them after he had put the victorious animal in the van but could only sip at a glass of bubbly because he was driving. The fat man handed them their winnings.

'This isn't right,' Becky said to Sean. 'We only had £20 on each – there's £300 apiece here. That's—' She struggled with the mental arithmetic.

'One hundred and eighty each extra. Put it away. It's a present.'

'You should have seen their faces when they realised they'd taken three bets together,' said Patzaki. 'What a caning.' His gold teeth glinted in a vulpine smile.

Eventually they took their leave and Sean offered to walk them to their car.

'In this envelope,' he said, 'is a cheque for Dermot's winnings. Can you give it to him for me?'

Becky stared at him. Sophie was noisily unlocking the jeep.

'Of course,' she said.

As they circled the roundabout looking for the central London turn-off Sophie asked, 'How much did Patzaki make tonight?'

'About six grand, Sean reckons.' Sophie whistled. 'The fat man got even more because there was £1,000 prize money. Sean picked up a couple of grand. And we didn't do so badly ourselves, considering how little we risked.'

'You're not kidding. What a thrill.' Sophie stretched back in her seat. 'Better than sex. What's that you're clutching?'

'Dermot's money.'

There was a gap while the implications percolated Sophie's brain, then a squeal and a sharp correction of the steering. 'I didn't know you'd decided to go out and see him.'

'I hadn't quite until tonight.'

'Brilliant. Stay at my place and we'll have a celebration of our own.'

Vanessa's dinner with Mikey had been, she reflected, an immensely civilised affair. Not, she corrected, actually an affair at all. He had taken her to Le Caprice, the black and white interior of which was reassuringly familiar from business lunches. Perhaps she was slightly disappointed that his choice was not more adventurous but as it was two years since a man had bought her a meal for reasons other than commercial even a Tandoori would have been unusual.

Thoughtfully he had warned her where they were going, guessing that what one might choose to wear to one restaurant was not what one would want to be seen in at another. She had deliberated ridiculously long before the mirror, rejecting one ensemble after another; too officey,

skirt too short, skirt too long, bit spinsterish, OTT ...
Eventually she settled for a pair of baggy trousers in richly
printed silk and a short, grey jacket with a mandarin collar,
which she knew had been a good choice as she hadn't
thought about them again until she was taking them off.

On Vanessa's way to meet him the problem of getting
through the evening without straying into a minefield by
mentioning Sophie or university had loomed large but once
they were sitting at the table the conversation flowed
effortlessly – their respective working lives, families,
music, films, holidays (dodgy because of Tuscany but no
accidents) – until the bill was paid and separate taxis were
waiting outside.

'Perhaps we could meet again soon?'

'I'd like to. When?'

'How about one evening this week?'

'You forget – with Josh evenings aren't really possible.'

'Next Saturday then?'

'Yes, that would be lovely.'

And he kissed her briefly on both cheeks and opened her
door for her.

Mikey had been depressed when he met Vanessa at the
ball. If he had had to describe his relationship with Sophie
words like tempestuous would have sprung to mind right
from the start. She was beautiful and outrageous and her
radical mood-swings – happy to sad, close to distant,
aggressive to defenceless – were exciting to begin with. But
her unpredictable behaviour gradually made him feel
permanently unsettled. Because his work as a freelance
was uncertain, and perhaps, he conceded, for other
indefinable reasons, what Mikey wanted was emotional
stability.

He suspected that he and Sophie could achieve this if

they spent more time together, perhaps lived together, but every time he had attempted to broach this subject in a subtle way, fearing rejection, the conversation had slithered from his grasp like a fish. He could never decide whether Sophie could see where it was leading and had manipulated it away, or whether she simply hadn't noticed and it was accidental.

She seemed to resist attempts for them to meet more often. No, not resist, just somehow avoid. He felt he knew her less well now than he had five months ago.

The sight of Vanessa crossing the dance floor of the Grosvenor House, cool, calm and collected, saved him from solitary drinking and what he suspected would have been the drunken ramblings of Billy. After their first dance he had watched her from the staircase while she disposed of her obligations and thought how controlled she was. Bringing up that child, dealing with all these tricky bastards ... Had he not drunk so much he would not have approached her again, all his social inhibitions militated against it, but it seemed quite natural, as did their coming together for that final, surreal, big band version of the old 10CC weepie.

Afterwards he had felt as pleasurably numb as a patient returning from a Novocaine slumber, his brain only processing certain bits of information so that, as he wandered down Brook Street, no overcoat, no sense of cold, there were great black gaps between the buildings and cars that he did see.

The next day he was frightened by this and rather inclined to pass it off as an alcoholic fugue, but felt threatened enough to attempt to force the issue with Sophie. However, when, at Rani's, he had suggested she moved in with him he had got nowhere. By now it seemed almost natural to add 'of course'. For the first time he began to feel that their relationship had nowhere to go, and that she was definitely misleading him.

At the Dolphin shoot he had only sufficient contact with Vanessa to admire her handling of the potential problem with the costume, but his nerve ends had jangled when she first appeared.

He saw her again at the editor's and within ten minutes had invited her for a drink. Later, when she wavered in accepting his dinner invitation, he told her he and Sophie were finished.

Mikey had already decided this. The problem was he hadn't been able to arrange a meeting with Sophie to tell her. Guilt marred his anticipation of dinner with Vanessa but, having failed to reach Sophie by Saturday morning, he panicked that if he told her now it would spoil everything so he put his answerphone on and stayed out until late afternoon. When he returned there were two messages from her and he felt morally obliged to dial the Camden number. He had resolved to let it ring five times – a bit of a cheat in a house where the phone is in the hall and the occupants mostly in their rooms – but on the fourth ring it was scooped up and he felt sick until he recognised Carol's voice.

Dinner was great, and he felt something important could be developing. Part of him said that this had nothing to do with Sophie – after all a meal was not tantamount to sexual congress, unless you were a foodie. The rest of him felt grubby and he rang Sophie again first thing. When he told her they were sitting in her room, the inevitable bottle of Frascati open and poured.

She was silent for a few moments – he couldn't see her face clearly as her head was bent and her hair obscuring it.

'You didn't give me very long to make up my mind,' she said finally.

'You wouldn't have said yes, Soph.'

'I might have,' she rallied. There were tears in the big green eyes, but she smiled. 'We'd have had some fun while I was deciding anyway.'

'I don't think I would.'

'I know. You want me waiting every night when you come home from a hard day's camera pointing.'

'No ... perhaps ... something like that.'

She lit another cigarette and stayed hunched on a corner of the mattress. He didn't know how to break the silence so after a few moments he got out his own packet.

When it was down to the butt she said, 'What now?'

'I'm not really sure of the etiquette.'

She laughed, but it was more of a snort than a giggle. 'Perhaps we should have met in a restaurant.'

'But then we'd have had to leave perfectly good food.' He tried to match her mood.

'You'd better help me finish this. Unless you've got something better to do.'

'No, of course not.'

'Why drink alone when you can drink together? I had some amazing luck on Saturday anyway.' And she told him about Becky and the bet. 'What did you do on Saturday?'

He felt lightheaded. 'Actually I had dinner with Vanessa.'

'Why?' She sounded incredulous.

'She can't really get out in the week because of Josh.'

'And my mum can only get up to London for the Harrods sale. But you wouldn't meet her for lunch. So why Vanessa? She's not Everest. I suppose you're buttering up the client. It's probably not worth it. I think you blotted your copybook by intruding on her holiday in Tuscany.'

131

He was surprised that Sophie could not imagine he would want to see Vanessa because he liked her. What sort of friends were they? Nevertheless, it was a relief that she could not see Vanessa as a rival, a potential – he hardly dared frame the word himself – successor.

When they had drained the dregs from the bottle he stood up to go.

'Don't.'

'It's late.'

She leant against him. 'Bye, then.' She looped her arms around his neck and kissed him. Her tongue parted his lips. She found herself counting and when she got to twenty his tongue began to push back. At thirty she could feel him stirring against her belly. She waited until he was completely stiff before she broke off and opened her eyes. 'Stay.'

'I can't, Soph. Not after what we've just said.'

'You want to.' She touched him.

'I'm not ruled by my prick.'

'More's the pity. I could do with a good screw.'

What a time to decide that, Mikey thought but stayed silent, staring at his shoes.

'Come on, I'll let you out.'

After he'd gone and she'd listened to his shoes clicking away down the pavement she went into the kitchen and put the kettle on. She squeezed her thighs together. The shock had reminded her she still desired him and she had proof that he still desired her. He wouldn't, couldn't just walk away. He'd been in her thrall. OK, she'd been through an iffy patch about the whole thing but this proved she wasn't ready to let it go.

Miserable, she tried to come up with a course of action, and failed. A special event to which she could invite him? Hardly credible. Begging phone calls? Hardly her style, and she knew from being on the receiving end that they very rarely produced anything more positive than pity closely followed by irritation. All she could do was hope he'd realise he'd made a mistake. She tried to summon up some anger with an experimental 'Bastard!' or two but knew she didn't really mean it. She'd somehow made a hash of it.

There was a thud from the room above and for the first time she registered the muted mumble of a TV. She got another Frascati from the fridge, went up and knocked on Carol's door. They were both surprised when they came down to go to the chippy that the windows were crying with condensation.

By the time Becky saw Vanessa she had had a reply from Dermot and had begun putting her plans into action. She saw a shocked headmaster and told him she would be leaving at the end of term. She apologised for leaving the school in the lurch and conceded that this unreliability would not help her career development. She accepted that she would not be able to come back with her tail between her legs. She disputed the view that what she probably wanted was a child of her own and that chasing rainbows would be no substitute. She narrowly avoided sweeping the assorted football trophies and framed family snapshots from his desk.

On her way home she went into the letting agency by the tube station and was told that there should be no trouble in finding six-month lessees for her flat subject to inspection.

Vanessa was also shocked, as Becky had expected, and pointed out pitfalls but stopped when it became obvious that Becky had already considered them.

'I mean, if the worst comes to the worst, which it won't, and I want to come home, and I haven't got any money left, then I'll just hitch. Thousands of students do it every summer.'

'Don't do that. If you're stranded ring me and I'll wire some money out.'

Becky hugged her. 'In loco parentis.'

'I wish I was. Then I'd forbid it.'

'And then I'd have a tantrum, do it anyway and never forgive you.'

'Aren't you a little bit frightened?'

'Of course. I've never done anything as stupid. Running away to the circus. At my age.'

'I'll miss you.'

'Likewise.'

'So will Josh. He'll make me come out and visit.'

'Until I saw Sean I hadn't really decided, you know. But then I knew I would as long as Dermot's letter was . . . encouraging. So if you'd been in on Saturday morning it might never have happened.'

'Don't say that. It's not true anyway. You only got his letter this morning and you've resigned your job and handed your flat to some Rachman within ten hours. You must have been plotting for weeks.'

'Well, a week maybe. Fantasising, not plotting. What did you do on Saturday anyway?'

'Went to Le Caprice.'

'I can't tell from the name whether that's swanky or some cheap pasta joint with big pepper grinders.'

'It's expensive. And nice.'

'Who with?'

'Don't laugh. I went with Mikey.'

'I'm not laughing. On your own? Vee, do you think that's a good idea? I mean, after all the angst over Tuscany. Sophie still doesn't know you slept with him, and I know that was twelve years ago but people get paranoid about their partners.' Vanessa had gone to the hob and was stirring the sauce. A strong smell of pesto crossed the kitchen. 'I'm sorry. I guess you had to for work, and anyway—'

'It wasn't work, it was pleasure. And it was just dinner. And anyway he and Sophie have split up.'

'From what she said on Saturday I don't think she knows that.'

The following Saturday Mikey took Vanessa to La Bastide. She knew that she might be reading too much into the choice but she approved of the progression. This pale room, which could have been the dining salon of a large Regency house, was quiet and more intimate than the upfront Caprice, but avoided the spurious romanticism of low lights, corner tables and candles.

During the week she had seen Sophie at their fortnightly get-together and discovered that although Mikey hadn't 'chucked' her until the Monday after Le Caprice they hadn't seen each other for more than a week so he hadn't really had the opportunity. Vanessa wasn't comfortable about that but it was simply another part of her ball of confusion and as Sophie seemed more angry than upset, apparently suffering from hurt pride rather than a broken heart, she felt relatively guiltless about accepting the invitation to La Bastide.

Sophie had been very amused by Mikey and Vanessa's last dinner date, as she called it, which was good but somehow irritating. Vanessa didn't think she knew about this one.

She dissected her sorbet of three fruits, sharp on the tongue and fragrant with mint leaves.

'Do you like Armagnac?' he asked, when the plates were a wasteland of broken biscuit and redundant coulis.

'What do you think?' she said slyly. 'Perhaps I'm more of a Tia Maria girl?'

'There's nothing wrong with that,' he said cautiously.

'Maybe not on ice-cream anyway. I would like an Armagnac but I'm not expert enough for you to impress me by ordering the 1932 and blowing the entire proceeds of your last film.'

Without being asked he once again ordered two taxis.

'Maybe the next time we meet we could do something with Josh? Then you wouldn't have to struggle with babysitters and your conscience.'

Thanks for mentioning conscience, she thought. I was doing very nicely without one. It was the first inappropriate move he had made all evening, and even that was far outweighed by his including Josh. Too good to be true?

Becky was watching a noisy late-night movie when she got home. 'We didn't even share a taxi in case you were wondering, my maiden aunt.'

'Just as well,' Becky grinned. 'As you seem to be squiffy. Boys will take advantage.'

'Not this one. A chaste kiss on the cheek at the moment of our parting, that's all.' She omitted to mention that the fleeting touch of their bodies had left her feeling like a cherry liqueur chocolate – hard and crisp on the outside but with a warm and liquid centre. She smiled to herself. Becky caught the sphinx-like expression and wondered but she didn't say anything.

The three of them met in Harrods on the assumption that the best Father Christmas would be there. 'Selfridges has got something called Uncle Holly,' Mikey had said on the phone, 'but I think that might be confusing, don't you?'

'Not to mention naff,' she had replied.

First they walked round the food hall, which Josh liked,

being particularly fascinated by the fish display with its glistening scales of mullet and wild salmon, and the submarine-grey hulk of a tuna whose red flesh bore no resemblance to the flaky stuff he ate from cans.

They weren't really shopping, not knowing one another well enough to expose their petty choices of soaps for sisters-in-law and vet's memoirs for distant cousins. After the toy department, which took up most of the morning, Vanessa bought some wrapping-paper and Mikey some extra cards.

'You can't give all the family the same design in case they spot them when visiting.'

They were of the Adoration of the Shepherds as depicted by the fifteenth-century painter Roberti – which reminded her that Becky would be gone by Christmas.

'Tell Mummy to cheer up, Josh,' he said. 'It's time for lunch. Where would you like to go?'

'He'll be happy if we can get ham and chips. We'll have to do the best we can.' Which was pretty well considering the swollen pre-Christmas crowds. She had fish soup with *croûtons* and *rouille* – halfway through she remembered the garlic, Jesus, was she out of practice – and he tucked into a big hamburger, stuffing copious quantities of every available relish under the lid of the bun.

She laughed. 'And I thought you were such a sophisticate.'

'Only after six,' he said.

'What are you doing this evening?'

'Well, nothing planned—'

'Only Josh and I thought you might want to come to the park with us and then back for supper. If you haven't had enough,' she added, indicating her small son's head closely engaging ice-cream with chocolate sauce.

'No, that would be great.'

'I haven't got anything in really, it'll be pot luck.'

'We could always go back to Harrods,' he said helpfully.

She laughed again. 'No, I've done my shopping in the supermarket. I was just being self-deprecating in case you said no or the meal turned out to be crap.'

It was cold in the park and the light was fading before they had done more than feed the ducks with a roll that Mikey procured from the cafeteria. They walked down to the riverbank and stood under the canopy of the Buddhist pagoda; the fountains were switched off and the zoo was closed but a crane obligingly stood on one leg for them. After they had visited the slide and swings they sat looking across the lake and drank steaming mugs of hot chocolate.

'It's like the whole of childhood crammed into one day,' he said.

Vanessa really hadn't known whether Mikey would come back or not, but she had tidied up and bought the ingredients for a chicken casserole, which could be flavoured once his likes and dislikes were known.

Before Josh went to bed Mikey produced a present – an Advent calendar which made up into a three-dimensional coaching inn with real lights in the windows from a tiny battery-powered bulb inside.

'A day late, I'm afraid, but I was never averse to opening more than one window at a time.'

Josh was enchanted, and too young to realise it was not customary to have more than one calendar. The one his mother had bought, a single cardboard sheet, was hanging on the back of his bedroom door. But she didn't mind.

By the time they had eaten the sitting-room was warm enough to encourage the discarding not only of sweaters but of Vanessa's shoes. Deciding where to sit had been a tricky diplomatic exercise; together on the sofa was what they both wanted but Mikey would not settle and hovered until, putting the Cointreau and cognac bottles down on the pine chest, Vanessa forced his hand by sitting there herself. He opted for the armchair opposite.

She put her feet up, and the evening idled away. It was nearly midnight before Mikey, returning from the bathroom, said that he had better go. Vanessa didn't stir. He knelt down at her side.

'Bye, then. Thanks for everything. I've really enjoyed it.'

'So have I.'

She ran her finger along his cheekbone. And that was the spark.

Feeling absurdly like a fourteen-year-old virgin rather than a thirty-two-year-old mother she stopped his hand between the thighs of her jeans and they both came up for air.

'I have to tell you I'm not the pushover I once was.'

He looked mortified. 'I suppose we had to talk about that sooner or later.'

'But not with you on your knees,' she said. 'Get up here,' and when he did she laid her legs across his to maintain some physical contact between them. Her body, unhappy about the interruption, buzzed its frustration to her brain.

Mikey was breathing deeply and sitting rigidly. 'Is it all right if I smoke?'

She realised that he had not had one since he had been in the house.

'I know that's a long time in the past,' she said once he had had a couple of deep drags, 'and if this isn't rude you seem like a different person. I didn't really know you then anyway, and now I know you as you are now what happened in 1977 is irrelevant. Except I probably couldn't

139

say this to someone I hadn't . . . I mean I didn't know what would happen between you and me this time but I think the last twenty minutes sort of prove something we both want.'

He looked relieved but said nothing, taking refuge in the tricky business of evenly spreading his ash around the tray.

She knew what she had to say next, but a decision taken quietly and alone, and buttressed by the possibility of the moment never arriving, was hard to put into practice with low lights and heightened libido.

She swallowed. 'But I've got Josh and I haven't made love with anybody since. Before I do I have to be sure that he's safe.'

'I like Josh.'

'I can tell. And you're good with him.' She blushed. 'But that's not what I meant.'

Trust a man to misunderstand. What did he think was worrying her? That he would ask her to get rid of Josh? That he was a child abuser? She had never imagined, hadn't got as far as . . . She pulled back from that abyss. Concentrate.

She could still feel his kisses on her mouth and neck as if they were nettle-stings. Her hormones sang a siren song. Don't worry. It'll be all right. You deserve it, want it, need it. She ploughed on in an attempt to drown out this internal dissent before it overwhelmed her.

'Look, this is hard, I'm frightened you'll be insulted and that will be that, but to protect Josh I have to know that you're safe.'

He watched her with genuine curiosity. She steeled herself to put the issue beyond all ambiguity.'

'I know that condoms are supposed to make it safe but if they're not a hundred per cent on pregnancy how can they be for anything else?' It seemed frivolous to add that she had never liked them much anyway. 'If this is going to happen I need total honesty and fidelity, and . . . and I need you to take an Aids test before' – what was the point of euphemism after what she'd already said? – 'before we can fuck.'

She'd blown it. How can you ask someone that on your third date? You can fuck them but how can you ask them if they're carrying, no, imply that they may be carrying a deadly disease? She forced herself to look up.

'I'm sorry,' she said very softly. 'It's not romantic, but it's sort of chicken and egg. I know it's probably too much to ask but . . . that's the deal.'

She waited. I'm going to pass out.

'No. It's not too much to ask. I'll take the test. I think you have to wait a certain number of weeks to be sure. I'll find out.'

Finally he returned her gaze, 'I love you.'

Sophie couldn't understand how it had taken her so long to see it. In retrospect she could picture that night at the wine bar when she had joked about Mikey and Vanessa's dinner date, and visualise clearly the momentary panic on Vanessa's face, the confusion on Becky's and the suspicious glance that Judy had thrown at the pair of them. At the time she had only seen puzzlement and surprise.

Sometimes she hated Mikey for doing this to her and then she considered that she hadn't been ready to commit and that he had.

Sometimes she knew that his offer couldn't have been honest if he was already seeing Vanessa and yet Sophie was sufficiently self-aware to recognise that she might well have oscillated in just such a way herself.

Sometimes she couldn't believe what one of her supposed best friends had done to her and at others she knew it wasn't treachery, just something that you couldn't help, and couldn't be blamed for if the other couple were already splitting up.

These reflections were private. In practice she found it impossible to see or speak to Vanessa and failed to turn up for their wine-bar meeting on the 5th. Judy rang her at home later to say that Vanessa hadn't been there, having started on the endless round of seasonal parties that the advertising business goes in for. Then Sophie had to pretend that she had been kept late at work and only just got in.

The real problem was she missed Mikey. The end of an affair always brings its minutiae into sharp focus and she seemed to have plenty of time to brood on the good moments they had shared. Sometimes there seemed to have been so many she wondered if she had loved him after all. The jokes, the messing about, the abandoned sex. How could he prefer uptight Vanessa? He would soon realise he'd made a big mistake and come crawling – well, at least loping – back. And then she'd tell him to get lost.

Hopeless fantasy. He wouldn't call, and if he did she'd take him. Unless she'd found someone better. She'd not realised before how much she disliked being alone, especially with Christmas coming up. Of course there were plenty of fish in the party sea but she wasn't desperate enough to accept a second-rater, not with the means of comparison so close at hand, playing happy families with Vanessa and the sprog.

December was turning into a freakishly bad month altogether. She had spent ages preparing for her interview for *Backdrop* – reading every review in the Sunday papers and ploughing through *Opera* and *Theatre Month* as well as the latest Arts Council funding reports and the catalogues of some extremely irritating Cork Street exhibitions. She developed two specific programme ideas – the iconography of the early Renaissance painters compared to that of the late twentieth-century designer; and a history of the Triumph Herald motor car.

Her board was on the 7th, luckily in a different building, and she changed in the toilets there. Boards were always awful; questions asked by a committee of whom at least one was a revered or household name, but she thought it had gone quite well and was wiping her still clammy palms on the back of her jacket when who should come round the corner but Kate, fingernails sharpened and gimlet eyes on the lookout for scandal, as usual.

Although she had put at least fifty yards of corporation corridor between herself and the interview room Sophie, cheeks flushing, felt as if she was wearing a lapel badge inscribed 'Desperately Trying to Leave Your Programme': nothing lost someone their place on a production team quicker than it being discovered that they were applying to join someone else's.

'Going somewhere nice?' Kate asked, clocking the smart black jodhpurs and matching, tailored coat.

'I hope so,' Sophie replied, as jauntily as she could manage. 'Otherwise borrowing this lot from Mary will have been a waste.'

'Yes, it is rather nice.' The talons tested the material and then flicked it back to read the label. 'Farhi. I was there myself only the other day. Thought I recognised the cut.' And she was gone.

Irrationally terrified that she would bump into Jerry next, Sophie locked herself in the nearest lavatory and smoked a St Moritz in record time. Had Kate been following her? There was absolutely no other bloody reason for her to be here – the coincidence must be a million to one. Well, maybe not quite but bloody high. Had she got away with it? Hopefully, if Kate's nose was as attuned to sexual subterfuge as she suspected. She wondered how much time Kate would waste trying to find out the identity of Sophie's implied BBC boyfriend or that of the fictional Mary. She must remember not to wear the black outfit again.

As the month went on not only was there no sign of an offer or a rejection from *Backdrop* but there continued to be an eerie silence concerning the renewal of her contract with *Churchill's People*.

This was good in that she didn't want to have to say yes or no to Kate until she had heard from the arts people, but what if they didn't want her on the chat show any more? Sophie couldn't reassure herself by asking, as that might reduce her options, so she worked on as efficiently as she could and lost no opportunity to butter up Mr Personality.

She told herself that they had simply forgotten to issue the paperwork, assuming she was happy to stay. Which of course she wasn't but if *Backdrop* didn't come off there were no other vacancies.

When she got into the office on the morning of Monday, the 18th, bright-eyed if not bushy-tailed, there was an internally-mailed envelope marked private and confidential sitting in her tray.

6

An Awfully Big Adventure

About the same time Becky was loading her luggage into the boot of Vanessa's car. She had a large backpack and an old canvas kitbag that had belonged to her father when doing National Service. Most of her clothes were stored in Vanessa's loft as they hadn't seemed particularly appropriate for the life of a ring-hand, and her jeans and sweater were topped by a black donkey-jacket she had bought ten years before to sail in at Hamble.

'It's not going to be very warm,' Vanessa had said doubtfully the day before when vetting the final selection. She came out now and clipped Josh into his baby seat.

'We'd better be on our way.'

They drove through the early morning gloom to the child-minder's, where Josh was casually dismissive in his goodbyes.

'He doesn't understand that he won't see you again for – well, for some time,' she said apologetically as she got back into the car.

'No, I know,' said Becky, 'but I do.'

She had butterflies in her stomach and her voice was difficult to find. The darkness of the car's interior concealed the little tears pricking at the corners of her eyes.

At Victoria they parked as close as they could to the entrance of the station without offending the sensibilities of the cabbies whose pitch this was.

Vanessa helped Becky remove her bags and they stood in the tidal flow of commuters.

'Don't come to the platform with me or we'll have that terrible problem of not having time to say goodbye, or saying it and then you hovering about awkwardly waiting for the guard to blow the whistle.'

'OK then. In that case I'd better give you your farewell present now.'

Vanessa produced a large carrier bag from the back seat. Inside was a heavyweight, sheepskin-lined leather flying jacket sporting a multitude of belts, buckles, pockets and zips. Becky burst into tears and Vanessa offered her a handkerchief 'to save you spoiling the sleeve'.

'I can't take this, it's yours.'

'There isn't time to argue, which is why I didn't give it to you yesterday. Just lift your arms up.' She was tugging at the donkey-jacket. 'It's probably going to be a little large but you'll need to wear several jumpers anyway and you can always turn the sleeves back. Good, that looks OK.'

'It's great but—'

'I hardly ever wear it.'

'But—'

'If it makes you feel better think of it as being on loan. Like a clothes library. That will make you come back to return it. Come on, you must go, otherwise I'll get tearful too and whereas you can get over yours on the ferry I've got to chair a meeting in half an hour and I don't want them thinking I'm suffering from the dreaded pre-menstrual tension.'

They hugged and Becky set off, admonishments to

telephone AND write ringing in her ears. When she reached the corner she turned and looked back and the BMW was still there. An arm came out of the driver's window, and gave a thumbs-up followed by a gesture which might have been the tail end of blowing a kiss. She waved frantically as it sped away and then scurried to her platform.

Only a certain amount of any journey can be spent in thinking about what's been left behind as opposed to what one is heading towards and in Becky's case it was about twenty minutes. Passing through Bromley South, so close to Beckenham, reminded her of school and how glad she was to be away from that, and crossing the high viaduct beyond Farningham Road, the street lamps of the villages of the Darent Valley strung out beneath, a sense of excitement and liberation bubbled up as it had done intermittently for the last fortnight.

She had never been to France other than in summer, and although she reminded herself that it could just as easily be raining there her soul refused to believe it and so the drizzle that collected on the windows of the empty, clattering carriage accentuated her elation. When they drew into stations she smiled at the glum faces waiting for the up-train; at Canterbury East she strained for a glimpse of the cathedral, and then she ticked off the subsequent village halts against the map on the wall until in a bad case of over-anticipation she got out at Dover Priory, a station early, and had to take a taxi to the terminal.

It was too wet to stand on deck for long so she had a cup of hot chocolate and a cognac because it seemed appropriate and slightly naughty to do so at ten in the morning, and went to the duty free shop to buy a bottle of Bushmills for Dermot and a carton of Silk Cut in case they were hard to come by. When they docked she binned the last copy of the *Guardian* she expected to see for a while and walked down the gangway.

It was pouring but somehow that didn't seem to matter.

Sophie didn't have long to recover from the news that she had not got the job on *Backdrop* as there was an editorial conference at ten. Depressed by the fact that this was now her fate for an indeterminate period she struggled to remain enthusiastic and constructive in the teeth of Jerry's hungover irascibility, and scarcely shared the covert amusement of her fellow-assistants at Jerry tearing a strip off Kate for being late. Immediately after she had to drive to Barnes to interview a fat maker of thinly-plotted films and abandoned her jeep in Knightsbridge in an effort to make her teatime rendezvous with an ex-pop star at the Ritz. That done, she picked up the Suzuki and toyed with the idea of going straight to Camden but as she wanted to be seen as a good girl at the moment she nose-to-tailed it back to Shepherd's Bush, only to find when she bounced into the office that everyone had gone home, or at least to the bar.

Frustrated, and with the prospect of another hour's drive ahead, she flopped at her desk and flicked through the small pile of mail and memos that had accumulated during her absence that day. At the bottom was the letter of rejection – folded but out on her desk rather than in her tray.

She swallowed a little spurt of fear. Surely she had tucked it securely away, and if so who had been poking about and reading it? She stuffed it into her handbag, and in a moment of paranoia vowed to burn it as soon as she got home. She sat uneasily for a while longer, wondering whether to go to the bar and try to divine from the expressions of her colleagues who, if anyone, now knew about her failed bid to fly the coop, but she couldn't summon up the courage in case it was obvious that everyone did. Instead she went to a Christmas party thrown by a girl at LWT, where she chatted up a man in light entertainment until she thought he was too drunk to remember her, at which point she went home to bed.

The next day Sophie was on tenterhooks but everything seemed totally average. She resolved to raise the question of her contract renewal after the broadcast on Wednesday.

Once the guests and staff were relaxing in the hospitality suite she waited for her opportunity. When Kate left the conversational orbit of the perennial game-show panellist with yet another book of reminiscences to promote, Sophie contrived to reach the drinks table at the same moment.

'I only realised this morning that Personnel haven't sent me a renewal for my contract,' she said, feeling that this was the most tactful way of reminding Kate that she had forgotten to ask them to.

The smile narrowed. 'Can we discuss this in the morning?'

'Sure, I'll remind you to chase them up,' Sophie said lightly.

'Let's talk tomorrow, OK?'

The sound of executive sidestepping activated alarm bells in Sophie's head.

'There's not a problem, is there?' Still light.

For a moment Kate's discretion wrestled with her pleasure in knifing a younger rival. She pursed her lips. Discretion lost.

'I'm afraid we shan't be renewing your contract.'

'But why?'

'We have reason to think you've lost interest in the programme and that we would be better served by some fresh blood.'

'You old . . . vampire. Have you been going through my mail?'

Although Kate said nothing her expression was a signed confession.

Sophie's voice stayed low but there is something in the intensity of a whispered argument that attracts the attention of bystanders more surely than a flaming row.

'Is this the royal we you're using or does Jerry know about this?'

'I am the executive producer of this programme—'

'He doesn't then. I want to discuss it with him now.' She marched over to where he was making small talk to the panellist and the panellist was nodding while trying to fathom what was going on between the two women.

'Hello, Sophie,' Jerry beamed, hiding beautifully his own curiosity. 'Have you met Giles?'

'Of course, I interviewed him.' Too peremptory. She tried a laugh to pass it off but it was strangulated.

'Relax, darling. Have another drink, unwind. Show's over.'

'It is for me. I've just been told my services are no longer required.'

Jerry's surprise was less well concealed and Giles salivated at the sight of gossip.

'I think you must be mistaken,' Jerry said.

'It was pretty categorical.'

'Excuse me,' said Jerry, guiding her by the elbow towards the door.

'Give you a job any time, love,' the panellist called after them.

'So what the hell's all this about?' hissed Jerry as they left the room.

'You tell me,' said Sophie. 'Kate just announced she won't be renewing my contract.'

The door reopened and Kate joined them. 'Yes,' she addressed Jerry. 'There are special reasons but if you think I'm discussing them now with a roomful of VIPs waiting for you—'

Smart move, thought Sophie.

Jerry hesitated, reminded of his priorities. 'Let's sort it out tomorrow, sweetheart. Don't lose any sleep. My office first thing.'

And he squeezed her bottom before switching on his smile and reopening the door of the hospitality suite, making his celebrity's entrance. Kate didn't look at her before prowling in his wake.

Sophie stood alone in the corridor and tried to decide whether it would do her more good to go home or to carry on as if nothing had happened. Would the old trouper or the vulnerable girl appeal more to Jerry's ego? She went to light a cigarette and realised they were on the window-ledge next door along with her handbag and car keys. The die was cast then. Nobody could look anything other than defeated going in, collecting their belongings and walking out. She might as well clear her desk. She fastened on her own happy face and followed the others.

Judy was just about to go out to Marks & Spencer for a sandwich when Sophie rang and asked if they could meet. It wasn't very convenient as she had planned a quick lunch at her desk, all her work wrapped up by tonight and a quiet morning tomorrow before breaking for Christmas, but Sophie sounded odd so she said yes. When she reached the wine bar Sophie, who turned out to have been in a callbox round the corner, was standing on the pavement.

'Office party inside,' she said.

'What's the matter?'

Sophie started to say 'Nothing' and then after the first syllable broke into wretched sobs.

On a bench under the plane trees and with the help of several grubby tissues Judy extracted the story of Sophie's sudden departure from the corporation, mixed up with her distress at losing Mikey and her disinclination to go back to Camden Road where a party was planned for that evening.

'Take my keys,' Judy said, 'and go to Islington. Make yourself at home and I'll be back as soon after six as I can manage. I'm not doing anything this evening so we can have supper and you can stay the night if that's what you'd like.'

'Yes, please,' said Sophie in a small voice, and Judy watched her trudge away with hunched shoulders that made her heart ache.

She made her excuses from her own office party and hurried to a tube crowded with late shoppers and early drunks. As she was going to her parents for Christmas her house bore no signs of festive spirit other than the few cards she had been sent outside of work and the bottle of vodka that was now open on the table next to another pile of tissues. Sophie was sitting in the dark with the TV on and puffy eyes, but she got up and smiled and they switched on some lights and some music and made supper.

Later they laughed about her saying to Jerry, 'I suppose if I'd let you fuck me I'd be doing her job,' thereby discovering that even if he hadn't done it with Kate one or both of them had wanted to.

'And then I said I wouldn't try it now if I were you because apart from her being too old the scratch marks from her talons would be infected.'

'So your boats are burnt?'

'I think so,' Sophie giggled. 'Particularly as I knocked the shoot off her rubber plant on the way out.'

They were both quite tipsy when they went to bed, but Sophie seemed more cheerful so when Judy woke up at three she thought at first that the strange snuffling sound was Bartholomew. She let it continue for a while, as she imagined you might with a child, and when it showed no sign of letting up she went to the spare bedroom.

'I'm sorry, I didn't mean to wake you up.'

'It doesn't matter.' She sat on the side of the bed and tentatively put out a hand. Sophie allowed her head to be cradled and after a while Judy felt the wet of her tears through the shoulder of her nightshirt. She stroked Sophie's hair and Sophie said indistinctly, 'Thank you.'

Judy's feet were beginning to go numb. 'Shove over,' she said, 'it's cold,' and she swung herself on to the mattress and beneath the duvet.

'I'm sorry, I don't know what's the matter with me,' said Sophie. 'It's not the end of the world after all.'

'No, but when it's dark and cold and a long time to morning it can feel like it. Shall we try and get some sleep?'

The sound of her radio alarm from across the landing woke Judy again at seven. She was lying on her back, which was unusual for her, and her right arm had pins and needles because it was beneath Sophie, whose head was pillowed above her breast and whose right leg was wrapped across her own. She could feel the delicate passage of Sophie's breath across her throat and breathing in herself meant tickling her nostrils with the ends of Sophie's hair. She shifted carefully and Sophie's sleeping hand caught at a fold of her shirt. In releasing its grip she woke Sophie up enough to slide from beneath her and go for a shower.

Bartholomew stood indignantly on the landing. Having obediently spent the night in his basket in the kitchen, or at least near it, he had ascended for his customary cuddle and found the bed empty. To make up for this he weaved between her feet while she was dressing and laddered a stocking for which she kicked him and so they were both in a bad temper by the time she had made coffee.

She took a cup in to Sophie who propped herself up in the narrow bed revealing a purple vest which Judy could not equate at all with the clothes she had been wearing the day before. 'You look amazing,' said Sophie, yawning. 'How come, after I put you through such an uncomfortable night? I feel like an old boot.'

'You don't look like one.' And she didn't. She looked frail and pale and the puffiness under her eyes was tinged with a dark shadow but the eyes themselves were as wide and bright as ever. 'What are you going to do today?'

Sophie's face fell.

'Not that you have to do anything, go anywhere, I mean. Stay here if you like – I'll only be gone till lunchtime.'

'Can I?'

'Of course.'

'Thanks, Jude.' And Sophie leant forward, hugged her and kissed her quickly on the lips. 'Oh God, I've smudged your lipstick. Sorry.'

'You can only stay if you absolutely promise to stop saying sorry.'

Sophie grinned and silently mouthed the word again.

The grey skies were mirrored in the faces of those who had attended the office party and were waiting for the dispensation to leave at lunchtime. Everyone knew it would come but as in offices everywhere it was the privilege of the boss to maintain the illusion that it was a last-minute decision of immense generosity. After a fragmented morning of fruitless waiting for bike messengers and failing to be connected to anyone that she wished to telephone, Judy was summoned to Hugo's office.

He offered her a drink which she declined, but to be polite she accepted a cup of over-percolated coffee and a factory mince pie. Hugo opened one of his many gifts, invariably bottles of single malt just as hers were of champagne or dessert wine.

'Friend all right then?'

'Oh – yes, thanks.'

'Just wondered. Knew it must be important to make you skip the shindig. You've always been mindful of your obligations to the troops.'

This was a rebuke. 'Very abnormal circumstances,' she said, finding herself, as she so often did in his company, adopting his clipped style. 'Lost job and boyfriend in one day.'

A white lie but . . .

'Tell you what. I think we might as well shut up shop now, so why don't you tell the lads and lassies and make it open house at the Masons. You take the chair and I'll be along in a minute.'

Punishment and redemption.

She escaped after a couple of rounds had been downed and, honour satisfied, returned to the office to collect her booty. What about supper? Her hamper contained only the beginnings and ends of a meal – smoked salmon and stilton, pâté and peaches in brandy. After a dive round the supermarket she drove home with a couple of steaks and some salad to fill the gap.

Her cottage was blazing with light and what sounded like the Huddersfield Choral Society accompanied by the massed bands of the Brigade of Guards blasted 'Hark the Herald Angels' through quavering window panes. She let herself in, to be met by Bartholomew, bewildered in a collar of pink tinsel. In the sitting-room Sophie was singing lustily along while decorating a tree which she had established in the terracotta pot usually inhabited by pampas grass.

'I hope you don't mind. I thought the least I could do was make a happy home for you to return to.'

'You seem happy yourself.'

'I went shopping and bought some exciting things for supper and some clean knickers and a toothbrush.'

'So did I.'

'You can't possibly need any. I've never seen a drawer crammed with so much exotic lingerie.'

'Don't say exotic. It makes it sound like scarlet basques and crotchless panties. What have you bought?'

'M and S plain white.'

'Food, you idiot.'

In the end they left the hamper untouched and Sophie, drawing on long-neglected training, produced asparagus with hollandaise, embellished the steaks to *en croûte* status, and finally served up a lemon tart which 'positively insists on the accompaniment of a bottle of your scrummy Beaumes de Venise'.

They played Scrabble 'to aid the indigestion' –

'Bloody cheek.'

'Well, overindulgence then.'

– and Mahler to soothe the senses but the combination of this and a brandy suddenly made Sophie tearful again so they decided to go to bed.

'Will you be all right?'

'Yes.'

'Sure?'

'Sure.'

But it wasn't long before Judy heard the tell-tale noises.
'Come on.'
'What?'
'I'm happy to share but why a single if we can use a double.'
Sophie shivered in her vest as they crossed the landing.
'If you weren't so thin . . .'
'You sound like my mother.'
'Get in. I feel like your mother,' Judy said. But she didn't. She wasn't quite sure what she felt like as Sophie unaffectedly snuggled up against her, but it wasn't the hard Cotswold hostess to whom she had occasionally been introduced. Protective maybe, happy yes, drunk not really. Perhaps it was just the time of the year.

It was like being in the middle of a Pre-Raphaelite painting – the colours glowing with that peculiarly over-real translucence – but this was a place with wind, and Judy was looking out through the bars of a prison, but moving. Not a gaol, then, but the visor of a helmet and the bouncing motion because she was on a horse and crossing a meadow with a stream and hanging on as the horse rose over the water and, just glimpsed below, a familiar face among the reeds, her hair caressed by the current and her white robe rippling beneath the surface. A bruising landing rattled Judy's armour. Then she was entering a wood with other shadowy figures in breastplates of a dull gold and the trees were entwined with vines of ivy and grapes and Dante Gabriel notwithstanding this was Burne-Jones country. She rode faster and faster, the branches smacking against her chainmail, and the others were slipping away and she was alone with the panting of the charger and the snapping of foliage underhoof until suddenly she was in a clearing with the sunlight shafting.

The princess was chained with heavy iron manacles to the trunk of a giant oak, her robe torn across one bony shoulder and her skin as white as ivory.

The horse stopped and pawed the turf. Judy swung over and down and pulled off her helmet. The weight of her pigtail pulled her head up into the celestial light. Approaching the princess, Judy drove the sword against the links of the chain and the sparks flew as they splintered with the pitch of a tuning-fork, which became the terrified shriek of the steed. Judy turned. Beyond the frothing jaws of the horse reared the blood-red head of the dragon.

The horse bolted; the princess groaned. Judy raised her sword and the dragon fixed her with its stony gaze. Drawing back its head as if to spit, it blew the hot breath that contemptuously whipped away her sword and threw her among the ferns.

Stiffly, almost politely, the dragon approached the princess. Her breath came in little gasps. The dragon dropped its scaly head and clawed at the trailing hem of her robe, drawing it down. She tried ineffectually to protect her body with her bare arms. Judy screamed. Distracted, the dragon turned. Its yellow eyes and teeth flashed, and then it blasted fire at her. Flames licked around her feet, not hot but cold as ice and . . .

Judy jerked up in the semi-darkness. Her legs were shaking. Needing the reassurance of some proper light she hauled herself from the covers and staggered to the bathroom, pulling at the cord and subsiding on the side of the bath, and then Sophie's arm was round her shoulders and her voice was saying, 'It's all right. It's all right,' over and over like a mantra. 'Jesus, that must have been some nightmare.'

'I don't know,' Judy said, 'it was—'

'—at eight o'clock,' announced the radio alarm, and they laughed with the nervous mirth of relief.

The bedroom was illuminated by a pale glow that had nothing to do with the golden stripe cast by the bathroom light.

Sophie said, 'There's something odd—' and, taking Judy's hand, led her across the bedroom and pulled back a curtain. 'Yes.'

The street and the cars were coated with bright snow. Only a couple of sets of footsteps and one of tyre-tracks had broken its perfection and the snow driftingly laboured to obliterate those. They watched in silence; Sophie gathered the duvet and wrapped it round their shoulders.

'What are you doing today?'

'Nothing,' said Judy, not mentioning the party invitation she had accepted without knowing why. 'Apart from wrapping my presents.'

'Neither am I. Shall we go for a tramp and then have our own Christmas dinner?'

'OK.'

So while Sophie went back to Camden Road to collect her stuff Judy, mesmerised by the moment, rang Paul and Sue to say that unfortunately she couldn't make their party as she had to go home a day early.

'I was well out of the Camden bash,' Sophie said on her return. 'My place looks like a bomb's hit it.'

'I thought that was how you liked it.'

'Bodies still in the living-room the morning after the morning after is too much even for me. I can cope with the odd spell of civilised living,' and she waved her arm around Judy's pseudo-rustic kitchen.

Muffled up, they walked across Highbury Fields and that wasn't enough so, mingling with the fans gathering for

Arsenal's home game, they headed north along slippery pavements to Finsbury Park. There they raced up and down the slopes until Judy fell and soaked her trousers and Sophie's ears ached. They went home on the painfully warm Underground.

'Great,' said Sophie, kicking her case which still lay in the hall. 'Now I can get into some fresh clothes. But you'd better have first bath, otherwise you'll catch your death.'

'I only want a shower. Shall I run yours?'

She left steam rising from the taps and shut herself in the glass cabinet beneath the scalding jet until her bones no longer felt chilled. Emerging she was surprised by Sophie saying, 'You're as pink as a lobster.' She pulled on her towelling robe.

Sophie's red hair floated on a sea of white bubbles. 'There's a mug of tea on your dressing-table. Not really decadent enough but better for the marrow than champagne, I thought.'

They opened the first bottle of that as Judy showed her how to braid her hair and finished it while wrapping their respective families' presents, Sophie displaying an alarming talent for creating elaborate bows.

'I don't suppose we've got any crumpets?'

'No,' Judy laughed.

'In that case I'll get changed for dinner.'

'Changed?'

'You don't want me to slut around in this dressing-gown all evening, surely?'

Judy looked at her own jeans and guernsey. 'Does that mean I have to?'

'Yes, turn up the heating and slip into something more luxurious. I'm not going to waste this hairdo you've created.'

They ate sitting in front of the fire with Bartholomew prowling between them and to his amazement receiving several pieces of smoked salmon and some succulent lobster flesh. Sophie had wisely draped an old gingham tablecloth across Judy's lap to protect the green ballgown last aired at the Awards from the depredations of mayonnaise. Her own sheath of black velvet she declared invulnerable.

She licked her fingers clean before gathering the spattered cloth and wiping Judy's lips with it.

'You can put your gloves back on for the dancing. Get your handbag to give us our bearings. I'll just liberate another of the benefits of corporate gladhanding to keep us topped up. Maybe we should mix it with some brandy and make cocktails.'

Pushing back the sofa to the wall gave just enough room to do justice to Judy's seventies soul and Tamla collection, wheeling and turning on heels which Judy would find had terminally depressed parts of the carpet, until they collapsed laughing and had a final restorative glass to see them up to bed.

Sophie kicked off her shoes, deftly unzipped her dress and wandered into the bathroom in her tights to clean her teeth. Judy resisted the desire to hang the dress up and simply placed it on the open suitcase in the middle of the floor.

'I don't know about you but I'm as high as a kite.' The voice was disguised by the brush and attendant froth.

'I think me too. Trying to take make-up off four eyes is very confusing.'

Sophie returned and, depositing her tights in a ball by its side, hopped into bed.

'You are a slut,' said Judy. 'Aren't you even going to put your vest on?'

While Sophie was saying something about being kept warm by bubbly she brushed her own teeth. As she stepped out of the gown Sophie said, 'What I wouldn't give for a body like yours.'

Aware of her breasts heavy on her ribs and her thighs rubbing together she said, 'Don't be silly,' and slipped the cold cotton nightshirt over her head.

'I mean it,' Sophie said sleepily once the light was out. 'You're Marilyn Monroe and I'm just Twiggy.'

'Nothing like. You're like—'

'Who?' Sophie turned to her. Their faces were very close. 'Who am I like?'

A shiver ran down Judy's spine. 'You're just beautiful,' and she leant forward and kissed her.

Jesus, thought Sophie. I would never have guessed in a million years that you were a dyke, but she kissed back and her hand found Judy's nipple steepled beneath the shirt.

Later she said, staccato, 'My turn now. It's not going to take much,' and it didn't but it was noisy enough to remind Judy of sounds overheard through a Tuscan wall.

It was still snowing when Sophie set off along an M40 crowded with irritable Christmas Eve traffic. Usually the prospect of a two-hour slalom followed by at least four days chez Attwood would have filled her with dread but today she sang along with Joni Mitchell, as much as anyone could, and only cursed other drivers in a spirit of fun.

After Moreton-in-Marsh the snow was really thick and she half-wished that Vanessa, who she knew sniggered at her for having a jeep, was there to see the four-wheel drive working. She waved chirpily at the policeman anachronistically pushing his bike at the top of their own village street, swung left at the Black Bull, past the church and did a handbrake turn into the drive of the Old Vicarage.

The Old Vicar must have been a fifteenth-century man of some substance as his residence was a handsome eight-bedroom stone house in an acre of gardens. The only blight on its social standing, now as then, was that the Manor itself was twice as large and clearly visible just up the lane. This afternoon both buildings epitomised a sanitised view of the season and of Merrie England itself, silhouetted as they were by a weak and setting winter sun, their white lawns pock-marked only by the feet of birds and dogs, their front doors bedecked by the regulation holly wreaths which, since everyone had them, Sophie presumed were hung by order of the parish council.

The drive of the Manor was empty but in her parents' own stood her father's Jaguar and Range Rover, and her mother's little Lotus sports car. Her father had made his money out of Land Rover and Jaguar, running a dealership in what was probably one of their best sales areas in the country. Lately he had taken an interest in a Volvo concession as well to cover what he described as the lower end of the market. He had long badgered her mother to demonstrate commercial loyalty by driving one of his own models, but Diana Attwood had been in her mid-twenties in the mid-sixties and somewhere beneath the Country Casuals still beat the heart of Emma Peel.

Experience had taught Diana that a family Christmas did not fill her daughter with joy and so she was unprepared for the manic gaiety with which Sophie entered into the spirit. Instead of asking her father for something specifically aggravating like a glass of 1981 Chablis (God knows how she knew what was, or more likely wasn't, in the cellar) she requested a dry sherry and settled down to watch the Bing Crosby film on the TV. She was friendly to her brothers and their wives when they arrived and to the Brize-Nortons over dinner.

When she announced after coffee that she intended to go to the midnight service Diana was bowled over.

'But we always go to the Sung Eucharist in the morning,' she said.

'I know, I don't mind going to that as well. The sermon's aimed at children of ten which is about my spiritual level,' she explained disarmingly to Mrs Brize-Norton, who she knew would secretly agree. Mollie Brize-Norton had held Sophie in low esteem ever since the party at which she had spotted the girl, then seventeen, dancing with her husband and deliberately inflaming, as she saw it, his menopausal libido.

'I'm only going for the candlelight,' Sophie added. Her brother Robin said he would come too, which she didn't really want, but he maintained a companionable silence as they trudged up the lane and, recognising that he was tone deaf, mumbled the hymns tunelessly by her side in the rear pew. Even the irreligiosity of the overspill from the pub and the once-a-year communicants could not detract from the magic of the occasion and they were both satisfied as they let themselves into the darkened house and settled by the hearth with a nightcap.

Sophie had often thought that the naming of Robin and his twin Roger was inverse, for Roger was a lecturer in geology while Robin thrusted in the city as a bond dealer. Needless to say it was only his family who used his full name; his colleagues and even his pretty wife, Victi, called him Rob.

It had been a matter of some concern to their father that neither of his sons had gone into the family business and inevitably the conversation turned to Daddy's imminent, or at least wished for, retirement.

'What I'm going to tell him,' said Robin, 'is that if he hangs on a year or so I might join him and he can show me the ropes before beating a retreat to the golf course.'

'Isn't flogging cars to gentlemen-farmers going to be a bit beneath the terror of the money markets?' asked Sophie, thinking of the Porsche and the flat in Docklands and the helicopters to Glyndebourne with clients.

'No. I've made a fair bit and they say you burn out after thirty, which gives me another fifteen months. I'd like to get out while I've still got some pizazz, buy a decent spread round here, have some kids, settle down.'

'How does Victi feel about these kids which, despite your undoubted talents, she is actually going to have to squeeze out?'

'Oh, mad for it. The old body clock's ticking away, she's ready.' He paused. 'Maybe you should put down some roots and have a baby yourself. After all, you're four years further down the road than Vicks, badly paid, worth thinking about.'

Instead of picking up the insult to her former profession she found herself thinking of cottage kitchens and saying, 'Perhaps I will. Not the baby, but the settling down.' She giggled. 'Perhaps I can be joint managing director of Attwoods' vehicle emporia.'

Robin looked alarmed. 'Well, I don't think you would really—'

The door opened and Roger appeared in his dressing-gown and slippers. 'Just come to take the statutory bite out of the mince pie and knock back Santa's port,' he said, indicating the offerings by the grate. 'Although if one of you would do it for me . . . I've already cleaned my teeth.'

'Sophie's thinking of coming home to claim her inheritance.'

Roger sat down. 'You have given up your job then. I

don't watch your show, of course, but Jane does and she said your name was missing from the credits on Friday.'

The old cow didn't waste much time, thought Sophie, and tried to remember why she hadn't watched it herself, as she had done some of the research. Then she recollected that she had been making hollandaise for Judy and felt a glow of happiness.

'Well,' she said lightly, 'my contract was at an end and I decided I'd had enough so I'm considering my options.'

'Very pleased to see you twice on Our Lord's birthday,' said the New Vicar, who lived in a bungalow at the other end of the village.

'Wish him many happy returns,' said Sophie, and he shook her hand as warmly as he could, swallowing an instinctive reference to sheep returning to the fold.

While they were walking up an appetite for the turkey, sizzling towards its date with a carving knife at eight o'clock sharp, her father said, 'Robin tells me you're out of work.'

'That's right.'

'You don't seem worried about it.'

'No. No, I'm not.'

'Good. Best not to mention it to your mother though,' he added as her nephew dragged her away to play snowballs. 'Unless you're thinking of getting married.'

And she gave him her secret smile as she shaped a missile between her leather gloves.

While the port was circulating and Jane was putting the kids to bed she stole into the study and rang Judy. 'Just wanted to wish you a happy Christmas.'

'Thanks.'

'Having a good time?'

'Yes, fine.'

'Any exciting presents?'

'Oh, the usual, you know.'

'If they're anything like mine you've probably got several books that will never grace your coffee table, another pair of rainbow-colour gloves, and a thing that looks like an Eskimo's nose-picker but is supposed to be for scraping ice off your windscreen. I've decided what to get you but it will have to be belated. When are you getting back?'

'Day after tomorrow – I'm working on the 28th.'

There was a lot of background noise. 'Is it difficult to talk?'

'A bit.'

'I'm sorry, I've been rattling on.'

'No.'

'Look, I'll go then. I can't wait to see you. Sleep tight.'

'And you.'

Sophie went to her room as soon as she could and thought of Judy. They had huddled in bed on the morning of Christmas Eve, eating boiled eggs. Judy was quiet and Sophie had asked her whether she had ever done what they had done before. Judy had said never, which was a surprise. Then Sophie had asked, 'But you liked it?' and Judy had said, 'Oh yes,' in a tiny voice and they had hugged for ages.

Sophie had always liked others to see her as a cosmopolitan, devil-may-care person but in her rare moments of self-analysis she had not been wholly convinced by this image. Consequently she was surprised by how little she was shocked by what she and Judy had done. Despite a couple of passionate attachments at boarding school, one of which had involved fervent embraces beneath a patchwork quilt, she thought she had given up girls for good as soon as boys became available. She had never been afraid of touching and hugging women friends but had never before felt any *frisson* of sexual excitement, even from Judy. Had she? She had always thought Judy astonishingly pretty but she'd never contemplated . . .

Perhaps it had only happened because they were such good friends? Then she thought of the absolute impossibility of making love with Becky or, God forbid, Vanessa. Circumstance then? It was true she had been down and lonely and Judy had protected her but . . . she sought a parallel. No, she couldn't imagine succumbing to the advances of say, Carol, her housemate.

The truth was Sophie couldn't understand how she and Judy had managed to avoid all this for so long. All those years when they had been in the same group, at parties, wine bars, concerts, dinners. How had they managed to keep their hands and mouths off one another? If only she had known how exciting it could be, not that she had particularly thought it couldn't be, just that it would be a sort of second best, which it most emphatically wasn't.

She knew that other people might have worried about such a fundamental reorientation, be frightened by all the boring baggage that society automatically sent along if you embarked on a lesbian adventure . . . lesbian. It sounded cold and dry, the exact opposite of . . . 'I'm a dyke,' she said experimentally to herself. She giggled. 'I'm in love.' The first had always been a jokey insult, the second a state that she had agonised over in the past – was she? wasn't she? – but now both seemed perfectly acceptable. There was no cause for alarm, only happiness, because she was Sophie and she could take anything in her stride. Amazingly, she was really as liberated as she had always insisted she was.

Sophie lay in the dark and imagined her next meeting with Judy, kissing her, undressing her, falling between silken sheets, and she remembered how, only the night before last, Judy had let out this one uncontainable sigh and that excited her and because she was incapable of coming quietly she rolled over so that her face was buried in the pillow.

A sizeable part of the north Cotswold business community gathered at the Old Vicarage for a buffet lunch on Boxing Day, a ritual that, since majority, Sophie had largely avoided by taking a long walk and repairing to the saloon bar of the Black Bull. Today she put on the nearest thing to a suit that she had with her and to her mother's mixed delight and jealousy behaved as an impeccable hostess should, right down to flirting ever so delicately with the more distinguished Rotarians. Luckily for Sophie Diana was not a witness to the moment when mischief overcame her and she goosed Bagley of Bagley's Agricultural Machinery who had earlier pinched her bottom by the cold pheasant.

Over the tea and almond biscuits she announced that she would be returning to London after breakfast the next day.

'Why?' said Roger, who was under pressure to stay himself and could not wait to get back to the sanctuary of his study in Lancaster. 'It's not as if you've got a job to go to.'

So then of course she had to explain to Mummy not only why she was unemployed but why Diana should have been the last to know and only mollified her with the promise of a day at the sales together. A short lecture on the virtues of marriage now that she no longer had the excuse of a career followed, culminating in the judgement that 'your looks have lasted well but you're entering a dangerous stage, darling. Decent men want children and for them you will soon be a risky choice.'

Robin collared her after supper to announce that he had talked to the old man about his joining the firm and he presumed, tension apparent here, that she had been joking about her doing the same because really . . .

'Don't worry. I only need to be here for a couple of days and a couple of parties to know that the dynastic crown will sit much more comfortably on your head.'

Robin looked reassured, then puzzled. Sophie went to pack.

Judy's euphoria lasted until she parked outside her parents' house in Nottingham. It was about the same age as hers and half as large again but her mother hankered after a new semi on an estate like her other daughter, Cheryl. When she had discovered that Judy was paying more than £100,000 for her terraced two up two down she had been profoundly shocked.

Although Judy would have handled the celebration of Christmas completely differently she had always enjoyed its undeviating observance at 21 Viceroy Road. She revelled in the silver-tinsel tree on its metal stand ('Needles take so much hoovering-up') and the bowls of Quality Street and Licorice Allsorts on the lounge table, the annual bottle of advocaat and the smell of sausage rolls from the kitchen. She played whist and explained yet again to her dad that she had liked port and lemon once but would prefer a gin and tonic this evening.

Yet inside her was a completely different person, separated from this comfortable scene as if by a thick sheet of glass. Being a deeply conventional girl she had never before had an experience that she could under no circumstances imagine discussing in any way at all with her mother. Of course the technicalities of her sexual relationships from the earliest youth club fumblings onward were no-go areas, but then so were the details of her job. She had always been able to talk about her boyfriends in general terms just as she had related her progress through O levels, A levels, BA Hons, and the various ranks of Pasco. But now she was in the midst of something that no generalities were sufficient to gloss over. And what's more, unlike the one time she had smoked cannabis, which was all right to mention because she genuinely had no intention of ever doing it again, making love with Sophie was something she could hardly contemplate not doing again.

On Christmas morning she helped her mum peel the vegetables and Dorothy pretended to complain about having Bartholomew's litter tray in the kitchen, although she had been cooing over him ever since they had arrived. As with most of her gripes she claimed merely to be voicing Don's objections but Judy had already caught her dad with Bartholomew on his lap so she took this with a pinch of salt.

She was upstairs changing into a dress and putting on her face, another unquestioned pre-lunch requirement, when Cheryl and her family arrived, and she could hear Darren and Kelly shouting over each other to tell Gran and Grandad precisely what they had found in their pillow-cases. She was still in her bra and slip when her sister popped her head round the door. It was too late to cover up.

'You still don't knock, I see,' said Judy. 'Happy Christmas.'

'Same to you.' Cheryl bent to kiss her. 'Blimey, they're some scratches you've got on your back.'

'What comes of living with a cat,' she replied jokily but she knew that Cheryl had seen her blush.

The dining-room table was really too small for seven but that did not explain why this, the biggest meal of the year, was treated as something to be dealt with as quickly as possible, rather than savoured and lingered over. The bacon rolls were crisp and fragrant, the Brussels not too soggy, the bread sauce inexplicably moreish considering that its colour and texture were so reminiscent of porridge, which Judy hated, but there was constant pressure to eat up.

Judy and her brother-in-law Pete drank the bottle of Châteauneuf du Pape that she had brought; the others stuck with Liebfraumilch. She knew that Pete would have laughed at her for paying more than three quid for a bottle of wine but as he wouldn't recognise the label, that was fine. Once she had opened champagne to go with the presents, and Pete and Cheryl's disapproval of this showing off was silent but very clear. She hadn't repeated the experiment, despite it having made her mum skittish.

Turkey was followed too swiftly by the pudding and washing up and the Queen's Speech and presents and then a quick game of Cluedo while Dorothy was assembling the pork pie and tinned salmon and sherry trifle that tradition demanded be consumed only five hours after a vast lunch.

Kelly doled out the characters – Colonel Mustard for Grandad, Reverend Green for Dad (here Pete, knowing what was expected of him, sang 'A-ah-mennnnnn', to his children's delight), Mrs Peacock for Mum, of course, because she was married but couldn't cook well enough to be Mrs White, and after some consideration Miss Scarlett for Aunty Judy.

Pete winked at her. 'That's a pretty high compliment. Means she still thinks you're glamorous and a bit of a devil, not over the hill like her old mum and dad.'

'She is still a bit of a devil, aren't you, duck?' said Cheryl and hooted with laughter.

When the phone rang at ten her parents stared at one another; nobody would ring that late, except in an emergency, on any day, let alone this one.

172

'Well, answer it then,' said Cheryl.

Dorothy went into the hall, saying, 'Perhaps it will be Aunty Ethel,' to reassure herself. The open door let in a cold draught; inevitably they all listened.

'Yes, she's here, hold on, I'll just get her for you – and a very merry Christmas to you too, dear. For you,' she announced to Judy on her return.

A spasm of mingled excitement and fear passed through her; she picked up the handset from the rickety hall table and sat on the bottom stair – the passage was too narrow for a chair.

Dorothy hadn't closed the door behind her and it would seem suspicious to do so now. From the lounge she could hear Cheryl asking, 'Boyfriend?'

'No,' her mum replied. 'It's a woman. Posh voice.'

'Hello?' Judy said.

The conversation was a blur because her awareness of her audience made it impossible to concentrate on what was being said and she had to be careful not to give any hint that she was talking to anyone special. When she went back into the lounge some explanation seemed to be required of this unusual event.

'Sophie Attwood who I was at college with,' she said. 'You met her at graduation.'

'Oh yes?'

'Just rang to say Happy Christmas.' A pause. More? 'Think she's a bit bored at home.'

Oh dear, not very tactful. Still, better they think that than . . .

Judy was in a tent with billowing walls, bound to the post in its centre. The ropes cut at her wrists and the pole pressed against her back. Bright sunlight beyond the canvas threw shadows against it; there was a murmuring of voices, people milling around outside. She looked down and realised she was naked. Panic. Her feet were more loosely tethered; she tried to twist round so that she faced away from the entrance – anyone could pull aside that flap and see her. It fluttered and rustled; someone had come in. She listened to their footsteps approaching, her heart beat faster and louder and then stopped as they caught hold of her plait and pulled back her head. Judy felt soft breath against her ear and opened her eyes. The princess stood at her side in hose and a sleeveless jerkin. She knelt before Judy and kissed her belly, and Judy felt the princess's wet tongue burrowing into her. Judy wanted to warn the princess about the darker shadow behind her, growing larger and larger against the wall, but she could not speak, only moan. Then the shadow coalesced into a long head with a flickering, lizard tongue and suddenly the walls were alive with flames and the fireball reached out for them both.

Boxing Day morning Don always went to the dogs at Colwick and then met his daughters in the Trafalgar for a quick one before lunch. They were sitting waiting for him now; Pete was getting the drinks. Dorothy had her grandchildren in front of the TV at Viceroy Road while she prepared the lunch.

A casual observer would have guessed that they were sisters, but might well have decided that Cheryl was the elder rather than three years the junior. Marriage and motherhood had left her the heavier by a stone, pushing her from adolescent voluptuosity into plain plumpness. Her skin was paler and her perm just obsolete enough to reinforce the impression of age.

To Judy she seemed happy; the early pregnancy that had ossified her ambition and capacity for adventure had also frozen her sense of humour, still strangely raucous. They were no longer close and their wholly different lifestyles had reduced any arguments or rivalry to the minimal area of their parents. But Judy had always been wary of forfeiting Cheryl's good opinion, partly through fear of her scathing tongue, not so much waspish as a nest of hornets.

The jukebox followed Bonnie Tyler with an old O'Jays number.

'Oh, I love this,' Judy seized a suitable cue. 'Do you remember that holiday in Anderby Creek? It was on all the time at those discos in the club.'

'I remember the one time you let me come with you,' Cheryl said sourly. 'You've probably forgotten that you told me I was too young to go 'cos I was only twelve.'

'Well, you went in the end.'

'Only 'cos I went on and on to Mum until she said that if you didn't take me you couldn't go either.'

'So as usual you got what you wanted.' This opportunity was slipping away. 'My new boyfriend's a musician.'

'What does he play?'

Good. 'The guitar.' Has she got it? Smile. 'Long fingernails.'

There was a pause. Cheryl grinned, 'You must tell him to pluck more gently.'

'What are you two laughing about?' Pete asked, returning with their halves of lager.

'I must just make a quick call,' Judy said, having now established a plausible alibi.

'You could do it from Mum's if you put the money in the box,' Cheryl goaded her.

'When did you ever ring him from our hall?' She pointed at Pete, quietly getting on with his pint. 'Until you got engaged, that is.'

The phone at the Old Vicarage was answered by a man,

perhaps one of the brothers. 'Is there any message?' he asked, having explained in a rather offhand way that he couldn't see Sophie anywhere.

'Can you just say that Judy rang?' She wanted to add, tell her I'm sorry about last night, but that sounded intriguing and in her present state she had visions of him asking why.

'OK,' and there was a click.

'Thanks very much,' she said to the dead receiver, and put it back.

Southbound on the M1 she felt sick; half anticipation and half fright.

For ten years Sophie had been a friend – not reliable or discreet or polite but funny and fun and just around. Then suddenly the world turned upside down. She had looked for pointers but there weren't any other than the circumstances of this extraordinary week to explain her transformation into ... well, lover. She had always admired Sophie's looks, had always found her open and physically affectionate, but without the catalyst of her sacking there might never have been anything more.

When she was at school, in the era of David and Angie Bowie, Marc Bolan and the rest, it had been very fashionable to describe oneself as bi-sexual and one or two of the more adventurous spirits had done so but without a shred of supporting evidence. Judy had always assumed that it was a pose – you were either hetero or a lesbian and that was that. Now here she was demonstrating precisely the opposite, let alone Sophie who had had more men than hot ... Sophie said she had had crushes on other girls at boarding school but thought it was something she had grown out of.

The problem with them being such good friends was that

you couldn't just forget it and put things back to the way they were before. Not that she wanted to. Did she?

What she could not imagine was anyone finding out. It was bad enough at home what with the scratches and the phone calls but at least the family were a hundred miles away and although uncomfortable and a little shameful a deception could be successfully practised during bimonthly visits.

But what about people in London? What would they say at Pasco when Sophie started ringing her, meeting her from the office, attending company functions?

'Yes, Sir Kenneth, this is my significant other.'

Taking her to dinner parties – 'But you know we always sit boy girl boy girl, Judy. Which of you is which?'

Becky and Vanessa. How would they react to the revelation that two of their best friends were having a love affair?

If you could just keep the bed bit private . . . but it would be impossible. It would stray over with involuntary looks and gestures; it would be obvious that they knew too much about each other.

Yet she wanted it – to go on and see what might happen. Already it had made her feel three-dimensional for the first time in ages.

When Judy got in she felt exhausted. She couldn't face speaking to anyone until she had had more time to think and had slept on her thoughts, so she set her answerphone and zeroed the ringer on the telephone itself so that she wouldn't feel guilty hearing it and not picking it up. Then she unpacked the supplies with which her mother had dispatched her – large chunks of Christmas cake, a tin containing cheese straws, six chocolate marshmallows – and made herself a plain omelette.

She lay on the sofa to contemplate but instead dozed in

front of a James Bond movie until woken by Bartholomew, who wished to be let out. Befuddled, she staggered upstairs to sleep properly.

7

Epiphonema

Sophie went to the most expensive place she could think of and browsed for some time before selecting a long night-shift in ivory silk with wide shoulder straps and a bodice of patterned lace. When she held it against herself the hem reached her calf and ought therefore to be the right length for Judy.

'Will this be comfortable for a 36C?' she asked the assistant, who darted a swift glance at Sophie's own slight bust. 'Don't worry,' she added, intercepting it. 'I'm not suffering from delusions of grandeur. It's a present.'

'It should fit very nicely, madam.' Caught out, the assistant was huffy. 'Would you like it gift-wrapped?'

'No thanks, I'd rather do it myself,' Sophie blithely added insult to injury. 'Now, have you got this one in a 32?'

'For you, madam?' Expressionlessly the assistant exacted her revenge. 'That will be an A, will it?'

There was no one else in at Camden Road so she luxuriated in a long and oil-scented bath. She fastened her teddy, shimmied in front of the mirror and decided that she looked very sexy. The effect would be enhanced by bolder than usual warpaint. She applied it and considered herself again, stepping into her stilettos to get the poise. Pleased with herself, she buttoned up the short-skirted russet linen dress that complemented her hair so well and rang Judy.

Not back yet.

She fiddled with her jewellery and experimented with piling her hair up. No, better down. She sat on the settee, carefully now that she had her gladrags on – linen creased so bloody easily – and had a glass of wine. Where was Judy? It was seven already.

After a while Sophie took the dress off again and wrapped herself in her kimono, but she couldn't settle, the adrenalin was flowing far too freely. She couldn't remember whether they had drunk all of Judy's champagne; she should take another bottle. She re-dressed, throwing her leather jacket over her shoulders, and stepped out to the off-licence.

She hadn't gone far before she regretted the stilettos; the pavements were still covered with a mixture of slush and impacted ice. As the traffic was very light she gingerly picked her way to the kerb and walked along the heavily gritted road itself. Every so often headlights threw a huge shadow of herself before her which abruptly vanished as each car passed. It was just before the railway bridge that she realised her shadow's length had remained constant for some time. She stopped, not wanting to look round but not wanting to pass from the glow of the street lamps into the dark beneath the bridge.

The car drew alongside her.

'How much, darling?' said an anonymous voice from inside.

She hesitated, unsure whether to try and climb over the piled slush to the pavement or continue on her way.

'You've got a lovely tight arse,' the voice continued. 'How much?'

She swallowed. 'I wouldn't go with you if you were the

last man in the world,' she said and, turning, marched back the way she had come.

The car's gearbox ground and it passed her in reverse. She turned again and began to run. It followed, its engine screaming and driver shouting, the words incomprehensible until it caught her when it slowed and she made out: 'You fucking little cunt. If you don't want punters why are you dressed as a whore? Probably pox-ridden anyway, no decent bloke would touch you with a barge-pole.'

She vaulted the pile of slush, twisted her ankle, stumbled and fell beneath the arches, choking with pain and fear.

The car roared off. She felt the wet soaking into her dress and, remembering how in warmer weather this pavement always smelt of piss, tried to push herself up but her palms slid on the ice and she subsided again. Her leg hurt.

'Can I give you a hand?' said a fruity voice belonging to the stained and smelly pair of trousers that had appeared from the darkness.

For a split second she thought it was the man in the car and opened her mouth to scream but then realised the voice was different and the trousers typical of those worn by the assorted winos who frequented these arches.

'Thanks.'

He took her outstretched hands and pulled her up so hard that she banged into his chest, knocking the breath out of her. She smelt pear drops and felt the rasp of matted beard on her cheek. 'Lovely,' he mumbled and as one of his horny hands pushed up her skirt the other grabbed at her breast. Her heart, as if to avoid his grasp, seemed to leap up into her mouth. For a moment she was paralysed with shock: surely it was only in the cinema that the helping hand turned out without warning to belong to the psychotic killer-rapist. Then fear kickstarted her. Still deprived of the air to shout but having a mouthful of saliva she spat as hard as she could into his eyes while pushing herself away.

Surprised, he let go and lifted his arms to his face, swearing. Grabbing at the railings for support she aimed a kick at his groin but it was far harder to lift her leg than she had anticipated and her shoe caught him a glancing blow on the kneecap. This turned out to be effective, if not symbolically as satisfying, and as he doubled up she hobbled away as fast as her one remaining shoe would allow. Round the corner and out of earshot of his befuddled imprecations she limped into the off-licence, wrenching the door open and then slamming it behind her with a force that brought the proprietor from behind his counter.

'Bloody hell!' he shouted, and then as he saw her dishevelled state, 'Are you all right, love?'

She leant against the fridge and realised that she was shaking. She sat on a pile of cardboard boxes of Bulgarian Cabernet Sauvignon and looked down at herself. Her stockings were torn and beneath the left one dark blood was running from a graze on her knee. Her hands were black with dirt and a couple of fingernails were broken. She couldn't even bear to wipe away her tears with them. She groped in her jacket pocket for a handkerchief. Her ankle throbbed now that the adrenalin of the chase was ebbing away.

'I'm sorry,' she said. 'Could you call me a taxi?'

'Where to?'

She gave him the address.

'I don't suppose they'll come out for that,' he said. 'It's not far enough to be worthwhile.'

'Well, I can't walk,' she said, indicating the stockinged foot. 'Tell them I'll pay a fiver anyway. Thanks,' she added as he went through the bead curtain into a back room.

'Not a bloody charity,' he mumbled audibly, transforming himself from pudgy Samaritan to Pharisee in one fell swoop.

On his return he said grumpily, 'A couple of minutes,' and sat on his chair eyeing her as though she was something the cat had dragged in.

'While I'm here,' she asked, 'can you give me a bottle of Lanson and—' what the hell, 'a bottle of Smirnoff.' Handing over the money she dropped two pound coins. 'Sorry, can't seem to stop my hands shaking.' She attempted a laugh. 'Or my voice.'

Mollified by her purchasing power, he essayed fatherly sympathy. 'Expect you're freezing, love. Coming out in that skimpy rig in this weather.' He adopted his man-of-the-world tone. 'What happened? Have a bit of a set-to with the boyfriend? Or did your old man find out about him?' He laughed.

Sophie prayed for the taxi to turn up and when it did the driver amazingly managed to forbear offering advice or comment and simply pocketed his money.

Sitting in the cab she had persuaded herself that Judy would have rung while she was out, and as soon as the door was locked she dialled her number, prepared to say, 'I am a stupid cow, guess what happened?' but the answerphone was still on and suddenly the smell of the tramp and the feel of his hands came back to her and she ran to the bathroom and retched into the sink.

In the mirror she saw that her make-up was smudged and her hair disarrayed and somehow greasy. Everything was ruined. Judy would ring in a minute and she couldn't drive on her ankle and her clothes were soiled. She burst into sobs, letting the scalding tears burn her cheeks until her nose was full of mucus and she had to blow it. Sophie ripped her clothes off, screwing them into a ball and throwing them into the dirty washing basket, pleased that one of the buttons on her dress burst as she did so, glad that one of her £50 shoes was lying in the gutter, purged by the hot shower which washed away every vestige of the sophisticated self that had preened in her bedroom only a couple of hours before.

Confused by her fit of mortification – after all, what had she done wrong for God's sake? – she nevertheless dressed in plain underwear, jogging pants and a shapeless sweater. Her hair she left wrapped in a towel while she sorted out her fingernails and applied antiseptic cream to her cuts. Christ, where was that girl? She had another glass of wine and turned on the TV to fill the silence but somehow the *risqué* remarks of Double O Seven were not appealing and the alternatives merely served to increase her concentration on the lifeless phone.

When she looked at her watch she could scarcely believe that it was only nine o'clock. She wanted to ring Judy again but there was no point – she would get the message as soon as she came in. It didn't look as if anyone else was coming back to the house this evening. She really needed to hear a sympathetic voice. Perhaps if she called someone for a chat it would encourage the one voice she wanted to hear to be there as soon as she put the phone down.

She got a refill and her address book, and discovered that nine in the evening is not a good time to call people over Christmas as they are out or away. Someone did answer at Stacey's but whoever it was, and she couldn't tell above the din of partying in the background, went off to look for her and she gave up waiting after she had listened to the distant jollity of Madonna for an entire 'Holiday'.

Finally, and without allowing herself to consider motive or consequence, she dialled Mikey. He answered quickly.

'It's me, Sophie. Happy Christmas.'

A little pause.

'Oh, hi. Yeah, happy Christmas.'

'How are you?'

'Oh . . . fine. And you?'

'OK – well, not so OK just at the moment,' and she proceeded to relate the events of the evening, minus any reference to Judy.

'That's horrid. But you're OK now, I mean it's only a scratch, right?'

'Yes, it's just a little tender, but I'm feeling a bit . . . well, miserable, and I don't want to be on my own so I thought if you were on your own perhaps—'

'I'm sorry, but I'm already on my way out. You only just caught me.' He now sounded curt and impatient.

'Off to Vanessa's, I suppose.'

'No, as a matter of fact. I'm going to a party at my sister's.'

'It doesn't matter then.'

She thought this had sounded fairly neutral but his response suggested otherwise.

'Look, I'm sorry I'm not free just because you are, but presumably you weren't, otherwise you wouldn't have been dolled up and buying champagne from the offy. Has your date stood you up?'

'What's it to you? You're happily screwing one of my best friends behind my back.'

'Not behind your back. We'd already split up, and anyway I'm not—'

'Why her, Mikey? Is she a better fuck than me? Not if practice makes perfect, unless she's been secretly working on her technique all this time.'

'I don't compare people like that and neither do you, do you?'

'Oh, come on, you can't help it, no one can help it.'

'Well, in this case I haven't even had the chance so all your accusations are completely—'

'Jesus, she's not holding out on you, is she? It's a bit late to play the wise virgin, surely.'

'If you must know I'm waiting for the results of an Aids test.'

'What?'

'She wants to be absolutely sure that I'm safe.'

'Why? I mean you're not, are you – not . . .'

'I bloody well hope not.'

'So why?'

'Perhaps she's worried about the company I've been keeping.'

In the short silence that followed Mikey was appalled at what he had said and Sophie computed the implications of his taunt. They came towards her and hit her like a heavy swing door.

'You bastard.'

She slammed the phone down. It rang again, and she snatched it up in case, please, it was Judy.

'Hello?'

'Soph, I'm sorry, I didn't mean—'

'Fuck off. Just fuck off.'

She didn't stop screaming but ran up the stairs, no destination in mind, deliberately banging her hand against the banister, to hurt something if only herself. On the landing was a poster Blu-Tacked to the wall, a vapid Post-Impressionistic rendering of a Parisian townscape which she had always mildly disliked. She grabbed at it and tore it down, ripping it almost in half and removing two sizeable chunks of ageing wallpaper. She scrunched the poster furiously into a ball and hurled it down into the hall but in running after it she lost her footing and bounced down the last four stairs on her bottom.

Sitting on the hall floor, breathless for the second time that night, sniffing and sobbing, her frustration imploded and was replaced by a dull desperation. She had no alternative but to ring Mrs Hucknell, something she had been putting off since eight, frightened because although it offered the faint hope of discovering that for some reason – broken car, a cold – Judy's departure had been delayed, on the other hand . . .

Judy's mum assured her that Judy had left after lunch and would be at home, did she have the number, well of course she would have, and a Happy New Year, goodnight.

The wine bottle was empty. Sophie opened the vodka. She had bought it in shock and then thought better of it, not wanting to be drunk when she . . . but as she wasn't now going to it hardly mattered.

When the alarm went off Judy thought about punching the snooze button but she used it so rarely she had to sit up and look for it and by the time she had found it self-discipline had reimposed itself. She got up and had a shower to wash away the grains of sleep. A dreamless night had left her feeling relaxed and in control of the situation – or at least not as panicky as she had been yesterday.

Judy fed the cat and ate her muesli and performed all the usual, comforting rituals of key-counting and handbag-checking. Together with the thaw announced by the dripping guttering they somehow made the whole Christmas experience seem very distant. Almost the last item on the list was to set the answerphone but it was already on, its red light winking. Messages. Why hadn't she heard the phone ring? Then she remembered that she had deliberately switched off its sound to avoid the guilt of not answering.

She had five minutes. There couldn't be that many messages just from the previous evening. She hit playback.

'Hi Jude. It's, oooh, about half-six.' The involuntary thrill that Judy felt at Sophie's voice relegated any doubts to the lowest division of her mind. 'You're not home yet ... obviously ... hope you're not having too bad a drive down ... really looking forward to seeing you, sweetheart—' Heart-stopping giggle. 'I'm feeling like a million dollars ... anyway call me as soon as you get in and I'll be straight round. Bye.'

Beep.

Guilt anyway. It couldn't be avoided. Never mind, she would call Sophie, they could meet for lunch ... Perhaps not with Hugo's inevitable post-festive puritanism, but this evening, which was only ten hours ...

Beep.

'Judith?' Her mother, cautious as ever in case the sepulchral voice at the other end should suddenly bite back. 'Why aren't you there? I expect you're having an early night which is sensible. Now I just rang to see that you were home safe so if you are don't bother to ring back but if you're not—' There was a long pause as her mother pondered the illogicality of her request and decided not to complete it. 'Oh, by the way, that friend of yours rang. I told her to try you at home. Thanks for the lovely presents. Better go now. Goodbye.'

Beep.

Well, at least Mum hadn't detected anything odd in Sophie ringing but if Sophie had called Nottingham ...

Beep.

'Hello. It's ten o'clock or something.' This was a different girl, a little slow, a little dull. 'You're still not there. But you should be, your mum said you would be, that you left there ages ago ... Where are you? ... I'm sorry I rang your mum but I couldn't think what else to do but now I wish I hadn't 'cos now all I can think is how can it have taken you so long and what if ... you've had an accident.' A sniff. 'Oh God, don't have one, I don't know what to do, I mean I could ring the hospitals, I suppose, but there must be loads between here and there—' She could hear the tears. 'The police might be better but they would want to know why I want to know and what can I tell them? That my friend's answerphone is on? ... I don't think I worried your mum anyway ... I mean, I know you're all right and I could prove it by coming round but if I did and you were, then why haven't you rung me? Anyway I can't drive because I've done something to my ankle and—' a sort of hiccup which might have been a laugh, 'now I've done something to my reactions and I can't say the Leith police dis-miss-eth us – well actually I can ... obviously ... but I don't think the police would take that instead of a blood sample ... mind you, if I told them I'd got Aids they wouldn't take it ... Look, this is bollocks, I could get a cab but I won't because ... because ... I look a mess now but earlier ... earlier I was a real femme fatale ... At least I'm not all dressed up with nowhere to go any more ... Either way I lose. If you're not in ... or if you are ... do you love me? I love you, I just want to see you but I can't ... if I go to sleep I know you'll be there when I wake up ... wake me with a kiss ... look, ring me whatever the time is ... please.'

There was a long gap which might have held breath along with the static but Judy couldn't tell. Then the receiver was replaced, almost as an afterthought.

She switched off the tape and dialled immediately. It rang. She counted ten rings, her business limit, and then another ten, her parental limit to allow for the journey from sitting-room to hall. But Sophie had to get up and come downstairs so she let the phone crow on, echoing against those gloomy walls. At thirty-seven rings she decided Sophie must still be asleep.

Or she'd gone out, having given up waiting. Oh God, don't let it be that.

Elbowing Barty aside she heaved herself from the floor where somehow she had ended up and charged out, fumbling with successive locks – front door, car door, ignition. She turned on the radio very loud to drown nauseating surges of panic. Zigzagging across Barnsbury in an effort to avoid the rush hour on the Holloway and Caledonian Roads she twice navigated herself into a dead-end and once scraped her paintwork on a bollard. When she parked illegally on the pavement outside Sophie's she was sweating inside her grey suit. The sudden wish to appear desirable made her powder her nose and forehead. She didn't notice the flesh-toned spillage it left on her collar. She tried to frame a convincing sentence along the lines of I wasn't trying to avoid you ... but she had to be truthful.

The doorbell shrilled on and on.

The truth was I was avoiding you but ... I love you, too.

Shit, she had gone out. Now what?

She hadn't got a job so where would she go at – Judy checked her watch – eight forty-five? She ought to ring her own office and tell them she would be late. Where to start looking when not even the shops were open? The truth was that she hadn't a clue. Disconsolately she settled back in her car in case Sophie had merely gone to get the papers or a breath of fresh air, unlikely as the latter seemed. But who knew what people might do when they were upset?

When the quick walk theory no longer held good Judy

retrieved the phonecard from her purse and went in search of a callbox to make her excuses to Pasco. She was away for ten minutes. Sophie had not returned in her absence.

Reluctant simply to sit but with no other plan she went to the side of the Victorian villa and forced the dilapidated wooden gate. The front windows had internal shutters to block an inquisitive gaze but the kitchen was without so much as a grubby length of net.

On the table was the inevitable empty wine bottle and a selection of dirty crockery for one. Over the back of a chair was a leather jacket and the strap of what could be, although its bulk was in shadow, Sophie's Mulberry bag. If so she definitely hadn't gone far. A tap was dripping. Beyond the door a yellowish glow suggested that the bare bulb in the back hall had been left on.

Hypersensitive, Judy heard the last couple of footsteps above the grumbling traffic. Shouting, 'Sophie, Sophie,' without in the least meaning to she rushed round the side of the house, winded herself banging into the gate, and surprised Carol on the doorstep.

'Oh,' she halted, disappointed and embarrassed.

Carol said, 'Are you all right? Is anything wrong?'

'No, not wrong. I just need to see Sophie and I thought you were her.'

'I just wondered because, as my old mother would say, it's an odd time of day to be paying social calls.' Carol's gaze rested significantly on Judy's grey suit and court shoes. 'Are you sure she's back from Sloaning Sodbury or whatever it's called?'

'Oh, yes.'

'You're right. She's bloody well gone out without double-locking the door. One day we'll be burgled and then she'll be sorry. Come in.'

Feeling the need to normalise this meeting Judy,

registering the suitcase, asked, 'Just back from the family yourself?'

'Like I said, my old mother.' Carol's mother, as Judy had been told by Sophie, was a brassy publican's wife not a day over forty-five. Her daughter was a chip off the old block. 'Bloody hell.' Carol had pushed open the door to the communal sitting-room. 'She's left the telly on again. Do you want some tea?' She switched off the set and the murmuring of a radio was revealed in the vacuum it left.

'Someone's in,' Judy said.

'Must be her, then. Wonder why she didn't answer the door?'

Or the phone, a small voice asked, but it was overtaken by a returning excitement.

'She must have got pissed,' Carol was saying. 'Go and give the lazy cow a shake and I'll put the kettle on,' but Judy was already climbing the stairs.

She hovered uncertainly on the landing for a moment before memory and the muffled radio guided her to the door at the end of the corridor. The brass-ball handle was cold against her skin.

The curtains were drawn and only a muted grey light redolent of cobwebs permeated the room. For a second the whole Sleeping Beauty scenario was there: Sophie's red hair spread across the pillow, the white skin of her wrist against the dark coverlet. And then Judy's eyes adjusted to the murk and she saw that Sophie was staring at her.

She started forward. 'Oh, Sophie, why didn't you—' but the fixed expression together with a sudden, sharp smell of sick silenced her. She pulled at the arm, which was cold and stiff, and then at the bedclothes, and her hand felt for a heart beneath the vest while she dragged the resistant head close to hers and saw the sour crust about the lips and then her voice came back and she screamed.

* * *

Afterwards Judy appreciated that she had been in shock, which accounted for her veering from rag-doll submission to calculated cover-up.

Carol, visibly weakened herself, had restrained Judy from interfering any further with what was obviously a corpse and dissuaded her from calling an ambulance, instead contacting the police.

While Carol was gone Judy saw the gold-wrapped parcel on the dressing-table and turned the tag over. It was for her, the message a euphoric protestation of everlasting love. It was very light but too large to fit in her pocket.

'They're on their way,' Carol said, returning to find Judy with tears streaming down her face, and apparently watching herself in the mirror. 'Come on, let's go and have some tea while we wait.'

In the kitchen the kettle had steamed up the windows, which reminded Carol of a night in December when they had come down to get fish and chips and found exactly the same thing, and that set her off.

In this no man's land between discovery and officialdom they did not talk because neither wanted to make the other feel worse by asking how and why. Carol wondered why Judy had been hanging around outside and Judy pictured that present, her present, with its tag and its contents, whatever they were, waiting to be pored over, pawed over by the police or someone. It was like knowing the location of a time bomb.

'I'm just going to get my bag from the car,' she said and having got it shouted 'Loo' as she ran up the stairs. In the tiny lavatory she scrabbled all the small items into her coat pockets and then, pulling the chain, walked briskly to Sophie's room, hoping the flush would cover her footsteps.

Knowing that she could not act if she looked at the body Judy averted her eyes from the bed and rammed the parcel into her bag just as the doorbell rang.

She told the fresh-faced constable that she had simply popped by on her way to work to give Sophie some names and addresses of possible employers and brandished her Filofax in support of this. She did not mention the answerphone message, stating that the last time she had spoken to the deceased was on Christmas Day.

She worried repeatedly about letting Sophie's family know and a patient sergeant explained that they were contacting them. She asked how Carol would cope with staying in the house and Carol, to calm her down, said she would go to her boyfriend's.

Back at home Judy fended off any thought for a little longer by feeding Bartholomew, overjoyed at receiving what he considered to be an extra meal in the middle of the day. Then she went up to change out of her suit and, at her own dressing-table, could no longer avoid opening the parcel.

Beneath the thick, gold wrap lay rustling sheets of tissue paper and beneath those was . . . the silk shift slithered free and draped itself across the bed.

How beautiful.

Thank God she'd rescued it, what would anyone else have made of it?

That was ridiculous: giving someone a present like this didn't necessarily imply . . .

Suddenly her petty selfishness slapped her face and a huge fist of longing and loss thumped her in the stomach and she fell against the pillows and howled.

Sergeant McKenna, a beat veteran nicknamed Dixon by younger colleagues, was interested by Miss (or Ms as he had to keep reminding himself) Judith Hucknell. His interest would have been official if there had been any suspicion of foul play but there was not.

Sophie Attwood's death was quite clearly due to the inhalation of vomit which itself was a product of the mixture of alcohol and Temazepam that the post-mortem revealed. These findings matched neatly with the evidence – an empty Muscadet bottle and a half-empty one of vodka, and in the bathroom cabinet with its jumble of discarded prescription items a brown plastic container holding only two sleeping pills.

Their owner, Karen Campbell, who lived on the floor above the dead girl, had taken her new bottle home to Kincardine for Christmas and thought there were only six or seven in the jar she had left behind. This corresponds with the pathologist's assessment. Any occupant of the house might have known they were there although Campbell had never been aware of anyone helping themselves before.

The deceased was alone in the house when Hucknell and Carol Brier had entered and both doors were locked.

The question was – suicide or accident?

McKenna had seen plenty of both but he was uncertain about this one. She would have had to be very drunk to have accidentally swallowed that many Temazepam and, although she had apparently liked a tipple, solitary drinking on that scale did not seem to have been her style.

On the other hand if she'd seriously wanted to do herself in she would have taken everything in the bottle and even then she was intelligent enough to know that less than fifteen or twenty tablets would not definitely finish her off. You couldn't bank on throwing up in your drugged sleep.

She might have just wanted to frighten someone, a lot of them did and some then miscalculated and went too far.

But if Attwood was one of those it was not obvious who she had set out to frighten and she had left no note to enlighten.

According to Brier she had split up with her boyfriend about six weeks before but she hadn't seemed overly upset and McKenna had got the impression that there had been plenty of boyfriends over the years.

Her parents had gone further and said that she was very happy over Christmas and was talking about moving back to the Cotswolds to live. None of these were the signs of a potential suicide.

She did have a grazed knee and some bruising to buttocks and ankle but these were entirely consistent with a fall on a snowy pavement as were the stains on the dress in the dirty linen basket. It was a very smart dress which suggested to McKenna that she had intended to go out but they had no clue as to where. In any case the fall had presumably changed her mind.

Which left Hucknell, apparently desperate to give Attwood the names of some potential employers, something that McKenna would have thought could be easily done over the phone but for which Hucknell had illegally parked and made herself late for work. Brier could not remember Hucknell ever having come round to the house before. An odd coincidence.

There was also a big discrepancy between Hucknell's opinion that Attwood was 'upset' to have lost her job at the BBC and the parents who didn't even mention it until prompted and then described her happiness as 'unaffected by her resignation'.

Obviously it was not unknown for children to hide their true feelings from their parents but the sticks being the sticks they even had the testimony of the village bobby who had seen the deceased in church on Christmas morning, looking 'as happy as Larry'.

Which was more than could be said for Judith Hucknell. Death affected people in different ways but he had rarely seen such sorrow in someone who described herself as 'just a friend'.

However, no hint of foul play and plenty of other jobs pending, so the coroner would have to decide whether the death was officially an accident or misadventure or whatever. Dreadful shame whatever the verdict. Pretty little thing – wouldn't have believed she was thirty-one to look at her.

McKenna was resigned to not getting to the bottom of things and so he was surprised when the case came back into his head months later. It was prompted by an actress on the TV with that same red hair and whose soap plot hung on a diary. It reminded McKenna that he'd never questioned Carol Brier about another inconsistency: the dead girl's diary (no revelations, just a listing of forward engagements) and parents had both stated that she went home on 24 December whereas Brier had implied that she left the house on 21 December. Three missing days.

Ah well, all done and dusted now. McKenna unwrapped another Everton mint.

Vanessa was very depressed. Her rational self said that Sophie could not have committed suicide because of her and Mikey. But it then added that she was bound to think that to assuage her guilt. So Vanessa felt guilty anyway. It was clear that Mikey felt guilty too; they had gone on seeing each other but the atmosphere was brittle and when they touched it was with the difficulty of repelling magnets. They had talked about their shock and sadness and sense of loss but the guilt skulked in the undergrowth, unmentioned yet palpable. She hoped the funeral would have some cathartic effect.

197

They had arranged to collect Judy from Islington, which was not exactly on their way but she seemed to have gone to pieces and Vanessa despaired of her getting there under her own steam. Quite why she had collapsed so completely Vanessa could not make out – not only was her sorrow disproportionate to Vanessa's own but in some indefinable way she too seemed to feel guilty.

'I'll just pop in and hurry her up,' Vanessa said when the sound of the horn had provoked no acknowledgement from the house.

Judy was wearing a beautifully-cut black suit and her hair was held back by black velvet but her eyeliner was already smudged by tears. 'Come in for a second,' she said. 'I just need to do something about this.'

Vanessa put her arms out to her and Judy let herself be drawn in. Vanessa squeezed her hard. It was good to hug someone who wanted to be hugged.

'Why don't you just wash it off for now?' Vanessa said eventually. 'No sense in doing it again if—'

'If I'm going to have another weep on the way.'

'Well, yes.'

They stepped into the living-room. The sofa was made up as a bed, with pillows and a large duvet. Bartholomew was lying on it.

'Have you got someone staying?'

'Oh . . . no. It's just a bit . . . cold upstairs. At night.' Judy went off to find cotton wool and make-up remover. While she was occupied Vanessa discreetly felt the radiator. Still warm, so the central heating was working.

The drive to Gloucestershire seemed to take for ever. Conversation was stilted and Vanessa was glad to have the excuse of needing to concentrate on the road. Mikey devoted far more attention to map-reading than was strictly necessary, and still called out a couple of turnings when it was far too late to take them, resulting in a repeated tour of a one-way system and a muddy reversal in a field. In the back Judy gazed steadfastly out of the window.

It had seemed somehow inappropriate to Vanessa to play rock or dance music on the way to a funeral, so she had bundled a pile of classical tapes into the car. She started them off with Bach, mathematical and safe, but when that finished and she asked Mikey to stick something else on he chose Chopin. This was far too melancholy but she hardly wanted to say that so after five minutes she tried, 'It's not very good driving music.'

'You'd better choose then,' Mikey said spikily. '*Madam Butterfly*? Wagner? Rachmaninov? Tchaikovsky's *Pathétique*?'

She could see his point. Death, gloom, doomed romance. Which was why they arrived with Ravel's *Bolero* blaring from the speakers.

Although Sophie was being cremated Vanessa had pictured a chapel of mellowed stone surrounded by yews. The acres of car park before the brick-built 1950s factory which claimed to be the crematorium came as a surprise. They were early and sat in the car while Judy redid her face.

'That's a wonderful suit,' Mikey said.

'I just want to look my best for her,' Judy replied tightly, apparently assuming the remark to be a criticism.

Other cars were drawing up, parking close together as if huddling against the bitter wind. 'Let's get inside before the coff – cortège arrives,' said Vanessa. 'If you're ready?'

In the chapel British reserve had reasserted itself and the mourners were spaced as equidistantly as possible about the pews.

Annoyed by the gaps near the front Vanessa had led them there where they might offer solidarity but when the family processed up the aisle she felt obliged to look at the floor. By the time she raised her eyes again the coffin was in place.

Judy had swayed at that point but held her composure until the Williamson quote about having just popped into the next room. Then she wept once more.

Finding that the eulogy hardly seemed to be about the Sophie she knew Vanessa imagined herself immune from tears until the purple plush curtains hid the casket and the shoulders of the fur-trimmed black coat in the front row gave a convulsive heave, and then she too was crying, her contact lenses swimming in the hot saline.

Mikey seemed unmoved, but when she looked more closely he was wooden with over-control. He shepherded them both out of the chapel and they joined a procession to the wreaths, which had been laid on paving slabs before a pruned rose garden of Japanese minimality. It seemed the form to inspect them closely enough to read the tags, so they did, although most of the names meant nothing to them and, judging by their age, the majority of the mourners were friends and acquaintances of the parents.

They located their own wreath with a tag in an unfamiliar, Interflora hand, which said: 'Becky, Judy, Mikey, Vanessa and Josh'.

A brother approached and discreetly invited them back to the house. Vanessa accepted politely and listened to the directions without the slightest intention of ever following them.

A hand tapped her on the shoulder.

'Hello, I'm Carol, one of Sophie's housemates.'

'Vanessa. I knew her—'

'Yes, I know.'

'Oh.'

'Judy still seems terribly upset.'

'Well, I think it must have been the shock of finding her – I'm sorry, I know you were there too.'

'Perhaps I'm harder.'

'No, I didn't mean—'

'No, I know you didn't. I did. Look, could I just have a word with you in private?'

'Well, sure.'

Vanessa was puzzled and a little frightened. She was not reassured when Carol asked, as they walked to her Volkswagen, 'How's Mikey taking it?'

'Badly. He—'

'Feels guilty?'

'Yes, I think so.'

'And do you?'

'Yes, although I know really that I have nothing to feel guilty about.'

'No, I don't think you do. Her death was an accident.'

'I don't just mean that, although I'm sure it was. It must have been. No, I mean she told me that she and Mikey were finished before I ever, not that even now I have—' she stopped, her sudden desire to unload her thoughts spent. She felt disgusted with herself for having offered the last spurious self-justification. 'I'm sorry,' she said.

Carol was looking at her with increased interest. 'Don't be. You obviously needed to say that to somebody. And maybe saying it to me would have got me to say that she didn't mind about what you did. That's not true. She did. But she didn't kill herself because of it.'

'But then losing her job on top—' Vanessa was compelled to continue, like a child picking a scab.

'Look, she died because she drank and then still couldn't sleep and she was unhappy and alone. And then she was

201

unlucky. You might as well say I'm guilty because I didn't come back a day earlier. She might have got drunk more happily then. But we don't know that. None of us is to blame.'

Vanessa realised that Carol too was defiant, and uncertain. 'You're right. Is that what you wanted to tell me?'

'No,' Carol sparked. 'That's what you wanted to tell me. The thing is, I've got some stuff of Sophie's I don't know what to do with.' She opened the boot of her car.

'Why can't you just give it to her parents?'

'I took it from her room to stop them seeing it.' She picked up a carrier bag and emptied it on to the floor of the boot. 'I didn't know what they thought their daughter was like. I just thought it might upset them more than they already were—' She tailed off.

There was an assortment of black-and-white prints which were clearly recognisable as Sophie aged about twenty or so. In some she was draped with a sheet, in others wearing nothing but a pair of French knickers, in others still draped naked on a *chaise-longue* or bent backwards across a desk. They were undeniably 'arty' but Vanessa was shocked. The extent of her shock surprised her. Perhaps, she thought, it's because their subject no longer exists.

The other item was a box which said 'Love Egg' on the side.

'Don't know that it's ever been used,' Carol said diffidently.

'How did you know she had them?'

'The photos came out one night when we were having a laugh. I think she went out with the guy that took them. Haven't you ever seen them?'

'No, she never mentioned them.'

'Perhaps she was more embarrassed with her . . . closer friends. The vibrator came from one of those parties, you know, where someone invites their girlfriends round to try on naughty négligés and stuff. She said the underwear was too hideous for words but she felt obliged to buy something. Promised to road-test it and report back but she never did, and I never felt able to ask somehow.'

'I didn't know she knew anybody like that.'

'Secretary at the Beeb, I think.'

'So why me?'

'What?'

'I mean, I think you did the right thing hiding them from Mr and Mrs Attwood, but why ask my advice on their disposal?'

'Didn't feel I could just throw them away. Thought maybe someone who'd been her friend longer should decide, or at least see the photos 'cos they're personal.' She was putting everything back in the bag.

'Why not Judy or ... well, Judy?'

'Look at the state she's in.'

'Of course.'

'And—'

'Yes?'

'Well ... when she brought the toy home she said that really she ought to give it to you as your need was much greater than hers.'

'The old cow,' Vanessa said eventually and then snorted with laughter. Carol joined in and soon they were guffawing to the disapproval of departing mourners.

'Look, I must go,' Carol said. 'I only took the morning off. Take this and you decide. Please.'

Vanessa accepted the bag. It didn't occur to her to say no, or to suggest throwing it away. There was something so death-defying about the pictures they demanded to be preserved.

'See you, then.' Carol wiped her nose against the back of

her hand and jangled her car keys. 'I hope it hasn't screwed things up for you and Mikey.'

'Bye.'

'Goodbye.'

They shook hands awkwardly and Vanessa made for her car. She didn't want Judy or Mikey to see the contents of the bag but luckily they were already sheltering in the BMW. She opened the boot and hid it beneath the blanket, resolving if asked to say that it contained some stuff Sophie had borrowed from her. But no one did.

She looked back at the crematorium. There was a thin plume of smoke rising from the chimney.

'Shall we go home?' she asked, starting the engine.

'We thought,' Mikey said carefully, 'that we would like to go back to the Attwoods, didn't we, Judy?'

'What, for baked meats?' Vanessa asked.

'Perhaps just a small sherry.'

'If you're sure?' She stared at Judy.

'Oh yes,' Judy said. 'I'm sure.'

Reggie and Diana Attwood were poker-backed and smiled like politicians coming to the end of an election campaign. Their son Robin seemed chiefly exercised by the fact that no one from *Churchill's People* had attended. Mikey excused himself from this conversation and helped himself to a ham sandwich and another Scotch. By the table Vanessa was talking to one of the sons' wives.

'So many beautiful flowers,' he heard her say. She had obviously switched on her business-reception automatic pilot.

'Yes. And one very mysterious,' replied Victi. 'Did you see it? That absolutely enormous bunch of white lilies which simply had "love J" on the card. Do you know who J might have been? None of us can think.'

Mikey had never been to the Old Vicarage before and as he never would again he wanted to see the room in which Sophie had grown up. At the top of the stairs he stopped to allow his eyes to adjust to the dark. A silhouetted woman in black emerged from the shadows of the panelled landing and Mikey jumped.

'Are you looking for the bathroom?' It was Judy.

'Er – yes.'

'It's the third door along,' she said. She had done another repair job on her make-up but it had not hidden the puffiness round her eyes nor the pinkness of the tip of her nose. When she passed him he caught a whiff of a perfume whose name he had never known but whose smell was unmistakably that of cucumber. It lingered in the bathroom, competing with the scent of Wright's Coal Tar soap. He waited a couple of minutes and then went back into the corridor and the smell of lavender wax. It was empty and so quiet that he could hear his footfalls on the drugget.

There were eight doors to choose from. The first was definitely either Mrs or both the Attwoods', peachily draped and swagged, the second and third were as clearly guest rooms with open suitcases on the floor and empty hangers in the wardrobes.

The fourth was an airing cupboard and someone was coming up the stairs. He opened the fifth, preparing himself to look like a man in search of a lavatory.

It was the fact that it was so self-consciously unoccupied in a house full of visiting relatives that made him immediately sure this was the one. Once he had closed the door other details confirmed this. The room was tastefully and anonymously decorated, but sanitised mementoes of every phase of Sophie's life remained. On shelves above the bed were a small collection of the type of glass animals that girls find appealing at nine and appalling at thirteen, and a selection of books from *Fourth Form at Malory Towers* to *Little Women* via *Heidi* and the *Jackie Annual* for 1972.

A school photograph of similar vintage hung on the wall between posters for an RSC production of *Twelfth Night* and a Sophie Attwood production of a college revue called *Once a Bishop*. He scanned the ranks of monochrome gym-slipped girls but at first none of them resembled her and then several did.

On the bedside table beneath the tassels of the lampshade stood a smaller frame holding Sophie beaming in academic gown and hood in front of Durham's Palace Green library. The degree certificate itself was above the dressing-table together with a sketch of a horse called Desert Prince. A blue gymkhana rosette was fixed to the corner of the frame. Presumably second was the best that Sophie and Prince had ever managed.

He went to the window and looked at the view that she had once described: the sundial on the lawn where they had hammered the croquet hoops for summer parties and the gap in the hedge through which she had kissed James from the Manor during a short-lived and frowned-upon teenage romance. Frowned upon by the Manorites, he presumed. Reggie and Diana struck him as the sort to encourage an alliance that would, by proxy, lift them up the ladder to the level of landed gentry.

This room was so different from the richly and junkily chaotic boudoir that Sophie had created in Camden that it was hard to believe they related to the same person. Then it struck him that this chapel full of relics was doubly sad because, although venerated by her mother, they were there only because they had been rejected by the daughter as excess baggage.

He lay down on the squeaky single bed and stared at the hockey stick on top of the wardrobe. The candlewick bedspread gave off that distinctive cucumber smell along with the mothballs. If only he hadn't argued with Soph on the phone. Why the hell had he and why the fuck had she?

Judy knew that she had to change the bedclothes. She couldn't sleep in either bed while they still harboured white musk, but deliberately eradicating this last physical trace of Sophie had seemed impossible before the funeral. Discovering that Sophie's own bed at home smelt of nothing more personal than mothballs and fabric conditioner helped.

She no longer believed that Sophie had killed herself deliberately, but deciding that had not been a relief. What had followed was the slow realisation that she had caused this accident as surely as if she had been driving a car and run Sophie down. And worse, it had not been unavoidable. If she had had the courage to answer the phone ... she steeled herself to strip the sheets and, bowing to the inevitable, went to clean off her make-up first. Run-proof mascara. She would get some tomorrow.

8

Bread and Circuses

... and so the coroner returned an open verdict. The family didn't look too happy at that because it doesn't rule out her having intended to do it but, as he said, no one can really know what happened. I think you're right. If anything tipped her over the edge it must have been losing the job but Mikey still thinks we're to blame. He says 'I' but he must mean the both of us because it takes two to tango. He came round on Saturday but he's really uneasy if Josh isn't with us. Don't think we'll ever get it together now, and I don't know if we can be just good friends with this between us. Oh, well.

Great to hear that you're producing a new number for the show. What's in it? Have you learnt any circus skills?

I might be in for a change of direction. Max Nicolson, our creative director, has taken me out for lunch a couple of times and I think he's testing the water for a breakaway agency. He's invited me to his house on Saturday – a first as he's notoriously unchummy with people in the agency outside normal working hours. Wonder whether it will be as decadent and bohemian as I imagine? Probably not but there might be a guilty secret. He's foppish enough to be a closet queen so perhaps there's a boyfriend lurking. Stay tuned for further instalments.

Take care of yourself.

Lots of love,
Vanessa.
XXX

PS Josh sends an extra hug and says he misses you madly. So do I.

Becky folded the letter carefully and zipped it into the lining of her flying jacket. Even in the bus that doubled as a box office they wore as many clothes as they could. There were only two warm places in the Cirque d'Apocalypse – under the lights in the ring during a show and under the blankets in bed if you were sharing with someone else. Which she was.

Dermot came in from the cold, bringing with him the pungent smell of onions from the hot dog stand outside. Becky retched involuntarily. She would never be able to eat another as long as she lived. For the first fortnight of her apprenticeship she had run the stand, frying onions and boiling frankfurters every evening and the steam from the cauldron permeated all of her clothes with their malodour. It lay greasily in her hair and seeped into every pore of her skin.

At the end of each shift she showered in the lukewarm drizzle that was the best the caravan offered, but it was the first scent on her nostrils in the morning, defeating the heavy applications of perfume that she hoped would spare Dermot. When asked he affected not to have noticed but it was a relief to be transferred to tickets and to see her epidemic of blackheads gradually disappear.

The communal existence of the circus reminded her of what she had imagined student life to be like before she went to university; conversations conducted in broken French and broken English with accents that gave the most banal exchanges a cosmopolitan air; the nightly high of a performance followed by analysis fuelled by cheap wine.

This nomadic lifestyle was bolstered by abundant char-cuteries and patisseries; the cramped caravan was a novelty not a source of frustration; and until New Year's Day the whole enterprise felt like a holiday. She had grown used to the hours and accepted the aching muscles and the grittiness compounded of too little sleep, too much booze and smoking and the never quite cleanliness of cold-water washing.

With the bleak realism that grey January inevitably brings her spirits might have fallen, but by then she knew that she would have the chance to work on the show itself. Being otherwise engaged during performances she had taken to watching rehearsals, saying nothing and remaining discreetly high in the tiered seating. She could offer no useful criticism of technique but felt there were places where a small change might create an image as arresting as those that had excited her when she first saw the show – the standard lamp on the wheelchair, the fiery glow illuminating the raggle-taggle procession, the exposed car engines.

Her first chance to discuss this came on New Year's Eve when, it being a Sunday and a sort of feast day, they had neither shows nor rehearsals. They woke late, Dermot first, as always, and Becky when he disentangled himself from her limpet-like embrace. She was surprised that she clutched on to him in her sleep. It wasn't something she had done to other lovers. She assumed it must be subconscious insecurity about her new life. He didn't seem to mind anyway.

'I'll go and get some croissants.'

'What's the time then?' she asked.

'After eleven. It might have to be bread. What do you want to eat later?'

'I don't know. Look, I'll go, then I can decide on the way.' She reached for her sweater and pulled it on over the T-shirt she slept in. One of the advantages of a caravan was that you could get dressed, even put the kettle on, without getting out of bed.

'So don't I have any say in this menu?'

'No.' She paused in the act of belting up her jeans to kiss him. 'You know you'll eat anything that's put in front of you.'

'That's true enough. We're out of toothpaste.'

What had make him think of that? she wondered, as she stepped out across the frosty turf. She ran her tongue around her teeth. Perhaps her breath had smelt when she kissed. She would buy some Wrigley's from the grocers. The cold was stinging her cheeks, wet from the hasty wipe with a flannel. Stopping to look in the window of the boutique (closed) she noticed that her hair was in rat's tails and attempted to comb it out with her fingers. Perhaps she should devote today to body maintenance. She wondered whether it would be possible to boil enough water in kettles and saucepans to fill a bathtub on the caravan floor. She had seen one underneath the seating stand.

She mooched on to the butcher's and then remembered the croissants. She hurried to the boulangerie on the square. There were three left so she knew it was going to be a good day and bought a glistening *tarte* faced with a mosaic of purple and green grapes.

The tables outside the café were sparsely inhabited as

mass was still in progress at the church opposite. Once the service was over the anti-clerics, atheists and agnostics already sipping beer and coffee in the cold winter sunlight would be joined by those who wished to top up the self-righteous warmth of the Lord's blessing with that of the Pernod company.

Sitting at one of the tables was Stephane Raspail, the nearest thing the Cirque d'Apocalypse had to a proprietor. He was its founder and the chairman of its executive committee. He took the largest share of the profits after expenses because, although democratic, the Cirque was not entirely egalitarian. He had an enormous caravan pulled by an ageing but powerful black Cadillac. Today he wore a black cape and wide-brimmed, soft hat in the style of Aristide Bruant; by tonight he might be modelling himself on Chairman Mao or Bruce Springsteen. The one constant in his appearance was a thick and lustrous black beard which made her want to suggest that he tried out Fidel Castro or Archbishop Makarios for size. He and his wife were the only performers to come from a long circus tradition; they were trapeze artistes.

Stephane waved to Becky and, having both hands full, she flapped the stick of bread in return. He beckoned her over. 'It is a lovely day, Becka. Have a drink with us.' He brandished his glass, disturbing the ice cubes in the opaque-yellow liquid so that she smelt the tang of aniseed.

'Thanks,' she said. 'But I'd better get back. With Dermot's breakfast.'

From somewhere in the folds of his cape he produced and consulted a pocket watch, although the enormous hands of the church clock were clearly in his line of sight. 'He will not need breakfast if he has lunch,' he said elliptically. 'You have plans for lunch, yes, no?'

'No, none.'

'Good. We make a lunch party here at one o'clock and you and Dermot will join us. I will go and increase the table. Now you have time for coffee, no, yes?' He disappeared into the café.

'There is a restaurant upstairs,' explained Mirielle who, as if in expiation of her husband's flamboyance, invariably dressed with a soft and understated chic which cleverly maximised the impact of her gypsy good-looks.

'Do not worry if you would rather have this day to yourselves.' She smiled. 'He won't be offended. Not for more than five minutes anyway.'

'No, I'm sure Dermot would like to. And so would I.' She hesitated, remembering how seriously the French take their Sunday lunch. 'What should I – we – wear?'

'Wear whatever you like. I'm sure Dermot will wear what he always wears.'

Becky laughed. He had plenty of jeans and shirts but they were all so similar that once the leather jacket and scarf had been added he might never have changed.

Stephane returned with a tiny cup of strong coffee which she gulped, burning her tongue. 'Thanks. I'd better go and see if I can squeeze enough water to wash my hair.' She picked up her shopping.

'Here.' Mirielle held out a key. 'Use ours. As much water there as you can think of a use for.'

'Thank you. If you're sure.' Out of the corner of her eye she had glimpsed Stephane's disapproval, or at least surprise, at this offer.

Mirielle simply nodded and smiled.

'Just don't tell anyone else,' said Stephane, magnanimous in defeat. 'I do not intend to become a public wash-house.'

It was not until she dumped her purchases on the draining board in the caravan that she realised one of the Flying Foxes, as the Raspails had been known when they

214

worked for Billy Smart, had torn off and devoured not only the end of her loaf but a chunk of the *tarte*.

They were nine for lunch. Apart from Becky, Dermot and the Flying Foxes there were Joachim and Ana, the erotic gymnasts; Straker, the band's keyboard player; Helga, the peroxide blonde administrator; and Fassbinder the dwarf.

She and Dermot were the last to arrive because she had been unwilling to skimp on the privilege of the Raspails' caravan. The place left for her was opposite Stephane, which she assumed was some sort of honour. Joachim was on her left and Straker to the right.

There were already several bottles of vin rouge on the table, although Mirielle appeared to be drinking champagne and Straker bottled beer.

This gathering was a circus powerhouse – only Becky, Ana and Mirielle were not on the executive committee – and it was the first time Becky had moved in such exalted company. Before this morning she had exchanged no more than a few words with the Raspails or the gymnasts. Straker was a drinking companion of Dermot's and she liked him well enough. Helga, who controlled the box office and front of house, was often in the groups in which they whiled away their spare time and even popped in and out of the caravan on business, but spoke to Becky no more than politeness demanded. Becky hadn't decided whether this was shyness of the sort to which bossy people can often be prone or plain rudeness and, if the latter, why.

She was relieved not to be sitting next to Fassbinder. At their first meeting she had been uncomfortably aware of trying too hard to behave 'normally' and suspected that he had manipulated the conversation to force her to refer to his size. Having reduced her to acute embarrassment he had said adieu and, as he passed her, pinched her bottom. He had judged perfectly that she was the sort of girl to object volubly to this kind of harassment but also the sort of liberal incapable of accusing a midget in a wheelchair. However, Dermot seemed fond of him so she had tried to reserve judgement.

While she ate her crêpe champignon Joachim asked her about her life in London, and she discovered how they had come to be in the circus.

'We meet in Amsterdam on a shoot; we are both models. We are also both dancers but not working – Ana is too tall for the chorus line. I had no such good excuse but anyway. The job we meet on is for a lingerie catalogue. Ana has the body for this but not for other clothes where they want boys. Lingerie is what you might call a borderline area; being Amsterdam there is a straight route from the catalogue into the pornographic videos and magazines, many of the same photographers. This one makes us an offer and being rational people we consider it.'

He took a sip of mineral water. She had noticed that Ana too was hardly touching her wine and was making hard work of a simple green salad. Perfect figures needed careful attention.

'The circus is in town. We go on a date. We listen to the clapping and remember how good it is to be in front of the audience. We see that they do not only have old-fashioned acts. We both want to dance again. We have an offer to show our bodies in this video. This does not appeal to us but we think if we make something beautiful like this then maybe the circus will be interested. They have nothing erotica in their show at this time. Maybe this is because they don't want it but maybe it's just that they never thought of it. So we work on it.' A ghost of a smile. 'And then we audition for Stephane.'

'And being the voyeur that he is,' said Fassbinder, who had apparently been listening in, 'he snapped you up.'

'Also,' said Joachim, unperturbed, 'we are both strong and I can erect scaffolding and drive a truck.'

Becky looked across at Ana. Bland, blonde, displaying her torso in a top taut as clingfilm, the script of her everlasting performance required her to go to the cloakroom. As she crossed the room, high-heeled boots extending very long legs coated in Lycra which revealed the workings of every muscle, a score of French patriarchs lifted their eyes from the dead flesh on their plates to feast on the live. Fassbinder did a three-point turn in his wheelchair to witness her progress.

'Get on with your meal, you old goat,' Stephane called good-humouredly.

She looked at Joachim, who had not turned to his partner. His grey eyes, clear, hardly lined, looked back at her. His sweatshirt defined his pectorals and its rolled-up sleeves exposed powerful, tanned forearms. She wanted to ask, although never would, what their sex life was like. They shared a caravan and talked about themselves in the way that lovers do but it was hard to imagine what was left to them after the delicate foreplay of their nightly public performances. Did they recreate those routines within the confines of their bed? As public property these moves could hold no clandestine excitement and might even suffer from the missing magic of heat, lights and the thrill of the audience collectively holding its breath. Maybe their kicks came from the contrast of clumsy fumbling – but could you learn to not be graceful? Perhaps then it was the one thing that wasn't in the act – penetration. A quick poke in the missionary position.

'A Pfennig for your thoughts,' he said, and she coloured, saved only by the arrival of their steaks and gigots.

Although Joachim and Ana were the most striking, working in a circus was clearly good for the body. Stephane was barrel-chested and Dermot wiry, but neither carried surplus fat. Mirielle was naturally lithe. Even Helga, who was broad-shouldered and heavy-hipped, could, unlike thousands of failed dieters, fairly use the description big-boned to explain her shape.

Diet was not an issue for Straker – he was forking away piles of allumettes heavily salted and smeared with mustard. Becky had never seen him take any exercise but, like many rock musicians, he was skeletally thin. This was partially disguised by his baggy, black suit but even his head was honed down to a bony minimum, his skull shaved with the merest hint of blue shadow on the cranium, the nose no more than a rest for his Raybans, the Adam's apple dancing attendance on his speech. He was arguing with Stephane now; something to do with a replacement for the band's lead guitarist. He was off to join a seventies group whose brand of pre-heavy metal was enjoying a revival in Germany but whose original axeman was unavailable, having stumbled into an early grave.

'What I'm saying,' Straker gesticulated with his fork, 'is it doesn't have to be a guitarist at all. Synths can play the tunes or we could get a sax, put some different textures into the music.'

'No, we must have a player of the electric phallus. A guy blowing down an old pipe is not so good to look at. And as for a man sitting behind a stack of black boxes like you do – that is . . .' Stephane gave an exaggerated yawn, then politely covered his gaping mouth with a large hand that he flapped delicately as if it was a fan.

'People shouldn't be looking at us. If the show was visually absorbing they wouldn't.'

Some of the others were taking notice now, as if the argument was a chess match in which Straker had just punched his opponent's clock.

Stephane took another swig of wine. 'If nobody is looking at you then perhaps we should have done with the band altogether and use tapes.'

'No spontaneity.'

'Is that so bad? No off-nights with tapes.'

'Tapes can't fill in when you miss an entrance, or need all those extra swings to get your old carcass from one perch to the other.'

Stephane laughed. 'Pax. Another glass of wine. No, I forget, you are an English philistine and drink only beer.'

'Wine for me,' said a voice to Becky's left. She ignored it.

'Perhaps, Straker, if you wish to be the frontman, you should get a keyboard that allows you to move about the stage and show off your body.'

'You mean like the new Yamaha. It's great, could combine the best of—'

Stephane was triumphant. 'I was actually thinking of an accordion. Then if we ever part company you can beg on street corners with a monkey.'

Everyone laughed including Straker.

'Fräulein, be so good as to pass the bottle even if you despise me.' Fassbinder had swapped places with Joachim who was now talking to Helga.

'Of course . . . I don't . . . despise you, I mean—'

He cut her off. 'Do you know what is the worst thing about being a midget?'

Just as she was about to say no he continued, leaving her with her lips redundantly parted. 'Not being able to drink so much. The alcohol gets round my body very quickly, there being so little of it, and so I become legless in yet another sense.' He chuckled mirthlessly. 'I'm glad you

219

have closed your mouth. I was beginning to understand why your name is Fish.'

'Fishman.' She took a deep breath. 'Are you always this rude?'

'That's better. Hit me back. It's what I like. Otherwise I would not be doing a job where I get thrown in a trashcan every night for the amusement of the populace.'

'How did you come to be in the circus?'

'I am a freak.'

'No, I didn't mean—'

'There is not a great deal of choice of occupation when you are a person of extremely restricted growth. I nearly became an academic but that is just a different kind of freak show and, besides, in Germany it is impossible to be academic without reference to Nietzsche. You know him?'

'Of him. I've never read any.'

'Don't bother. Oh no, it is OK. You are more than one and a half metres with all limbs intact and in the right place. When you are not, the idea of the Superman is just a bit depressing. It is an affront. But you know about these things. You are a member of at least one oppressed minority.'

'No, I don't think so.'

'It is OK. You're among friends. And a word of advice. If you don't want people to know you're Jewish try changing your name to something properly English like Smith. I don't think the nose will give you away. It's rather inadequate for a Jew.'

'That's because I'm not one. I just married one.'

'First a Jew. Now an Irishman. You must be kinky for minorities. Do you have to go with a Palestinian or a Kurd before you get round to me?'

'I'm hoping to stick with the one I've got.'

'And be a hot dog lady all your life?'

'No.'

'So what? You got some big ideas about this show that will get you away from all that pork?'

'As a matter of fact I have.'

'Hey, Stephane, this girl is not as stupid or as Jewish as I thought. She thinks you are a crap director and is plotting to take your job.'

And that was how Becky came to be rehearsing in the mornings. She had devised a sort of Count of Monte Cristo story around the trapeze act. Mirielle was to be frog-marched, kicking and screaming, into the arena by a mob carrying flaming brands, and locked in a small iron cage, which was to be hauled on chains high above the centre of the arena and suspended in mid-air, swaying and creaking with her anguished movements.

She would wriggle her way out of the hole in the top of the cage, looking for an escape route. She would be spotted by the guards below who would start to lower the cage. To stay out of their clutches she would climb the chains and eventually reach a point where she could jump on to one of the marquee's supporting struts. To cut her off Stephane would climb this pole and a chase would follow along the struts and trapezes, Mirielle's escape routes successively blocked by groundlings swarming up the poles.

It would culminate in her scrambling around the outside of the cage attempting to evade the grasping hands of guards from within and Stephane only inches behind. At the last moment she would drop into the open bed of a truck driven across the arena by Dermot and they would disappear in a blaze of explosions, leaving her captors stranded.

It was impossible to use safety nets for this routine and, although Becky knew that the Raspails did not always use them, her discomfort at deliberately jeopardising Stephane and Mirielle had prompted caution about the wilder excesses of the action. But the enthusiasm of the principals brushed aside her doubts and even watching it with the house lights up and the diminishing effect of the empty marquee was exciting. Given the extra lift of performance atmosphere and the music that Straker was assembling to accompany it she felt that for five minutes it would beat any adventure movie that the audience had seen.

She wanted to use women as the chief guards. Helga was suitable, enthusiastic and, given her position on the executive committee, Becky thought it would be impolitic not to offer her the part.

'Why don't you do the other one?' suggested Dermot.

Becky wavered. 'Will anyone mind? I'm a bit of a new girl.'

'Why should they? You devised the whole piece.'

'People quite often resent directors who cast themselves.'

'This isn't *Hamlet*. You're just a sadistic warder in a thrills and spills routine.'

'You're right. I don't really look outlandish enough though.'

'Costume will take care of that.'

'No, it's my hair.' She thought for a moment or two. 'It would look good if we were a matching pair.' She went to the tiny mirror on the back of the cupboard door. 'I wonder what I'd look like with it that short?'

'You'd look great,' Dermot said.

So didn't you think I looked great before? The thought bubbled instinctively and suspiciously to the surface. She turned to him as he sat on the bed. He smiled his soft smile at her.

'It's a very good idea,' he said.

222

* * *

Making-up for her first performance was the only thing that normalised Becky's new haircut. As the real markings of her face disappeared beneath the pancake and cupid's bow lips, the eyes of a racoon and blusher as harsh as Prussian duelling scars, so the bright crop that belonged to an albino Neapolitan urchin or an ambiguous female rock star gradually ceased to shock her. This was, after all, what it was intended for.

It had shocked Helga too. When Becky walked into the box office on her return from the hairdresser's Helga had seemed shaken, almost frightened by its similarity to her own, coarser cut.

Now they were both dressed in black boots and breeches and white Cossack shirts. Between them Mirielle stood barefoot, a ragged wraparound skirt and torn blouse over her brown leotard. Her hair was tousled and her face and legs smeared with dark streaks to suggest that she had been kept in terrible conditions. Already into her role, her eyes flashed defiantly and she hung from their arms with the suffering of the eternal blameless victim.

Paolo, the backstage supremo, handed out torches and lit them. 'Save it for the crowd,' he said. 'Don't peak too soon.' He winked at Becky.

'Break a leg,' Helga said sourly.

'So charming.' He blew them a kiss and passed down the line.

Applause and laughter came through the curtain on a current of warm air just ahead of the jugglers. 'All yours,' one of them said and she heard the first booming chords of their music as Paolo hauled the curtain fully aside and out they strode off the edge of the known world.

She felt the sawdust beneath her soft-soled boots and the oil on the hasp of the cage door. As it was lifted away she focused on Mirielle's toes curled around the metal mesh of its floor. The heat of a torch flame stung the nape of her shorn neck. She jeered at the tragic figure clinging to the bars, and tried to sound suitably outraged as Mirielle insinuated herself through the gap in the cage roof, her skirt being left behind as planned to waft in the wind which always blew up there. Then it was all a blur – Mirielle scrabbling up the chains, slipping once although whether by accident or design Becky could not tell, and making her first jump safely in a perfectly placed gap in the music which allowed the crowd to hear their own gasp. Drums flailed, hand-held spotlights criss-crossed the marquee to accentuate the Raspails' speed and daring, and Becky felt her stomach lurch as she and Helga, now in the cage themselves, swayed upwards.

For the first time she looked at the faces upturned to hers and was relieved that they were mere pink blobs whose eyes she could not catch. They jolted to a halt. Becky's fingers, slippery with sweat, lost their grip and she fell, banging her knee painfully on the cage floor. Blinking away the tears she watched as Mirielle came swooping towards her along the length of the auditorium, Stephane a blur behind as he caught each empty trapeze bar on its back swing. Then she was flying at them, hands like talons, legs wide and Becky and Helga screamed as she hit the side of the cage and hung on.

It was their big moment. Helga opened the door of the cage and leant out as if to grab Mirielle, who scrambled away along the cage wall. When she turned the corner Becky, braced against the tilting caused by uneven weight distribution, had to claw at her blouse, the poppers of which were designed to burst, leaving Becky with the blouse and Mirielle swinging below the cage floor. Their faces were inches apart, the Frenchwoman's breath coming in short rasps. Her head was thrown against the bars by the impact of Stephane hitting the cage in his turn.

'*Merde*,' she whispered. 'Pull, pull,' and Becky pulled so hard that the fabric ripped and her nails cut into Mirielle's skin. As Stephane's feet came into the uppermost part of her vision she saw the fleeting twitch of pain, the swelling bubbles of adrenalin-rich blood welling from Mirielle's shoulder, and felt the momentary caress of long black hair as she slid away.

Then Becky was stamping on the floor of the cage to loosen the fragile hold of the fingers by which Mirielle was suspended, with only some subconscious barrier stopping her really breaking them, for she so believed in the drama that the roar of the truck, headlights and horn blazing, was as much of a surprise to her as it was to the audience.

Mirielle, with a shriek, dropped the thirty feet into the net in its trailer and bounced up. She seemed to fall again so slowly that Becky was certain the moving truck would have passed from beneath her and she would break her back on the dirt floor of the ring. Becky's heart was in her throat as the body drifted into the rearmost corner of netting and flapped like a fish on the deck of a boat. Then it was slammed higher, somewhere inside her brain, as the cage was released and fell with a rush of chains and hot air and the lights were cut.

In the terrifying dark she remembered to brace her legs but bumped her head savagely on the roof as the hoist halted them inches from the ground. There was clapping and shouting and Helga was pushing her from the cage and suddenly they were back behind the curtain with Paolo grinning and handing her a cigarette as the truck returned to the arena, carrying Mirielle and Stephane to take a bow.

She sucked down smoke and felt the humming in her temples almost immediately. The Sam Browne pulled her shirt between her breasts as she panted. She accepted pats on the back and crushed the butt beneath her booted heel. Part of her was the successful impresario, part the brutish guard and part woman reduced to frightened child.

She was excited. Now she saw why they lived in a world of their own. If you could fly through the air every night and never fall to earth, what couldn't you do?

. . . and I have decided to take the plunge, on the understanding that I can work any extra hours at home and that if we take off – I mean WHEN we take off – we can eventually have a crèche on the premises. So maybe Max isn't a secret mysogynist after all.

It's really exciting. We have six clients committed in secret, including two of mine – Gateshead Foods and Dolphin swimwear. On top of that Max has done so much work for Orion that he's sure we can get some NPD from them.

What was NPD? Becky wondered. It sounded like a toxic chemical or a monetary unit, but presumably couldn't be.

Going to look at some premises this weekend and if they are suitable we hand our resignations in at the end of the month. Hip hip hooray.

Saw Judy on Tuesday. She never calls but in the end I twisted her arm to go out for a drink. She wouldn't go near our old place and we ended up in this really noisy dump instead, which didn't help the conversation. And boy, did it need helping! She hardly said a word unless forced and she looks really tired and washed out. She says it's because she's working so hard – on some top secret new shampoo thing – but I think it's as much to do with Sophie as that. I mean, she's always worked hard

but it's never left her like this. I can't understand why it's
had such a terrible effect on her. I know they were
friends but so were the rest of us and without wishing to
sound callous it's not like losing a parent or something.

Sorry, I do sound like a bitch but you can't grieve for
ever. Not as badly as that. Or I can't but she can. If
you've got any ideas for lifting her out of the doldrums
please say. Soon.

Still missing you madly.

Loads of love,

Vanessa and Josh.

XXX

PS Have just done a jargon check. NPD is New
Product Development.

Becky smiled. Just when you thought she was losing her
grip. No mention of Mikey. Did that mean she had stopped
seeing him altogether or that nothing had changed or that
they had finally got their act together and done it? With the
satisfaction of those in comforting coupledom Becky did
not like to think of her friend permanently outside, gazing
through the window. Particularly not tied to a small child
for company. Of course her solitary state was of her own
making but the Mikey thing showed that she hadn't ruled
out involvement.

The potential offices of Bennett Nicolson Tierney were at
the western end of Soho in the hinterland of Carnaby
Street, an area once inhabited only by the type of tailor who
had swathes of Lurex and faded, signed photographs of
Herman's Hermits in his window. The strip clubs had never
crept this close to the dignity of Liberty's and Oxford
Circus; now even the handwritten notices reading 'Busty
young model. Third floor. Walk Up' had been replaced by

discreet brass plaques announcing the presence of a somewhat younger profession.

'Not that we aren't prostitutes,' said Max, as he unlocked the door, 'just that we don't get screwed on our backs.'

'Neither do they necessarily,' said Peter Bennett. 'I think a broader range of techniques is available these days, Max. You should try one again.'

'But are they value for money, Peter?' Max aped his partner's most frequent question.

Vanessa pointed down at Josh's flaxen head and placed a finger to her lips. '*Pas devant les enfants*, as they say in old sitcoms.'

'Whoops-a-daisy,' Max cried. 'I'm excused on grounds of bachelordom but you should know better with that enormous brood at home.'

Bennett, like many advertising men, had married young and his four children were stabled in Esher. He was still only thirty-seven and the New Business Director at Breughel Thomas. Ironically it was his success in the job that had brought about the present situation. After three years he had had enough but the company didn't want to waste his pitching skills by returning him to account management. He had considered moving to another agency until his insurance broker had implanted the idea of setting up on his own. He had broached this idea to Max on one of the interminable journeys that they shared to prospective clients.

Max was keen. At forty-five he had begun to feel that he had missed the boat of fame and fortune. Of course he had collected his fair share of awards, his job was very well paid and the vintage Aston Martin was a comfort, but he was never going to be a millionaire working for someone else. Or have his name over the door.

On the other hand he knew he was not one of life's

natural entrepreneurs. But Peter was and they had worked together often enough for Max to feel confident that they made a good combination. Starting a new agency was a risk but Max had no responsibilities and his house was paid for. When they decided they needed an account director who inspired loyalty in staff and clients he had thought of Vanessa, even before Peter had mused that a woman would 'look good in the mix'.

Vanessa was flattered but had plenty of misgivings to counterbalance the excitement expressed in her letter to Becky. These flowed directly from her love for Josh and the enormous responsibility she felt for him. First was the potential loss of the limited time they had together. Despite the agreements about her doing some stuff at home she knew her working week might well be substantially longer than at BT, and the crèche was a dream until they were bigger, probably long after Josh had started school.

That was why she had brought him today, although her child-minder could have had him; to start as she meant to go on, whatever the others' reactions. Which were not adverse; Peter was so used to the background chatter of kids that he took no notice and unselfconsciously behaved as if Josh were not there. Max had been stiff at first but this evaporated when he stumbled on the stairs and Josh said in imitation, 'Whoops-a-daisy.'

If time was one worry the other was money. Not just the loss of a fairly safe salary for the uncertainty of a profit share but the requirement to put risk capital into the business. That meant using all her savings and taking out a larger mortgage on the house. Occasionally, and the occasions were becoming more frequent, Vanessa woke at four in the morning and sweated about this. Visions of her and Josh trudging to some Dickensian workhouse played over her father's advice: never in any circumstances put all your eggs in one basket. What would he say if he knew she'd put them in a basket that was no more than a handful of twigs?

The suite of offices, in what had been a nineteenth-century hat factory, had lots of big windows and very little wasted space. So many of the places they had considered needed constant artificial light and had vast reception areas, which at £35 a square foot was money thrown away – all they needed was room for a desk and a couple of sofas. The layout here was more or less what they wanted and the bare white walls and grey carpet tiles were anonymity crying out to be personalised.

'What do you think?' asked Peter.

'The lift is very small,' said Max. 'It will be a job getting furniture in.'

'Vanessa?'

'Is that room big enough for meetings? It looks enormous now it's empty but the rooms in my house did too and they're really poky.'

'OK,' Peter said. 'Let's come back to specific details, but what about the feel of the place, location and so on?'

'Good.'

'Shall we go and have a coffee in that place across the road?'

'Yes, all right. But what do you think, Peter?'

'Oh, I think it's perfect so I shall tell the estate agent we are quite interested and look for a deal on the lease.'

In the café they sat with a bunch of early American tourists and a couple of girls taking their tea-break from Liberty's.

'Oh God,' said Vanessa. 'I've suddenly realised there's no parking.'

'That's all right,' said Max. 'We won't have any cars once we leave BT.'

'But I must have one. How will I drop him off and—'

'Don't panic,' said Peter. 'We'll lease. We just have to decide what.'

'BMW.'

'Why?'

'Well, my childseat fits and the vanity mirror is just the right height to—' she giggled. 'You two. Completely taken in. All too ready to believe I'm just a little woman underneath. Whatever's cost effective. A Ford Fiesta, I don't mind. Max?'

'As anything's going to be a comedown after the Aston I hardly care. But I draw the line at brown paintwork.'

The conversation drifted along from one minor topic to another, more a displacement activity than anything else. Eventually Vanessa said, 'Look, sod the built-in hi-fi and video unit. Are we going ahead?'

There was a pause. Peter, boyish in his weekend blouson and cords, ran his hand through his thinning hair. 'Oh yes, I think so, don't you?'

'Of course,' Max said.

She grinned. 'Come round to dinner next Saturday to celebrate. Not to talk business, just to – awful word – socialise. I've never met Penny.'

'Lovely, if we're free. Penny's the social sec in our house. I'll call you tonight and let you know.'

'Is there anyone you want to bring, Max?'

'That makes me feel about fourteen. Can't I just come by myself?'

'No, it will make Penny feel odd, and we will end up talking shop.'

'I'll have to think.'

'OK, you've got until Tuesday. If you haven't thought of anyone I'll invite someone for you.'

'She's so domineering,' Peter said. He looked down

at Josh, twisting some imaginary implement between Vanessa's shoulder blades. 'Are you winding Mummy up?'

Josh gave them his most beatific smile. 'Screwing on her back,' he explained and Peter snorted *cappuccino* down his perkily-patterned sweater.

Judy had decided that the only way to get through, if she ever did get through her grief, was to devote herself to work. She threw herself into Project Doublehead, the development of the combined shampoo and conditioner, with a vengeance and volunteered for any other task that came along.

As a consequence she found herself on the milkround – visiting provincial universities along with David from Personnel in the interest of recruiting the pick of 1990 graduates for the Pasco cause.

The anonymity of the hotels she stayed in provided her with greater peace of mind than her house. It was hard now to think of the Islington cottage as anything other than a venue for crying herself to sleep, an activity which alienated even Bartholomew, who had at first been pleased to take advantage of the unaccustomed pleasure of sleeping on his mistress's duvet. There was an improvement. To begin with she had suffered outbreaks in the office and had to retreat to the loo for privacy and repairs, runproof mascara notwithstanding. Now she told herself that grief had been supplanted by self-pity and sometimes she believed it. Occasional surges of anger at Sophie for having been so stupid simply reinforced her guilt.

Because she could share none of these feelings with her friends she had taken to avoiding them, only agreeing to a meeting when the determination of the other to fix it resulted in an open-ended offer that could not be side-stepped.

She had been in two minds as to whether to refuse to go to Durham, scene of their studenthood, but could think of no good reason to turn down this one stop on the itinerary. She had thought it would be the supreme test of her ability to disguise her feelings from David, the graduate recruitment manager, but soon realised that as Sophie the student had been more an acquaintance than a friend what actually came flooding back were much happier memories.

As a consequence dinner with David was more fun than usual and alone in her room afterwards Judy found herself wondering if what she needed to shake herself out of melancholia was no more than a sexual experience – not necessarily a relationship, just an experience.

Over breakfast she asked David if, as it was nearly the weekend, he fancied a night on the tiles. They could check out some of her erstwhile haunts. He seemed surprised but keen so after work, changed into their most casual clothes, they explored several pubs that she remembered and with closing time upon them made for a club on the river.

'God knows what it will be like,' she said as they descended an ill-lit flight of stairs to the towpath. 'It seemed rather cosmopolitan to me as an undergraduate.' It wasn't, but it was hot and dark and smoky and they drank some more and danced separately and together. Judy, her inhibitions blown away by alcohol and music, entwined herself sinuously around her partner, but her libido failed to respond. Unprepared to admit defeat she persevered until David suggested they returned to the hotel.

Back in the cold night air he slipped his arm around her and she leant against him but knew she had made a mistake. She had to disillusion him about his prospects before they reached their landing. She tried to suggest by rigidity and mundane conversation that there was a difference between the dance floor and the street. But there was too far to retreat. At his doorway he hardly let her go to unlock, assuming she would join him.

'Thanks very much for this evening. I've enjoyed it, but I ought to be getting to bed now.' His grip on her tightened momentarily but he had not mistaken her meaning. Lucky he wasn't more pissed.

'Oh.' He turned her face on. 'Thank – you.' And he kissed her with ardour. Realising that he had not fully comprehended the scale of his defeat she yielded to the pressure of his tongue and parted her lips but when his hand found its way to her breast she indicated, with the remembered wriggling of herself at fifteen, that he had gone too far. He desisted and delicately she released herself.

'Goodnight.'

'Goodnight. I'm sorry if I misunderstood,' he said mechanically.

'No, don't apologise. I got carried away dancing. I'm sorry if I misled you.' She turned away and as she searched for her own key heard his door slam.

He had every right to be angry, poor bugger. Another forgotten phrase from her teenage years came back to her. Cockteaser. She had been a real cockteaser and lucky to get away with it. If she had got away with it.

Breakfast confirmed she had. They had both clearly resolved to behave as if nothing unusual had happened, as if they had eaten their customary meal and retired separately to make phone calls or watch TV.

But Judy had rekindled something last night, if not what she intended. While talking to another batch of aspirant marketeers – serious, studious, boring – she suddenly wondered why she was returning to London this evening. Perhaps she should stay here and really wander down memory lane. At lunchtime she told David that she would get the train back. He looked disturbed.

'It's nothing to do with you,' she said gently. 'I just want to look up my old tutor, that's all, now we've finished work.'

She booked back into the hotel, changed and went for a long walk up the hill to her old college. She stood in its gardens and watched the windows lighting up as students returned from supper. In some, small groups were obviously settling down for coffee, in others lone figures hunched over desks. The occasional flimsy curtain was pulled across to conceal the occupant's preparations for a night out.

A few of the people wandering back from the main block looked at her quizzically. She realised that she had been idly imagining that she looked like, almost that she was, another student, whereas she was fifty per cent older than these girls. What they probably saw was a middle-aged woman, possibly an unknown tutor, hanging about the rose bushes for no good reason on a cold March evening.

She hurried back to the centre of town and the warmth of the snug of the Saracen's Head. It was already nearly full. She sat at the last empty table and rang for service. It had been a mistake to stay on. All she had achieved was to remind herself how old she was, how much of her life had already passed.

'Is anybody sitting here?' He was tall and thin and dark and very young. He wore jeans and a leather jacket but the haircut would not have disgraced a merchant banker. She shook her head, thinking of unruly undergraduate haircuts of her own period. 'I'd have thought you'd have gone by now.'

She looked up, startled.

'We must all look alike to you. You interviewed me yesterday.'

'I'm sorry. It must be like the policemen getting younger.' He looked puzzled. 'I'm feeling my age this evening.'

'Can I get you another drink? I promise I don't want to discuss my job prospects. I've already decided that Pasco is not for me.'

She felt relieved and riled at the same time. 'I'm off duty so I won't ask you why not.'

'Oh.' Finally he was nonplussed. 'Would you like a drink then?'

'I would, but I can still remember how small grants are. Let me buy you one. Ring the bell.' She felt completely in control and it was a good feeling.

He was waiting for friends – well, she had hardly expected him to be on his own on a Friday night – but when they arrived she was effortlessly absorbed into the loose circle that formed at her table, and unlike her own friends none of them were ostentatiously coupled. Hours passed without her noticing; the conversation was amusing and not only for the naïvety that lurked beneath a veneer of sophistication. It was refreshing to escape any reference to mortgages or babies. When the group began the slow rousing that precedes departure she was sorry.

'Why don't you come?' Ian asked. 'Unless you've got something better to do.'

She laughed as she realised that he really thought she might have.

'It's nothing special,' someone else chipped in, touchingly concerned that her expectations should not be too high. 'Just, you know, a few tapes. Bring a bottle.'

'Are you sure they won't mind?' she asked, and then realised what a stupid question it was.

'They won't even know,' one of the boys said.

'They could hardly miss you,' Ian said. He seemed to view her as an embodiment of metropolitan glamour, which, as she was wearing Levis and a guernsey, made no sense. She sometimes forgot the effect of impeccable make-up and her piled and pleated hair.

The party was in a draughty and unkempt house along the street with the grubby, bare boards and echoing hallway that characterised student accommodation. The temperature rose along with the noise level and the partygoers' spirits. She was hot in her jumper but loath to expose her figure in the midst of wraiths in black Doc Martens and Lycra bodies. She drank to cool herself down and at some stage passed the point where it mattered what anyone else thought. She dumped the guernsey and Ian, still the courtier, asked her to dance.

Perhaps, she thought, as they bobbed about in a crowded sitting-room, it would work with someone I don't know at all. No possible repercussions. Besides which he is quite good-looking. Gilded youth. Gild the lily. Her mind floated. Anticipation tingled, and then throbbed. She announced that she was leaving (your one and only chance, boy) and on cue Ian offered to walk her back to the hotel.

The night air struck with liberation not inhibition. Somewhere inside an exterior that she recognised as giggly and flirtatious her mind worked lucidly. She asked him in for coffee and strode him past the night porter. She sat him in her room with the kettle boiling and retraced her steps to the ladies' cloakroom on the ground floor. She bought, after a struggle with the dispenser, a packet of condoms. She poured them both cognacs from the minibar in the fridge.

When the moment seemed right she kissed him. He must

have expected it but she sensed an uncertainty. With her confidence at full throttle she thought it best to clear that up. 'I'd like you to stay.'

'I'd like to, too,' he said, a touch gruffly.

'Good,' she said and pulled him down on to the bed. After a bit she said, 'I'm going to take your clothes off and then you can undress me.' She took her time, hoping that the gradual exposure of his body would raise her libido. It did. Getting the message he proceeded with caution, the caresses making up for the fumbling of tense fingers with buttons and catches. Naked, she reached for her handbag and got out a condom. As she rolled it on, long out of practice, worried that it must be painful, banishing the mental picture of a bank robber, features squashed beneath his stocking, Ian gave a little grunt which should have warned her but didn't. As he attempted to enter her he came with a groan, whether of ecstasy or shame or simply irritation she could not tell.

The aftermath was horrid. Him in and out of the bath-room, both of them apologising, both trying to preserve some shreds of dignity. She pulled on her wrap while he dressed but was all too aware of her discarded underwear sprawled undecorously over the carpet.

The bluff had been called on the euphemism 'stay'. After he had gone she wondered whether he would have trouble getting past the porter, but he didn't come back so she presumed he must have managed somehow. Picking up her clothes she nearly overbalanced and realised how drunk she was. A pity he had not been more inebriated; they might have achieved a satisfactory conclusion.

She splashed cold water over her face. Where there had been goosebumps of desire her skin now crawled. Already she felt a kind of disgust and knew she would feel far worse in the morning when she had sobered up. Two lucky escapes. She must have been mad, but at least someone up there had recognised it as an aberration and let her off with a warning. There was to be no salvation through sex.

9

Games Without Frontiers

'The problem is,' Vanessa said, 'choosing a menu that doesn't mean skulking in the kitchen while your guests amuse themselves – or don't amuse themselves – without resorting to avocado prawns.'

'I didn't realise you were the sort of woman who got nervous about dinner parties,' said Judy. 'Anyway I thought amusing your guests was my and Mikey's job.'

'I've never had a works dinner before. It's suddenly become ridiculously important for it to go without a hitch.' She laughed. 'You don't have to entertain anybody. You've been invited to make up the numbers and look decorative. Want a sherry? I've got fino, or a dark-brown one – oloroso I think it's called – in case Penny's a medium-sweet person.'

'Neither, thank you. You can start offering me sherry when you've moved to West Bridgford. Until then I'll have a gin and tonic.'

Paradoxically the fact that Vanessa was so strung up about this evening was going to make it easier to cope with, Judy thought. More an assignment than an occasion where your host was watching you to make sure you were enjoying yourself. Even at the best of times pleasure tends to wilt under nervous scrutiny; it was comforting to know that for once she would be last on Vanessa's list of worries.

'When's Mikey coming?' she asked, when Vanessa returned to the kitchen with their drinks.

'He's supposed to be here now. But I guess he's waiting until he's certain someone else will definitely have arrived.'

'Why?'

'Avoiding the continuation of a conversation we had on Thursday.'

Judy waited.

'About the fact that we seem to be stuck up a creek without a paddle.'

'Will he be OK tonight, do you think?'

'Oh, he'll be fine. Perfectly well-behaved. He could be one of those walkers that escort women like presidents' wives to concerts and parties while their husbands are away saving the world or whatever. That's the trouble. He acts like a social stand-in, which would be fine if you had an original but I don't. I thought he was going to be it, not first reserve.'

The doorbell rang. It was Mikey. He kissed them both delicately on the cheek.

'You two go and disport yourselves on the sofa,' said Vanessa, 'while I get the swordfish out of its marinade. And try not to mess the place up.'

When there are only six people at a dinner-table they can sometimes remain in one conversation for most of the evening, too few in number and too close to each other to fragment. At larger gatherings occasional snippets of more interesting discussions are at the furthest reach of earshot, whereas around a domestic dining-table they can be ruinously, magnetically obtrusive, drawing you inexorably back to the mainstream.

Judy therefore expected the evening to consist chiefly of anecdotal set-pieces – and for some while this was the case, with the contestants politely waiting their turn to contribute a finely-honed story about the subject in hand. Then Mikey, performing well and sensing that Penny was withdrawing from the field of battle, took advantage of the lull provided by the collecting of plates to engage her in a consideration of the merits of private schooling. Peter and Vanessa were quickly submerged in the changing face of supermarket wine-labelling, which left Judy and Max, sitting to her left, to their own devices.

He was a pen-and-ink drawing of a man – strikingly handsome but physically insubstantial, all fluid lines and fastidious movement. His conversation fluttered in banners, seemingly knowledgeable on any subject but his opinions were cloaked in sufficient jest to signal that they should not be taken seriously.

'Vanessa tells me you have a cat,' he said.

'Yes.'

'Is he old and wise, or young and skittish?'

'Young but not so skittish. Only when he forgets himself. He's very moody.'

'Sulky but silky then. Is he nursing any particular grievance?'

'He's been neutered.'

'Ah well. I expect that's it. They say you can't miss what you've never had but I think cats know they've been deprived of something. Still, a dignified if disgruntled eunuch seems far more appropriate for your harem than some buccaneering old tom creating nocturnal havoc around the dustbins. You probably don't have dustbins in any case. Or shouldn't. Mysterious beauty and waste disposal don't go hand in glove.'

The words suddenly conjured up for him the image of her

jade evening gloves the first time they had met at the Grosvenor House.

Judy pictured herself in Marigolds and blushed at the compliment. 'Oh, I've got a dustbin. Have you got a cat?'

'No, but if I had an animal then a cat it would be. At least you can delude yourself that they're intelligent and discriminating. Unlike the average slavering dog.' He took a sip from his glass. 'I'm not really a man for pets. Just pet hates, and pet loves.'

'And what are they?'

'The hates or the loves?'

'The loves. You seem to be interested in just about everything cultural from acid house to expressionism, but I suppose that's just the job?'

He laughed. 'You mean the ability to steal ideas from anywhere.'

'No, not steal. Adapt. Use. I'm the last person to mind. Not that shampoo advertising is very adventurous.'

'There's a place for adventure, but the haircare business doesn't seem to be it. Could be, should be maybe, but that's another topic for another time, I think. No, it's not just the job that's made me inquisitive – or rather, I'm in the job because I'm a natural dabbler. But mostly with me the tip of the iceberg's all there is. All surface flash and nothing beneath the waterline. Passing enthusiasms.'

'There must be some that have stuck. Tell me one.'

'Wagner. Richard not Robert.'

'A pity. At least I know something about Robert.'

'What?'

'Pronounced wag not vaag. Minor American film actor. TV detective. Married his wife twice. She drowned.'

'I bet you know at least as much about Richard.'

'I bet I don't.'

'Try.'

'Long operas featuring fat ladies in Viking helmets.'

'Anything else?'

'Wasn't he a Nazi?'

'Too early. But he was anti-Semitic. Anything else?'

'Um . . . no, that's it.'

'Never heard any then?'

'Not that I know of.'

'You should. Given the right tune fat ladies are surprisingly moving, with or without armour.'

'Do you think it went well?' Vanessa asked Mikey.

'Of course it did. You're just fishing for compliments and everybody's already said at least once how marvellous the walnut and mushroom soup was, how subtle the goat's cheese dressing on the spinach salad, how wicked the stem ginger *bavarois*, how divinely you hand-rolled your own after-eight mints, how you are, in short, the living embodiment of—'

Vanessa laughed. 'Belt up. You know if it's your own do you only register odd bits and even if they're good you're afraid you might have missed great chunks of people being bored and looking at their watches or insulting each other.'

'Well, we were bored, of course,' said Judy, 'but that's only because we know you so well. I'm sure your new friends were most impressed.'

'Yes, you positively terrified poor old Penny with your handsome son and your *cordon bleu* and your career, and there's her like the school matron in her Laura Ashley smock.'

'That dress was not Laura Ashley,' said Vanessa, mindful of Judy's predilection for the label. 'It just happened to be rather flowery. Now stop winding me up.'

'Stop is what I must do,' said Mikey, 'or rather, stop talking and go home.'

The mood was completely broken. Judy had been about to suggest that it was time she made a move. Instead she said, 'I've forgotten exactly where in Scotland you're going,' and his explanation, which she remembered quite clearly from dinner, covered the awkwardness of Vanessa getting his coat.

The two of them went into the hall and Judy heard the soft mumble of goodbyes. They did not take very long.

'Another coffee,' Vanessa said somewhat brusquely from the kitchen and Judy did not have the heart to decline. Realising that she could not leave for some time she accepted a Drambuie to go with it.

'I didn't really frighten Penny, did I?' Vanessa asked.

'No, but I think she's been a career mother for too long. She's frightened of not having anything to talk about to women like you and me. She doesn't realise that I think bringing up four children is far more daunting than holding down a job in marketing.'

'You don't really think that, do you?'

'Yes. I don't know. That's not the point. It is an achievement and it's not directly comparable with my achievement. She has marriage and kids, I have a job and a kitten. Separate. But you threaten that by muscling in on her territory. You manage to combine the career with having a child and what's more bringing him up without the help of a husband. You and she are comparable and what you've done completely undermines the scale of her achievement.'

'Blimey. I didn't realise she was competitive.'

'She is but the game's about how well the offspring are getting on. You compounded your villainy by not playing that game when she asked you about Josh.'

'What do you mean?'

'When she was comparing him with James and William at the same age. You were completely offhand.'

'It's not polite to boast.'

'That's as may be but you were implying she was small-minded to care. That's not playing the game.'

'Oh God, I didn't even notice a game had started.'

'For a smart woman you're very unobservant. Worse still—'

'Please, please . . .'

'Worse still, Penny is one of those women who went from being a sweet young girl to being a middle-aged mumsy about the time that the head of her firstborn engaged.'

'She's quite pretty.'

'I know, but she's not slim and svelte and powerful and dangerous like you in your slinky black dress. You look less like someone who's had a baby than me . . . actually you're enough to threaten anyone.'

'I'm not.'

'Miss sickeningly perfect.'

'Shut up. So have I blown it with Penny completely? Could it be any worse?'

'Well, don't have an affair with her husband, that's all.' She sniggered. 'Uurgh, can you imagine it?'

'He's very good with clients.'

'He may be but I don't fancy his bedside manner. He's so squeaky clean. She probably checks that he's washed behind his ears before she lets him in.'

'Matron, can we do it now? Only if you drink up your syrup of figs.' Vanessa took a gulp at her coffee. 'I'm not perfect anyway. Otherwise I wouldn't be stuck in this rut with Mikey. Perhaps you could turn the beam of your psychological insight on to that problem.'

'I don't think I'm qualified to act as an agony aunt.'

'Have you been in love?'

'What, ever?' Judy could feel the familiar churning of the tear ducts. If they didn't change the subject ... but she couldn't think how to.

'Don't count adolescence. I mean recently.'

A pause. 'Yes.' The tears welled, right on cue. She felt for a handkerchief. 'I'm sorry.'

Vanessa brandished a box of tissues. 'No, I'm sorry. Do you want to talk about it?'

'Not really.' She blew her nose.

'I know I'm good-looking,' Judy said, as Vanessa unobtrusively topped up her glass. 'People have said it for as long as I can remember, and I somehow thought that true love would be easy to find, but it wasn't.'

'They've always been queuing up.'

'I know but I think my type of looks attract the wrong men.'

'What do you mean? If my memory serves me correctly all your suitors were handsome.'

'They'd have had to be that to ask, according to the surveys.'

'And what surveys are these? Ones personally conducted for you by Gallup?'

'No. You know, those that say people tend to look for a partner about as good-looking as they are themselves. They don't play out of their league. So I got these handsome lads asking me out but they always seemed to expect something I'm not.'

'Like what?'

'Well, I think they equate being blonde and pretty and big-titted with being meek and mild and subservient and stupid.'

'Perhaps other women do, too,' said Vanessa. 'It's the only consolation we've got. Sorry. So you see looks as the sole determinant of luck in love, then? If you don't conform to type you've got no chance.'

'Not really. It just seems to have been like that for me.'

'Are you sure your ideals aren't too high?'

'Probably. Still, no matter now. I've decided I'm wedded to my work. That's it.'

'Never again?'

'Well, I'm not looking. Or holding my breath.'

'Definitely no children then.'

'No, I couldn't do what you've done. Couldn't cope.' She smiled. 'Must tell Penny. That will make her feel better. God, look at the time. And all we've done is talk about me, or rather all you've done is interview me.'

'Stay. You can't drive now anyway. Have another.'

'OK,' Judy said. It was a relief not to have to go home. 'So what about you and Mikey?'

Vanessa made some commotion with bottles and glasses. 'Once I'd had Josh,' she eventually began, 'all my love went into him. I didn't really think about . . . about his dad at all. If Josh has, or had, a surrogate father then it's Becky. It was at least a year before I even started . . . noticing men again and even then I never thought about doing anything practical. Just liked seeing the occasional bum in the gym. I don't think I'd resigned myself to being a spinster but I certainly had no ambition to fuck.'

Vanessa's forthright use of the 'F word' always made Judy wince.

'Then I met Mikey. And soon I felt that old irrational stirring of the hormones. To me that means "in love". I still didn't do what I would have done before Josh; I waited and checked out that the two of them got on, and they did, and even though my body said yes I said no, not without an Aids certificate. I know that sounds like a shitty thing to do but I was paranoid for Josh in case I caught the virus—'

'No, it doesn't sound shitty,' said Judy but her mind was on Sophie's answerphone message and its reference to Aids. She had never understood it and assumed it must have been prompted by a TV programme or article that Sophie had seen that evening. She made no connection now with what Vanessa was saying.

'—wish I hadn't been so stupid. If we'd been to bed together before Sophie died it might not have been such a big issue but now it seems like it's sacrilegious for him.'

'Don't say that. You did the right thing to wait. So he still thinks it's his fault?'

'Yes.'

'Because he left her for you?'

'More or less.'

'It's not true.'

'I know that, you know that, but how can we convince him? We can't prove it.'

'No,' said Judy. But she could. 'Perhaps he just needs a bit more time to get over it.'

'I don't think so. We're for ever tainted by it. And the thing is, I don't think I can have him around as a kind of sociable capon. It would be a reminder of what might, no, what should have been.' Vanessa took another slug at her cognac.

'There's something I ought to tell you,' Judy said carefully. 'Sophie was in love with somebody else when she died.'

'Who?'

Judy swallowed some Drambuie to gain time. She hadn't thought this through but she had to make an attempt. As long as she didn't cry.

Luckily Vanessa changed tack, adding, 'I mean, how do you know?'

'She told me.'

'When?'

'She rang me Christmas night. She was very happy. She said she was in love.' She searched for a form of words that would not be an outright lie, not 'That's all I know' ... 'I can't tell you any more.'

'You've never said before.'

'No ... I haven't told anybody. My memory's only just sorting itself out.'

That didn't sound very convincing, even to her. Please, she thought, let this stop soon.

'Well, I'll tell him when I have it out with him. It might, should ease his conscience. I wonder who it was? It must have blown up very quickly.'

There was no meeting fixed for 2 April so when Hugo sent for Judy she assumed it must be something to do with Doublehead. She had circulated her Stage Three report the previous Friday. It was unlike him to have read it over the weekend but it was a nice piece of work and as its findings were so encouraging perhaps he was going to bring the presentation forward to this month's board meeting. She picked up a copy and trotted down the corridor.

It was only nine fifteen but Trish, Hugo's secretary, had, as always, laid out a plate of assorted biscuits to accompany the coffee.

'Sit down, sit down,' Hugo indicated the low leather suite by the window. She perched on an armchair, aware that the angle and lack of support afforded by these seats encouraged an undignified posture. If there were just the two of them Hugo usually sprawled across the sofa but today as if in solidarity he also sat upright.

She waited for him to begin, but he busied himself with their cups and saucers.

'Do you agree with my conclusions?'

'About?' He offered her the biscuits.

She shook her head. Obviously not Doublehead then. 'I thought you might have read my report.'

'No, no. Looking forward to it, of course. Must be good news if you're keen to discuss it.' He popped a pink wafer into his mouth.

'Is there a problem on Erotin?' She ought to play him at his own waiting game but they didn't usually fence like this and she was anxious to get on.

'No, not as far as I know. Coming to the end of its cycle, of course, so it will probably need more advertising support next year . . .'

What on earth was he going on about? She knew all this – even the office junior knew it.

'Sorry, Hugo, but I've got a briefing, so—'

'Yes, get to the point. I am retiring.'

Perhaps he was contracting Alzheimer's or an early dose of senile dementia or something.

'I know. In October.'

'No, at the end of June.'

'But that's only three months,' she said stupidly.

'Yes,' he said. 'But it doesn't do to announce these things too far in advance, even to your right-hand man. No point in having a lame duck director.'

'But I won't have got board agreement to launch Doublehead.'

'No, but that won't be affected.'

Suspicions started to rush in on her.

'It would make a difference to my CV . . . your job hasn't been advertised, not anywhere that I've seen.'

'No. The appointment was made by headhunters.'

Appointment? 'Appointment?'

'Klaus Weerman is replacing me. He's done amazing things with Protocol in the States.'

'Yes, I know who he is.'

'I want to arrange a meeting for the two of you, perhaps dinner.'

She had to get out before she exploded. 'I'm sorry, I haven't got my diary. I'll get back to you after my meeting . . .' She forced herself to add, 'If that's all right with you?'

'Of course, of course.' He seemed anxious to assist her departure.

An hour later when she felt less in danger of appearing hysterical she rang Trish and requested another meeting with Hugo that morning.

'He's a bit tied up, Judy.'

'If he's there can you tell him it's absolutely essential?'

There was a long pause. 'Will quarter to one suit?'

Just before lunch, the implication being no more than fifteen minutes. Still, she didn't need long. 'Fine.'

This time Hugo had stayed at his desk, either as an assertion of authority or a means of protection.

'Something come up at the briefing?'

'No.' She concentrated. 'Your decision to retire early has deprived me of the chance to succeed you. You must have known that seeing Doublehead through would have improved my reputation and if you'd waited until the statutory time, which is only another seven months—'

'Four until my notice period – August to October—'

'OK, four then.' She forged on. 'I would have been ready anyway and they couldn't have dismissed me as a lightweight; I would have been the obvious choice.'

Hugo splayed his hands as if to demur but she ignored him.

'Sometimes people have to take early retirement for ill health or whatever and if that had happened and spoilt my chances, then I would have been upset but understood. But if that happens it's sudden, and this obviously wasn't sudden. It was planned. It was planned so carefully that the first I hear of it the new man's already appointed. It's a *fait accompli* and I can't see it as anything other than a deliberate betrayal.' For the first time her voice wobbled but she controlled it. 'After the years I've worked for you, Hugo, I just want to know why.'

She looked at him. He gazed back, furled and unfurled his hands a couple of times.

'I've seen too much frustrated ambition to be angry, Judy, but I am sorry that you should imagine I would stitch you up, as I think the expression has it. You are right – I've known for some time that I would go in June and I haven't told anybody. But I have never said that I would stay until October. I can only imagine that you worked that out for yourself on the basis that I would stay until statutory retirement. But if you'd consulted Personnel you would have found out that my forty years' service are up in June so I gain nothing in pension by staying any longer. I'm looking forward to spending a whole summer on the yacht.

'Now you can blame me, but the extra time you would have gained by my staying on would not have affected your hopes of being appointed director in my stead.'

'So you're saying mine is a hopeless case.'

'Don't be melodramatic, Judy. You've done a good job for me, and despite the odd hiccup, as in January this year, I don't think there are any doubts about your stability as well as your commitment.'

The very fact that he mentioned it confirmed what she had known – that her depression after Sophie's death would count against her.

'But you're very young for a full directorship,' Hugo continued, 'and in any case you've got your hands full with this potential product launch. I should have thought you would have been satisfied with that for the moment.'

'How old is Weerman?'

'Weerman? Forty-two or forty-three, I think.'

'So this post may well not come up again for another eighteen years. By which time I'll be—'

'Oh, come along, Judy, a lady never reveals her age. Besides it's very unlikely that he'll stay that long, an ambitious man like him.'

'But they wouldn't have appointed him without an assurance of what – five years at least?'

'Yes, I concede that.'

'By which time I'll have been deputy for nearly nine years.'

'Yes, I suppose you—'

'And we all know what the career prospects of long-term deputies are. Nil.'

'It's not impossible for the bridesmaid to become the bride.'

She could tell that he regretted that particular simile as soon as he had used it.

'Hugo, be frank. To progress I am going to have to find another job.'

He nodded. 'I hope you'll see Doublehead to its conclusion—'

Which, she thought, will conveniently allow me to nursemaid Weerman through his acclimatisation.

'—and then apply to Personnel for another posting within the group. It shouldn't take too long, particularly if you're prepared to go overseas, and as you have no ties, that's worth considering.'

'Funnily enough,' she said, looking for something to say that would terminate this interview on a lighter note, now that there was nothing but a dull inevitability about it. 'Funnily enough Personnel waved a completely unsolicited job at me only last year—' He was blushing. Realisation dawned. 'You knew about that, didn't you?'

His expression was almost tender. 'I proposed it. I shouldn't tell you, couldn't have told you then—'

'But?'

'I wanted to spare you the disappointment of not taking over here.'

It was that clear-cut then.

'Thank you. I was too dense to see it.'

'Too optimistic, perhaps. But don't lose your optimism.'

'Hugo, will Pasco ever make a woman a director, in any of the companies?'

'They are an equal opportunities employer.'

'Hugo.'

'There's always a first time.' She remained silent, provoking. 'Who knows, if you stick at it it might be you . . . It must happen—'

'Eventually. I see.'

'What are you doing for lunch? I think we've been closeted here long enough, don't you?'

'Too busy, I'm afraid.' He seemed unsurprised at the snub. 'Thanks for your time.'

She stood and extended her hand. He shook it gravely. She left.

Outside she could think of nothing, absolutely nothing, that she wanted to do. Just when you thought you had some pattern, some plan sorted out . . .

* * *

Becky was happy.

Travelling with the circus gave her the same perspective on towns as might be experienced briefly on a train journey. Because they were almost always camped on the periphery, they gazed into what amounted to the back yard of a place, absorbed into its gut rather than its heart.

'Surely you mean arsehole,' Fassbinder said, when in a fanciful moment she had attempted to explain this to him. 'That's the back door of my system.'

From Paris they had headed north to Brussels and Antwerp before embarking on a trek south that would bring them to Marseilles and Nice for the height of summer.

They had played Lille, Rouen and Orleans before driving west to Rennes where they were established on a site between an enormous Renault dealer and a hypermarket. Within a year a furniture store was destined to open here but for the moment they looked out on to green fields.

Becky had spent a very pleasant day wandering the broad boulevards of the city itself, replenishing in bars and cafés the posters that had either never gone up when sent on from Orleans or subsequently disappeared beneath later contestants for the space.

Rennes was a university town as well as the Breton capital, and its evening promenaders in the first warm spell of the year exuded chic with an intellectual edge. Raspail was banking on large audiences here for a troupe with an anarchistic reputation.

Dismissing the image of the half-eaten cassoulet in a pot on their cooker and the paper bags containing goodies from her early shopping spree at the hypermarket, she suggested to Dermot that they should eat in one of the restaurants clustered in the cobbled squares behind the Hôtel de Ville. This would be their only chance, for tomorrow they were rehearsing and another stint of performances began on Wednesday.

As always he agreed with her.

She ordered snails and *coq au vin*. 'Do you know why?'

'Why snails? Not really, they're best in Burgundy, or so Stephane assures me.'

'No, the other.'

'No.'

'It's our anniversary dinner.' He raised an eyebrow. 'Seven months. Exactly. From the day you bought my car.'

'Seven is not a conventional celebration period, is it? And why *coq au vin*?'

'Because that's what we had the night you first ex-perienced my cooking—' she looked down, 'and me, which, in case you were wondering, was six months on Saturday. But we couldn't have gone out then, we had an audience.'

'I should have guessed there would be some tortuous logic behind it.'

He raised his glass and touched hers. It chimed. Becky knew better than to try and coax any description of his feelings from him.

If she had one reservation about them it was that she felt no closer to Dermot now than when she first joined him in France. She had heard the bare bones of his life story back in Clapham and he had not elaborated on that. He was always prepared to speculate about the wider world but otherwise entirely reactive in conversation. He never offered anything of himself and drawing him out on any personal subject was harder than prising apart the halves of a bad mussel.

He was affectionate, attentive and amusing but some-how remote. She had thought that the distance might be lessened by her increasing involvement in the councils of the Cirque – she had been co-opted on to the executive committee, which they now attended together – but if anything that had made him less inclined to discuss its workings.

She had been responsible for several additions or adaptations to the show since the success of the new trapeze routine, but none involving Dermot more than tangen-tially. Perhaps they could develop a routine together.

He was ordering another carafe of wine. That one had gone quickly.

'What's going on in your head?' he said.

That's rich, she thought. Imagine the response if I asked you that. She decided to follow his tactics: when asked a personal question, don't only sidestep it but use it to start an entirely different ball rolling.

'I was wondering about escapology,' she said. 'Only on a small scale, not to Houdini standards. If it was easy to learn how to slip some knots there's a thing you could do with the jugglers and those flaming clubs and someone suspended from a rope.'

'And who had you in mind for this?'

'Maybe Joach. I was just remembering Richard Harris in *A Man Called Horse*. Did you ever see it?'

Dermot shook his head. A great deal of the inspiration for the look and the context of the Apocalypse show came from genre movies, of which Stephane and Fassbinder were both avid fans. Becky, who had recognised the references to *Mad Max*, *Spartacus* and the rest peppering the show had brought a new fund of ideas to their ongoing party and the three of them spent many afternoons swapping remembered scenes.

'However,' he added, 'I can do it. I'll show you when we get back.'

They found Straker sitting on the step of their caravan, the headphones of the Walkman across his bald cranium and dark glasses transforming him into an alien creature, half-lit by the flicker of Calor gas lamps.

'There you are,' he shouted, as those under headphones invariably do in an effort to hear themselves clearly. 'I've got something good on the music for this opening to the second half.'

'Not now, Straker,' said Dermot affably.

Becky, resting comfortably against his shoulder, was glad. He must have some sense of occasion.

'First thing then?'

They agreed and Straker dematerialised.

Inside Becky made some coffee. 'OK,' she said. 'Demonstrate.'

Dermot looked for some rope but couldn't find any. 'I'll show you tomorrow,' he said.

'Won't it work with a scarf? You've got plenty of those.'

He rolled two long bandannas into tubes and used the first deftly to bind his ankles together. 'You'll have to do my wrists,' he said. He held them out and she followed his instructions, 'Left over right ... loop ... pull tight ... convinced I'm tightly tied?'

She nodded, smiling. 'I never had you down as a member of the Magic Circle.'

'OK,' he said and let himself fall on to the bed. She had expected him to concentrate on freeing his hands and use them to loosen the bonds about his feet, but he bucked and writhed in a frenzy of activity and within half a minute was upright having wriggled out of both apparently simultaneously.

She was entranced. 'Again.' This time she concentrated on the construction of the knots, and timed him. 'Twenty-seven seconds. Beat it.'

He did, clocking twenty-four and then twenty-three.

'I think it's easier than you make it look.'

'You try then.'

He pulled the scarf so tight on her wrists that she could hardly flex them. 'OK?'

'I'm sure I didn't do yours so hard.'

'Making excuses already,' he said, finishing off her ankles. 'I've given you more leeway there. Off you go.'

After a minute of rolling back and forth all she had succeeded in doing was make herself red in the face and very hot under the collar.

'Not so easy after all,' he said, watching speculatively from the end of the bed.

'No.' She was about to add 'You'd better untie me then' but something about his expression changed her mind.

She lifted herself on her linked arms. 'Well then,' she said coquettishly. 'I seem to be completely at your mercy.'

Afterwards, wrapped in his arms, her back curled against his stomach, she felt not only sated but triumphant. His lovemaking had always been subject to the same rigorous control that he applied to everything from bike riding to laundering. Sometimes she had desperately wanted to pull him into her but had never risked breaking his delicate rhythm. But tonight there had been no such restraint on his part. Inadvertently she had stumbled on a key that unwound his protective skin.

She thought she might use his vulnerability to draw them closer still. 'Dermot?'

'Yes?'

'As we've got so much space here, behind the Renault place—'

'Yes?'

'Will you teach me to ride the bike?'

'Did you not have one as a girl, stabilisers and all?'

'Not the pushbike, the Kawasaki. Will you?'

It was a chilly afternoon but Vanessa preferred wearing her coat and keeping the window open to enduring the smell of wet paint which lay throughout the building as gas must have lain in the trenches. Metaphors of war abounded during this, their first month of trading. Or not trading.

They had a company (and certificates to prove it), they had premises (in the process of decoration), they even had staff (if that was the correct term for Debbie, their receptionist and general factotum, and Nasil, the bookkeeper on secondment from their accountants). What they did not as yet have was any business.

It was nearly five weeks since, on the last Friday in March, she, Max and Peter had delivered their letters of resignation from Breughel Thomas to the managing director's office.

'What now?' Vanessa had asked as they waited for the lift on the fifth floor.

'He'll read them,' said Peter. 'Even Vernon can't fail to spot this as a conspiracy. Send for our contracts to see what leverage he's got, and then send for us.'

'Together?'

'One at a time, I should think. Let's keep each other posted.' She returned to her office and tried to read the paper. Max rang. 'Peter's on his way up.' The clock ticked on.

Even though she was expecting it the electronic burble made her jump.

'Ask not for whom the bell tolls, it tolls for me,' said Max.

'Is Peter out then?'

'Don't know. Haven't heard. Don't forget to tuck a book down your knickers – it's a corporal offence, going into competition.'

The next time the phone rang she snatched it up. 'Yes?'

'Vanessa, it's Billy.'

'Oh. What is it?' she asked, although she had already remembered that she had arranged a creative meeting on the Krunch account.

'Graham and I are in Conference 1 with all the artwork and stuff but we've lost Max. We thought he might be with you.'

'No. Er . . . I think he's up on the fifth.'

'Oh. Well, are you coming anyway?'

This was difficult. 'I'm just waiting for a call, Billy.'

'Oh. There's this rumour going round that Peter Bennett's been sacked or something. Have you heard?'

She could almost smell the copywriter's curiosity. 'Well . . . not sacked.'

'Jumping ship then?'

'Well—'

'Bloody hell, is that what old Max is doing, too?'

'You'll just have to—'

'Jesus, it is true.'

She could hear Graham in the background saying, 'What, what?'

'Shut up, in a minute. Vanessa, how do you know?'

'Billy, I've got to go. I'm waiting for a call.' As she put down the receiver she could hear him hooting, 'And her. The whole bloody place is baling out.'

And they were out by lunchtime. Peter, rightly suspected of being the prime mover, was not even allowed back to his office unaccompanied although, as he pointed out, had he wanted any of the information it contained he would already have taken it. Max had been left alone but with the injunction to vacate the premises by midday – his many possessions would be sent on. This resulted in an unseemly row about whether the statuettes commemorating his successes at Cannes and elsewhere belonged to him or Breughel Thomas.

Vanessa had been kept waiting most of the morning and then subjected to a syrupy attempt to retain her. When this had failed it was followed by a harangue about the making of big mistakes. Then she was instructed to clear her desk immediately, and walked back to her office amid a babble of speculation and curious glances.

They celebrated in a restaurant a taxi ride away ('Any closer and we'll be surrounded by BTers wanting the inside story'), where the head waiter concealed his irritation at the number of plastic carriers and outsize folders they had with them.

Vanessa was secretly chuffed that such efforts had been made to dissuade her, very much the junior escapologist, but when she tried to mention it in the guise of a dismissive aside Peter said, 'Damage limitation. They know that you wouldn't be doing it without us and they can pinpoint the business that might be going with you. I don't suppose they're so bothered about Dolphin but Gateshead have a sizeable spend, and a high creative profile. If they could stick a spanner in the works for us there they would. Did they offer you much extra to stay?'

'Ten. And a bigger car.'

'Max?'

'Fifty and some share options.'

That puts me in my place, thought Vanessa. 'What about you, Peter?'

'Oh, nothing for me. I'm a leper as far as they're concerned. I could tell how much they hated insisting that I fulfil my notice period by staying at home on full pay. Writing the cheques will choke them but it's the only way they've got of buggering up our launch – delaying it anyway – and buying themselves some more time.'

'To shore up the client base against our wicked depredations,' said Max. 'Another bottle of the Clicquot,' he instructed a passing waiter. 'And then I'll definitely start pulling my horns in,' he promised Peter.

The upshot of their legal separation from their former employers was that both Peter and Max were held to three months' paid notice but Vanessa to only one. Effectively this meant that in the first month, although they could announce the existence of their new agency to the trade press, it had to be given an official launch date of 1 July. Until that date the only work that Bennett and Nicolson could be seen to be doing was sorting out their new offices. Which is why they were currently spending money at a frightening rate and not making any.

Even Vanessa's client contacts had to be discreet and her visit to Gateshead was conducted in a state of perpetual fear that she might bump into an erstwhile colleague on the East Coast mainline.

Like their other putative clients Gateshead's boss, George Doherty, had not yet informed Breughel Thomas that he would no longer be requiring their services and although he had promised Vanessa and Max his allegiance every phone call provoked a *frisson* of fear in case it heralded a change of heart.

Today's was on a surprising subject.

'I've been thinking about appointing a marketing coordinator.'

Previously Doherty had acted as de facto head of marketing with individual product managers reporting to him directly, so this train of thought was alarming. A new marketing chief very often followed the dictum about new brooms and swept old suppliers, including the advertising agency, clean away.

Where would this leave them, not an old supplier, not even appointed but still the creature of the *ancien régime*? Down a crack in the floorboards?

'And I was thinking about the lady you were telling me about. Judy Hackford.'

'Yes?'

'Was that her name?'

Trust him to call her bluff.

'Hucknell actually. But I knew who you meant.'

'If she's looking around, ask her to give me a ring.'

Before Judy arrived, having been summoned by a phone call, Vanessa had discussed the implications with Max but not Peter.

'He's got enough to worry about,' said Max, 'without thinking our most committed client has gone haywire.'

She felt obliged to explain Judy's circumstances – how after being told that the possibility of significant advancement at Pasco was zero she had resolved after ten years to move on and had started ringing recruitment consultancies – but Max hardly seemed to be listening.

'Why tell Gorgeous George?' he asked.

'Just something to talk about over lunch. You know, how sad, and how stupid of them to throw away someone so talented who would never leave them for domestic bliss. I wouldn't have mentioned it if he hadn't met her once – at that awards bash at the Grosvenor House.'

Max smiled faintly. 'The belle of the ball, saving your presence, of course. If he's set his heart on having somebody we couldn't do much better than an old friend of yours. She's hardly likely to sack you, is she?'

'No. Might put her in an awkward position though.'

'He must have considered that. If she wants to do it and he appoints her, two very big ifs, I would have thought, then we can see it as a very strong affirmation of his belief in us as well.'

Judy traced the etching of Vanessa's name across the shiny new brass plaque and announced herself on the entryphone. Debbie buzzed her in. She had to hold the door open with her foot while she rubbed away her smudged fingermarks.

They shared the street door with the other occupants of the building and the lobby housed only the staircase and lift, a set of padlocked mail boxes and a board giving names and floor numbers. She took the lift to the third, and emerged into chaos.

The landing was littered with builder's rubbish. Men in white overalls were fitting sliding glass doors to the entrance of their reception area. The glass was etched with the initials BNT in a vaguely oriental script. She picked her way past them and found the area beyond occupied by painters. The sofas were swathed in dust sheets and Debbie's marble-topped desk was dripped with gloss.

Max appeared, the epitome of elegant ease – soft leather jacket, soft cashmere sweater, soft suede loafers – and swivel-hipped his way between wet walls and cardboard boxes to her side.

'What do you think?' he asked, gesturing at the desk. 'Not too much like a fishmonger's slab? I'll show you through. Mind your coat.'

He ushered her into what was going to be their meeting-room. At one end of the long elm table the floor was taken up by the entrails of a video and hi-fi system awaiting installation. At the other, Vanessa was on the phone. She grinned and put her hand over the mouthpiece before whispering, 'Mother.'

Judy did not know whether she wanted to work for Gateshead, but she could see no reason for not ringing Doherty.

'He does realise my experience is in haircare and detergents, does he?' They assured her that he did. 'This isn't some sort of charitable act, is it?'

'Of course not,' Vanessa replied. 'You might have been dealt a rotten blow by those sexist bastards but you don't need charity where jobs are concerned. Loads of people will be crying out for you.'

'So, isn't George Doherty a sexist bastard?' Judy asked.

'The terms client and sexist bastard are not compatible when you're a struggling start-up agency,' Max said. 'Everyone's a knight in shining armour to the likes of us.'

'I don't think he's a chauvinist really,' Vanessa said. 'He's always treated me with respect.'

'Even if he does like your legs,' Max said. 'I must go. See you tomorrow, Van. Bye, Judy.'

'Don't forget Saturday,' Judy said.

'What are you two doing on Saturday?' Vanessa asked, too surprised to temper her curiosity.

'I invited Max to a day at the races laid on by my agency,' said Judy. 'I shouldn't have done really but it was in a fit of pique. It should put the cat among the pigeons.'

'Yes,' said Max, 'I think the sight of a director of a hungry rival escorting their client should put the wind up a few complacent Miller Markwick execs; spoil their enjoyment of the quails' eggs and salmon. Toodlepip.'

'What made you think of asking Max out of the blue like that?' Vanessa asked as soon as he was gone.

'Oh, it wasn't out of the blue. He took me to the opera last week.'

'How extraordinary.'

'The obvious question would be which opera and the answer is *Tristan and Isolde*. I don't think I'm that unsuitable a consort for a civilised musical evening and a late supper at the Ivy.'

'No, I just thought he would have had a friend for that sort of thing. I mean, I can understand him not wanting to bring him to a company dinner with Peter and Penny—'

'Perhaps he feels the same about Covent Garden.'

'So you think he's gay too?'

'I don't know. He didn't try to grope me in the cab.'

'I've always assumed he was. OK, I've got no evidence but you know he's so charmingly effete ... If he was a hairdresser you wouldn't doubt it for a moment.'

'As I'm not looking for a stud it really doesn't matter to me.'

'Perhaps he only likes rough trade who aren't suitable for taking anywhere. I do hope he's being careful.'

'Nessie. Control that fantasising.'

'Well, I'm fond of him. I suppose we're getting to that dangerous age for single women.'

'What dangerous age?'

'Where it would be so easy to become fag hags; no problems, no temptations, no disappointments.'

And from that Judy deduced that Vanessa and Mikey were no more.

Much as she would have liked to, Vanessa hadn't believed Judy's story about Sophie's mysterious and anonymous new lover – it was far too convenient and unspecific – but she appreciated her efforts to help.

She had invited Mikey to lunch, avoiding all the mantraps that he might see in dinner *à deux*, and they had talked only after a boisterous Josh had been persuaded to take his afternoon nap. The conversation was punctuated by the sound of his restless form testing the solidity of his mattress overhead.

Mikey thought that the tale of a new lover might be true; after all, in that last phone call Sophie had said she had been attacked on her way to the off-licence dolled up to the nines. But without shape or name it could not outweigh what he had heard with his own ears, that she hated him for dumping her for Vanessa. The fact that he had not done anything with Vanessa other than take her out to dinner before he and Sophie split, that he would probably have split with Sophie regardless; all these arguments seemed jesuitical now.

Sometimes he polished up his morality with the reflection that he still hadn't done anything with Vanessa, that in a sense he had remained faithful to Sophie, but it was a sham. He would have done if Vanessa had let him; he was after all fundamentally flawed.

He was sure that what he had done, and then said to Sophie on that fateful evening, had contributed to her death. He deserved to be punished for it, and the punishment was not that he deprived himself of Vanessa's body but that he no longer wanted it. He could not tell her this but he still enjoyed her company, in which he felt an innocence for the first time. Even last summer there had been an element of subterfuge about their situation.

Vanessa was not interested. She explained that she could not cope with a relationship whose boundaries were dictated by a dead person, and if they had lost the intensity that they had both shown in December then she was sorry but anything less was worse than nothing.

He understood.

He said goodbye to Josh who awkwardly came downstairs as he was leaving. It was all so clipped and overlaid with notions like duty and principle that he felt like some romantic Noël Coward character.

The novelty of this tranquillised Mikey until he reached home. Then, tidying the flat, he attempted to convince himself that it was a relief that it was over, all for the best. But, try as he might, he could not get out of his head that he had lost something very special. Not today – it was gone long before that, the day he heard of Sophie's death. But it was so unfair. Mikey well understood the movie notion that romance involved sorrow, tragedy even. But usually there was a happy ending and, if not, as in *Brief Encounter*, the lovers' self-denial had some purpose – to avoid hurting others. Whereas here the hurting of others had already happened, nobody else could be hurt but themselves. Futile. Hollywood would not have ordered it so.

He thought oblivion through drink might help and poured himself a large Scotch but it only seemed to concentrate his mind. What he needed was something to overpower his senses until the whisky had time to work, so he stuck the bottle in his coat pocket and went to the cinema where two hours of mindless violence bridged the gap.

When Mikey had gone the house was deadly quiet. Where was Josh, Vanessa thought, when she needed his clatter? Playing quietly with his ark.

She wanted to ring someone but realised the only someone she felt like talking to was uncontactable. Where was Becky when she needed her chatter? Hundreds of miles away in France.

Feeling claustrophobic, Vanessa persuaded an initially unwilling son that what he really wanted was not the ark but the park, and bundled him into the car, around the lake and, eventually, on to the swings.

She had, she realised as she pushed Josh to and fro, entertained very little hope that her ultimatum would turn the relationship around. To distract herself she searched for analogies. An oil tanker approaching rocks in a force ten gale would have stood more chance of survival. An advertising agency that told its client the unadulterated truth. A sheer stocking drawn over jaggedly-cut toe-nails. The last chocolate in the box, unless of course it was a tangerine cream. Fudge, on the other hand . . .

'Josh, shall we go home and make some sweeties?'

God forgive me for all the hypocritical times I've told him no, bad for the teeth.

As they busied themselves about the kitchen she attempted to convince herself that she had done the right thing in forcing Mikey to choose all or nothing at all. She had, the in-between was too frustrating. But, who knows, given time, and he was so nice. No, better to start afresh. But start where? Her life seemed to have closed in, to the point where she had no one to confide in, let alone to offer her some physical affection. Hugging Josh fiercely merely emphasised the fact that within a few years he would spurn her embraces.

'Do you want some more, sweetheart?'

'No.'

'No what?'

'No, thank you. It tastes funny.'

'Never mind,' she said, giving him a chocolate finger instead and helping herself to another square of achingly sweet fudge. 'It wasn't really for you.'

10

Great Escapes

The top of the generator truck was high enough off the ground for no one to notice her as they passed, and Becky had taken to spending the occasional half-hour, sometimes longer, up there where she could watch the life of the circus unobserved. Inside the claustrophobic caravans, or even within the charmed circle of the ring lights, it was impossible to get any perspective on what she and they were all doing.

Previously she had wriggled up here in the still of early afternoon and lain with the sun on her back and the occasional insect buzzing about her head. This was the first time she had retreated to this refuge after dark, and the difference was disturbing enough for her to half-wish she hadn't.

For a start, the way that people coalesced out of the warm blackness and then dematerialised again was surreal, and they spoke to one another in hushed, conspiratorial tones that made Becky feel more than ever like a spy. Not that she had heard anything more incriminating than the usual bitching of one faction about another, but the night lent it a more sinister air.

There had been no show that evening so the encampment was illuminated only by the rectangles of light from caravan windows. Becky tried to work out which was which. The pink-curtained glow, she knew, simply from the size of the squares, must be the Raspails'. Behind and to the left she could see Ana, gently swaying, presumably to music, as she did the washing-up, looking every inch the perfect model-wife of the TV commercials.

Dermot's caravan was parked further round, by the box-office bus, and as he had said he was spending the evening with Straker, Becky was surprised to see a light where she expected its window to be. Perhaps, she thought, she had miscalculated. It looked like the inside of their caravan but those cupboards were the same as several other people's. She was counting along again when his head appeared quite suddenly in the window and, ridiculously, she ducked down. Of course he couldn't see her out here but he was staring straight at her.

Dermot stayed like that, his expression – hints of worry, puzzlement, irritation – frozen as in a miniature portrait for at least a minute, and then he swung half-round, features redrawn to anger. Someone must have come in, Becky realised, as his face withdrew through annoyance to politeness.

There was a conversation but she was unable to make out any of the words from the shapes of his mouth. She assumed the other participant was Straker but then a peroxide blonde head came into the frame and for one fantastic moment she thought she was looking at herself, in her natural habitat – it was, apart from the fact that she knew she was elsewhere, logical.

Helga was animated, her hands popping in and out of the pockets of her dungarees. At the end of one upswing they came to rest on Dermot's shoulders and Becky saw him tense, but then the hands were withdrawn and they seemed to be taking their farewells affably as they drifted from view. Helga was socially maladroit, Becky thought. She hadn't noticed how much Dermot disliked casual physical contact, whether hail-fellow-well-met or to emphasise some debating point.

Becky had had enough of watching. She scrambled down and strolled back to the caravan, approaching it from behind, giving Helga enough time to have got clear. She opened the door and seemed to have stumbled into an action replay – same event, different angle.

Dermot was at the window and as she entered he turned, his face tight with anger. But this time there was no subsidence.

'Where have you been?'

She knew that now she could never tell him about the top of the generator truck. It would be obvious she had been spying on him.

'Just for a walk,' she said, but she was aware of a fatal hesitation.

'Where? You've been gone ages.'

'Just . . . about.' Horrified with herself, she fell back on the clichés of domestic argument. 'Look, what is this? Can't I go for a walk if I want to? Anyway, I thought you were with Straker.'

'Oh yes, I know you did,' he said significantly.

There was an awful thudding in Becky's chest. 'What's that supposed to mean?' she asked, wishing she could find some way of escaping from this pre-ordained script.

'Who is it?'

'What?'

But she already knew what he meant. She could hardly believe it but she knew.

'Is it Paolo?'

The script called for her to say, 'Is what Paolo?' Instead,

with an effort, she forced out, 'You think I'm having an affair with Paolo.'

The genuine incredulity in her voice must have penetrated the certainty of his suspicion because he said, 'OK, so not Paolo. Who then? Stephane?'

'Why should it be anybody?'

'You're hiding something, you're always off on your own,' he said, all of a sudden more sulky than angry.

Her breathing slowed. The potential flashpoint had passed. She knew better than to be angry herself, even though she thought she had every right.

So she said, as lightly as she could, 'I'm entitled to a few secrets, surely.' She restrained herself from adding, 'There's plenty about you I can't find out.' Instead she said, 'After all, you don't own me.'

'I know,' he said, and then he gave her the ghost of a smile. 'But I'd like to.'

And he'd demonstrated that, Becky thought later, lying awake in bed, with Dermot, as far as she could tell, asleep by her side. When they made love he had pounded into her as if internally branding her might ward off the attacks of marauding pricks. How could he have imagined she was being unfaithful without any evidence or even a prime suspect? She had hardly spoken to Paolo outside the big top, and Stephane had been Dermot's friend for years. Anyway, she thought, why would he want me with the beautiful Mirielle at his disposal? Perhaps that was the only saving grace of the evening. Dermot clearly did think that any man would find her more desirable than the competition, even though it suggested he could do with a visit to the optician.

All that suppressed passion. And to get him to reveal anything of himself she had always had to give. She let him sleep with her, and the next day he had revealed his brother and the greyhounds. She let him tie her up and he let go for the first time. Bondage to secure motorbike training. Becky yawned. She knew there was something wrong with this argument but she was tired. As she drifted off she recalled a snatch of their earlier conversation.

'I was alone, contemplating,' she had said. 'Don't you contemplate?'

'Oh, yes,' he had said. 'I contemplates.'

And apart from the odd 's' he had given it a strange, lilting pronunciation so that now she found herself wondering what templates, exactly, he was conning?

If Judy got the job this was a journey she would be making often. The 125 pulled out of Newcastle station and reflexively she looked for the view of the five bridges over the river, just as she would later look for the cathedral at Durham and the minster at York. She couldn't think of any landmarks in Doncaster or Peterborough but doubtless she would get to recognise other signs – a signal box two hours from home, a trackside tree that meant Darlington approaching. If she got it. If she accepted.

She had travelled up to Gateshead on the Thursday afternoon and had dinner with Doherty at a rather smart restaurant in Newcastle city centre. The fact that they were not eating in the hotel he had booked suggested that he was making some point by choosing this particular restaurant but at first she was not sure what it was.

Not that he was a down-to-earth bloke, which he was, although the occasional bluntness was camouflage for subtler manoeuvring. Not a demonstration of his taste for exotic food, for the menu was international conservative. Surely not to prove that he could afford the prices; that had to be taken as read in the founder of an expanding and prosperous manufacturing company. In the end she concluded that it was simply to prove that such places existed in the north-east, in case she had acquired the southern assumption that London held a monopoly on expensive table linen.

That first evening he delicately steered the conversation away from any detailed discussion of the business, extolling the virtues of the area in an understated way while questioning her about her own interests and enthusiasms. As she had no fixed idea as to whether she wanted to work for him or not it was easy to be frank and ask plenty of questions in return. By the time they had finished coffee she felt that she liked and could work with him but couldn't guess whether he felt the same.

In the morning she took a taxi as instructed to the factory and he showed her round. Inevitably there was a soupçon of pride in his tour but the questions he asked were infinitely more probing than his explanations and she was glad that she had done what homework she could on the snack food market and its technological developments.

They had lunch in the canteen – 'No separate managers' dining-room here; the Japanese have got that right' – and then went to his office. He introduced her to his PA, Sandy, an expansive blonde with an expensive perm who looked her up and down with the unconcealed curiosity which Judy had come to expect from Geordies.

For an hour he picked her brains about her career to date – he had done at least as much research into her business as she had done on his – and then asked her what she thought was lacking in the marketing of his own products.

This was the crunch. To be opinionated or circumspect?

She wavered for a fraction of a second before plumping for her original plan. 'It's far too early for me to say.'

He nodded and outlined the salary, car and so on that he had thought appropriate. 'I wouldn't decide to offer you a job now any more than I would expect you to accept but I don't hang about. I'll let you know next week.'

Which implies that he wants a similarly prompt response, thought Judy.

'Any questions about terms and conditions?'

She asked about relocation expenses if it proved difficult to dispose of her London house immediately; the property market was falling.

'Let's cross that bridge when we come to it.' A tight smile. 'If we come to it. I'm sure we can work something out.'

When she indicated that there was nothing else he asked which train she was catching.

'I'm not going back tonight. I thought I would stay over the weekend and have a look round.'

'Staying on at the Post House?'

'Yes.'

'You'll need a car then. Arranged it yet?'

'No, I'll hire one this evening.'

'Don't need to. I'm sure our insurance will cover you to use one of the pool cars.'

And so she had spent the weekend touring the byways of Northumberland in a company Cavalier, leaving it as requested in the car park nearest St James's Station before her departure on Sunday afternoon.

Her train was nearing Darlington and she decided to get a coffee before the queue for the buffet lengthened. In her case were a mass of Pasco papers that needed reading before her return to work but far more alluring were the sheaf of property particulars that she had collected from estate agents. Would it be tempting fate to take another look? He might not want her. She might not want it. But the faster the landscape flashed past the more she thought she did.

He had hypothesised a salary no larger than her present one without bothering to point out that its purchasing power, especially in property, was significantly higher. Presumably he thought that if she could not work that out for herself then she was unsuitable. As in other areas he was selling but not too hard.

So she would gain financially and in titular prestige. Admittedly, Gateshead Foods was smaller than her division of Pasco but it had as high a public profile. Compared to the bustle of the West End the working environment was somewhat soulless – clean, metal-clad toytown buildings surrounded by dwarf shrubs and vast expanses of car parking – and there would be no lunchtime shopping; the nearest newsagent was a good mile away.

But then getting away from London and her present circumstances was one of the main attractions. She was played out at Pasco and the house harboured bad memories. Already she was depressed at the thought of returning there. Instead of which she might be in a cottage in the heart of the countryside. Barty would love that. She would put Marmite on his paws to stop him getting lost and they would grow old together.

Judy had no friends up here but that could hardly make her any lonelier than she had felt, or chosen to be, in the last few months. The only people she looked forward to seeing were Vanessa and Max, and this was the one job where their attendance was guaranteed.

Being their client would inevitably have an effect on their relationship but Doherty had already pre-empted any awkwardness by saying that the one option not available to his new marketing director was to change agencies and that any future change must be a joint decision. Assuming that Vanessa and Max continued to perform as satisfactorily for Gateshead as they had done for five years it should not be an issue. She had no qualms about Vanessa taking advantage of their friendship.

It would be tempting fate to reconsider the various 'des. reses' that she had in her case. Instead she started on *Cosmopolitan*, bought for the journey, but the jamboree bag of sex surveys and pocket psychology which had often been so entertaining failed to appeal. She tried the back page of the *Sunday Times* held aloft by the man opposite until he realised what she was doing, and then had no alternative but to settle to 'Doublehead: Production for Test Markets'.

'So, shall we have a realistic run-through?' Dermot asked. 'No one else is using the arena, and Straker and Helg can help me set up the course.'

'OK,' Becky said, although she felt a little queasy. He was full of energy this morning; had been up and out while she was still dozing.

They had been working on the new act for a week – ever since he had pronounced her competent with the bike. Not that it involved her controlling the bike, she was merely riding pillion but Dermot was now confident that she had mastered balance.

Getting him to teach her to ride the Kawasaki had been hard work. He had begun in Rennes, continued in Nantes and finished the job here in Bordeaux. Some days he had been happy to do it and others he had made unreasonable excuses in his reasonable way. The first time Becky had taken it for a circuit of the field alone he had come charging from the marquee where he had been tuning one of the cars and flagged her down.

'It's OK,' she had said. 'I'm taking it gently.'

'Maybe.' He was touching the petrol tank. 'You should have asked.'

Trying to make light of it she had said, 'Not worried about me or the monster then. Just a little boy who's jealous when someone borrows his cricket bat.'

He had turned and walked away without another word.

'Dermot,' she called. 'I'm sorry, I didn't mean to be rude,' and she would have gone after him but she had to prop the machine on its stand and the weight and stiffness meant that took time. When she looked round he had vanished and although she had searched Becky couldn't find him.

But at lunchtime he had suddenly appeared as she was talking to Stephane and Mirielle and said, 'We'll have to get you up to thirty tomorrow. I thought you'd better have your own helmet so I bought you this.' It was black, full-face, heavy.

After that she had always asked his permission.

She had a lukewarm shower in the hope that it would perk her up and looking at her pale face in the mirror decided to apply full make-up. She felt really nervous despite having completed the course twelve times yesterday.

The act had been Dermot's idea. She had been developing her escapology scenario and attempting to involve him and the bike when he had said, 'Why don't we incorporate you into my act?'

'But I don't ride anything like well enough.'

'No, you don't, but all you would need to do is sit on the back, and you've learnt enough to lean with me or stay still depending on what's required.'

'What will we do?'

'The slow circuit of the obstacle course. It will be a challenge to do it with the extra weight.'

And they had – Dermot experimenting at first with a heavy kitbag strapped to the saddle to represent her, then with her in person but with the planks and poles only six inches from the ground. Finally, yesterday, they had attempted the circuit at its correct height, more like six feet above the sawdust of the ring. After the first couple of successful circumnavigations her knuckles had regained some colour and at the end of the session she was able to swing down from the machine with only a faint wobble as her legs touched the ground. He had not made a single mistake. But then she had been free to jump clear had something gone wrong – today she would have no control.

The artistic gloss that had her bound and gagged was also Dermot's idea – and it made sense. 'If you're free you will look like an expert assistant but any stooge can end up trussed to a machine against their will. It will help them identify. Add to the thrill.'

'And for you,' she had wanted to say but he never joked about his routines so instead she had said, 'You've listened to my half-baked justifications too often. But I think it's good. Really good. What about costume?'

Becky put on the short leather skirt and the fringed black brassière top that Mirielle had made. Together with her high leather boots they added up to a pastiche somewhere between cowgirl, go-go girl and *Easy Rider*. Inspired by this theme Becky had made Dermot a papier-mâché German helmet, of the type sported by the Wehrmacht and Hell's Angels.

Her face looked fine now, a confident face, but her exposed arms and legs were pallid. She wondered whether

Ana used tanning solution or a sun bed. Could you run one off a car battery? Whatever, if she was going to appear in this rigout she would have to follow suit. She took some gel and ran it through her soft peroxided hair to lift and spike it a little. The roots were showing dark. They would need doing again soon, and her armpits, which held the faintest blue shadow.

'Very good,' said Dermot, re-entering the caravan. She wasn't sure whether he meant her costume or posture, standing as she was with hands through hair and jutting hip. She gave him the classic dancer's pelvic grind, making her fringes swing, but he was already changing into his own gear and didn't seem to notice.

She smoked a Gitane as he strapped on his bandoliers and heavy, studded belt.

'Ready?' He picked up the helmet and swung it by its frail strap as they crossed the compound.

Becky wanted to crack a joke to reduce her own tension but he had that closed-off look and anyway now that the moment had come she couldn't think of anything funny to say about a tin hat made from old copies of *Le Monde*.

The marquee was empty and the afternoon sun had intensified the smell of the canvas. The planks along which the bike was to run looked impossibly high and ridiculously narrow. The only light was that coming through the sides and roof of the tent and the course was sunk in soft and murky shadow.

'Aren't you going to put the spots on? You can hardly see in this.'

He looked dubious but they could hear the sound of the generator truck idling outside and he went behind the curtains to switch them on. If anything the sharp relief into which they threw the arena was more frightening.

'OK then.'

She swung astride the bike and the leather of her skirt creaked against the plastic of the saddle. He bent down to tie her ankles to the rear struts but the boots were too baggy to give a firm grip. 'I think you'll have to go barefoot.'

'And me feeling so like Nancy Sinatra,' she said.

He pulled them off and secured her. The knotted red and white cloth squashed her flesh against the cold metal and the breeze tickled the soles of her feet.

He pushed her gently against the high backrest and pulled her arms behind her, fastening her wrists to each other and the backrest's chrome supports. He came back into view. 'Last one.' The thickly rolled bandanna he placed over her mouth and pulled tight against the base of her skull. 'OK?'

The scarf had pressed her ears so tightly that his voice was muffled and when she tried to reply she could not shape her lips and couldn't tell whether he had heard the formless grunt she emitted, sucking in wet cotton in the process. So she nodded and waggled her eyebrows.

He nodded in return, put on his gold-rimmed, dark glasses and the German helmet and swung on to the saddle in front of her. He let the bike drop off its stand. She stared at his back, concentrating on the knobbles of his spine outlined by the thin black vest. She wanted to put her arms round his waist but she could not move. Even her legs were pinioned away from his. He turned the ignition and the engine rumbled. Now she could not hear him, call to him or even see his face. She had never been so close to anyone and yet so completely out of communication with him.

They moved off and, just like yesterday, did a couple of preparatory rounds of the ring. Becky wanted a pee or a cigarette, it barely mattered which. Her muscles were tense and she wasn't leaning with the bike. Relax. It's just a matter of trust.

They approached the ramp and began to climb. She stared straight ahead until they levelled out and she knew they were crawling along the first length of planking. Out of the corner of her eye she looked to the side and immediately felt dizzy. The ground was miles away; it was like peering over the parapet of St Paul's. She closed her eyes tight and a firework display danced before her. There was a bump and, Pavlovian, she leant left to compensate for the first bend. On to the scaffolding straight. The breeze was cold, striking the rivers of perspiration running from beneath her arms. She concentrated on Dermot. Dry as a bone. How come?

ᵀ ᵉan. Straight three. So far so good but ... she swallowed a mouthful of saliva and entwined her sweating fingers as the bike shuddered and he stood up. Still to plan but always the most heart-stopping bit – what if his foot slipped? Tilt for corner three and he lowered himself back into the saddle, putting her directly into the beam of a spot. She closed her eyes again. Home straight.

She didn't so much hear the increased power of the engine as feel it beneath her. That wasn't right. The sound and vibration of every yard of the course were imprinted on her memory. A fraction of a second before she was thrown backwards she realised what he was going to do and she knew she had screamed although no sound suggested so. In his solo turn he always did the fourth straight on the rear wheel only and this was what he was attempting now.

She lay rigid against the backrest, her spine almost parallel with the planking, staring up at the straining tendons of his arms and beyond them the silhouetted handlebars and the slack trapezes in the roofspace. She focused furiously on their changing perspective as at a snail's pace the bike juddered along, its engine roaring against the brake and clutch.

Oh God, oh Jesus, oh Christ, oh Mary Mother of God ... a distant picture from last summer of that stubby Florentine priest working the rosary flowered and wilted, rivers of blood pounded inside her head and then suddenly they were lurching on to the descending ramp and a spurt of bile, released in relief, threatened her throat.

They hit the floor and once again he stood in the saddle, letting out a whoop of triumph along with the throttle, and they were surging out of the marquee and across the bumpy turf towards the car park.

She couldn't believe he was doing this with her powerless behind. It was as if he had forgotten her completely. What was he doing anyway? Becky looked towards the caravans, hoping to see people flagging him down but her movement coincided with the bike swinging away and the whiplash made her feel sick. They were moving so fast the air was battering her eyes and nostrils. He performed a huge skidding turn and the concrete was so close to her right leg that she felt its warmth and for a second imagined that it had scraped away her defenceless skin, felt the hot blood coursing over her feet, before she realised it was simply the exhaust vapour on her sweat.

Then they were racing back to the marquee, through its dark entrance beneath its blinding lights and he was taking the ramp again, this time at speed. Becky was too panicked to remember to lean. Whether she did she had no idea. Her lungs felt empty, bursting. They swayed and lurched, the planks bouncing beneath their wheels as he repeated the circuit.

He was bareheaded although where the helmet had been lost she did not know. Mercifully it was all over very quickly, a blur of sound and light and they were coming to rest.

The engine was switched off and despite her fear and

anger she felt a soft wave of relief. Her fingers were locked together. Her gag was wet against her lips, her thighs were stuck damply to the saddle. She shifted to break the suction as he jolted the bike back on its stand and dismounted.

He turned and stood over her and she experienced a sudden, very different anxiety. His body menaced, his features were impassive, his eyes masked by twin reflections of herself in his glasses.

And what did she look like?

A powerless victim, her pupils dilated and breasts heaving with fright?

Or an eager supplicant, her pupils dilated and breasts heaving with passion?

Did it matter to him? He could do anything he wished to her and she was incapable of preventing it. She could not reason or fight.

She stared at her selves in his lenses, willing him to relax and untie her. Time passed.

He bent forward and stroked her hair and her cheekbone, his fingers dry and firm against her scalp.

And then he was slipping the knot on her gag. Her jaw was so stiff from grimacing that at first she could not speak.

'Perfect,' he said. 'Or at least nine out of ten.'

She had to personalise him again. 'Take your glasses off, Dermot.'

He smiled, perhaps at the irrationality of this remark, but took them off. His eyes were watching but not open to her.

'You bastard,' she said, only it left her as a shriek. 'You stinking bastard.'

He put a hand out to her shoulder.

'Don't touch me,' she shouted, and that was irrational because he twisted away and walked out leaving her still tied to the bike.

She sat, half feeling faintly silly and reluctant to call for assistance, the other half reeling from the magnitude of what had just happened. She had genuinely believed that Dermot was going to . . . without her consent . . . well to . . . to rape her.

And why had she believed that?

Because she had seen him really out of control.

Because for him she had ceased to exist as a person to be taken into account. Become baggage, nearly a baggage, nearly dead weight.

Because he had broken their trust. He had had her in his power and abused that.

She could not trust him again.

She sensed an observer and looked up. The lights were still on so it took some time to distinguish a figure high up in the seating. When she did she was momentarily frightened (or relieved?) that it might be Dermot.

But why would whoever it was stand still up there while she was so obviously trussed against her will down here?

The figure coalesced and it was shorter and dumpier and very blonde.

'Helga,' Becky called, hoping to sound nonchalant. 'Can you give me a hand?'

And then it moved but not towards her. Instead the figure slipped away into the outer darkness.

Becky was astonished. She listened to the silence. Had she imagined it? Was it her alter ego? Then the lights went out with a thump and a crack that made her squeal and left her in the comparative gloom of early evening. It was Helga then; illusions didn't switch switches and neither did most circus performers, only pedantic authoritarians and born organisers.

In the void left by the generator's grumble she could hear

the distant sound of caravan radios, the occasional shout or clang of utensils but no one came to the marquee.

If she shouted someone would hear and set her free, but how could she explain away her predicament? On the other hand, if she just waited she would be found by whoever had booked the evening rehearsal slot; inevitably not one person but an entire group, not a single explanation but a whole string with cross-questioning and ribald humour.

Or Dermot would come back.

She did not want to see him even when she could move. Which meant she could not stay in the caravan. And if she was too embarrassed to explain this, how could she explain that she wanted to move in with . . . well, who? Not Helga, not Straker and the band, certainly not Fassbinder. It would have to be Joach and Ana or the Raspails. Becky pictured their well-meaning attempts at immediate reconciliation. All too clearly. She would count to a hundred, just in case, and then start hollering.

At seventy-three she heard the hum of an electric motor and seconds later the wheelchair hove into view.

'Andromeda chained to the rock never looked so fair,' said Fassbinder, drawing alongside.

'What are you doing here?'

'I am your Perseus and not, as you so obviously imagine, the sea monster.'

'How did you know I was here?'

'A little bird told me.' He hopped down and began to untie the bonds on her right ankle.

'Dermot?'

'No.'

'Helga.' She stretched her leg out and flexed her toes. His fingers, as delicate as the paws of a mouse, pattered across her other ankle. 'Why didn't she help me herself?'

'I cannot say.'

'But she—'

'Or rather, I should not say. This knot on your wrists is very stubborn.'

'But will you?'

'I rather think she felt you had got your—' He searched, as was his pleasure, for the correct English idiom, 'your just deserts.'

He pulled the scarf away and she inspected her arms. Her wrists were striped a livid red where the cloth had cut into them and her hands, when she rubbed them together, fizzed with the pins and needles of returning circulation.

'Or perhaps come-uppance is better,' he mused.

Becky dismounted but her legs were shaky and she staggered, falling on to her hands and knees.

'Sit down,' Fassbinder said, gesturing at the wheelchair, and she accepted. It was oddly comforting, probably because the standard lampshade above reminded her of a certain armchair at Granny's.

'Why just deserts?' She massaged her palms as vigorously as she could manage. Fassbinder stood with his head downcast like a small child and it occurred to her that his gaze had been averted ever since he had dropped from his chair. Uncharitably she had assumed that he would at least have taken advantage of her predicament and proximity to look up her skirt.

'I think Helga's view would be that you have invaded Dermot's space. Not content with sharing his bed you entered the compartment that was his work by getting yourself co-opted on to the committee and then you tried to share his bikes. In her view it is hardly surprising that he should . . . crack up.'

'How does she know what happened?'

'She saw you racing round the car park, came over to

take a look. I don't know if she got here before or after Dermot stormed out.'

'Where is he now?'

'He's left the site. Who knows where? I am sure he'll return.'

She's wrong anyway, Becky thought. He asked me to join the circus, he ... but, in truth, in all subsequent developments Dermot had merely acquiesced, sometimes with a smile, sometimes with only a nod.

'He is a very private person, I think,' Fassbinder was saying. 'He has to be in control.'

And that, she thought, is true. And she had gradually removed those levers from him, stripping away his command and exposing his weaknesses, until he had reasserted control in spectacular fashion. The act had been his idea – had he developed it with this demonstration, this humiliation in mind? That was too clinical but perhaps no less comforting than the thought that his feelings were so suppressed that they could only burst out in this sudden, violent manner. She decided to think about something else.

Fassbinder was looking at her quizzically. She had no idea how long she had been silent.

'What's it to do with Helga?'

'She has always carried a torch for Dermot.'

That was understandable. But even so, why the detestation?

'And what about him?'

'In what respect?'

'Was there anything between them?'

'I do not think she had captured his heart—'

'But?'

'But yes, they too shared a bed at one time.'

Dermot and Helga? She could not imagine it, did not want to imagine it.

'When?'

'Oh, finished before you came on the scene.'

Helga hanging around Dermot's caravan when she first knew him, presumably the rejected lover, still hoping. No wonder she disliked her and ... Helga's shock when she had appeared with her hair cropped and dyed; oh God, in Helga's eyes she hadn't only stolen her man, she had stolen her very appearance. It was like offending against some primitive superstition, a flesh and blood version of stealing someone's soul by taking their photograph. And Dermot had acquiesced, even encouraged her in that.

She wanted to get away and think for a bit. She stood up. The light was fading.

'Thanks,' she said. 'Thanks for helping me out but I'm all right now.' She took his hand.

Fassbinder didn't ask what she was going to do, he simply squeezed her hand back and climbed into his vacated wheelchair.

'Don't do anything you might regret,' he said and drove away.

Outside it was brighter than she expected, the sun still orange towards the sea. She approached their caravan carefully and peered through the window but it was empty. She couldn't stay here at the moment – she would stick a few things in a duffel bag and spend the night in a hotel. She had enough cash for that. She pulled on jeans and a sweatshirt, and then the flying jacket, which was too hot but the only thing she had with plenty of pockets.

She ought at least to leave Dermot a note. She searched for paper and pen, but when she leant on the draining board to write her brain seized up with panic that he might come back.

'I need a break,' she wrote, after some consideration. 'Don't worry.' She didn't mean that, it would do him good

293

to worry but she didn't want him trying to track her down. She would return when she was ready. She had to think what day it was. Monday. There were the usual run-throughs tomorrow prior to their Wednesday opening. 'Carla can stand in for me in the cage if I'm not back. Becky.'

Then it occurred to her that she had a responsibility to the Raspails as far as the routine was concerned and she started again on another piece of paper. She left his above the sink and closed the caravan door behind her. The twilight was scented with the smell of the south which had been with them ever since they had passed La Rochelle. The Raspails' trailer was dark – she slipped the note under the door and headed for the road. It was only a mile into town.

'Where are you going?'

He had her note in his hand. He must have been watching her even as she was writing it. It was too dark to see his face properly but the voice was relaxed. Her pulse leapt. She kept moving. 'I just need a breather. I'll be back soon.' Her own voice was shaking. Her hands were shaking.

Dermot skipped to stay in front of her, walking backwards. 'Don't go. You can't go.'

'I can if I want.'

'Don't. I want you to stay. Please.'

'I'm not going for good. I just must have some time.' They were nearing the band of trees that hid their site from the road. He glanced over his shoulder. He stopped. 'No.'

She changed direction and he moved to block her, as if the cause would be lost if she reached the border. She changed direction again but maintained a brisk walking pace. His arm shot out and he grabbed her. Becky shook him off and ran. The dumbshow was over. He caught at her duffel bag and it pulled her round. She flailed at him, unable to shake his grip.

'Leave me alone. Leave me alone. Leave me—'

He slapped her face very hard. The pain was excruciating, but to do it he had let go of the bag. She ran again and as he caught up with her she swung it at him as if it were a mace. It caught him a glancing blow on the side of the head and he stumbled. She rushed into the trees where it was really dark. Should she go into the light on the road or try and hide here? She pressed herself against the trunk of a tree and held her breath. She heard him swiping at the undergrowth and then the clicking of his quarter-tipped heels on the tarmac beyond. Too late. He had cut her off.

A car cruised past and she used the cover to take another gulp of air and adjust her stance. This was stupid. She should appeal to his reason.

Her cheek now felt anaesthetised. What reason?

Her foot touched something that moved. An empty wine bottle. Drawing on her stock of movie memories she considered throwing it to distract his attention. It had worked in countless war epics. She carefully bent and picked it up.

The footsteps had stopped. Where was he? What to do? She drew the bottle back to throw.

'Becky.'

His hand clamped on her left shoulder, no warning sound or smell, his head loomed up at hers. Fear and fury boiled over. She brought the bottle round with all of the force of her backswing and hit him in the face. The face jerked back and she ran again, staying in the dark of the wood, until she was out of breath and buffeted by the bumping of the bag against her back, until she could no longer bear the suspense of not knowing where he was. She turned, still gripping the bottle by its neck. In the distance she could hear a sobbing sound. It must be him and she must have hurt him badly. She looked down at the bottle. It was unbroken so she could not have cut him. Perhaps she had bloodied or even broken his nose. It had been a sickening crack. Oh God, she hoped it wasn't too bad.

As her eyes grew accustomed to the dark she could clearly see the undergrowth and encampment beyond, and all the while she could hear him she was safe. She squatted on the ground. She knew now that she wanted to get as far away from here as possible. Even if she could get into town, and she couldn't rely on a passing motorist to pick her up before he did, had she enough money to buy a rail ticket before the banks opened? She felt in her pocket for her purse and found a key. It was an ignition key, not for the display bike but the heavy Kawasaki parked in the lee of the generator truck.

When you fell off a horse the best therapy was to get straight back on, or so she had read. Her urban childhood had not extended to ponies. A terrifying experience on a motorbike was not so very different. It was not even the same machine.

Voices and the beam of a torch were approaching from the caravans. Fassbinder and Helga. Not coming in her direction but heading for Dermot by the opening to the road. Helga's exclamation told her that they had spotted him and she scrambled to her feet and scurried away, knowing that they would not hear her above their own racket. She followed the thicket round until she could dodge from the shadow of one caravan to another.

Her helmet was hanging from the Kawasaki's handle-bars. She put it on, but it rendered her deaf so she reslung it from the tail rack. Starting the engine would be very noisy and Dermot would immediately recognise it. When she did start it she had to get up sufficient speed before she reached them not to be stopped. With an effort she dropped the bike from its stand and pushed it to the edge of the cover afforded by the caravans. The open road, beyond the only gap in the trees, was two hundred yards away. A little to its right the yellow glow of Helga's torch, surprisingly powerful from this distance. What if they blocked the gap? She could hardly ride straight through them, could she?

From the marquee the jangling of tuning up which had hardly impinged on her suddenly gelled into a count of drumbeats and the power chords of what Straker always referred to as his Overture. The band was rehearsing at a blessedly high decibel level. She climbed on to the bike and teetered, her feet barely touching the ground on either side. She was committed now. She didn't have the strength to stay like this for very long and the only way the Kawasaki would support itself was at speed. She turned the key and the bike roared into life. Now she could hear nothing but it and the music anyway. She found the headlight switch and readied her thumb against it, hoping to make use of another Hollywood stratagem. She revved the engine and released the clutch.

She shot across the turf so fast that she barely had time to point the bike at the gap before she was upon it. She bounced in the saddle as if she was riding a rocking horse. She hit her headlight and illuminated a tableau of three figures huddled in some ghastly parody of suburbia beneath the wheelchair's standard lamp. Their astonished faces gawped at hers but, as she had hoped, the blast of sound and light to which she had subjected them induced a temporary paralysis and it was only as she passed that they came to life.

Becky nearly killed herself on that first bend, just bringing the bike round as she hit the dirt verge on the far side of the road and straightening with inches to spare before the trees, but she accelerated away with a screech of tyres and minutes later was heading north on the autoroute to Saintes.

For such a significant, life-changing letter it was very short. The florid company logo at the top of the sheet was far larger than the few terse lines of black prose neatly positioned in the middle.

Despite having weighed the pros and cons over and over again Judy did what her old tutor would have called the statesmanlike thing and sat on it over the weekend, which she spent with her parents in Nottingham. She said nothing to them about the Gateshead job offer; secrecy was becoming a habit that extended even to her own family.

On Sunday evening, after one last look through the accompanying terms and conditions, she got her portable typewriter out of the cupboard under the stairs and hammered out an acceptance. She put it on the breakfast bar for posting but, sitting with Barty and the colour supplements, she was as aware of it lying there as if it had been a carelessly abandoned iron burning a ring in the Formica. She put her coat on and took it to the pillar box on the corner.

Then she felt able to go to bed and with the aid of Horlicks, the purring mass of the cat on her legs, and the soft glow of the nightlight on her radio alarm, all staples of her nocturnal ritual these days, she slept.

She arrived at the office, rested but strangely detached, as if in an air bubble, and immediately made an appointment with Hugo.

He was disappointed that she was leaving Pasco's protective fold but being demob happy himself – his own notice period was up at the end of the month – did not try very hard to dissuade her. In a way, of course, it merely demonstrated his own capacity to inspire devotion if his lieutenants found it impossible to serve under anyone else.

At lunch, having ascertained that she did not want any more time to consider her resignation, he wished her the best of fortune, and clasped her hand over the sugar-snap peas with patently heartfelt sincerity.

Before her afternoon conference she rang the estate agents whose boards were most prominent in her part of Islington and made an appointment for them to value.

The subject of the meeting was Total Quality – this year's hot favourite in conglomerate concepts. Judging by the messianic enthusiasm with which this notion was being discussed one would have thought that all but the most dimwitted had previously been irrevocably committed to Partial Quality, not a position which any multinational had admitted. When she said as much her cynicism attracted several raised eyebrows and she sat out the remainder of the meeting in silence. All of a sudden, now that she had performed the necessary obsequies, she wanted to celebrate.

She rang Vanessa. 'Are you busy? Can I come over?'

'No and yes. But it's only five. Very unlike you to knock off early. Is everything all right?'

'Oh yes, it's just a lovely summer's day. I'd like a walk.'

'Down Oxford Street? Through the petrol fumes?'

'Yes.'

'You'd better not dawdle too long, Mary Poppins, or you'll be brain-damaged before you get here.'

The sun was hot and, surrounded by shoppers in summer dresses and tourists in T-shirts, Judy regretted the taupe suit which she had thought appropriate to the termination of her eleven years with the firm. Vanessa's crisp cotton shirt and culottes emphasised her own stickiness.

'You're looking enviably cool,' she said.

'And casual,' said Max, lurking at the far end of the room.

'It's only because we're in legal gestation until 1 July. Then it's back to the *Dynasty*-style shoulder pads and the five-inch-spike heels for our Mata Hari.'

Vanessa raised one finger in an unambiguous gesture. 'As you're dressed for the verandah of the Raffles Hotel the least you could do is fix us a couple of gin slings or something.'

'You could hardly say that the sun is over the yard-arm,' Max said, but he made for the door. His linen suit was the sort of garment that Ivor Novello might have affected had he been called upon to play a Malayan planter.

'You've got something to tell,' Vanessa said. 'Out with it.'

'I'm going to be the marketing director of Gateshead Foods.' The words all tumbled out in a rush.

'Wah.' Vanessa leapt up and flung her arms around Judy. 'Well done.'

In his turn Max planted a featherlight kiss on her cheek and then drew back in mock consternation. 'My God, that makes you – a client.' He pulled out a chair. 'Please, sit down. You may have assumed that we were simply lolling about at your expense in the middle of a working day but in fact we have been slaving over a presentation which my esteemed partner will now deliver without the aid of overheads or even flip charts while I go and find something more in keeping with your new and exalted status for us to drink. Vanessa.'

The door slammed behind him.

'He's mad,' she said. 'But a real pet. God, Judy. Isn't it exciting? When do you start?'

Drawn by the commotion Peter emerged from his office

to find Max returning from the wine bar with three bottles of Veuve Clicquot.

'I know,' he said. 'I know I promised to kick the habit, Peter, and spritzers are my methadone, but this is different. Client entertainment. You'd better come and meet her.'

For the first thirty or forty miles Becky concentrated on driving as fast as she could within what she thought were the speed limits. She did not want to get pulled over on what might already have been reported as a stolen bike.

On this big road, the Kawasaki seemed remarkably easy to control but things still flashed by much faster than they would have done in a car. She tried to detach herself from her situation. The visor helped; behind it she could almost believe she was playing a video game. It was hard to decide what was paranoia and what reasonable suspicion. Would they have rung the police? Would they be pursuing her at this very moment? And in what? The bike, even ridden by a novice, could comfortably outrun the Cirque's motley collection of vans and trucks, but the Cadillac, or Joachim's Audi, or worse, Dermot's other bike, the Suzuki, could all catch her. She notched up the throttle a little more.

When she had set off she had not thought about destination but she knew now that she wanted to be with someone, or at least able to be with someone, and in France she knew no one outside the circus. She had to get back to England.

The obvious ferry ports were Calais and Boulogne but they were right at the other end of the country. Presumably she could stay on the autoroute for Paris and follow the signs from there but she had no idea how long it would take. Le Havre was nearer but her mental map of France did not mark it. However, if she retraced the Cirque's route along the N137 to Rennes in southern Brittany, then St Malo was directly above it on the peninsula's northern coast. Boats went from there to Portsmouth or Plymouth or somewhere.

Approaching Saintes she had to make a decision. Autoroute or N137? If they were chasing her and assumed she was making for England wouldn't they also assume she was making for London and therefore the Channel ports?

It was a one in two chance. Becky took the exit.

That night seemed to last for ever. The occasional towns and villages stopped her riding on autopilot, and the booming of the exhausts was so loud when reflected by houses at the roadside that she expected to be succeeded by a firefly trail of windows lighted and opened and the outraged complaints of mesdames and messieurs in their night attire.

After the first couple of hours her back ached terribly and her legs felt locked but she pressed on and, searching for something comforting to occupy her unquiet mind, settled for the sofa in Vanessa's front room with Josh in his fluffily-scrubbed post-bath persona on her knee, a large gin and the smell of something very English like roast beef drifting from the kitchen. Not that she could ever remember having roast beef at Vanessa's but . . .

Such domestic and prosaic fantasies sustained her until the long, straight stretch between St Fulgent and Montaigu where, with her headlight illuminating nothing but endless lines of bleak poplars she became convinced that somewhere in her wake, just out of sight of her snatched, over-shoulder glances, he was coming, tracking her by the engine note of his stolen Kawasaki, waiting for a series of bends to slow her down so that he could sneak up behind.

In the end this thought was so oppressive that she had to run the bike off the road and park it behind the trees. She leant against a thin trunk, watching and listening. Nothing for several minutes but the sound of the wind, her own breathing, and an odd clicking which turned out to be the bike cooling down. Then the faintest gleam of light, which became two lights and a powerful motor. She shrank down. By now Dermot or even her ex-husband could probably have identified not only the make but the year. To her it could still be anything from a Porsche to a Volkswagen Camper.

It shot past, the diminishing whine of its Doppler effect lingering after the red strip of tail-lights. It had been an anonymous executive saloon with French plates. I knew all along that it couldn't be him, Becky said boldly to herself, but found herself crying with relief just the same. She sat on the ground and let the tears flow until they were exhausted. Having no handkerchief she was forced to wipe her face on the front of her sweatshirt.

When she restarted the bike, and looked at the dials properly for the first time, Becky realised she was nearly out of petrol. A vision of the machine hiccuping and then stuttering to a halt in the middle of nowhere – which might well have happened had she not stopped deliberately just now – sent her heart into a Fred Astaire routine, and she rode at a steady fifty into Nantes where she wasted half an hour looking for an all-night filling station.

As she approached Rennes there was a grey light in the sky to her right and, on the ring road, the first smattering of traffic. Then the direction signs which she had counted down – Rennes 106, Rennes 65, Rennes 4 – switched to Dinan 48, St Malo 69 and her spirits soared. Almost there. She forgot the ache across her shoulders, and the nausea, and the fatigue which had been pulling at her eyelids, and raced on as the rising sun brought the soft Breton landscape into focus.

It was hard to slow down once she had her first sight of

the Rance Estuary and it took the indignant parp of an elderly Renault van, forced to apply its uncertain brakes very sharply as she cut in front, to remind her that she was in a town.

The narrow streets of shops and warehouses gave way to the open space of the harbourside car park, almost empty, and she stopped the bike at the water's edge. Immediately she felt desperately sick with relief and there was a struggle to get the helmet off before she vomited.

She padlocked the Kawasaki, went to the ferry terminal, and bought a ticket for the morning sailing. The sea breeze and the ozone began to restore her composure. It was six o'clock.

To get the maximum of air she walked the ramparts of the old port, and then because in a strange way it felt like the last day of a holiday she went down to the beach. The sand was firm and wet and smooth, newly washed by the receding tide. She picked a length of seaweed from a rock and carried it with her. She was hungry, hardly surprising as she had not eaten since lunch the day before. Inside the town walls she found a bar and ordered café au lait with croissants but when they came they were so rich with milk and butter that she felt sick again. To the surprise of the waiter she paid and left, finding another place down the street where she had black coffee and a Gitane, sitting outside where the air could continue to cleanse her.

Two hours had passed and she had not thought about Dermot at all. She had a *frisson* of panic at the Porte St Vincent and peered around the stone archway in case the Kawasaki was surrounded by circus people or police people but although the car park was less empty the bike still stood in splendid isolation.

She had to let him know about the Kawasaki, but not until she was ready to go.

She rang Stephane's mobile phone from a callbox on the quay, not fifty yards from the gangway.

'My God, Becca, where are you?' Mirielle roused herself from her initial torpor very quickly. 'We were so worried when we saw your note, and Dermot's nose.'

'Is he with you?'

'No, not here in the trailer—'

'No, with you in Bordeaux.'

'Yes, he is in his – in your caravan of course. Bec—'

She had to lean against the glass wall. 'Is he all right? I mean, not too badly hurt.'

'His nose is maybe broken. He will go to the hospital today but he is too concerned that you have an accident—'

'Listen, Mirielle, I haven't got much time, can you pass on a message for me? Tell him not to try and find me, I will write. Tell him the bike, his motorbike, is in St Malo—'

'Where?'

'St Malo, in the car park by the Tourist Information. Have you got that?'

'Yes, but—'

'Mirielle, I'm sorry. Thank you for everything. I will write to you, too.'

'Becca, don't go, Stephane is bringing Dermot, you must—'

She put the phone down immediately.

For most of the crossing she stayed on deck, watching the gulls wheeling above the turmoil of the propeller, for the saloons were swarming with French schoolchildren whose luggage and ebullience occupied every seat. She ate some bread, having thrown the fatty ham within to the birds, and finished her cigarettes.

Before they docked she thought she would clean up and get changed, as far as she could with the meagre resources of her duffel bag, but the sea had been rough and the lavatory floors were unsavoury so she contented herself with wiping off most of yesterday's make-up and redoing something more subdued in the mirror of her compact.

On the train to Victoria she noticed the seaweed still hanging from her jacket pocket but of course the deep, rich colour that the sea gave it had gone; it was shrivelled and black. She left it in a bin at the station and tested her old cashpoint card. It still worked so she got £20 and a taxi.

Vanessa, unused to unexpected callers and fearing Jehovah's Witnesses, opened her front door warily. The bleached and cropped hair, bright-red lips, and heavily kohled eyes, bloodshot and lemured with the bruising of tiredness, were a disguise she only penetrated when something about the leather jacket rang a bell and an unmistakable voice said with a failed attempt at aplomb, 'I'm sorry to land on you but my flat's full of tenants.'

Then it was a blur of hugs and garbled explanations and making sandwiches and Becky for some reason gasping for a gin and tonic which wasn't really her drink.

'Do you want to get changed before you eat?' Vanessa asked, eyeing the crumpled sweatshirt stained with the effort of living up to its name.

'Not until I've had a bath,' said Becky, who could still feel the salt stretching the skin across her cheeks, 'but I will get rid of this.'

Vanessa gaped at the swaying tassels of the top that Becky revealed. 'I thought you were doing the tickets,' she snorted, 'not dancing at the Folies-Bergère.' And then, 'Bloody hell, Becky, how did you get those muscles?'

11

Creatures of the Chase

Becky stirred when Vanessa and Josh left the next morning but not enough to drink the tea that was left by her side. She found the cup cold and scummy when she woke for the second time. It was a bright, sunny afternoon but she had no desire to go out. This house was familiar and safe but neutral; an airlock between her and the real world.

She made herself the most English lunch she could find the ingredients for – Heinz tomato soup and a toasted cheddar cheese and Branston pickle sandwich of sliced white bread. Thus fortified she lay in the bath and read the *Independent* and the previous week's *Time Out*.

A note informed her that Vanessa would be home at seven with the ingredients for supper so she couldn't even prepare that. She did have to make some decisions, but framing the questions, let alone the answers, felt beyond her and she passed the time watching TV.

The news seemed practically unchanged – Northern Ireland, balance of trade, Common Market. The local bulletin carried the usual mix of private murders and public misdemeanours. The same minor film stars and airport bookstall fillers settled on the grey sofas to become the latest batch of *Churchill's People* ... but a Lucinda had taken Sophie's place.

All the while she had been overseas Sophie's death, while shocking, had seemed remote and she hadn't cried at all. Now, back in London, where Sophie might reasonably be expected to breeze in at any moment, trailing white musk, extreme opinions, and sharp put-downs, Becky was suddenly aware of how much she would miss her and what a waste of exuberant life it was. She thought of the time they had spent on the hot, cobbled streets of Florence, arguing about the best route to the synagogue or San Spirito; of the scented night by the pool when Sophie had pulled her sundress over her head and jumped into the water, hauling Judy, squealing in an expensive frock, after her; even of Sophie in a ridiculous Paddington Bear hat emptying confetti over Becky as she got into the Rolls outside the register office. The tears coursed down Becky's cheeks. How could that girl have been so unhappy as to want it all to stop? It would be better to think that she hadn't, that it was all an accident, but, impetuous as Sophie was, she wouldn't have taken sleeping pills on top of masses of booze unless she wanted to blot absolutely everything out.

It suddenly occurred to Becky that the chief reason Sophie's suicide seemed so fantastic was that she could not imagine herself in any circumstances contemplating the same thing. Some life was always better than no life, wasn't it? Strangely heartened, she resolved to disguise her sorrow from Vanessa.

When they got home Josh and Vanessa were both over-excited so teatime and bathtime were protracted and noisy. Becky would quite happily have joined Josh in fish fingers but it was clear that Vanessa had bought something special so she read the *Tales of Mrs Tiggywinkle*, *Mr Jeremy Fisher* and, for good measure, *Pigling Bland*, by which time the boy's golden lashes had knitted together and the smell of smoked haddock floated up the stairs.

'I figured,' said Vanessa, pouring an egg and watercress sauce over the yellow fish, 'that you might have had enough of French recipes.'

The wine was Italian, Pinot Grigio, the strawberries were presumably English and when the cheese was laid out – with biscuits rather than French bread – Becky identified Red Leicester, German smoked, and Swiss Emmenthal. No Brie or Camembert, no Port Salut, no Normandy butter.

'At this time of the year it must have been hard to resist the temptation to buy French beans or mange-tout,' Becky said provocatively.

'What? . . . Not really.'

'Would it destroy your meticulous planning if I said I fancied a Cointreau?'

'Do you?'

'No, not really, but whatever happened to me I'm not going to break down at the sight of an escargot or a frog's leg,' she laughed.

'It sort of got out of hand,' Vanessa said, smiling herself.

She could tell that Becky had been crying but her attempt to conceal it was so heavy-handed that it seemed unfair to refer to it. Vanessa only had the bare bones of the story, and they didn't really make sense. Something had gone wrong with the act that had frightened Becky, who had decided to leave. Dermot had forcibly tried to stop her, leaving her with a badly bruised cheek and an almost perfect set of fingerprint bruises on her upper arm. Little bastard. All the reservations that Vanessa had held about Dermot had been amply justified, a strung-up creep who should be strung up. Becky had been right to walk away but she had sworn that this was the first time he had hit her, so she hadn't left because of the violence and, given that she had subsequently driven a motorbike all the way across France, it was hard to believe that motorbikes were responsible for her decision to depart. There had to be more to it but Vanessa knew she would have to wait for Becky to tell of her own accord.

'What's the situation with your flat?' she asked instead.

'Terrible. My timing couldn't have been worse. I agreed to another six-month let at the end of May so I won't be able to get back in much before Christmas. I'll have to look for a place as well as a job if I'm staying.'

'You don't need to look for anywhere else. Live here.'

'For five months? I couldn't.'

'See how it goes. Stay for a bit anyway.'

'Well . . . that would be great. But I feel guilty cluttering up your living-room every night.'

'If you're going to be here for a while we could clear out the spare room. Underneath the junk there is a perfectly good bed – it's just that I've never needed it.'

'Well . . .'

'Even for a week it's worth it.'

'OK. Shall I shift the stuff tomorrow?'

Vanessa had dourly predicted that it would take Becky all day to rehabilitate the room, but she was done in a couple of hours. Perhaps, Becky thought, everyone should get someone else to do this kind of job for them; if the detritus was your own it was bound to sidetrack you. At home she had spent ages reading old newspapers in the hope of establishing why she had saved them in the first place, but other people's junk was just junk, shorn of emotional connotations. Or, even if it wasn't, you resisted the urge to pry. Mostly.

With an effort of will she put away the batch of Vanessa's

old school reports which had fallen from a battered satchel. They contained a string of 'Excellents' dipping through 'V. Good Work' to a relatively ignominious 'Satisfactory Progress' for fourth-form Latin. But it was fascinating to discover that the perfect hostess's early attempts to master the domestic arts had not impressed T. Jackson, the home economics teacher, and the occasional veiled reference to bossiness that appeared in the comments of her form mistresses. 'Vanessa is a strong-willed girl who should make her mark . . .'

She started the vacuum cleaner, ran over the carpets and bumped something under the bed. On hands and knees she peered to see what. A carrier bag. She pulled it out and was about to stick it in the cupboard when she thought she recognised the eyes gazing over the rim. She edged the glossy, black-and-white prints out. Sophie, a very young Sophie, posed like a high-class tart. With her thin hips and insignificant breasts she could almost have been a beautiful child, but the smouldering expressions and beckoning limbs were so knowing. She had seen Sophie naked before, even seen her sprawled, clothed, in a parody of sexual abandon but not the two together as they were here, and never without humour. This was disturbing, almost frightening.

She couldn't help but take out the box as well.

It would not take a tabloid journalist to draw the conclusion that the girl in the pictures was the sexual-fantasy object of the owner of the sinisterly named 'Love Egg'. But Becky simply could not bring herself to accept this. It would have been ludicrous even if they were magazine pin-ups but these could not have been obtained without Sophie's consent and enthusiastic participation. It implied some kind of sexual relationship between Sophie and Vanessa that had been going on for ten years. If that was true it threw an entirely different light on ... everything. She was consumed by an intense feeling of betrayal at the deceit it put at the heart of her own relationship with Vanessa. Betrayal and, she had to admit it, jealousy. Not that she, for one moment, had ever ... but she had seen her friendship with Vanessa as special, as a mutual love that this relegated to second place in a way that no male lover could have done.

She felt sick. Don't, she thought, don't get carried away. This just cannot be. I would have sensed it, surely, before. There is an innocent, or at least silly, explanation.

But what?

After some thought Becky put the carrier bag in Vanessa's room rather than the cupboard. At least now Vanessa would know that she had seen it and maybe offer that explanation.

The telephone rang and she stiffened as she had every time, afraid that it might be him. Whoever it was they rang off when they heard the answerphone but it pushed Vanessa and Sophie into the background. What was she going to do about Dermot? Sometimes, like this morning when she was in the no man's land between asleep and awake, she thought she should go back to him. They had, after all, had six months. She had loved him. It was redeemable.

Then the phone would ring or the doorbell and she was frightened. Not that he would be here, not yet. But it might be the postman with a registered letter and she didn't even want to read his writing.

She was sure he had already started hunting her. Unable to abandon the Cirque until they had rearranged the show to his satisfaction, he would be on the phone, polite but persistent. Establishing that she was at Vanessa's would not take him long and unless she contacted him or responded to his entreaties he would take a leave of absence and come to find her.

She made herself sit at the kitchen table and once again attempted to draft a difficult note.

Vanessa found her still there when she got in from work and attributed the tense atmosphere to the letter. With difficulty she restrained herself from asking Becky what she was writing to the bastard and instead inspected the newly spartan spare room.

'It's a bit monkish. We could get some of your stuff down from the loft.'

'We'll have to get the clothes,' Becky said. 'I can't go on borrowing yours.'

'Let's get some books and stuff as well.'

'Oh no, not yet.'

'OK. I'll just get changed before we do. Fancy running the boy wonder's bath?'

Josh was clinging to Becky's arm.

'Fine.'

Vanessa went to her room. Becky busied herself with the taps, getting Josh to sing her once again the song he had learnt at nursery school. Above the running water and the runaway train 'blewwww'ing she heard an exclamation. Vanessa's head poked round the door.

'You've found my guilty secret, then? Aren't they extraordinary? I'd forgotten all about them. When Carol – you know, Sophie's flatmate – gave them to me at the funeral I just stuffed them in the boot and they stayed there until I cleared out the car to go back to Breughels. Good job they didn't snatch the keys off me the day I resigned otherwise rumours would have been rife.'

Through the steam she finally registered Becky's red face. 'Becky. You didn't think – you did, didn't you? That they were mine!' Vanessa snorted.

'No,' Becky lied fervently and then changed her mind. 'Well, I mean, why not the . . . you know . . . vibrator . . . it was just finding those photos with it I couldn't—'

She stuttered to a halt, bathed in confusion, relief and guilt. How could she have believed it?

Vanessa chattered on. 'I know – very exhibitionistic. She obviously fancied herself as a femme fatale – shit, I didn't mean that – oh, Becky, come here.'

'So I shall stay here and see if I can get some supply teaching.'

'It's definitely over between you then?' Judy asked.

'I think so. I've written explaining—'

'It is over,' said Vanessa coming in from the kitchen. 'Don't have second thoughts. If a man hits you that's the end of the road. No second chance.'

'I should think it's difficult not to keep rethinking it,' said Judy. 'Something as complicated as that.'

'What's complicated? A black eye's a black eye. There's no excuse for it, even if, and I find that hard to believe, the woman likes being beaten up.'

'I'm not talking about that specifically,' said Judy mildly. 'I just meant any relationship that's lasted several months is a complex thing even if you're not living together, let alone if you are.'

'Makes no odds. Violence is—' she paused.

'Look, you two,' Becky interrupted firmly. 'Whose emotional crisis is this? It wasn't a black eye, just a bruised cheekbone.'

'Just?'

'And I hit him back. Probably broke his nose.'

'Good,' said Vanessa. 'But you were lucky.'

She disappeared to tend her lamb.

'I'm sorry I set that off,' Judy said.

'It's all right. She's been tiptoeing round me all week full of anger and outrage. It had to come out. She's just doing her mother hen and protecting me. I love her for it.'

'Oh, so do I – and I'm sure she's right about not going back to him.' Then Judy giggled. 'But it can't be good for her blood pressure to get so worked up.'

'You're right, too, about how complicated it is, but I think the fact that it all happened in such unreal surroundings makes it easier to distance. Now I'm back with all this—' her gesture encompassed the neat furniture, the comfortable pictures, the scattering of toys on the rug, 'the whole experience is a bit dreamlike. Mind you, I haven't gone up to the Common yet or past my old flat. That's bound to do something. Remind me it might have ended in tears but it started with – oh, you know, stars in my eyes, all that.'

She looked so wistful Judy attempted to change the subject by degrees. 'Will you miss being in the circus?'

'I expect so. Can't see supply teaching pumping the old adrenalin – although if I get a class of teenage thugs to subdue—'

'I thought you had definitely gone off teaching?'

'I had. I'm just going to do it to pay my way until I've sorted out what to do next, and it's too early to say that yet.'

Vanessa peered round the door. 'Becky, can you come and give me a hand for a sec?'

'I'll do it,' said Judy.

'No,' Vanessa said quickly. 'Can't risk your frock.'

'Oh, thanks a lot,' Becky vamped, 'I know mine's old but—'

'And you're a guest, Judith. Whereas you, Fishman, are now family.' Vanessa caught Becky's arm and swept her off. 'If you're at a loose end,' she sang over her shoulder, 'you can devise ways of upping your future advertising budget.'

There was no immediately obvious chore in the kitchen. Becky looked questioning.

'I suddenly panicked,' Vanessa hissed, 'that you might tell her about the photos.'

'I'm sure she'd cope. It's six months but I see—'

'Not just that. I didn't tell her at the time, you see, because she was so upset, and she might be angry that I didn't even though I was thinking of her . . .'

The door swung open. 'If I'm to be idle can I top up my spritzer?'

Vanessa would not have credited Becky with the dexterity for subterfuge that she displayed, whipping open the oven door and hauling out the casserole while animatedly discussing the optimum cooking time of Jerusalem artichokes.

Sometimes Judy's friendship with Max seemed so like the ordered surface of a Jane Austen novel that she could only think of him as Mr Nicolson. They were not frequent companions but their meetings were always an elegant pleasure.

They had been to the Royal Academy and were intending to have tea at Brown's but when they arrived there was a queue of tourists in baseball caps and garish slacks, the women smirking as their recalcitrant husbands were helped into obligatory ties the colour of Windsor soup. Max, knowing the rules, was sporting a dashing silk number patterned, it appeared, with tasteful representations of the warrior hordes of Genghis Khan.

He looked at his watch. 'Waiting for this lot to trough might be a little trying,' he said. 'Unless you're desperate for sticky buns and clotted cream we could have a pot at my house and go on to the National from there.'

'Fine,' she said. This would be the first time that she had been to Max's place in Pimlico; Vanessa's reports of her own visit to Maunsel Street had been tantalising.

'We could walk across the park. Are your shoes up to that?'

She smiled. No other man she knew would have asked that question. They were low-heeled, suede pumps but new enough to rub at the heel.

'Let's.'

Green Park was littered with young lovers and old ladies in deck chairs. Pigeons picked their way among the debris from myriad picnic lunches. Max swung his jacket insouciantly over his shoulder but, true to form, made no attempt to loosen his collar.

'It's an unusual tie,' she said.

'Flatters to deceive, I'm afraid. Present. When I first got it I thought it was a bunch of Mongols galloping across the Steppes. Turns out to be an entirely different set of savages playing a chukka on Smith's Lawn.'

Judy stopped and lifted it towards her. At once it was clear that they were polo players with mallets and pith helmets, and the purple and green seemed rather vulgar.

'I know,' he said, as if her opinion was flashing above her head. 'Who would have thought a change of meaning could affect the value of an object so meaningless? I shall have to throw it away.'

She slipped her arm through his. His lavender shirt was cool against her skin. 'I thought all consumer items contained hidden meanings? According to you communications gurus.'

'Not me, lady, I just like pretty things. You're the one on an endless quest for the perfect lifestyle.'

They stopped on the balustrade above the lake in St James's Park and watched the fountains. 'Don't they make you feel parched?' she said.

'Yes. "Water, water, everywhere, but not a drop to drink".'

'Excuse me.' A diminutive Japanese, equipped with the normal gamut of cameras but unusually flying solo, beamed uncertainly at them. 'Will you take my picture? Please.'

'Certainly,' Max said. 'If you stand here then the lake's in the background and Horse Guards—'

'No, please. With palace.' He stood on the edge of the pavement. Max looked dubiously through the Canon, moved slightly to the left and then to the right. He was, Judy thought, flustered.

'Problem?' asked the subject through a rictus of gleaming teeth.

'Oh no, no.' Eventually Max knelt on the pavement, said unnecessarily, 'Smile,' and the job was done. His subject announced that he was off to Burberry's and bowed out with a volley of handshakes.

'You seemed strangely reluctant to press that button,' Judy said.

'Well, it was terrible. All this street furniture—' he tapped the modern crash barriers on the kerb, 'and the flagpole sticking out of the middle of his head. At least by taking it at ground level I got a nice angle on the Victoria memorial and – don't laugh at me, you horrible girl.'

Max bought a cucumber and some pastries and when they arrived descended to the kitchen to make tea.

The room into which she had been ushered occupied the whole of the raised ground-floor of his narrow, four-storied house. At the front the window looked on to wrought-iron railings and street lamps with an identical terrace beyond. At the back french doors opened on to stairs leading down to a tiny yard full of shrubs and lichen-covered statuary. In between were faded sofas, clubbable armchairs, two fireplaces beneath ancient gilt mirrors, and walls clustered with water-colours and the occasional strong abstract of the type where the paint has been applied with a trowel.

A grandmother clock in the hallway competed with the ormolu on the mantel to chime the half-hour. Otherwise all was shaded and still. She negotiated the narrow stairs to the kitchen, one half of which had been isolated by shelves loaded with eclectic *objets* to create a dining area. In the other half Max was quartering minute sandwiches.

'What a lovely house. A retreat from everything.'

His eyes flicked up. 'Explore if you like. There's a lovely rooftop view from upstairs.'

'Well, I'll use the bathroom at least.'

'Top landing.'

Ascending the stairs reminded her how painful her feet were going to be by the end of the evening. She would have liked to take her shoes off but bare toes, even nail-polished, seemed the wrong type of informality for Max's and anyway there was the terrible prospect of not being able to force the shoes back on.

The half-landing held a lavatory, and above it a cluttered study with a computer and a lightbox sitting amid a profusion of magazines and videotapes. The door was propped open with a gold trophy inscribed 'Cannes 1977'. It was the only room in the house that could have been described as disordered.

Next – she took just a peek – was a guest room cheerful with paperbacks and exhibition posters but nothing revealing. She was in uncharted territory now – Vanessa had been no further than the loo.

The bathroom was deep and soft and striped by sunlight through the Venetian blind. The thick towels and carpet, the gold taps and silver shaving kit, the oils and unguents arrayed on the shelves, all exuded opulence. She washed with seductive Floris soap.

The door of what had to be his bedroom was hardly ajar. She gave it a nudge. Here was the promised view – a jumble of chimneypots and weatherworn slates, the coils and capital Hs of ancient TV aerials, very British but exoticised by the distant campanile of Westminster Cathedral.

In the foreground a bed, a monstrosity of mahogany, the scrolls and curlicues of its headboard rearing above a Chinese-silk bedspread. A Georgian tallboy, an enormous wardrobe displaying her in its central mirror. On the worn Turkey carpet a stray pair of black brogues; on the bedside table a silver frame.

She walked around the bed. Beneath the fine specks of household dust highlighted by the sun a young man stared nobly at a point just above and to the right of the camera. Monochrome emphasised the delicately chiselled nose, the high cheekbones flushed as with blusher, the treacle eyes and sweeping lashes, the tight Graeco-Roman curls above a high forehead. So Vanessa was right.

'Handsome, isn't he?' He must have floated up from the kitchen, she had heard nothing.

'Very.'

'It's the opposite of the Dorian Gray story.' He sat on the window-ledge.

'What?'

'I run to seed while keeping this picture in my attic.'

'This is you?'

'I know. A shock. It's not vanity having it by the bed but an intimation of mortality. A constant reminder to try and preserve what shreds remain.'

'I didn't mean that. It's just . . . the hair.'

'Oh, a play, while I was at Oxford. Forget quite what. Aristophanes, something.' He looked out of the window. 'Do you like the view?'

'Yes, sort of Peter Pannish.'

He laughed. 'I've always thought Coronation Street twinned with Siena. It's God's factory chimney that does it. Come and have some tea, otherwise it will have stewed.'

Later, on the concrete terrace of the theatre complex, he said, 'Is that how you see me? Peter Pan? The boy who never grew up?'

'I hadn't thought. It must have sounded rather rude.'

'It needn't have done but now that I can see you understood the implications, of course—'

'No,' she said. 'Not Peter Pan. You're actually much more like Captain Hook. Or the crocodile.'

They went back in for the second half.

Becky's cycle was so long and irregular that for another month she didn't give it a thought, and it was only Vanessa's flippant remark about her being off-colour – 'Anyone would think you'd got morning sickness' – that prompted her to buy a pregnancy test. When it proved positive she was mesmerised.

'How many weeks?' Vanessa asked.

'Well, nothing's a hundred per cent safe, right? . . . But I know the first time that I did it without my cap was the 23rd of April.'

'The first time?'

'There were others.'

'How can you be sure of the dates? Unless you were thinking about this?'

'I couldn't tell you them all. It's just that this one was an anniversary.'

'And you weren't prepared?'

'Lay off, Vanessa.' Becky turned away, lit a cigarette. The whole house smelt faintly of Gitanes. Vanessa wanted to tell her to think of the baby and stub it out but now was not the right time.

'I'm sorry. It's just that I know from experience our motives are sometimes confused, or ambiguous.'

Becky looked at her sharply. This was a major admission; Vanessa had always maintained that her pregnancy was a result of the one per cent pill failure rate.

She said carefully, 'Not mine. Just got carried away.'

Tied up. Her shiver should have been of revulsion but it wasn't entirely.

Vanessa was calculating. 'If it did happen then, you're nearly eleven weeks.'

Becky's diary was out. 'If. But I think that was too soon after my last period.'

'What are you going to do?'

'Go to the doctor's and make sure. I'm still registered, I think.'

'But you're sure really, aren't you? I know I was.'

'No,' Becky said. For a moment or two, as she had stared at the indicator, she had imagined she could feel it, as solid as a stone within her, and that the subsequent mingled spurt of excitement and disgust had shifted it as if she might sick it up, but the sensation had faded. 'I don't know what I'm supposed to feel like.'

Vanessa did not ask whether she was pleased; it was clear she was not. 'If he confirms it, what will you do?'

'I don't know that either.'

And she still didn't when Dr Cronin assured her that she was 'with child'. According to Vanessa's collection of books about childbirth and rearing, one-third of all pregnancies miscarry within three months. So waiting for nature to maybe take its course seemed less like indecision until week fifteen when the foetus was still in place.

She had managed to get some teaching before the end of the summer term but now that was over. She had a lot of time on her hands and yet no time at all in which to take action if she was going to stop this thing happening to her.

Apart from the doctor she had discussed her condition with no one but Judy and Vanessa. Both believed they were being neutrally supportive but their true feelings were obvious.

Vanessa clearly thought she should have it, assuming that it would be a carbon copy of her own experience with a happy ending, and seemed excited at making use of what she had learnt in her own solitary gestation.

Judy's antipathy seemed equally personal. In the same predicament she would, or thought she would, have had no doubts about abortion. Like the doctor, she sweetened this pill by referring to it as a termination.

As the weeks went by it was Judy who reminded Becky of the necessity for a solution, 'Unless you're happy to have it, of course. The limit's twenty-four weeks and I've read that under the NHS it can take several weeks to get a referral.'

Alone in her room, Becky gazed at her stomach as if by concentrating she might see through the placid white skin to the supposedly frenzied activity beneath, but she could not relate the bland exterior to the highly-coloured films she had seen of the cell division that scientists claimed was going on in there. Her paralysis of thought continued.

It was Dermot's – she carefully avoided the use of emotive words like baby or child to herself – and she had broken with him. Her blotchy explanation of her feelings in a letter had provoked a long and reasoned reply. He apologised for his behaviour that day and understood that it was unforgivable. Nevertheless ... he amplified in his understated way how much he missed her, how suited she was to circus life, how he hoped she would return. She would be amused by the kink in his nose. Holding the letter was like opening the door of a freezer and watching the smoke chill your fingers. The kink in his personality had been put back in the jar and the lid screwed firmly down. She knew for certain that she would not be the one to reopen it.

Should she have a ... that would never have a father because the father would never know ... it ... existed?

How could she explain to ... thing ... her refusal to discuss or name ... its ... other parent?

How could she bring up her – all right, this was ridiculous – her child on her own? Vanessa had managed it but Vanessa was strong, Olympian. What would she do for money, for comfort, for intellectual stimulation even?

On the other hand, how could she kill it?

Dermot's brother Sean rang to say that he had a parcel for Becky. It contained her clothes and books and a cheque from the Cirque. Could she meet him at Hackney Stadium to collect it? She was glad to be getting her things back and the money would be useful but, suspicious, she asked where Dermot was now. Back in France, Sean said. The fact that Zakis Minotaur was running clinched it. If Sean recommended it she would have another flutter.

Hackney meetings were daytime rather than evening but it wasn't just the critical blanket of sunlight in place of the selective floodlighting that made it so different. If Walthamstow was greyhound racing's Hollywood, then Hackney was its crackly Ealing comedy.

The stands, built in the 1930s to accommodate many thousands, were largely deserted, the hard core of punters congregating by the bookies' umbrellas. Although the stadium was half derelict, the façades peeling, the towering old neon scoreboard perpetually dark, the price of admission would not justify opening the place. Races at Hackney were now run for the benefit of a satellite TV audience in the betting shops with as much money placed in Arbroath as was wagered at the track itself. With the exception of the cameras there was no new equipment; the place was as much of a dinosaur as the empty gas storage towers to the west and the docks to the south, waiting to be cannibalised by an alien culture.

Vanessa, having driven through a wasteland of redundant factory premises and left the car on an expanse of concrete where the amount of broken glass was testament either to a large number of crashes or of break-ins, looked dubious. Becky herself felt cheated of the tacky glamour that she had somehow pictured surviving the eleven o'clock start, but led them up to the covered gallery of the main stand.

Inside, the stale smell of the bar, offering an unappetising selection of keg beers, competed with that of the refreshment counter where urns hissed and spat and a pair of grandmotherly women assembled toasted bacon sandwiches and crusty cheese and onion rolls. Becky bought Josh a bottle of Vimto and a Wagon Wheel. Vanessa, reminded by these of her school tuckshop, softened and had a polystyrene beaker of marmalade-coloured tea.

Sean had grown a beard but Becky, attuned to the family characteristics, would still have recognised him anywhere. He said a polite hello to them all, and then Vanessa tactfully led Josh away to watch the runners parade.

'How are you keeping, then?'

'Fine. And you?'

He nodded. There was a silence. The tannoy chuntered on, a race came and went.

'Is Smokey going to win today?'

'Don't know. It's only his second try over the hurdles. He's a trier though. Can't ever count him out.'

'Why hurdles?'

'He's too old now to do a decent job on the flat, well past his sell-by date. But he's got the trackcraft and he loves racing. The jumps reduce the advantages of youth and pure speed. Perhaps you'll bring him luck. It worked last time. Your stuff's in the van. Come down to the car park afterwards.'

'Thanks,' she said. He seemed more awkward, jumpy even, than her. It was windy out on the terraces and the loose-fitting dress that she had deliberately worn to conceal her bulge was pulled back against her body, emphasising the swelling. Sean's gaze seemed drawn down to it.

'What is it, your van?' she asked to distract him.

'Blue transit. You can't miss it. It's got an air-conditioning vent in the roof.' He glanced down again. 'Don't catch cold. I'd better go and sort the old boy out.'

'He couldn't possibly have guessed,' said Vanessa. She put her hand on the bump. 'It's no worse than some women get every month, or after a bingeing Christmas.'

They watched the chalked prices oscillate and then settle with Z. Minotaur at six to one. Afraid that she might miss the start Becky put a tenner on and Josh was lifted up to hand over a fiver.

'That's it, sweetheart,' said a strawberry-nosed neighbour. 'Start him young.'

When he won at Walthamstow Smokey had been wearing the yellow-five jacket and Becky saw it as a good

omen that he had it again today. She didn't appreciate
the significance of there being another wide runner on
Smokey's inside in Trap Four. Unless he made a snappy
start he risked being squeezed between four and six which
is why the bookies had marked him high. They doubted his
early pace.

The rail hummed. 'Hare's running,' the tannoy coughed.
The dogs in the boxes yelped in excited anticipation. The
bunny hurtled past and the lids jerked up. Smokey trapped
well, and this advantage took him over the first fence a nose
ahead, but by the second the six dog was passing him on the
outside and the number four on his left shoulder. As
Smokey landed, the four, drifting inexorably wider, hit him
in the ribs and he cannoned into the six. They both fell to
the ground, rolling over and drawing groans from the
spectators.

Becky closed her eyes, unable to watch in case they were
badly hurt. Then Vanessa said excitedly, 'He's up again,'
and he was, frantically chasing the railers who were by now
rounding the next bend. It was impossible for him to catch
the pack but he tried so hard, reducing the deficit to a
couple of lengths, that Becky shouted him home and tore
up her ticket with pleasure rather than disgust.

'Why's Sean carrying him?' Vanessa asked.

On the other side of the track, where the handlers were
putting their jubilant charges on to leads, Sean with
Smokey in his arms was making unsteady progress towards
the tunnel.

'That's his lot, poor old sod,' said one of the men leaning
against the rails.

'There can't be anything wrong with him,' Becky said.
'He was running so well.'

'Perhaps he's just exhausted,' Vanessa said, but when
they made their way to the car park she suggested that she

and Josh wait in the BMW. She had told him that the doggie was perfectly all right and didn't want him to discover otherwise.

The blue van was already parked by the trainers' gate. Its rear doors were open and Sean was sitting on the tailgate in his white coat, his sneakers scuffing at the fragments of someone's rear light. In the darkness behind him she could make out six cages, five occupied. Sean looked up listlessly.

'How's Smokey?'

'Mr Patzaki's with the vet now.'

'What's the matter with him? I mean, he looked fine, he ran on as if nothing had happened.'

'They do that though, even if they've broken something. There's so much adrenalin pumping round they don't feel the pain. So they keep going and do themselves far more damage.' He sounded bitter.

'Will he be all right?'

'No, not all right. I don't think they'll put him down but he'll never race again. His owner won't want to pay his keep any longer. We'll have to find a home for him.' He got up. 'Here's your stuff.' He reached into the depths for the bag and her eyes followed.

The driver's seat was unoccupied but someone was sitting on the passenger side, outlined in silhouette by the sun streaming through the windscreen. She blinked. The rearview mirror was at an odd angle and reflected back at her were a pair of gold-framed sunglasses.

Becky was transfixed; the hairs on her arms and the back of her neck rose. Sean was saying something; his voice perfectly normal. The passenger sat still.

'. . . let me know if you're coming again.'

She tore her eyes away.

'I will.' She took the bag. 'Thanks.'

She looked back. The passenger seemed not to have

moved but now the mirror showed only herself. 'I'm sorry,' she said. 'Goodbye.'

'It must have been your other friend who was the lucky one,' she heard Sean say as she walked away.

She sat silently on the journey back to Battersea, letting the prickling under her skin subside.

'Don't fret,' Vanessa said as Josh seemed to be absorbed in the passing traffic. 'I'm sure the dog will be OK.'

'I'm fine,' Becky said, making an effort. 'I'm sorry you lost your fiver though.'

'You were the one behaving like a riverboat gambler. Is that what's making you uncomfortable?'

'No.'

'What then?'

'Nothing.'

'It must be something.'

Becky could not bring herself to tell the truth – that she thought, was almost certain, that she had just seen the father of her child for the last time. Unless Sean told him or he had guessed for himself that she was pregnant. Then what might he do?

She tried to swallow the panic. This was paranoia. He had just been having a final look. If he was going to make a move he would have made it then. There was nothing to worry about, or rather there was plenty to worry about without that. That was all over.

'Becky? Are you going to be sick? Do you want me to stop the car?'

Becky searched for an explanation that would lighten the atmosphere and, finding one, sighed theatrically. 'No, I'm all right. My chest hurts—' Vanessa frowned, 'but because my bra's really tight. I know you said they would get bigger but I didn't realise you meant this much.'

Vanessa hooted. 'And you're complaining? Make the

most of it. Buy a low-cut dress – it's heaven having a real cleavage and if you breastfeed you'll hang on to it. For a bit. Unfortunately when you stop they wither away again like mine did.'

Judy had finished at Pasco on Tuesday and the removal men were coming tomorrow to put her furniture into storage. She and her clothes would move into a hotel on Sunday, as she started at Gateshead Foods on the Monday but hadn't yet exchanged on her new house.

Given the gathering recession she had been lucky to find a buyer, or so the estate agent said. She had been forced to accept an offer similar to the price she had paid for the house. That meant no return for the kitchen and bathroom that she had fitted but it left enough for the small stone cottage in Teesdale.

Its slate roof would need attention before long; the last owner had a fondness for Vymura and swirly carpets that might have been expressly designed to induce migraine; the Ascot had probably dripped in time with Mr Chamberlain's declaration of war; in short there was work to be done. But Judy liked that – the making of a silk purse out of a sow's ear. In any case this was a silk purse that had been disguised as a sow's ear. There was an open fireplace, a tree in the garden, and a beautiful view along the valley from the bedroom window.

She finished clearing the drawers of jumpers and methodically started on the suits and dresses. Bartholomew, blissfully unaware of the month in a cattery that awaited him, lay on the duvet, occasionally batting at the stray edges of garments dangling from the suitcases.

When she got as far along the cupboard as the evening dresses she broke off for tea.

The September sun was still bright but the warmth had

seeped out of the afternoon and she put on her guernsey before packing her shoes and clear the bathroom cabinet.

When that was done there was only an hour before she was due to meet the girls for their farewell dinner so she had to finish the dresses.

She took down the black taffeta and the blue satin with the fishtail skirt which she suspected was less than flattering to her bottom and had consequently only worn twice. Then the jade silk and she reached, as she knew she had to, the ivory shift. It had been hidden at the back of that cupboard, untouched and unobserved, ever since she had brought it home. It couldn't just stay there any more – she had to decide whether to take it or dispose of it.

It swung from its hanger – elegant, emptily chaste, its perfection only marred by a watermark of tears. And yet there was something indecent about the exposure of such delicacy; it was an exquisite symbol of her guilt.

How to get rid of it was a problem; she did not want anyone else to have it, so the charity shops were out and the dustbin was too sordid. All she could think of was burning it but her company car had been repossessed along with its petrol and she didn't keep paraffin. Would it burn unaided?

She couldn't bear scorched fragments all over the place. Burning was so melodramatic; redolent of funeral pyres or murderers disposing of their victims' remains.

She knew she should not take it to hang unregarded in Teesdale but could not abandon it unworn and that was why she had delayed this moment.

Judy stripped hastily and took it from the hanger. It slithered in her hands as she pulled it up, cold and ticklish on her skin. Its smell was the smell of a shop but it reeked of intimacy. It lay on her lightly, barely touching but idealising the shape of her body. It caressed her. She experienced a flood of desire so intense that she had to lean against the wall for support, hugging herself.

She groaned. Bartholomew stared.

But then it was ebbing and she had not cried. Instead she felt a tranquillity that was entirely unexpected.

She dressed again. She retrieved a box and some tissue paper from the living-room. She laid it carefully to rest. And put it in a crate with her books.

12

The Feast of Purification

Out on the landing Judy's mother was chivvying Dad out of the bathroom. 'I told you – be done by nine. She mustn't feel rushed.'

No, she mustn't. She knew she would get a cup of tea in a minute. She still had the itch between her shoulder blades. Honestly, the last time she had spots on her back she was fifteen. It must be nerves. There was a disturbing, subterranean ache in her nose too – the sort that presaged the eruption of some monstrous blemish.

A pimple.

A boil.

A goitre.

By the time she got there she would be like Quasimodo, hunched to keep the back spots below the top of her dress. 'The bells, the bells.' That at least was appropriate.

Judy rolled on to her side and half-strangled herself on the silver chain around her neck. On it was the thimble that he had sent her in a box together with the card reading 'A kiss'.

At the end of her bed hung the dress – ghostly white in this half-light but so full, so sure of itself that it hardly seemed to need her to get out of bed and into it to validate its existence.

Her parents' reactions to the marriage had see-sawed; delighted that she was settling down, disturbed that it was with someone fifteen years older, dumbstruck when they met him. He of course had been immensely charming but not overly familiar, appreciating that they would like to stand on their dignity a little.

The four of them had gone out to dinner – 'Nowhere too posh,' she had said, 'otherwise they'll be nervous' – and so they went to a steakhouse and Max ordered prawn cocktail and rump steak without batting an eyelid.

Everything was going swimmingly until her mum, thawed by the champagne at home and the Martini and Blue Nun in the restaurant, had said, 'Will you try and get a job in London again or are you going to become a lady of leisure like me?'

'I'm keeping the job I've got, Mum,' she had replied, a mite aggressively.

Max, leaving the two of them to have this conversation alone, was regaling Don with a racing anecdote.

Dorothy fixed him with a stare. 'Will you be moving to Gateshead then, Max?'

'No,' he said, 'my business won't allow that at the moment, but equally Judy can't abandon her boss.' She was pleased to see her choice presented as duty. 'For a while we shall have to content ourselves with the weekends, and of course work will sometimes bring us together between times.'

Judy knew that in her mother's eyes this hardly constituted a marriage at all. Dorothy temporarily contented herself with the comment, 'You're very lucky, Judy, to have such an understanding husband.'

Her tone did not imply approval of Max's sensitivity and for once he had not helped by saying, 'Don't forget that your daughter is my client as well as my fiancée.'

She could have hugged her dad who, whether wittingly or not, turned the flak on himself by saying jovially, 'When you've lived a while as a bachelor I should think you're quite grateful to have the place to yourself every now and then.'

Her mum, having planned on putting Max in the boxroom, had wavered at the sight of the middle-aged sophisticate she was condemning to the narrow mattress beneath Cheryl's old Queen and Rod Stewart posters, but this incident rehardened her heart. Judy was relieved. The thought of sharing this bed with Max, even after their wedding, was nerve-racking.

There was a tap on the bedroom door and Dorothy entered, carrying a tray on which she had arrayed the *Daily Mirror* as well as tea and a boiled egg.

'Thanks, Mum.' Judy struggled upright.

'You'll be needing something to keep you going,' Dorothy said defensively as her daughter eyed the egg. 'I've got your dad out of the bathroom so take as long as you want.'

'Thanks, Mum.'

'I'll be off to the hairdresser's in a minute so if the florist comes while I'm out can you make sure he leaves eleven buttonholes? There's nothing worse than being one short.'

'Yes, Mum.'

Dorothy had taken a lot of convincing that Judy did not need the ministrations of Jacqui at Salon Valerie and once Cheryl had unkindly pointed out what her sister had avoided saying – that she would sooner risk a pudding-basin – her attention turned to the investigation of more 'with-it' establishments. Only reluctantly had she accepted that Judy's hair would require nothing more than washing and pinning, neither of which needed professional assistance.

'Do you need anything while I'm out?'

'No, Mum. Don't worry yourself with shopping. We've checked everything a hundred times already. Off you go.'

Her mother's gaze had settled yet again on the dress.

'Yes,' said Judy, anticipating. 'It's gorgeous ... and worth every penny. Get your skates on. You don't want to be late.' This did the trick.

She was glad her mum was so excited. She knew that, left to his own devices, Max would have chosen a register office followed by a long lunch at Le Gavroche, but her parents deserved this. At Cheryl's wedding the bride had been visibly pregnant which made it a hole in the corner affair, not to be boasted about to the neighbours. The least Judy could do was to regularise her unorthodox union with a church service and reception for a hundred and fifty at the Spivey Hall Country House Hotel.

And secretly she had been looking forward to it herself until this morning, when she felt decidedly shaky. She took the tray with her to the bathroom and, breaking open the top of the egg, scraped its contents into the lavatory bowl.

To give Becky five minutes alone in their shared room Vanessa bundled Josh down to breakfast as soon as he was dressed. He was bubbling with excitement about his starring role in this afternoon's production.

Judy had tentatively suggested that he might like to be a pageboy. Vanessa doubted it but let Josh decide. With the perversity for which small children are renowned he had accepted enthusiastically. Judy's niece Kelly, aged eight, was the bridesmaid proper and Vanessa a sort of matron of honour, having made it conditional on her wearing an outfit of her own choice.

'Otherwise,' she had said to Becky, 'God knows what I might end up in. It's well known that people lose all inherent taste when it comes to a white wedding.'

It being the first Saturday in February the dining room at Spivey Hall was sparsely populated. The advertising crowd who had kept the bar open till two in the morning were presumably still abed, nursing their hangovers. There were one or two businessmen, unexpectedly delayed and instantly identifiable by their formal Friday suits; the clan Nicolson who had trekked in convoy from Dorset; and a semi-detached aunt and uncle of Judy's who were well enough liked to receive an invitation but not so popular that the local branches of the family had offered to accommodate them.

Hovering in the doorway, lenseless and short-sightedly wondering where to sit, Vanessa was beckoned by a lemon-yellow golfing jumper which, once she had fished her glasses out of her pocket, became George Doherty. His wife, a birdlike Trappist who had been toying with some toast, gave Vanessa a cursory nod but only broke her silence to coo over Josh.

'Watch him,' Vanessa said as he started on a bowl of Rice Krispies. 'He's liable to scatter them around.'

'Oh, it won't hurt these old things,' she replied of an expensive-looking twinset. 'He's an angel, isn't he? All that golden hair.' Her meaningful glance at Vanessa's black locks rendered 'He must take after his father' redundant.

George, who seemed to be stolidified by the presence of his other half, made ritualistic conversation just as by rote he consumed his full English breakfast. Journey down. Sausage. Weather prospects. Bacon.

'And where are they going on their honeymoon?' he asked after the grilled tomato. 'Do you know? Judy won't tell. Says it's bad luck but I think she's just frightened the faxes will follow her round the world.'

Vanessa did know because she had seen the brochures and the tickets on Max's desk.

'I cannot believe that a canny lass like you has not found out, even if you haven't been told.'

'Promise me you won't disturb her.'

'He wouldn't dare, would you, Georgie?'

Georgie? Judy would like that.

'No. Come on, Vanessa, spill the beans.'

'Thailand, Hong Kong, Australia.'

He laughed. 'Your business must be doing all right then. I shall take a very jaundiced view if you try and double my budget come April.'

'We're keeping our heads above water,' she said cheerily, as she always did when asked how it was going. The fact was that was about all they were doing. Their start-up had coincided with the onset of a recession which showed no signs of bottoming out. There had been no new clients of any size and the office space that they had intended for an expanding workforce remained largely empty. Their salaries as partners were enough to live on but hardly allowed for the extravagance of this wedding reception or honeymoon. Max was philosophical about it – 'Trust me to go solo at the worst possible time' – but she assumed that he must be digging into some secret nest-egg for this lot. If his finances were like hers then the bank certainly would not let him borrow any more.

She caught sight of Becky and waved. Pregnancy had treated Becky kindly. Apart from the pod pushing against her baggy pullover and the ungainly, stiff-legged walk she was as much the gamine as ever. George leapt to his feet to help her into a chair, receiving a sweet smile in return.

Vanessa introduced her. No reference was made to

Becky's condition but the appearance of a second single mother seemed to have startled Maureen Doherty back into silence.

'How are you feeling?' Vanessa asked solicitously.

'Fine. Do you think they have any kippers?'

The Hucknell house was seething with relatives. Josh, for safety's sake still in his dungarees, was pounced upon and removed by Kelly. In the kitchen Dorothy, her hair set in a newly-lacquered helmet, was making tea in rubber gloves to protect her professionally varnished nails.

'Hello,' she said. 'You do look nice.'

'Thank you,' said Vanessa.

'I said to Judy she was making it very difficult marrying in the middle of winter – all those layers to co-ordinate.'

'You know that she couldn't get the church on a Saturday in the spring or summer, Mum,' said Cheryl.

'And just like us she couldn't wait,' Pete chipped in, winking at Vanessa. His wife glared at him.

'It's not the same thing at all,' snapped Dorothy, breaking off abruptly as Darren, her eldest grandchild, entered the room.

'She'll be the one feeling the cold most anyway,' said Vanessa emolliently. 'Shall I take her up a cup?'

Judy sat before the dressing-table, one of her mother's housecoats over her petticoat, her face already immaculate, her hair coiled and pinned to expose the nape of her neck, still pink from the bath. The giant-hound's-tooth pattern of Vanessa's matching coat and dress seemed to fill the mirror. She turned round. 'You look nice.'

'You're the third person to say that.'

'Count yourself lucky.'

339

'Count myself middle-aged, you mean. Your grandma looks nice in her floral Crimplene.'

'All right. You look . . . striking . . . daring . . . original.'

'More, more.'

'Maybe a touch too much the sloe-eyed vamp.'

'You cow. You've completely spoilt it. So you don't think I'll get off with one of your cousins then?'

'No. Apart from the fact that none of them are eligible enough, you'd scare them to death. If you take to the dance floor tonight watch them run for the gents.'

'How are you feeling?'

'Petrified. I've run out of things to do. And I've got enormous spots on my back.'

'How can you tell?'

'I can feel them.'

'I bet they're invisible.'

'They're not. Look,' she shrugged off the dressing-gown, 'if I stand here they're as clear as anything.' She had positioned herself so that she could see the reflection of one mirror in another.

Vanessa peered. It was unlikely that anyone would notice the little rash but better for Judy to be occupied by that than for her to be remembering forgotten invitees and mislaid passports or having second thoughts.

'Give me that stick.' She worked away with it. 'There, completely gone. I'll do them again after you've got the frock on.'

Judy inspected as best she could. 'OK.'

'Next.'

'Do you think I should wear this?' She held up a blue suspender belt the colour and texture of a Tory rosette.

'You're not wearing stockings, are you?'

'Yes.'

340

'Blimey, you're a better man than I am, Gunga Din. You'll freeze. Even so, why this? Where did you get it?'

'Cheryl gave it to me. Something blue. It's good luck.'

'It might be good luck but it's not good taste. Haven't you got something virginal and white?'

'Yes, of course.'

'And you'd be happier in it?'

'I'm already wearing it. It's just getting the proverb right.'

'Are the others sussed?'

'Uh huh.'

'Something old?'

'This slip for starters.'

'New?'

'Dress, shoes . . .'

'Borrowed?'

'Lace for my veil.'

'Got a blue hanky or something?'

Judy shook her head. Vanessa thought for a minute and then rummaged in her handbag.

'Carry this,' she said, throwing over a tampon. 'It's got a blue string.'

Josh and Kelly had been changed and declared adorable in dark-green velvet. Vanessa and Dorothy had coaxed Judy into the dress and the tight-fitting green velvet cossack jacket and she had, as commanded, given them a twirl.

'You look wonderful,' Vanessa said. 'Really gorgeous,' and her mum had nodded in agreement, not trusting herself to say anything in case she got emotional and set them all off.

And then those four had got into the Rolls and gone, leaving Judy and her dad alone in the house. Self-conscious in his morning coat, he was standing in the middle of the sitting-room, frightened to sit down in case he creased his tails. He didn't look like himself at all. But then neither did she, she reflected, taking another sideways glance in the hall mirror.

'Nervous?' he asked.

'Uh huh.'

'Me, too.'

'What about?'

'Speech, of course.'

She attempted a laugh. 'That's nothing. Five minutes, a swig of champagne and it'll all be over. Mine's for the rest of my life.'

'You've picked a good bloke though,' said Don and gave her arm a hesitant pat as if she was a piece of porcelain that he might easily break. 'He'll look after you.'

There was a hoot from the street. The limo was back.

On the way to the church she thought how well her dad had taken to Max. She hadn't necessarily expected him to. A lot of men didn't, perhaps because they assumed he was queer. She had heard some of the boys in her office say 'Backs to the wall, lads' when he passed by, although in their eyes la-di-da southern vowels alone probably made a man a poofter. Unless he compensated by playing great soccer, or rugby or something. And Max didn't do that.

Her marrying him must have been a shock, she knew how they secretly leched after her. Even Vanessa was shocked for she too had surmised that he was gay. And perhaps he was. Had been. She didn't know. They had not discussed their sexual pasts at all. Should they have done?

He loved her, he had told her that, told her with an

eloquence that would have seemed over the top from anyone else. 'A perfect woman. The divine made flesh.'

He made her laugh and she felt safe with him, content. Somehow she believed that fortune could only shine on them as a couple; in that restful Pimlico townhouse and quiet Teesdale cottage they were untouchable, protected from the slings and arrows.

The car pulled up outside St Mary's and she gathered her wits and her skirts. The photographer capered about, the chauffeur lit a fag, a couple of old ladies with tartan shopping trolleys stopped on the pavement to spectate and reminisce. In the porch Vanessa made minute adjustments to her bouquet and train and her mind seemed to be floating ahead. She wanted to shout, 'Quickly, quickly', to slap away the hands that fiddled with her and restrained her. Instead she adjusted her impatient feet to the ponderous pace of her father as the organ swelled and Vanessa whispered 'Good luck' before slipping away down a side aisle.

Through the sea fog of the veil the nave looked as long as a runway, as high as the Albert Hall. The faces, all turned in her direction, seemed to thrust at her as if on extendable stalks. She felt the pull of Kelly and Josh dawdling with her train. Then she was there, with Max more like a literary hero than ever in his waistcoat and stock, and the vicar impersonating John the Baptist, all soulful eyes and heavy beard. And at that point she might have lost touch with reality altogether had Max not given her the ghost of a wink.

Becky had recognised Danny's back when she entered her pew, broad in its sober suit. The pink, padded shoulders roughly on a level with his waist must belong to the second wife. While they were taking the photos she had positioned herself so that she could get a better look at the new Mrs Fishman.

Becky considered that on the whole she had withstood the ravages of pregnancy better than her successor. The girl's bust and bump were both enormous but there the attractions of fecundity stopped. Her ankles and her face were puffy and her bulk tottered on black patent stilettos. She clung to Danny's arm all the time. Her paintbox make-up deteriorated visibly during the meal, her hair was lank beneath her hat.

'When I wrote the date of this do in my diary,' began the best man, Adrian, an art director with whom Max had worked in his gilded youth, 'I discovered that the 2nd of February is also the Feast of Purification. Funny, I thought. Sanctification maybe. Purification . . .' He gave an exaggerated shrug. Knowing what was expected of them his audience gave an apprehensive titter.

Becky sipped at her glass of champagne and thought that as it was such a special day she might have a cigarette. Giving them up had been the most hellish thing about being pregnant, otherwise she had, as the old wives put it, blossomed. Under Vanessa's tutelage she had gone regularly to the pool and the gym, rubbed oils into her skin, and carried on teaching until forced to give up by the education authority. It was finally uncomfortable to move around or even sleep but not yet so familiar that she longed for the birth to put an end to it. She hoisted herself up and plodded to the lavatory. It would be wonderful to regain a normal capacity bladder.

As she washed her hands the baby gave her a kick. 'Oh, give it a rest, Sophie.'

The anonymous foetus she had at first kept out of philosophical inertia – after all, how could you abort something whose existence you didn't really believe in? –

had acquired its name on the bus back from the hospital where Becky had been told its gender. It had seemed like a good idea, sitting alone on the top deck, but Vanessa had been horrified.

'Becky, you can't. It's – it's bad luck.'

'What? Naming a child after a dead person. Why? People do it all the time. Statesmen, relatives and stuff.'

'But not, well not someone who died . . . unhappily.'

Becky had been upset that what had seemed such a wonderfully uncomplicated expression of friendship was clearly going to be viewed as insensitive and in poor taste.

'I expect pregnancy has skewed my brain or something, but I don't understand.' She did, of course, but knowing that for Vanessa the name raised the spectre of guilt had only made Becky more determined. Giving the name another context might finally lay all that to rest. 'It's not as if it's going to affect her personality. Look, if it makes you unhappy then I won't but I'm not just doing it in memory. I mean, if Sophie had been called Ethel or Doris or something I couldn't have named the baby after her but Sophie's a nice name.'

And Vanessa had eventually said, humouring her, thinking that she would change her mind, 'You're right. It is a nice name.'

Judy had clearly been equally shocked but managed to say, 'I think it's a lovely idea.'

And Becky hadn't changed her mind. She no longer thought it would achieve anything; she considered it an illogical choice; nevertheless the name Sophie had stuck. Neither Vanessa nor Judy used it, but then how many people did refer to someone else's unborn baby by name?

Standing at the washbasin, Sophie pressed against its rim, Becky flicked her hair, recently redyed white-blonde, and retraced the line that made her eyes look bigger and deeper still. She really did feel good, better than good, in a strange way she felt sexy.

While she was contemplating the unsatisfactory choice of cigarettes in the machine in the corridor Danny emerged from the gents and approached her. She had seen him look at her a couple of times, outside the church and across the several white-clothed tables that separated them in the dining-room, but whenever their eyes had met he had looked away.

'How are you?'

'OK. You?' She began to register the differences about him – new smell, the first hint of a paunch to come, more hair at the throat of his shirt . . .

'You finally decided to have one then?' He gestured at the bump.

Go on, touch it, she wanted to say. She wanted to touch him.

'Yes. And you've got yours. How is . . . I'm sorry I don't know her name.'

'Heather.' He paused. 'You look completely different.'

'It's the size.'

'No, I mean the hair and stuff, very . . . good.'

'Thank you.' She looked up. He looked down.

To distract herself she asked, 'When's yours due?'

'Three weeks.' He smiled ruefully, his little-boy-lost smile. 'And then Heather's mum's in charge.'

Suddenly it had evaporated, that echo of the old attraction. She could see the hairs protruding from his nostrils, and realised that his scent was not purely lust but fear. He might be drawn to the new her but he was frightened of it too.

She felt sorry for poor Heather in her bovine maternity, desperately trying to please this philanderer. How could she have envied her, thought such bitchy thoughts about her? She put in her coins and pulled out a packet of Embassy. She wanted to shock him now, to be shocking. 'Have you got a light?'

'No, I don't, you know I don't . . . Should you be?'

'What the hell . . . If it makes her a bit stunted I'll just have to feed her up.'

He stared at her.

She said, 'You'd better get back. I'll give you a couple of minutes so that Heather doesn't guess you've been with your ex.'

'Right. Er . . . see you.'

'OK,' she gave him a little wave.

He walked away. She lit her cigarette with the lighter that she still carried in her handbag and sucked greedily on it. When it was no more than a stub she returned to her seat.

It wasn't the first time it had happened and the fact that it happened at all only emphasised how quickly the memory blurred. The swing doors to the kitchens were opposite the top table and when the waitresses were charging in and out with the lobster bisque she had seen Sophie's auburn mop bent over a vat out there. Except of course it wasn't Sophie, just some kitchen hand who was breaking the regulations by not wearing a cap and bore a fleeting resemblance to Sophie. She knew it was her mind playing tricks but at one time she would never have mistaken such an impostor for the real thing, even for a moment.

The speeches passed, they cut the cake, the flash bulbs popped along with the champagne corks. They filtered through to the ballroom where a jazz band pottered leisurely through some standards, waiting for the call to arms of the first dance.

She floated about having happy non-conversations with people, accepting compliments, refusing drinks. Then they were on the dance floor and Max was leading her gently through a waltz. Then she was in a bedroom with Vanessa easing her feet from her shoes and her arms from the dress. She allowed herself to be zipped into her going-away outfit.

'You look exhausted,' Vanessa said. 'Shame you've got such a long drive.' They were going back to London.

'It'll be relaxing. We can compare notes.'

Max knocked on the door. 'Ready?'

'As ready as she'll ever be.'

'Bye, Van. Thanks for everything.' He kissed her cheek.

'It's been fun. Don't be late back to work, you lotus-eater.' She turned to Judy and hugged her as hard as she could.

Judy squeaked, the breath leaving her body. Vanessa kissed her and leaning forward whispered very quietly in her ear, 'Be happy.'

They ran the gamut of farewells and then they were out into the night.

'Oh God,' said Judy. 'They've done the car.' It was strung with cans, and the windows were a baroque fantasy in foam.

'It's all right. We're going in that hired Rover over there,' Max said and marched her past the BMW, to the groans of those, Billy and Graham chief among them, who had decorated it.

'You were always too clever by half, Nicolson,' someone shouted.

Judy threw her bouquet, which was caught in a fit of absentmindedness by her cousin Anne, already married with three kids and a budgerigar. In her subsequent embarrassment Anne handed it to Darren and it was never seen again.

The dark roads were empty. The car, like so much else that day, smelt unfamiliar but the pale glow of the instrument panel made it almost cosy. She slumped in her seat.

'Glad it's over?'

'In a way,' she said. 'It was all such a rush. I hardly spoke to anyone. Did you?'

'Hundreds of people. Remember very little about it. Doesn't matter. Whether we did or not they'll all think they talked to us. You were a beautiful bride. That's what they'll be saying.'

'And you were a handsome groom,' she said, suddenly shy.

'Oh, I don't think that's half so important.'

'It is to me. Thanks for going through with it.'

'It wasn't a punishment.'

'Good.'

'Just a labour of Hercules.'

She punched his forearm. They drove in silence for a while.

'Max?'

'Yes?'

'We've never talked about ... previous—'

'About previous what?'

'Relationships.'

'Do you think we should?'

'I don't know. I don't think we should have secrets, do you?'

'Have you got a secret?'

'Yes.'

'Where do you keep it? It's not a love child, is it?'

'No,' she said, surprised. 'It's a box. In my wardrobe.'

He had a way of prompting you to say things you didn't expect to.

'Can it escape?'

'No.'

'Then I think your box should remain a secret, don't you? As long as we're happy now, with each other, why rake over the past? What have we got to gain?'

To herself she said 'Understanding?' but didn't know if she believed it, even as a question. Out loud she said, 'Nothing', and stroked his hand on the gearstick.

He did not reply, just gave her a quick smile before looking back at the motorway.

'Have you got a secret box?'

'Several, but they're locked. They can't hurt me or you.'

'Good.'

She felt peaceful in love. When he'd asked her if she would marry him she had barely hesitated.

She'd been through the phase when, after moving to Teesdale, she had wondered if she had, after all, discovered her true nature with Sophie. Was she a lesbian who had deceived herself with men until she was thirty-one? She didn't know but she'd studied the personal ads in the Newcastle listings magazine and been unable to follow any up, let alone place one herself. Then, one night, nervous but desperate to establish something, she had gone to a women-only disco. Being appraised and approached raised her temperature but she had shrunk from any greater intimacy. Even with the very striking woman in black she had been unable to move on from a slow dance. She didn't belong, she was set apart, in-between.

Rather like Max. Or, at least, as Max seemed. They had grown quickly but imperceptibly, unthreateningly closer until his proposal seemed quite natural but so other-worldly that she suspected they might not have had sex until after they were married unless she had, that night in the Pimlico house, made it clear that she was waiting for him to make love to her.

And it was sweet. She couldn't help, afterwards, thinking of Sophie but she knew the comparisons had to stop. Sophie had been snatched from her or, rather, she had thrown Sophie away so she would never know whether the pure elation, the stunned happiness that she had briefly experienced and which was undoubtedly refined by memory, could have continued. It might have got better but, then again, she had to believe it could have turned sour or faded to indifference.

Sophie was a one-off. This was the rest of her life. Nevertheless she wished, just for a moment, as she sat on the motorway, that she was a virgin so that she had nothing to compare him with.

Vanessa and Becky were sharing a table at the furthest edge of the ballroom with Peter and Penny, and taking it in turns to keep an eye on Josh, who looked innocent but was probably making mischief with some small Hucknells. Penny had taken Becky under her wing and was discoursing earnestly on child-rearing. Vanessa was trying not to discuss business with Peter and attempting to keep her housemate within some mainstream conversation. The jazzband had temporarily given way to the 'discomachine' of a sallow local youth recommended by the hotel who used him for their dinner-dances.

'Would anyone like to dance?' Peter asked.

'Well, poor old Rebecca is in no state, are you?' said Penny. She was in full sisterly flow. 'And I'm quite happy. Take Vanessa,' she decreed magnanimously.

So they jigged, in the self-deprecating way that polite English people do, to the Supremes. When they returned to their seats Mikey was there.

He and Vanessa had worked together again in the autumn at the behest of Dolphin swimwear who had been so pleased with their first commercial that they had wanted to use the same director for their second. Vanessa knew better than to let personal complications jeopardise commercial arrangements and had to concede that it had been less difficult than she expected. But outside the studio and the cutting-room they had no contact.

'I'd better put Josh to bed,' she said when he offered to buy another round. When she came back half an hour later he was still there and, as these things do, the party atmosphere had cranked itself up several gears. They seemed to have returned to champagne.

'Toasting the happy couple again?'

'No, although why not?' Peter asked. There was a general raising of glasses. 'The real reason,' he went on, 'is that young Michael has just announced that he's been chosen to make the new Ford commercial.'

Mikey grinned.

'Well done,' Vanessa said. 'Big league.'

'A long shoot anyway. Death Valley, three weeks. Keep the wolf from the door.'

'It'll buy you a woodman to chop off his head, I should think,' Peter said.

'I think it's brilliant,' Becky added. 'If you'll excuse me I'm going to take the weight off my feet.'

'You poor love, of course you must. We know what it's like, don't we, Vanessa?'

Vanessa, surprised that Penny had admitted her to the sorority, laughed. 'Do you want me to come with you?'

'No, you know me. I'll probably be back soon. Have

some bubbly for me. I'm over my ration.' She waddled away.

'She must be ... well ... about ready to—' Mikey began.

'Pop it out,' Peter hooted.

'Officially it's overdue but Becky thinks they've underestimated.'

'I'm surprised she was allowed to travel,' Penny said.

'She wouldn't have missed this for the world. Besides, I was coming and I wouldn't have wanted to leave her alone.'

'Is there no father?' Penny leant forward conspiratorially. Peter chuckled.

'I mean,' she jabbed at her husband, 'is there no father around?'

'No.' Vanessa was not prepared to elaborate.

'Parents?'

'Dead.'

'Oh, poor child.'

The speakers blasted out Freda Payne's 'Band of Gold' and Peter, keen to end the interrogation, leapt up.

'Come on, darling, we can't miss this. It's our tune,' he explained.

Penny went, somewhat reluctantly.

'It really is good news about the film.'

'I know. They haven't exactly been thick on the ground recently. I would have got a proper job but I'm not qualified to do anything. And this one's thanks to you. Having that latest Dolphin on my showreel clinched it.'

Vanessa decided to be honest. 'Don't thank me. I didn't put you forward. Not,' she continued, seeing how this could be misinterpreted, 'because of your work but because of us. Luckily for you – for everybody – the client was more professional about it and being a craven bag-carrier I always do what my client says.'

He smiled. 'I was a tad surprised to get the call. But it wasn't so bad, was it?'

'No, it wasn't so bad.'

'How about you? Businesswise? You picked a tough time to go it alone.'

'It's been pretty awful. I think Peter feels it most because he's always had this shit-hot reputation for winning new accounts, and they're not coming. But we've all felt depressed. Max has had Judy and the wedding to take his mind off it, of course.'

'And what have you had?'

She thought. 'Looking after Becky has helped a lot. I don't exactly mean looking after her but I feel responsible for her in some ways. And there's always Josh, of course, a handful but I worship him . . .'

'I don't think he really recognised me,' Mikey said wistfully.

'Maybe not, but at that age they forget very quickly. Don't take it to heart, see him a couple more times and—' she lapsed into embarrassed silence.

Fortuitously the Bennetts returned, flushed from their exertions. Penny became quite frisky, the bottles circulated, the company expanded and contracted.

'OK,' the DJ announced matily, 'we have to say bye-bye now, but before we do let's have a last earful of the careless whisper of Mr George Michael.' He faded it in. The floor filled. Vanessa and Mikey stayed put.

'Come on, you two,' Peter said. Vanessa did not know whether he was privy to their previous entanglement but if so he was past diplomacy. He gestured at the abandoned tables and the smooching couples. 'You can't be the only two wallflowers.' He tugged Mikey upwards.

There was a beat and then Mikey shrugged and held out a hand to her.

He felt very tense. She closed her eyes. Their slow rotation with the music acted like some reverse centrifuge, sucking them closer; a touch, a press, a crush.

'Same old magic.'

'Except last time we took a wrong turning somewhere.'

They kissed until it was hard to breathe, and found themselves abandoned in the centre of the room, the lights forlornly up. Vanessa could see Penny staring at them from the sidelines.

'Mikey—'

'Let's . . .' he flapped his arms ineffectually, 'go for a walk.'

'OK,' she said uncertainly. 'I must check on Josh – and – er – get a coat. It's cold.'

'Yes, yes,' he said and then they were almost running up the stairs because it seemed very important to keep moving.

In Room 219 Becky was propped up in bed, rereading some Trollope. Josh was fast asleep. Vanessa burst in and then dithered.

'All over then?' Becky asked. 'As you can see I—' The door was still ajar. She was puzzled. 'What's the matter?'

'I want to . . . is it all right if I go for a walk?'

'A walk?'

Vanessa nodded.

'Of course.' Becky pointed at the door and mouthed silently, 'Mikey?'

Vanessa nodded again. 'You don't mind keeping an eye on—'

'Don't be stupid. Wrap up warm. Don't wake us.' She blew her a kiss and waggled her eyebrows.

Vanessa was gone.

Mikey was leaning against the wall, drumming with his palms, sustaining as much momentum as he could while standing in one spot. He caught her arm. As they approached the corridor's end he began to speak softly and urgently.

'The thing about Sophie, I was wrong and I'm over it now, have been for ages, I—'

'Shut up.' She slammed him against the wall and closed his mouth with her own.

A stray reveller opened the fire door, striking her a sharp blow in the back. 'Ooh, sorry,' he mumbled automatically, weaving away.

'Oww. You are over it,' she said. 'Mikey, it's too cold to walk. Can we . . . go to your room?'

He whirled her round and they ran, bouncing off corners. He fiddled with the key, cursing under his breath. She pummelled at him, 'Come on, come on.'

They stumbled into the room and she was pulling at her coat as he switched on the lamp. He turned to find her kicking off her shoes, leaning against the door as she unzipped her dress. He moved to her and she caught his face in her hands, kissing him, then making him touch her as she tugged at his shirt.

'Quick, quick, or I'll realise I haven't done this for so long I don't really know how to.'

Afterwards he squirmed in the tangle of sheets and said, 'You're just the same as I remember.' He was kissing the top of her head and stroking the fur on her belly.

'That's not flattery, that's downright lying. I'm a middle-aged woman now, not an amateur starlet.'

'You're just as . . . angry.'

She levered herself on to her elbows. 'I wasn't angry then, at least not until you went on to the next strumpet, you bastard.' She grinned. 'If I'm angry now it's because I've just been reminded of what I've been missing. Can you get this up again?'

'Don't you want to see my safety certificate?'

'Not if you've got another rubber.'

'I've got two.'

'Chance would be a fine thing.'

Becky had been dozing, playing back the events of the day. How strange that flicker of excitement for Danny this afternoon. Ridiculous. What an enormous prick. She hadn't realised that till after she'd left him, of course.

There was a sharp pain, enough to jolt her awake. She decided to ignore it and think about the pictures of Piero della Francesca, as she had done to distance herself from gynaecological examinations.

Time passed; she knew how much because without wanting to she could see from the corner of her eye the blinking red digits of the radio alarm clock. The pain faded, a one-off. Like this afternoon, a flicker. Situation normal.

Then it happened again.

For a while she was sure the contractions were some kind of false alarm. She had felt as if there was a coconut lodged between her legs all day but she could not believe that fate would send her into labour in a hotel a hundred miles from her hospital. She waited for Vanessa to come back and tried to concentrate on Renaissance painting.

The trouble was wherever her mind roamed on the remembered canvases she kept running up against the Madonna and Child or worse still, blood; blood in trickles on the muscled legs of saints, blood in lakes on the shrouds of the dying. Blood presided over by the soldiers and torturers, their cold eyes like the remote gaze of doctors dehumanised by white masks.

Quietly, so as not to wake Josh, she got up and hobbled around, leaning and crouching in a variety of positions all of which seemed comfortable for a short while until the next tightening of the vice.

She should never have had that cigarette, that second, no, third glass of champagne. If something terrible was happening she had brought it on herself, oh GOD.

She tried to recite the names of Form 2C as they had appeared in the register, concentrated until she could hear their lazy voices and see their bored faces. She did as much as she could of *A Midsummer Night's Dream* – fragments of speeches, the cast list, the dates of performances. Where was Vanessa? They were getting closer.

She knew where Vanessa was and good luck to her. You can't disturb someone having their first screw in – three? – four? – years for a false alarm.

Hits of Rolf Harris – 'Sun Arise', 'Tie Me Kangaroo Down, Sport' ... 'Jake the Peg' ... 'Two Little Boys', of course. Bugger. Back to square one.

She wanted to turn the light on. She got back into bed, pulled the duvet up tight.

It was after two. She rang reception and asked for Mr Rodgers' room number. But she didn't dial it until the bed, already marshy with sweat, became a swamp and she knew her waters had broken.

Vanessa was lying awake.

Her legs ached.

Her body was sleepily sated.

Her brain scurried about.

Of course it was nice to have sex again; she truly had forgotten how different it was from self-satisfaction. Not always better, could be much worse but ...

The thing was, she was a working mother with a recessed business and Becky and her baby to look after. Was a sporadically-employed commercials director a sensible acquisition? No matter how attractive. They couldn't all share her house.

She touched his sleeping flank. A log. Dead wood?

No, he was great with Josh. Great with her. Did she love him?

Pass. Something anyway.

Was he reliable?

Had she made a terrible mistake? Who knew? Think of the romance, the passion.

She whistled softly, through her teeth, a snatch of some half-remembered tune.

'What are you doing?'

'Whistling in the dark.'

'Why?'

'It's an expression.'

'I thought that was whispering in the dark.'

'No, you've misheard. The victim of a Chinese whistle.'

'I thought that was . . . Jesus, this is far too complicated for the middle of the night.' He rolled over. 'You're mad, do you know that?'

'Yes.'

The bedside phone rang, and she sprawled across him to pick it up, quite forgetting it was his room, operating on maternal anxiety reflex. She should have gone back to 219.

'Hello?' A quavery voice.

'Becky, what's up? Is it Josh?'

'No . . . oo-oo-oo . . . I'm having, I think I'm having—'

'Hang on, I'm coming. Just hang on.'

Vanessa shot out of bed.

'Mikey, I've got to go. Becky's in labour.' She found her dress and stepped into it. 'If she is, you can't go back to sleep, you'll have to look after Josh.' She kissed his forehead as he nodded. She wasn't sure whether he'd taken it in but she'd more or less zipped up her dress so she ran barefoot, blundering around the identical landings for several lifetimes before she found their room.

'I'm sorry,' Becky was saying, 'I'm sorry but I was frightened.'

Vanessa hugged her. 'It's all right, I'm here now, I'll take care of you, don't be frightened.'

She tidied Becky up and moved her to the other bed and rang the desk to find out where the nearest hospital was and rang the hospital to announce their arrival and dressed properly and comforted Josh and summoned Mikey so that he and Josh were reacquainted before she left them alone. Then she got the car and Becky was transferred to it with the assistance of the worried duty desk manager.

As Vanessa wrapped a rug around Becky she gently patted the bump and said, 'Great timing, Sophie. As always,' and Becky hazily recognised this as a breakthrough but somehow the name didn't seem very important any more.

Under the cold lights of the empty bypass they cruised slowly to minimize bumping. Vanessa hunched over the wheel, looking for the promised signpost.

Becky, trying to be brave, smiled a wan smile and said, 'I can't help wondering if I've made a terrible mis—'

All Vanessa's insecurities reprised in a Technicolor flash. She battened down the hatches on them. 'Don't say it. Don't even think it. We've done the right thing.'

There was the sign. She indicated.

What did she mean, 'we'? Becky wondered. 'You ... sound very sure.'

'I am.'

She seemed so confident that Becky said no more, just listened to Vanessa's irritating, tuneless whistle.